LEGION OF THE DAMNED

ALSO AVAILABLE FROM WILLIAM C. DIETZ AND TITAN BOOKS

WILLIAM C.
DIETZ

LEGION OF THE DAMNED

A LEGION OF THE DAMNED NOVEL

TITAN BOOKS

Legion of the Damned
Print edition ISBN: 9781783290369
E-book edition ISBN: 9781783290376

Published by Titan Books
A division of Titan Publishing Group Ltd
144 Southwark Street, London SE1 0UP

First edition: June 2014
1 3 5 7 9 10 8 6 4 2

A CIP catalogue record for this title is available from the British Library.

Printed and bound in Great Britain by CPI Group Ltd.

DID YOU ENJOY THIS BOOK?
We love to hear from our readers. Please email us at:
readerfeedback@titanemail.com or write to us at Reader Feedback at the
above address.

To receive advance information, news, competitions, and exclusive offers
online, please sign up for the Titan newsletter on our website.

www.titanbooks.com

This book is dedicated to Marjorie: friend, lover and buccaneer.

1

There is nothing more dangerous than an honest man falsely accused.
LIN PO LEE PHILOSOPHER EMERITUS
The League of Planets
Standard year 2169

Worber's World, the Human Empire

Colonel Natalie Norwood stepped out of the underground command post and into the elevator. Though normally spotless, it stank of vomit and was littered with bloody bandages, used hypo cartridges, and empty IV bags. Medics had used the elevator to ferry an endless stream of wounded soldiers down from the now devastated surface.

She nodded to the guard and watched the armor-plated doors slide closed. Blood had been spattered on the shiny metal. She noticed that the dots were uniform in size and thicker towards the bottom.

The soldier touched a button, machinery hummed, and the elevator rose. Norwood felt self-conscious in her dress uniform, gleaming medals, and polished boots. They made a marked contrast to the guard's fire-scorched armor, cracked visor, and battle-worn rifle.

Both had fought and both had lost.

The alien Hudatha had taken less than five days to destroy the four battle stations that orbited Worber's World, to decimate the three squadrons of antiquated aerospace fighters the Navy had sent up to protect it, and to lay waste to all of the planet's major cities.

One of them, the city of Helena, had been home to the governor and headquarters for the general staff. They had been in a meeting, trying to decide on what to do, when a subsurface torpedo had burrowed its way *under* the command post and detonated.

The resulting explosion created a crater so large that it diverted the south fork of the Black River, formed a new lake, and left a heretofore obscure Army colonel named Natalie Norwood in command.

What a joke. In command of what? The shuttle that would carry her to the enemy battleship? The stylus that she would use to surrender?

The elevator came to a stop. The door slid open. The guard flipped his visor up and out of the way. He was no more than seventeen or eighteen, a kid really, with soft blond peach fuzz crawling over his cheeks and chin. His voice cracked as he spoke.

"Ma'am?"

She paused. "Yes?"

"Why don't they stop?"

Norwood searched for something to say. The soldier had put his finger on the very thing that bothered her the most. The Hudatha had won the battle many times over. So why continue? Why attack objectives already taken? Why bomb cities already destroyed? It didn't make sense. Not to a human anyway. She forced a smile.

"I don't know, son."

His eyes beseeched her. "Will you make them stop?"

Norwood shrugged. "I'll try." She forced a smile. "Your job is to keep the slimy bastards out of my liquor cabinet."

The soldier laughed. "No problem, Colonel. I'll take care of it."

Norwood nodded. "Thanks. I'll see you later."

She felt guilty about her inability to answer the guard's questions. Officers knew everything, or were supposed to anyway, but the Hudathans were a mystery.

An Imperial survey ship had encountered them two years before, had established rudimentary contact, and learned very little other than the fact that the aliens were technologically sophisticated, and very wary of strangers.

Why they attacked, and kept on attacking, was unknown. Her only chance lay in communicating with the Hudathans, meeting whatever demands they made, and waiting for help.

She stepped off the elevator and into the underground aircraft hangar. It was a huge place, made even larger by the fact that the aerospace fighters normally housed there were gone, along with the crews that flew them. Not "gone" as in "gone out on patrol," but "gone" as in "gone and never coming back."

They had left their marks, though. Yellow lines that divided one bay from the next, grease stains that resisted even the most ardent crew chief's efforts to remove them, and the eternal stink of jet fuel.

The walls were covered with a maze of conduit, equipment readouts, safety slogans, and there, right in the middle of the back wall, a twenty-foot-tall three-dimensional holographic of the squadron's insignia, a skull wearing an officer's cap, and the motto "Touch me and die."

It seemed a bit ironic now.

The sound of Norwood's footsteps echoed off cavernous walls as she made her way towards the darkly crouching shuttle. It was a large V-shaped aircraft, originally intended as a VIP toy, now comprising roughly 25 percent of the planet's surviving Air Force.

They appeared like ghosts from the shadows. Power techs, com techs, weapons techs, and more. Some came on foot, some on ground-effect boards, and one wore a twelve-foot-tall exoskeleton.

These were the men and women who had armed the planes, traded jokes with the pilots, and sent them out to die. They looked at Norwood with pleading eyes, not expecting good news, but hoping for it anyway.

She nodded, forced a smile, and marched across what seemed like a mile of duracrete.

The ground crew watched her go, absorbed her silence, and faded into the shadows whence they'd come.

Captain Bob Ellis stood waiting by the shuttle. He was a

reservist and, like many of his kind, incredibly sloppy. His battle dress hung around his body like a deflated balloon, his sidearm threatened to pull his pants down, and his left boot was only half-laced. Ellis tried to salute but looked like he was summoning a cab instead. Norwood returned it.

"Captain."

"Colonel."

"Did you get through?"

Ellis nodded miserably. "Yes, ma'am."

"And?"

"And they refuse to grant you safe passage through the atmosphere."

"But that's outrageous, it's…" Norwood was about to say "uncivilized" but caught herself. The Hudathans were aliens and what seemed outrageous to her could be normal practice for them.

"So they refuse to see me?"

Ellis shook his head. "No, they're willing to *see* you, but they won't *protect* you."

"Says who?"

"That's another thing, Colonel. Their spokesperson is human. Some guy named Baldwin. Colonel Alex Baldwin."

The named sounded familiar but Norwood couldn't place it. "Terrific. A goddamned traitor. Well, get on the horn and tell *Colonel* Baldwin that I'm on my way."

Ellis bobbed his head obediently. "Yes, ma'am. I'll get on it."

Norwood smiled. He would too. No matter how Ellis might *look*, he was sincere, and a helluva lot more competent than some of the regulars she knew.

"Thanks, Ellis. How 'bout the message torps?"

"They were launched two hours ago, just as you ordered," Ellis replied. "Twenty-two at random intervals."

Norwood nodded. Given the fact that the scientific types had yet to develop any sort of faster-than-ship method of communications, the torps were the best that she could do.

Maybe a missile would find its way through the Hudathan blockade. *Maybe* an admiral would get up off his or her ass long enough to mention the matter to the Emperor. And *maybe* the

Emperor would make the right decision.

But, given the fact that Worber's World was just inside the rim, and given the fact that the empire was contracting rather than expanding, Norwood had her doubts.

"Good. We gave the bastards a chance… which is a helluva lot more than *we* got."

Ellis nodded soberly.

"Major Laske will assume command until I return, and Ellis…"

"Yes, ma'am?"

"Lace your fraxing boot."

"Yes, ma'am."

Ellis bent over to lace his boot, realized that he should have saluted, and straightened up. It was too late. Norwood had turned her back on him and was entering the shuttle. She looked terribly small for such a big job. Why hadn't he noticed that before?

The hatch closed behind her and Ellis felt a hollowness in the pit of his stomach. Something, he didn't know what, told him that he'd never see her again.

Repellers roared, a million pieces of grit flew sideways through the air, and the shuttle lifted off. Norwood looked out a window and saw Ellis. His hat was centered on his head, his back was ramrod straight, and his salute was textbook perfect.

"Well, I'll be damned. He got it right."

The pilot rotated the ship on its axis. "Did you say something, Colonel?"

Norwood made a small adjustment to her headset.

"No, talking to myself, that's all."

The pilot shrugged, knowing that Norwood was to the rear and couldn't see through the back of his seat. Brass. Who could figure 'em anyway?

The shuttle rode its repellers up one of six massive ramps, paused while armored doors slid open, and lifted straight up. The aliens had become quite adept at nailing low-atmosphere aircraft, so the pilot applied full military power.

G-forces pushed Norwood down into soft leather which had until recently served to cushion an admiral's rather ample posterior. She was certain that he would have disapproved of a mere colonel using his private gig, but like all of his peers, the admiral was entombed under Black Lake and unavailable for comment.

The G-forces eased and Norwood looked out the window. This was the first time that she'd been outside since the initial attack. She'd seen most of it before, but secondhand, via satellites, drones, and helmet cameras. This was far more immediate and therefore shocking.

The shuttle had climbed to about five thousand feet. High enough to provide a good view but low enough to see some detail. What had been some of the most productive farmland on Worber's World looked like a landscape from hell.

Clouds of dense black smoke rolled away towards the horizon and were momentarily illuminated as a nuclear device went off hundreds of miles to the east. Lightning flickered as bolt after bolt struck the ground and added its destruction to that already wrought by the aliens.

Fires burned for as far as the eye could see, not in random order as one might expect, but in carefully calculated fifty-mile bands. That's the way the Hudathans did it, like suburbanites mowing their lawns, making neat overlapping swatches of destruction.

First came the low-orbit bombardment. It began with suppressive fire intended to keep aerospace fighters on the ground, and was almost immediately followed by an overwhelming air assault, and landings in force.

Norwood had seen video shot from the ground, had seen a thousand carefully spaced attack ships darken the sky, had seen the death rain down.

And not just on military installations, or on factories, but on each and every structure that was larger than a garage. Homes, churches, libraries, museums, schools, all were destroyed with the same plodding perfection that was applied to everything else.

The Hudathans were ruthless, implacable, and absolutely remorseless. Such were the beings to whom she was about to appeal. A tremendous sense of hopelessness rose up and nearly overwhelmed her. Norwood pushed it down and held it there. She felt tired, very tired, and wished that she could sleep.

The pilot jinked right, left, and right again.

Norwood tightened her harness. "What's up?"

"Surface-to-air missile. One of ours. Some poor slob saw us, assumed we were geeks, and took his best shot. I sent a recognition code along with instructions to look for another target."

Norwood imagined what it was like on the surface, cut off from your superiors and hunted by remorseless aliens. She shivered at the thought.

Norwood noticed that the copilot's seat was empty. "What happened to your number two?"

The pilot scanned his heads-up display and felt feedback flow through his fingertips. The shuttle had no controls other than the implant in his brain.

"She took a flitter and went home."

Norwood was not especially surprised. While some continued to fight, thousands of men and women had deserted during the last couple of days. She didn't approve but understood nonetheless. After all, why fight when there was absolutely no hope of winning? Of course the Legion had sacrificed more than a thousand legionnaires on Battle Station Delta, but they gloried in that sort of thing and were certifiably insane.

"Where was home?"

"Neeber's Knob."

"It took a direct hit from a twenty-megaton bomb."

"I think she knew that," the pilot said evenly.

"Yes," Norwood replied. "I suppose she did. So why stay?"

The pilot ran a mental systems check. It came up clean. "Different people react in different ways. She wanted to go home. I want to grease some geeks."

"Yeah," Norwood agreed. "So would I."

The pilot sent a thought through the interface, felt the G-forces pile on, and arrowed up through the smoke.

Baldwin screamed, and screamed, and screamed. Not with pain, but with pleasure, for the Hudathan machines were capable of dispensing both. He lay naked on the metal table, muscles rigid under the surface of his skin, gasping for air as another orgasm rippled through his body. His penis was so rigid that he thought it would explode. Sometimes he almost wished it would.

Part of the human sex act involves release, but the aliens had bypassed that function in order to prolong his pleasure, and in so doing were unknowingly torturing him.

But there was no alternative. The Hudathans believed that it was important to dispense rewards and punishments in a timely fashion. By associating pleasure or pain with a particular event, they hoped to reinforce or discourage the behavior in question. Since Baldwin had provided them with some excellent advice concerning the attack on Worber's World, he deserved a reward. Never mind whether he *liked* the reward, or *wanted* the reward, he *deserved* the reward and had to receive it.

So Baldwin screamed, the technician waited, and a timer measured the seconds. Finally, when the allotted amount of time had passed, the pleasure stopped. His body tingled all over. The human was only vaguely aware of the 350-pound alien that stepped in to remove his restraints. The straps were intended to protect rather than punish.

There were no wires or leads to disconnect, since all of the necessary circuitry had been surgically implanted into his brain, and was radio-controlled.

That was the part of the bargain that Baldwin liked the least, the knowledge that the aliens were in total control of his body. But it was absolutely necessary if he wanted to continue his relationship with them. If a single word could be used to describe the Hudathan race, it would be "paranoid."

Except that humans classify "paranoia" as aberrant behavior and Hudathans considered it to be normal. Normal, and desirable given the nature of their home system.

Baldwin knew that Hudatha, their home planet, was fairly Earth-like, and rotated around a star called Ember, which was 29 percent more massive than Terra's sun.

So even though both stars were about the same age, the gravity generated by Ember's greater mass had compressed its core, which led to higher central temperatures and more rapid nuclear fusion. That in turn had shortened the star's life span and caused it to grow significantly larger, redder, and more luminous over the last few million years. The result had been warmer temperatures on the surface of Hudatha, the loss of some species, and increasingly bright sunlight that hurt the eyes.

Having observed these changes, and being scientifically advanced, the Hudatha knew that their sun was headed for red-gianthood and that they would have to move.

Making things even more complicated was the fact that the planet Hudatha was in a Trojan relationship with a jovian binary. The jovians' centers were separated by only 280,000 kilometers, so their surfaces were only 110,000 kilometers apart.

If there had been no other planets in the system, Hudatha would have followed along behind the jovians in a near-perfect circular orbit, but there *were* other planets, and they tugged on Hudatha just enough to make it oscillate around the following Trojan point. The upshot of it all was a wildly fluctuating climate.

Hudatha had no seasons as such. Major changes came in response to the ever-changing distance between Hudatha and Ember. The changes took place on a time scale of weeks, rather than months, and that meant that at any given time of the year it could be searingly hot, frigidly cold, or anything in between.

And that, Baldwin knew, explained why the Hudathans felt the universe was out to get them, because in a sense it was.

All of which accounted for the implant. If the Hudathans could control a variable, they were sure to do so, knowing that control meant survival. And, to a race like the Hudatha, the very existence of another sentient species was an unendurable threat. A threat that must be encountered, controlled, and if at all possible, completely eliminated.

It was this tendency, this need, that Baldwin was determined to exploit. The only problem was whether he could survive long enough to do so.

The technician released the final restraint and Baldwin sat up. The alien backed away, careful to protect his back, always ready to defend himself—a reaction so ingrained, so natural, that the Hudathan hadn't even thought about it.

He was seven feet tall, weighed about 350 pounds, and had temperature-sensitive skin. It was gray at the moment, but would turn black under conditions of extreme cold, and white when the air surrounding it became excessively warm. He had a large humanoid head, the vestige of a dorsal fin that ran front to back along the top of his skull, a pair of funnel-like ears, and a frog-like mouth with a bony upper lip, which remained stationary when the creature talked.

"Do you have needs?"

The human swung his feet over the side and addressed the technician in his own tongue, a sibilant language that sounded like snakes hissing. "Yes. A cigarette would be nice."

"What is a cigarette?"

"Never mind. May I have my equipment, please?"

The Hudathans had no need to wear garb other than equipment such as armor, which explained why the word "clothing" had no equivalent in their language.

The alien made a jabbing motion that meant "yes," and disappeared. He was back a few moments later with Baldwin's clothes.

"The war commander requests your presence."

Baldwin smiled. The humans had arrived, just as he had predicted that they would.

"Excellent. Inform the war commander that I am on my way."

The Hudathan made no visible response, but Baldwin knew that his message had been subvocalized and transmitted via the technician's implant.

He zipped the uniform jacket, wished that he could see himself in a mirror, and made his way out into the corridor. It was taller and wider than a human passageway.

His guard, a huge brute named Nikko Imbala-Sa, was waiting (still another precaution to make sure that the human-thing remained under control). Baldwin moved towards the core of the ship. Imbala-Sa followed. The Hudathan equivalent of argrav had generated a rather comfortable 96.1 gee.

This corridor looked exactly like every other passageway on the ship. There were evenly spaced light strips on ceilings and bulkheads, identical junction boxes every twenty feet or so, and gratings that could be removed to service the fiber-optic cables that lay beneath them. Baldwin thought the sameness was boring, but knew that the Hudatha found comfort in the uniformity, suggesting as it did a well-ordered universe.

They arrived at an intersection, waited while a lance

commander and his contingent of bodyguards passed by, and approached the lift tubes. There were eight of them clustered together. Four up and four down.

Baldwin waited for an up platform, stepped aboard, and knew that Imbala-Sa would take the next. Each platform was intended to carry one passenger and no more. The human had noticed that Hudathans had a tendency to avoid unstructured group situations whenever possible.

The platforms never actually came to a stop, so it was necessary to watch for the deck that he wanted and jump. Baldwin made the transition smoothly, waited for Imbala-Sa to catch up, and headed for the battleship's command center.

There were four sentries outside the war commander's door. All were members of the elite Sun Guard and were heavily armed. They made no attempt to bar Baldwin's way but omitted the gestures of respect that would be afforded to a Hudathan officer. Baldwin ignored it. He had no choice.

The airtight hatch disappeared into the ceiling and Baldwin strode through the newly created opening. Imbala-Sa was right behind him.

The command center was oval in shape, with fifteen niches set into the outer walls, one for each member of the war commander's personal staff. The cave-like seating arrangements gave the aliens a sense of security and served to protect their backs. Seven of the seats were filled. Baldwin felt fourteen sets of cold, hard eyes bore their way through him.

The fifteenth seat, the one that belonged to Niman Poseen-Ka himself, was empty.

The center of the room contained a huge holo tank, presently filled with a likeness of Worber's World and the surrounding system. The holo was at least twenty feet in diameter and looked absolutely life-like. Baldwin knew that if he watched the simulacrum closely enough, he would see tiny fighters strafe the planet's surface, lights flash as nuclear bombs were detonated, and cities glow as they were burned to slag.

But his eyes were focused on a far more satisfying sign of victory, a woman in the uniform of a full colonel and a man dressed in a flight suit.

Indescribable joy filled Baldwin's heart. This was it! The moment that he'd been waiting for, the moment when they groveled at his feet, the moment when his revenge was complete! He looked to the right and left.

"Where are they?"

The woman was about his age, pretty, with gray-streaked auburn hair. She was small, five-four or five-five, and very shapely. She projected an aura of strength.

"Where is who?"

"The admiral. The general. The officer they sent to surrender."

The woman shook her head sadly. "That would be me. The rest are dead."

Baldwin felt the joy drain away like water released from a dam. "Dead?"

The woman frowned. "Yes, dead." She gestured towards the holographic likeness of the planet below. The cloud cover was streaked with black smoke. "What did you expect?"

Baldwin struggled to forget long-harbored fantasies and deal with things as they actually were. "Yes, of course. I'm Colonel Alex Baldwin. And you are?"

"Colonel Natalie Norwood. This is Flight Lieutenant Tom Martin."

Baldwin nodded to Martin and turned back to Norwood. "You had a pleasant trip, I trust?"

"No, we didn't," Norwood replied. "Two of your fighters jumped us in the upper atmosphere. We managed to shake them off. Now, let's eliminate the small talk and get down to brass tacks. You attacked and we lost. What do you want?"

Baldwin smiled. The line came straight from his fantasies. Never mind the fact that the governor or an admiral should have uttered it, the words were perfect.

"Nothing."

Norwood's eyebrows shot up. "Nothing?"

"That is correct," a new voice said. It spoke standard with a hissing accent. "Colonel Baldwin desired nothing more than the satisfaction derived from your arrival."

Norwood turned to find herself face-to-face with a 450-pound Hudathan. He wore a belt and cross-strap. The strap bore a large green gem. It sparkled with inner light.

Baldwin made a sign of respect. "Colonel Norwood, Lieutenant Martin, this is War Commander Niman Poseen-Ka."

Norwood held her hands palm-out in the universal gesture of peaceful greeting. She looked the Hudathan in the eye. She saw intelligence there, plus something else. Curiosity? Empathy? A little of both? Or were his emotions so different, so alien, that she could never understand them? But she must try. An entire world was at stake.

"It is an honor to meet you, War Commander Poseen-Ka. Am I to understand that there will be no discussions? No opportunity for a cease-fire?"

"That is correct," the Hudathan replied evenly. "There is no need to negotiate for that which is already ours."

Norwood felt a heaviness settle into her stomach. She chose her words carefully.

"But why? Why attack that which you have sacrificed lives to conquer?"

Poseen-Ka blinked, and for a moment, and a moment only, she saw what looked like doubt in his eyes. But was it? There was no way to be sure. His answer was measured and seemed empty of all emotion.

"We will attack as long as there are signs of resistance. Resistance cannot and will not be tolerated."

"And it's good practice for the troops," Baldwin put in cheerfully. "Sort of a warm-up for battles to come. We let all the message torps through, you know. Here's hoping the Emp responds."

Norwood looked at Baldwin the same way that a scientist might examine a not altogether pleasant specimen. She saw thick brown hair, parted in the middle and swept back on both sides, a high forehead, intense eyes, patrician nose, and an expressive mouth. A handsome man except for what? A weakness of some kind, which, like a flaw within a metal blade, reveals itself when stressed. Her eyes narrowed and her voice grew hard. "So this is a game? A sop to your ego?"

Baldwin's eyes flashed with pent-up emotion. A vein started to throb just over his left temple. "No! It's proof! Proof that they were wrong! Proof that I'm fit for command!"

Suddenly she had it. Colonel Alex Baldwin. Of course! She should have remembered earlier. His court-martial had been big news on Imperial Earth, and even bigger news in military circles, where it was widely believed that he'd been railroaded. Something about a massacre on a rim world, drug addiction, and the Emperor's nephew.

"Yes," Poseen-Ka said, as if reading her mind. "Colonel Baldwin betrayed his people in order to prove his competence. That is what he claims anyway. There is an alternative explanation, however. Some of our best xenopsychologists have examined Colonel Baldwin and concluded that his true motive is revenge."

Norwood didn't know which surprised her the most. The Hudathan's calm, almost clinical description of Baldwin's psychology, or the subject's lack of visible reaction.

It was as if the war commander had never spoken, as if Baldwin could filter things he didn't want to hear, as if he was not entirely sane.

Norwood looked at Poseen-Ka. There it was again, that ineffable something that she couldn't quite put a finger on. Sympathy? Understanding? What?

"Well, that about covers it."

The voice belonged to Martin. They turned. Norwood frowned. "Covers what?"

Martin shrugged. His eyes were dark and flashed when he spoke. "What we came for. You heard the geek... no negotiations until resistance ends... and that means we have nothing to lose."

"Now, Martin, don't do anything..."

But the flight lieutenant closed his eyes, activated his implant, and sent a thought towards the shuttle. And, on a deck half a mile away, relays closed, power flowed, tolerances were exceeded, and an aircraft exploded. It was Martin's ace in the hole, a little surprise that he and a crew chief named Perez had dreamed up.

It worked like a charm. The first explosion caused a Hudathan attack ship to blow as well, which triggered more explosions, which caused the deck under Martin's feet to shudder in sympathy. A series of dull thuds followed moments later and served to confirm what had happened.

Martin opened his eyes and a lot of things took place all at once.

Imbala-Sa put two low-velocity darts through Martin's heart.

Klaxons began to bleat, orders were issued over the ship's PA system, and the surviving humans were dragged from the room.

Norwood tried to memorize the maze of seemingly identical corridors but was soon lost.

Crew members ran in every direction, shouted orders at each other, and did the multiplicity of things that they'd been trained to do.

It was hard to think in the midst of all the confusion, but one thing was clear. Martin *had* managed to kill some Hudathans, and in doing so, had unintentionally reinforced their xenophobia. It would be a long time, if ever, before the Hudathans would agree to meet with human beings again. Other thoughts might have followed, but were lost when she was shoved into a freight elevator and herded into a corner.

Then, after a very short ride, she was pushed, pulled, and prodded into a hallway, led to a small compartment, and secured to some wall-mounted rings.

Baldwin was stripped, forced to lie on a metal table, and strapped into place. He said something in Hudathan and the technician made a hissing reply.

Norwood was very, very frightened but did her best to hide it.

"What's going on?" she asked.

Baldwin tried for a nonchalant grin but wound up looking sick instead.

"The Hudathans believe that immediate reward or punishment can alter subsequent behavior. And, since I was the one that brought you here, responsibility for your actions rests with me."

"What will they do?"

"They forced me to accept an implant. Through it they can dispense pleasure or pain."

Norwood thought about that for a moment. "You deserve some pain."

Baldwin nodded understanding. "Yes, from your perspective, I suppose I do."

The technician started a timer and touched one of the lights on his control panel.

Baldwin screamed, arched his back in agony, and started to convulse.

Norwood thought of the planet below, of the people he had killed, and tried to take pleasure in Baldwin's pain.

But the screams went on and on, and no matter how much she tried to do otherwise, Norwood couldn't help but feel sorry for the man who made them.

2

Planet Algeron, the Human Empire

It was a beautiful day. The sun was out, the air was crystal-clear, and the mountains seemed so close that St. James could reach out and touch them. The Towers of Algeron. That's what the Naa called them and they deserved a majestic name. Some of the higher peaks soared 80,000 feet into the sky, higher than Everest on Earth, or Olympic Mons on Mars. So huge, and so heavy, that they would sink right through Terra's planetary crust.

But Algeron was different from Earth. Very different. Almost all of the differences stemmed from the fact that Algeron completed a full rotation every two hours and forty-two minutes. A rotation so fast that centrifugal force had caused a larger-than-normal bulge at the equator.

In fact, while Algeron's mass was virtually identical to Earth's, its equatorial diameter of 16,220 kilometers was 27 percent larger than Earth's. That, plus the fact that its polar diameter of only 8,720 kilometers was 32 percent smaller than Earth's, meant that Algeron's equatorial diameter was almost *twice* that of its polar diameter.

And that's where the Towers of Algeron came in. They were the topmost part of the world-spanning bulge, and thanks to the gravity differential that existed between the poles and the equator, weighed only half what they would on Terra.

All of which had nothing to do with Camerone Day, or the legionnaires waiting for St. James to speak, except that it pleased him to think about it. That was one of the privileges that went with rank: long silences, and the assumption that they were in some way profound.

Legion General Ian St. James smiled and ran his eyes over the assembled ranks. There were thousands of them, white kepis gleaming in the sun, weapons at parade rest. They were a treat to the military eye.

There were ranks of cyborgs, "trooper IIs," in front, each one standing eight feet tall, carrying enough armament to take on a platoon of marines. They had no need of uniforms, but many had received medals for valor, and wore them on ceremonial harnesses designed for such occasions.

Behind them St. James could see the assault quadrupeds, or "quads," four-legged walkers that could function as artillery, tanks, or antiaircraft batteries. They towered over the troops and provided what little shade there was.

Then there were the "bio bods," men and women with their hair cut so short that they were almost bald, their kepis gleaming white in the sun. Their uniforms were khaki, as they had been for thousands of years, and would be for thousands more.

Each wore the epaulets, green shoulder strap, and red fringe that had been standard since 1930, the green ties that had been adopted in 1945, the scarlet waist sashes authorized in 2090, the collar comets added after the Battle of Four Moons in 2417, and the hash marks that indicated their length of service.

He saw divisions of the 2nd Foreign Parachute Regiment, the 3rd Foreign Infantry Regiment, the 4th Foreign Infantry Regiment, the 13th Demi-Brigade de Légion Étrangère, and the 1st Foreign Regiment, which supplied administrative services to the entire Legion.

This was the day, April 30 on Earth, when the entire Legion came together as they were doing now. Not physically, because their duties didn't allow for that, but spiritually, as man, woman, and cyborg joined in a union that bound together the past and present. The mystical *something* that made the Legion more than a group of soldiers.

Nothing was more symbolic of that union than Camerone Day. It was a remembrance, a celebration, and a reaffirmation all rolled into one.

St. James lifted the old-fashioned paper from which he was about to read. It was hundreds of years old and sealed in plastic. The story of the battle was read once each year, and this year it was his duty—no, his *privilege*—to perform that function.

St. James cleared his throat. The sun had already rolled halfway across the sky in the relatively short time since the ceremony had begun. He would have to hurry to finish the story before another one hour and twenty-one minute night fell. Amplified by the PA system, his voice startled a pair of roosting brellas, and they squirted themselves up and into the air.

"In the spring of 1863, on the planet Earth, in a country then known as 'Mexico,' a war was fought. Now, thousands of years later, it doesn't matter *why* the war was fought or *who* won the war, except that the Legion was there.

"About 150 miles inland from the Gulf of Mexico, and 5,000 feet above sea level, the Mexicans decided to hold the town of Puebla. The French surrounded the city and a siege ensued.

"To reinforce their forces and break the siege, the French sent a supply convoy up towards the highlands. The convoy consisted of sixty horse-drawn wagons loaded with guns, ammunition, food, and gold."

St. James paused and let his eyes drift across the parade ground.

"Elements of the Legion were available to march *with* that convoy... but they were relegated to guard duty along the Gulf of Mexico."

St. James looked down at the paper.

"General Élie-Frédéric Forey put it this way: 'I preferred to leave foreigners rather than Frenchmen to guard the most unhealthy area, the tropical zone from Vera Cruz to Córdoba, where… malaria reigns.'"

St. James grinned. "Sound familiar?"

The roar of laughter confirmed that it did. The Legion had always been handed the short end of the stick and, so far at least, had always been willing to take it. He waited for silence.

"And so it was that the Legion's commanding officer, a colonel named Pierre Jeanningros, sent two companies, their strength diminished by illness, to meet the convoy and escort it to his base on Chiquihuite Mountain.

"Two days later a spy brought some disturbing news. The convoy would be ambushed by several battalions of infantry, cavalry, and local guerrillas. Hoping to avert disaster, Jeanningros sent another company down the road to warn the convoy or make contact with the enemy. He chose the 3rd Company of the 1st Battalion which had no officers fit for duty.

"That's why Captain Jean Danjou, a member of the headquarters staff, volunteered to lead the patrol. Two subalterns agreed to join him. Out of a normal complement of 120 men only 62 were fit for duty."

St. James looked out at his audience and knew that even though most of them had heard the story many times before, they were still enthralled. Similar battles had taken place since Camerone and would take place again. And the next story could center on them. He drew a deep breath.

"The company left before first light on April 30 and marched towards the coast. They made good time during the darkness and reached a post manned by the battalion's grenadiers before dawn. After coffee and some black bread the march resumed.

"Danjou led his men out just before dawn, which was just as well, since it was going to be an extremely hot day.

"They passed through a number of settlements during the next few hours. One such settlement was a run-down collection of shacks called Camerone.

"Danjou, a veteran of the Crimean War, led the column. Had someone been watching, they would have noticed that his left hand had been lost in an accident and replaced with a handcarved wooden replica. It did nothing to slow him down.

"The legionnaires entered Palo Verde about 7 A.M. There was no one about. They brewed some coffee and were drinking it when Danjou spotted an approaching dust cloud. The cloud could mean only one thing—horsemen, and lots of them.

"'Aux armes!' Danjou shouted.

"The company was terribly exposed, so they fell back towards Camerone and looked for a place to make a stand."

St. James looked up and continued from memory. "A shot rang out and a legionnaire fell. They rushed a tumbledown hacienda but the sniper had escaped. Danjou gathered his men and started them towards a nearby village. But the firing had alerted a contingent of Mexican cavalry. They came at a gallop.

"Danjou waved his sword in the air. 'Form a square! Prepare to fire!'

"The Mexicans split their force in half and approached at a walk. And then, when they were sixty meters away, they spurred their mounts and charged.

"Danjou ordered his men to fire, and thirty rounds hit the tightly packed horsemen. He gave the same order again and a second volley rang out. No sooner had the charge broken against the legionnaires' square than the Mexicans prepared for another charge. Danjou instructed his men to fire at will.

"The Mexicans took time to regroup. That allowed Danjou and his men time to break through their lines and reach the walls of the deserted hacienda.

"During the subsequent confusion the pack animals were lost along with most of the legionnaire's food, water, and ammunition. Sixteen legionnaires were killed. Danjou had two officers and forty-six men left.

"In the meantime the Mexican cavalry had been reinforced by local guerrilla fighters who had infiltrated themselves into the farm. They fired on Danjou and his men as they ran for a stable or took cover along a half-ruined wall. A sergeant named Morzycki climbed to the stable's roof and reported that 'hundreds of Mexicans' surrounded them.

"The ensuing battle was an on-again, off-again affair in which periods of relative quiet were suddenly shattered by sniper fire and sneak attacks.

"Meanwhile, about an hour's march away, three battalions of Mexican infantry received word of the fight and headed for Camerone. At about nine-thirty, a Mexican lieutenant approached under a flag of truce and offered the legionnaires an honorable surrender. 'There are,' he said, 'two thousand of us.'

"'We have enough ammunition,' Danjou responded. 'No surrender.'

"It was then that Danjou visited his troops, asked them to fight to the death, and received their promises to do so.

"Danjou was shot and killed two hours later. Second Lieutenant Napoléon Villain, a medal for gallantry shining brightly on his chest, assumed command. By noon, the two youngest members of the company, Jean Timmermans and Johan Reuss, were dead.

"A bugle sounded and Morzycki announced that approximately one thousand additional soldiers had arrived, each and every one of whom were armed with American carbines. The Mexicans called for the legionnaires to surrender and were refused once again.

"At about 2 P.M., a bullet hit Villain between the eyes and killed him instantly.

"The legionnaires died one by one. Among them were the Sergeant Major, Henri Tonel, Sergeant Jean Germays, Corporal Adolfi Delcaretto, Legionnaire Dubois, and the Englishman Peter Dicken. The survivors searched their clothes for ammunition, food, and water.

"By five o'clock there were nine legionnaires left alive. The Mexicans had suffered hundreds of casualties.

"When evening came, the Mexicans piled dry straw against the outside wall and tried to burn them out. Smoke billowed, and unable to see, the legionnaires fired at shadows. Another surrender was called for and summarily refused, after which fresh troops assaulted the hacienda and fired hundreds of rounds at the legionnaires. Sergeant Morzycki fell, as did three others.

"There were five men left: Second Lieutenant Maudet, Corporal Maine, plus Legionnaires Catteau, Constantin, and Wenzel. Each soldier had one bullet left.

"Maudet led the charge. Catteau tried to protect his officer and fell with nineteen bullets in his body. Maudet was hit and gravely wounded, but Maine, Constantin, and Wenzel were untouched.

"They stood perfectly still.

"A colonel named Cambas stepped forward. 'You will surrender now.'

"'Only if you allow us to keep our weapons and treat Lieutenant Maudet,' Maine said.

"'One refuses nothing to men such as you,' Cambas replied.

"They were presented to Colonel Milán shortly thereafter. He looked at an aide. 'Are you telling me that these are the only survivors?'

"'Yes, sir.'"

St. James looked down, careful to get the Spanish right.

"'*Pero, non son hombres, son demonios!*' ('Truly, these are not men, but devils!')

"Days passed before the bodies were buried, and during that time a rancher named Langlais found Danjou's wooden hand and eventually sold it to General Bazaine for fifty piasters."

The walls of Fort Camerone were high, high enough to contain the sound of General St. James's voice, and it took a moment for the echoes to die away.

The sun had begun to set and was little more than a reddish-orange smear.

Gas-fed torches, one located at each of the fort's three corners, popped as they were ignited, and the central band, a traditional part of the 1st RE, struck up a solemn dirge.

Lights came on, illuminating the gigantic globe that stood at the exact center of the parade ground, its base guarded by four bronze figures, each representing a different period in the Legion's history. The most recent was a cyborg.

It was at that point that an honor guard, comprised of one person from each of the regiments stationed on Algeron, carried the box containing Captain Danjou's wooden hand to the Monument to the Dead, and lowered it into an armaplast case. It would remain there for the duration of the festivities.

Then, one by one, the regiments were formed up, marched onto the large platforms that would carry them below, and released to take part in the celebration. It would, if past experience was any guide, last for the next six to eight hours.

General Ian St. James remained for a while. His eyes were on the Monument to the Dead but his thoughts were on a woman who was light-years away. General Marianne Mosby. Like him, she would be called upon to read the story to her troops and attend the ensuing festivities.

Would she think of him when the ceremony was over? Of the nights they had spent together on Algeron? Or had someone else caught her eye? The stars twinkled but gave no reply.

Slowly, deliberately, and with great respect St. James saluted those who had died, turned, and went below.

Booly groaned as the alarm went off next to his head. It took three tries to hit the off button.

He lay there for a moment, swung his feet over the side of the bed, and sat up. The duracrete floor was ice cold.

"Shit."

His head hurt and Booly cradled it with both hands.

"Shit. Shit. Shit."

Booly had promised himself that he would remain sober and had failed to do so. His bedside console included a clock. The readout said 0502, and the patrol would leave at 0700, hangover or no.

He stood, saw that his roommate, Sergeant Major Chin, was still passed out, and headed for the can. His bare feet made a slapping sound as they hit the floor.

Vomit had splattered across the toilet seat, dripped down the side, and pooled on the floor. It smelled and Booly wrinkled his nose. Damn Chin anyway. The bastard always missed.

Booly opened the cabinet over his sink, grabbed a bottle of pain tabs, and shook two of them into the palm of his hand. A gulp of water washed them down.

The face in the mirror had blue-bloodshot eyes, a flattened nose, and thin lips.

Booly ran a hand over his head to assure himself that it was nearly bald, stepped back, and checked for fat. There was none. His chest was broad and thick with muscle. Each rib was clearly defined. His stomach was flat and hard. There were tattoos on both of his forearms.

His right arm bore the winged-hand-and-dagger emblem of the 2nd REP, the Legion's elite airborne regiment, Booly's first love, and his left arm featured a grim reaper, with the caption "Death before dishonor."

Booly looked one more time, gave a grunt of satisfaction, and headed for the shower. The hot water felt good.

He took the opportunity to empty his bladder as well, and if Chin didn't like it, he could damned well barf *into* the toilet for a change.

It took more than fifteen minutes to clear his head and feel halfway human again. He stepped out, dried himself off, and dressed for combat.

First came thermal underwear, followed by half-armor, starched utilities, and lace-up boots. Then came the combat harness, complete with radio, knife, first-aid kit, sidearm, and spare magazines. And then, to top the whole thing off, the *képi blanc*.

Booly looked in the mirror, nodded approvingly, and turned. The room was a mess, but Chin would order some poor jerk to clean it up. That's how it was, and would forever be, amen.

Booly opened the door, stepped outside, and let it slam behind him. If the noise bothered Chin, then so much the better. A few steps carried him out of the side corridor, through one of the zigzag defensive points that interrupted the hallways every hundred feet or so, and out into the main passageway. It was busy as usual.

A pictorial history of the Legion lined both walls. Booly had examined most of it and been struck by the fact that there were almost as many losses as victories, a reflection of the fact that the Legion had been poorly used down through the years. As far as he could see, that trend hadn't changed much.

Unlike the rest of the Imperial services, the Legion's noncommissioned officers rated a salute, so Booly saluted his way down the corridor and into the mess hall.

He grabbed a tray, ignored the bins full of scrambled eggs and greasy meat, choosing toast and coffee instead.

To reach his table, Booly had to make his way around a series of life-sized Camerone Day displays. They stood like islands in an ocean of tables and chairs. There was one per regiment, and all had common themes, the most popular of which was glorious death.

His regiment, the 1st Foreign Cavalry Regiment, or 1st REC, had constructed what looked like a jungle, and populated it with a badly damaged Trooper II and twelve fanciful aliens. It was clear from the way the figures were positioned that the cyborg would die, but only after killing most, if not all, of his attackers. The display had been quite popular the night before and had won second prize in the overall contest.

Booly stopped, removed the pair of pink panties that had been draped over the Trooper's left missile launcher, and tossed them toward a trash can.

Four legionnaires saw Booly coming, jumped up, and moved to another table. Sergeant majors ranked just below god and could sit wherever they pleased.

Two pieces of toast and five cups of coffee later, Booly felt nearly human. Human enough to carry his coffee cup over to a cart himself... and smile at a sergeant with the largest breasts that he'd ever seen.

It was a relatively short walk from the mess hall to staging area 4, where the members of his patrol were running through last-minute equipment checks. It was a large rectangular room, filled with greenish-blue light and a lot of noise: the whine of servos as the cyborgs tested their electromechanical bodies, the chatter of a power wrench as a weapons tech tightened the bolts on a Trooper II's ammo bay, and the sound of profanity as a bio bod ran a systems check on her blast rifle.

The staging area smelled too, a heady mix of lubricants, ozone, and hot metal. Some of his fellow NCOs complained about it and submitted recs demanding a better ventilation system, but Booly liked the smell. It was part of what he did.

Booly stepped over to a wall terminal, entered an access code, and watched while names and serial numbers filled the screen. This was a routine "roust and reconnaissance," or R&R, patrol, designed to keep Naa bandits on the jump and detect tribal movements should any occur. Not that anyone really expected anything to happen, since both sides adhered to a long-established policy of almost ritual combat, in which skirmishes were the rule and pitched battles were studiously avoided. By doing so, both sides were able to reinforce the warrior-based values they held in common, confer status on individual members, and keep casualties down.

The Naa accomplished this by admitting adult males to the circle of warriors *after* combat with the Legion, and the humans had adopted a similar system in which recruits were brought to Algeron, where they were bloodied in battle.

The key to all of this was that Algeron had been given to the Legion by the Emperor himself, and that subsequent to that gift, the Legion had decided to forbid further colonization of the planet. So, with the exception of some early settlers, the legionnaires were the only humans around, a presence the Naa had learned to tolerate and even make use of.

Scanning the screen, Booly saw that he'd been given a quad whose official name was "George Washington," but was better known as "Gunner." Not that "George Washington" was his *real* name, since recruits were allowed to take a *nom de guerre*, and most did. It was a link to the distant past when the original French Foreign Legion had been home to people from many countries, most of whom had been on the run from the law, from a failed relationship, or from themselves.

Booly felt the floor shudder and looked over his shoulder. A quad had entered the bay. It stood twenty-five feet tall, weighed fifty tons, and had huge bull's-eyes painted on both of its battle-scarred flanks.

Booly shook his head in amazement. Gunner was a longtime legionnaire and one crazy sonofabitch. Some people thought the bull's-eyes were some sort of joke. Booly knew better. Gunner *wanted* to die but seemed destined to live forever. No matter how thick the battle, no matter how many legionnaires fell, Gunner survived. It was both his blessing and his curse.

Booly moved his eye down the list. He had the quad plus a full complement of Trooper IIs. Three were prime, with at least a battle a piece under their camouflage, but one, a newbie with a *nom de guerre* Napoléon Villain, was straight from Earth. He'd keep an eye on her.

A half-squad of five bio bods under the command of a sergeant known as "Roller" completed his force and would ride on Gunner. So, while Booly would have welcomed another quad, or double the number of bio bods, the force was adequate. Or so he hoped.

He wiped the screen, jumped down to the floor, and found that the patrol had formed up. Roller took a certain kind of perverse pride in allowing his people to run every which way right up to the last minute, and then, just when it looked as if he'd be caught short, bringing them together into perfect formation. Quads to the rear. Trooper IIs towards the middle, and bio bods in the front. It drove officers, especially junior officers, stark raving mad. Booly ignored it as if so serenely blessed that the world always fell into place around him.

Roller fumed but kept a perfectly straight face. He stood at quivering attention two paces in front of his troops.

"Sergeant Major."

"Sergeant."

"The troops are ready for inspection."

"Thank you."

Booly stepped past Roller and headed for the first legionnaire on his left. Her name was Kato. She'd been in the Legion for five years, wore a nose stud, and had a dotted line tattooed around her neck. Booly stepped in front of her, ran an experienced eye over her gear, found it to his liking, and moved on.

The next trooper wasn't so lucky. His name was Imai, and it took Booly less than a second to notice that the emergency locator beacon that should've been attached to his belt wasn't.

"Sergeant."

Roller appeared at Booly's right elbow. "Sergeant Major?"

"This man's emergency locator beacon is missing."

Roller treated the offender to a thunderous expression. "I'm glad you brought that to my attention, Sergeant Major. I'll take care of it."

Booly said, "See that you do," and knew that he had sentenced Imai to a week's worth of punishment. Unpleasant, perhaps, but preferable to being lost in the wastelands with no chance of rescue.

The rest of the bio bods, O'Brian, Wismer, and Yankolovich, passed muster, and Booly started in on the Trooper IIs. They had a more humanoid appearance than the Trooper Is plus heavier armament.

Each was equipped with a fast-recovery laser cannon, an air-cooled .50-caliber machine gun, and dual missile launchers. They could run at speeds up to fifty miles an hour and could be adapted for a variety of environments including vacuum, Class I through Class IX gas atmospheres, underwater use, desert heat, and arctic cold.

On the other hand, Trooper IIs had a tendency to overheat during prolonged combat, consumed ordnance at a prodigious rate, and were vulnerable to a variety of microbot-delivered computer viruses.

Their greatest weakness, however, lay in the fact that they were only as smart and capable as the human brains that lived inside of them. Brains that had been connected to human bodies once, and then, in retribution for an act of criminal violence or as the result of some terrible misfortune, had literally died. Died, and been dragged back from the great abyss, to live in electromechanical bodies where they might very well die again.

This common experience made the cyborgs different in ways that bio bods couldn't understand. A bio bod might *imagine* what it would be like to live in a mechanical body but couldn't really *know* it. Couldn't know the feeling of isolation that came with looking like a freak, the yearning for physical contact, or the pain that a malfunction could cause, which was why a gulf existed between cyborgs and bio bods, and why the media sometimes referred to all of them as "The Legion of the Damned," and why an aura of mystery surrounded them.

Booly was six-two, but the Trooper IIs towered over him. Most of their equipment had been built into their bodies, so readiness was ascertained by checking tiny readouts located at different points on their armor.

The first Trooper II in line had the name "Rossif" stenciled on his right chestplate, a 1st REC insignia on his left arm, and a heart with an arrow through it on what would have been his right biceps. By long tradition the cyborgs were entitled artwork in place of the tattoos worn by bio bods.

Each Trooper II came equipped with no fewer than ten small inspection plates. Booly picked five in random order, thumbed them open, and examined the readouts. Power, 92%. Coolant, 98%. Ammo, 100%. Life support, 100%. Electronic counter-measures, 85%.

Booly looked up towards the Trooper II's massive head. "You have an ECM readiness reading of 85 percent. Explain."

The cyborg's speech synthesizer sounded like a rock crusher in low gear. "There's a shortage of high-end filters, Sergeant Major. The techs have them on back order."

Booly nodded. Parts were a constant problem on Algeron. Thank god the Naa were relatively low-tech. The chance of an electronic attack was next to nothing. He moved on.

Troopers Jones and Wutu got off with little more than a superficial inspection. But by virtue of being a newbie, Trooper Villain came in for special attention.

Although she had chosen a male name, and was just as asexual as the rest of them, she had elected to use the title "Ms." in front of her name, indicating that she still viewed herself as female. Booly knew this was a touchy subject with cyborgs and made a mental note to use a female pronoun whenever he referred to her.

He checked all of her readouts, scanned the floor around her massive feet for any signs of leaks, and gave a grunt of satisfaction. "A nice turnout, Villain. You and I will take the point position."

Villain started to say "Thank you," remembered what they had taught her in boot camp, and said, "Yes, Sergeant Major," instead. She remembered something else too. She remembered that point was one of the most dangerous slots, if not *the* most dangerous, in patrol formation, which meant that she had nothing to be thankful for.

Booly nodded and moved on. Gunner had lowered himself to the floor, a position that allowed Booly full access to his mechanical anatomy, but the inspection was for show. The cyborg was far too complex for Booly to evaluate from readouts alone, and far too wily to let any of his faults show. Besides, any problems with Gunner's systems would reflect on the techs who maintained him, and they weren't about to let that happen.

So Booly went through the motions of an inspection, climbed down, and returned to the point from which he'd started.

"Sergeant."

"Sergeant Major."

"Not bad. Not bad at all. We leave ten from now."

In truth it took more like fifteen minutes to complete the final checklists, download the latest intelligence summary, and form up.

Roller had taken one hit already, so Booly ignored the difference.

Booly found Villain, used the steps built into the back of her legs to climb level with the back of her head, and strapped himself into a recess designed for that purpose. He pulled his goggles on, adjusted his headset and inserted the lead from his radio into a jack panel located at the base of Villain's duraplast neck.

"Villain?" Booly's voice seemed to echo through her head.

Villain cursed her rotten luck. Going out on her first patrol was bad enough, but doing it with a sergeant major strapped to her back was even worse. It was one more indignity, one more unit of pain, one more thing to avenge. The legionnaire forced a response.

"Yes, Sergeant Major?"

"Give me a radio check."

Villain knew what the sergeant major meant. By plugging his radio into her communications system Booly had doubled his range. If there was a problem, her testing circuits would find and identify it. She ran a check.

"The com system is green."

"Good," Booly replied. "Be sure to let me know if any of your systems turn yellow or red."

Hell, yes, she'd tell him. What did he think? That she was stupid?

"Yes, Sergeant Major."

A new one-hour-and-twenty-one-minute day was dawning as they rode the lift up to the parade ground. Villain and Booly left the elevator first, followed by Rossif, Jones and Wutu.

A work party stopped to let them pass, practiced eyes

skimmed their equipment, and salutes snapped back and forth.

Gunner's head darted this way and that as his legs took large mincing steps. The cyborg was very much aware of the legionnaires inside his belly. He was honor-bound to protect them while they were under his care, but the obligation ended the moment that they left the squad bay, and gave him an opportunity to die.

Ah, the cyborg thought to himself, how wonderful that would be. To fall into eternal blackness where memories could not find him, where the past could not haunt him, where peace would be his. He'd been there once, but the medics had reached down into the darkness and saved him from the very thing that he wanted most. Damn each and every one of the bastards to hell!

Massive gates rumbled open. The right side had been hit by a shoulder-launched missile the month before. Metal had buckled under the force of the explosion and grated where it rubbed against the fort's outside wall. Not a serious attack, but a reminder that the Naa were around and could inflict damage when they chose to do so.

The memory caused Booly's stomach muscles to tighten. Chemicals entered his bloodstream and everything grew more intense. The blueness of the sky. The warmth of the sun on the back of his neck. The whine of Villain's servos. The pungent odor of Naa incense.

The Naa had an extremely acute sense of smell and used the incense to obliterate the odors that seeped out of the fort. They burned the stuff in small ornamental pots, so that a hundred fingers of smoke pointed up towards the sky, where the wind caught and pulled them towards the south.

Booly turned to exchange salutes with a legionnaire on top of the wall, checked to make sure that Wutu had cleared the gates, and signaled accordingly. Servos whined, doors rumbled, and metal grated as the gates slid closed.

The smell of incense was more intense now as the domes of Naa town closed in around them. The domes were low, gently curved affairs, that served as roofs for the mostly underground dwellings. Light gleamed here and there where it reflected off metal that had been scavenged from the fort's garbage dump and used to reinforce the adobe-style construction.

Cubs chased each other around Gunner's huge plate-shaped feet while their parents watched from a distance. Most people agreed that the Naa were attractive in an exotic sort of way. The males stood six to seven feet tall. Females were a foot or so shorter. Both were covered with soft, sleek fur, which came in a wide variety of colors and patterns. Their heads were extremely human in shape and size, as were their ears, noses, and mouths, although their dentition was different, featuring chopping teeth in front, grinding teeth in back, and no canines.

Like humans, the Naa had four fingers and an opposable thumb, but had no fingernails. Their feet were different too, having no separate toes, and being longer, broader, and flatter than humans'.

Booly watched them from his position on Villain's back. These were tame Naa, of course, outcasts, misfits, and thieves for the most part, unwilling or unable to make a living out in the wild, huddling around Fort Camerone for protection from their own kind, while eking out a living based on alien scraps and day labor.

Still, there was something about them that Booly liked, a fact he had kept to himself, since many of his peers called them "geeks" and other disparaging names, a practice that seemed more than a little strange, for many of the same men and women who called the Naa derogatory names praised them for their valor and considered them worthy opponents.

The seeming contradiction stemmed from the Naa's status as respected enemies. In order to kill, it was first necessary to hate, and calling the Naa names helped the legionnaires accomplish that. But there's little glory in killing someone or something weak, so it was simultaneously necessary to build the Naa up, making them worthy opponents. Booly saw it as a piece of psychological flimflammery, and was often tempted to say so but had managed to hold his peace. After all, what difference would it make? One person says this, another says that the whole thing was bullshit.

The domes had thinned now and were dropping behind.

Booly swept the horizon from left to right. Nothing. Good. He activated his radio.

"Rossif... Jones... take the flanks. Wutu... watch our back trail. You'll be first to die if we take it in the ass.

Gunner... give me full scan on your detectors. Okay, everybody... let's move out."

Back at the edge of Naa town a male watched them go. His fur was spotted with age, and missing where an energy beam had sliced across his chest twenty-odd years before, but his eyes were bright with intelligence.

He watched the patrol until it became little more than specks. It was a two-klick walk to the garbage dump and the com set that was hidden there. A com set that had been liberated from a similar patrol six years before. Used sparingly, and kept where no one thought to look, it had already accounted for sixty-two legionnaires.

The old one smiled and took the first step of his long journey.

3

To sup with the devil… you must first enter hell.
DWELLER FOLK SAYING
Circa 2349

Planet Earth, the Human Empire

Everyone knows they're going to die but few know when. Angel Perez knew, right down to the day, the minute, and the second.

And if he managed to forget somehow, or used contraband drugs to push the information out of his brain, it was there on the wall screen to remind him. The words appeared in different fonts sometimes, and changed colors every hour on the hour, but the content remained the same.

"At approximately 1830 of day 4, standard month 2, you killed Cissy Conners. Having been tried for this crime and found guilty, you will be executed at 0600 on day 15, of standard month 4."

The words never varied, but the digital readout located in the lower right-hand corner of the screen did. It showed his life expectancy in hours and minutes. What had originally been thirty-one days had dwindled to little more than an hour. They'd send for him any moment now.

He'd been in prison for more than a year while the criminal

41

court's centralized computer system took his case through the automatic appeals process. Then, having found no grounds for a retrial or an adjustment of sentence, an artificial intelligence known as JMS 12.1 had transferred him from carousel 2, tower 4, to carousel 16, tower 9, better known to inmates as the "death stack," or DS for short.

Perez was glad that he'd refused his last meal. An empty stomach made it less likely that he'd throw up or shit his pants. He thought of his mother and wondered if she knew or cared.

Servos whined and his cell moved. Sideways at first, then downwards, dropping so fast that it made his ears pop. Air came in via thousands of tiny holes. None were large enough to look through, but Perez knew what was happening.

JMS 12.1 had rotated carousel 16 until his particular cell was aligned with one of the tower's four elevator tubes and dropped it down a shaft. The cell slowed suddenly, making him feel heavier, and throwing him sideways as it was rotated out of the elevator tube.

There was a commotion outside. Other prisoners, with life expectancies only slightly longer than his, shouted obscenities and banged on the steel walls. The ritual had no effect on the guards but made the inmates feel better.

Machinery hummed, dead bolts snicked, and the door opened.

There were four of them. Just the right number to handle a desperate prisoner without getting in each other's way. They wore black hoods, shirts, and pants. Perez was naked. That, like everything else in the prison, was part of the punishment.

The guard furthest to the left spoke.

"Perez?"

Perez found his throat was very, very dry. He mustered some saliva and forced it down.

"Wrong cell. He's on carousel five."

There were appreciative chuckles from the nearby cells.

Their thoughts, their memories, were the only epitaph Perez could hope for.

One of the men had a black truncheon. He tapped it against a thigh. "Cute, Perez. Real cute. So what's it gonna be? Vertical? Or horizontal?"

Perez forced himself to stand. His knees were shaking. The digital readout said he had 42:16 left. "Vertical."

The man with the truncheon shook his head disappointedly. "Okay, vertical it is. Ito and Jack will go first. You'll come next and Bob and I will bring up the rear. Questions?"

Perez tried to think of a flip comment, failed, and shook his head.

"Good. Let's go."

Perez waited until two of the guards had passed through the door, got a nod from the man with the truncheon, and followed along behind.

The hall was brightly lit and smelled of industrial-strength disinfectant. The floor felt cold beneath his bare feet. Perez was painfully aware of his nakedness and complete vulnerability.

There were catcalls and comments from men and women he'd never seen and never would.

"See you in hell, Perez!"

"Take care, asshole."

"Sweet dreams, shithead."

It went on and on until they reached the checkpoint. The party stopped, one of the guards placed his palms against a print reader, and the doors slid open.

The first pair of guards went through, Perez followed, and the others came along behind. There was another hallway, shorter this time, followed by a second checkpoint. This one required two sets of prints, one from a guard and one from Perez. The substance inside the reader looked and felt like gray modeling clay. He put his hands against it and looked towards a guard, who nodded his approval.

"It's for your own protection, Perez. We wouldn't want to grease you freaks in the wrong order."

Perez removed his hands from the reader and the doors slid open. "How very considerate."

"Yeah," the guard agreed. "Ain't it just?"

Perez saw that all four of the guards had placed themselves between him and the hall. This was it, then, the infamous death room, where justice would be administered. Justice that came straight from the Old Testament. An eye for an eye, a

43

tooth for a tooth, a bullet for a bullet.

Perez felt his bowels loosen and his knees start to shake.

"You need some help?" The voice was gruff but sympathetic.

Perez shook his head, turned, and forced himself through the doors. The room looked the way it did on television, only larger. And why not? Live executions were a regular part of the news. He'd seen plenty of them. So many they didn't mean shit. Not until now, that is.

"Show 'em what death looks like and they won't do it."

That was theory... but judging from the long waiting lines in death row, it seemed as if things were a bit more complex than that.

Perez was a case in point. He hadn't *planned* to murder Cissy Conners. He had pointed the gun at her, demanded money from the till, and fired when her hands dipped below the countertop. Just like in the vids, where blood spurted out and the actor lived to star in another show. Except this bullet was real and the woman was dead.

The guard was polite. "Step over here, please."

Perez did as he was told. He stepped over to the chromed framework and waited while his arms and legs were strapped to cold metal. It was shaped like a huge "X," as in "X marks the spot," and occupied the exact center of the cube-shaped room.

Perez looked around. The walls, ceiling, and floor were made of seamless easy-to-clean stainless steel. Dark-clad images rippled across them as the guards moved.

Perez felt an unevenness beneath his feet and looked down to see what it was. His penis had almost disappeared into his abdomen, and beyond that, his feet rested on a chromed drain. A drain that could handle a lot of water, or water mixed with blood, or...

Perez looked up and around. Now he saw the hoses that hung on all four walls, the nozzles that would spray disinfectants into the room, and the television cameras carefully placed to record his death. He wanted to give them the finger but it was too late. The restraints held his arms and legs in a rigid embrace.

A voice filled the room. It was solemn but somewhat bored as well.

"Angel Perez, having murdered the woman known as Cissy

Conners, and having been found guilty of said murder, you are about to die. Do you have any final words?"

"Yeah. Frax you."

"Not especially original, but heartfelt nonetheless," the voice said calmly. "Now, you are doubtless aware that a small percentage of the criminals executed in this room are chosen for resuscitation and enlistment in the Legion. Would you like to be considered for resuscitation? Or do you choose certain death?"

Like most of the people who found themselves in his position, Perez had considered certain death and rejected it. Somewhere, just beyond the walls of the death room, other facilities waited. Medical technology so sophisticated that it could bring all but the most massively injured back to life. And life, even half-life as a cyborg, was better than death.

His voice came out as a croak. "I wish to be considered for resuscitation."

"Your choice has been noted," the voice intoned.

"And now, in concert with Imperial Law, you will be executed in a manner similar to the way that you killed Cissy Conners. A bullet in the arm, followed by a bullet in the shoulder, followed by a bullet in the chest. Do you have any questions?"

Perez felt something warm dribble down the inside surface of his leg. "No."

"May god have mercy on your soul."

Only one guard remained. He wore full body armor to protect himself against the possibility of a ricochet. He had a long-barreled .22-caliber pistol. It was equipped with a laser sight, reactive grips, and special low-velocity ammunition.

He stepped forward, raised the pistol, and sighted down the barrel. Perez felt every muscle in his body tighten against the expected impact.

The guard did something with his thumb and Perez saw a red dot appear on his left biceps. Seeing the dot, knowing exactly where the bullet would hit, was more than he could stand.

"Oh god, please don't…"

The slug hit his arm, tore its way through, and flattened itself against the steel framework. The sound, like the pain, came a fraction of a second after the impact.

Perez screamed, fought the restraints, and lost control of his bladder. The urine was still splattering across his feet when the second dot appeared on his shoulder.

"No! No! N—!"

This bullet went through, hit the far wall, and smeared itself across the harder metal.

Perez was still in the process of absorbing the shock, and feeling the pain, when the guard corrected his aim.

Perez saw the dot slide up across his chest, slow, then stop.

He was starting to scream when the last bullet hit.

Rain drummed against the limo's roof and ran in rivulets down the windows. The palace was a smear of bright light blocked here and there by the statues that lined the drive, and the fancifully shaped topiaries that dotted the lawns.

The limo threw up a wave of water as it turned into the drive. Sergi Chien-Chu shook his head sadly. He felt sorry for the people at Weather Control. Someone or something had chosen the night of the Imperial ball to screw things up. Within a month, two at the most, they'd be counting icicles on an ice planet, or sorting sand on a hell world. The Emperor had very little patience with incompetence, other than his own, of course, which generally fell under the heading of "bad luck."

A massive portico jutted out over the drive. The rain vanished as the limo came under its protection and slowed to a stop. A footman appeared and waited for the door to open.

"Buzz me when you're ready to leave, sir. I'll be in the parking lot."

The voice came via the car's intercom and belonged to Chien-Chu's chauffeur-cum-bodyguard, Roland Frederick. He sat twelve feet forward of the rearmost passenger seat and was invisible behind black plastic.

Chien-Chu gathered the ridiculous toga around his rather portly body and prepared to leave the limo.

"Don't be silly, Frederick. Go home and get some sleep. I'll take a cab home."

"I'm sorry, sir, but madam would never forgive me."

"What if I *order* you to go?"

"No offense, sir, but I'm a good deal more afraid of madam than I am of you."

Chien-Chu knew it was true, and knew something else as well: that Frederick *wanted* to stay and would do whatever he pleased.

Chien-Chu touched the door release. It hissed open. "Well, suit yourself, but it's damned silly, if you ask me."

The driver's-side rearview mirror provided an excellent view of the foppish footman and the now open door. Frederick watched his boss heave himself out of the backseat, refuse a helping hand, and gather the toga into some semblance of order. Chien-Chu was a short man, and what with the gold bracelet, white robes, and leather sandals, looked the spitting image of a Roman senator.

Frederick shook his head sympathetically. The boss hated this kind of crap and would be miserable all night. He'd welcome a ride when the ball was over and Frederick would be there to provide it.

Chien-Chu waved toward the driver's compartment, turned, and joined a couple dressed as twenty-second-century air dancers. It took him a moment to recognize them as Governor French and her husband, Frank.

"Sergi! It's good to see you! I *love* your costume!"

"And I yours," Chien-Chu replied, eyeing the governor's next-to-nonexistent attire. She was close to fifty but very well preserved. He leered at her.

"Why, Sergi... you old goat! Have you met my husband, Frank?"

"Of course," Chien-Chu replied, exchanging nods with a handsome youth thirty years the governor's junior. "Frank and I had drinks together during the in-system speedster races last year. A nice finish, by the way... you nearly won."

This comment was sufficient to stimulate a highly technical dissertation on Frank's loss and his prospects for the current year. A somewhat boring conversation but sufficient to carry them through the main doors, down a brightly lit hallway, to the entrance of the Imperial ballroom. Brightly uniformed marines stood along the left side of the wall, eyes front and weapons at port arms.

During this seemingly innocuous journey, all three were aware that batteries of scanners, sensors, and detectors were probing their bodies, clothes, and accessories for any sign of weapons, explosives, or toxic chemicals. Should anything even remotely threatening be discovered, they knew that the marines had orders to fire. Which explained why there was one line of marines instead of two, why all of them wore a receiver in their left ear, and why they stood against the inside wall. Stray bullets, if any, would be directed out and away from the ballroom.

A pair of carefully matched Trooper IIs formed the last line of defense. Like all military cyborgs, they were members of the Legion and stood like statues to either side of the ballroom doors.

They had two missions. The first was to provide the marines with fire support in the case of a massed assault, and the second was to kill the marines if they moved more than a foot out of position.

There was the theoretical possibility of a joint assassination attempt, of course, but, thanks to the carefully orchestrated interservice rivalries that the Emperor had worked so hard to encourage, such an alliance was extremely unlikely.

It was, Chien-Chu thought to himself, a simultaneous measure of the Emperor's brilliance and paranoia.

They paused while a pair of brightly befeathered aliens preceded them into the room, then they stepped through the door. A truly resplendent majordomo lifted his staff from the highly polished floor and brought it down with a distinct thump.

"Governor Carolyn French, of the Imperial Planet Orlo II, her husband, the Honorable Frank Jason, and the Honorable Sergi Chien-Chu, Advisor to the Throne."

The sound of his voice was amplified and could be heard by anyone with a pulse.

Chien-Chu had no idea how the majordomo managed to get all the names and titles correct but assumed electronic wizardry of some kind.

The ballroom was huge, large enough to hold a thousand people at one time, and six or seven hundred of them had already arrived. The combined sound of their conversation, laughter, and movement came close to drowning out the ten-piece band.

Though normally light and airy, the room had been transformed into what seemed like a subterranean cave. Columns of light reached up to explode across the ceiling. Multicolored lasers slashed the room into a thousand geometric shapes. People appeared and disappeared as floor spots speared them from below. Their brightly colored costumes and expensive jewelry sparkled with reflected light. Some wore suits and dresses that had been decorated with stardust, the fabulously expensive substance that could only be obtained from the corona of one particular brown dwarf, and was of considerable interest to Chien-Chu Enterprises.

Most of the guests had ignored the announcement, but Chien-Chu knew that at least fifty or sixty had paid close attention and were headed his way. Each one of them wanted something. A favor, a deal, reassurance, information, or variations on those themes. That, after all, was what sensible people did at such affairs, leaving the drugs, sex, and vicarious violence to those with little or no self-respect, a group that was consistently overrepresented of late.

The three of them descended the stairs together, promised to see each other later, and separated.

Knowing that various associates, customers, and suppliers were headed his way, Chien-Chu sought to temporarily avoid them. A newcomer was present tonight, an individual with enough power to influence the Emperor, and therefore someone to know.

Such relationships were necessary for the well-being of Chien-Chu Enterprises, and more than that, for the continuation of the somewhat fragile alliance that sought to counter the Emperor's less rational moments. Moments that seemed to arrive with ever greater frequency.

The merchant murmured a steady stream of hellos, excuse-mes, and how-are-yous as he wound his way across the floor. The air was thick with expensive perfume, cologne, and incense. His destination was the clump of people that always seemed to gather near the largest of the ballroom's four bars.

These were the men and women of the Imperial Armed Forces, in mufti tonight, but clearly identifiable by their carriage, jargon and tendency to form tribal groups.

There was the Navy, known for their loud braggadocio, the marines, unimaginatively dressed in a variety of ancient uniforms, and the Legion, standing back-to-back as if besieged by the other services.

But these were functionaries for the most part, lower ranking generals, admirals, captains, and colonels, jockeying for position and holding court for lesser lights.

Their superiors, the group in which Chien-Chu was primarily interested, had no peers other than each other: men and women who understood what it was to deal with Imperial whims, tight budgets, and corrupt bureaucrats. It was to them that he gravitated, feeling sure that if Legion General Marianne Mosby was anywhere to be found, it would be here among her peers. And he was not disappointed. The military *crème de la crème* stood all by themselves, protected by a moat of unoccupied floor, turned in on each other.

Admiral Paula Scolari, chief of naval operations, was a tall, angular, and rather gaunt-looking woman dressed in medieval armor. Her choice of costumes struck Chien-Chu as symbolically appropriate for someone who lived in fear of the Emperor, the court, and, he suspected, of herself.

General Otis Worthington, commandant of the Marine Corps, stood to her right, dressed in little more than a jockstrap, lace-up boots, and a sword. His carefully maintained body rippled with muscle and pent-up power. He had black skin, bright inquisitive eyes, and a quick laugh. Though an excellent officer and well intentioned, Worthington hated politics and ceded more power to Scolari than he should have.

Standing to the admiral's left was the woman Chien-Chu was looking for. Unlike her associates, General Marianne Mosby had chosen the guise of a well-known holo star, and the likeness was remarkable.

She had long brown hair which the merchant assumed was part of the costume, a heart-shaped face, and full, sensuous lips. And, like the star that she'd chosen to impersonate, Mosby was ever-so-slightly overweight, as though she was inclined to take her share—and a little more.

But whatever extra flesh the general allowed herself was

located in all the right places. The bodice of her gown was cut low and wide, so low that her nipples, rouged for the occasion, appeared and disappeared as she moved, and caused every male within fifty feet to watch her from the corner of his eye. Mosby's attire was conservative compared to that worn by many in the room, but was outrageous by military standards, as was clear from Scolari's rather pronounced frown.

Chien-Chu summoned his most engaging smile and stepped across the invisible barrier. It was necessary to yell in order to make himself heard above the noise.

"Admiral Scolari, General Worthington, how good to see you."

Scolari glowered and inclined her head a quarter of an inch. "And you, Sergi. Have you met General Mosby? The general has assumed command of the Legion's forces on Earth."

Mosby extended a hand, but rather than shake it, Chien-Chu lifted it to his lips.

"My name is Sergi Chien-Chu. I had no idea that generals could be so beautiful. The opportunity to kiss one, if only on the hand, is too good to pass by."

"Sergi has a way with words," Scolari said dryly. "He owns Chien-Chu Enterprises... and is one of the Emperor's most trusted advisors."

Mosby smiled and subjected Chien-Chu to the same lightning-fast evaluation that she used on raw recruits. What she saw was a relatively short man, five-nine or five-ten, who was at least twenty-five pounds overweight. His features had a Eurasian cast to them, which made an interesting contrast to his piercing blue eyes and olive-colored skin. He radiated confidence the way the sun radiates heat. And, unlike most men, Chien-Chu had managed to maintain contact with her eyes rather than her breasts. He was, she decided, a force to contend with, and worthy of her attention.

"It's an honor to meet you, Mr. Chien-Chu. I'm familiar with your company. One of the few that make promises and keep them."

Chien-Chu bowed slightly. "The honor is mine... and thank you... we place a high value on the Legion's business."

Mosby extended her arm. "I don't know about you, but I'm

famished. Would you care for some refreshments?"

"I shouldn't," Chien-Chu responded cheerfully, "but I will." He took her arm. "If you two will excuse us?"

Scolari gave a barely perceptible nod and Worthington grinned widely. "Nice work, Sergi. Move in on the most beautiful woman in the room, steal her right out from under my nose, and make your getaway."

Chien-Chu smiled and shrugged. "Some of us have it... and some of us don't. General Mosby?"

Mosby nodded to her peers and allowed herself to be steered across the room. This was only her second visit to the Imperial Palace, the first having been for a short ceremony years before, and she was amazed by the goings-on.

She had chosen the gown with every intention of being provocative but was outclassed by those around her. Some of the guests were clad in little more than a sequin or two. Many were engaged in casual sex, pairing off on the floor or heading for side rooms where more comfortable furnishings could be found.

In some of those rooms, acrobats staged live sex acts and the audience joined in. In some, drugs were served on silver trays. In others, even darker activities were said to take place.

One part of Mosby, the part that had been raised on a conservative planet named Providence, was repulsed by what she saw. Another part, the part that had driven her off-planet to look for adventure, was titillated. What would it feel like to take her clothes off and roll around on the floor with a perfect stranger?

Damned uncomfortable, she decided, eyeing one such couple and sidestepping another.

She made eye contact with Chien-Chu. "Has it always been like this?"

"Like what?" Chien-Chu asked distractedly. His mind had been elsewhere.

"Like this," Mosby said, gesturing towards the rest of the guests. "I've been to some wild places, and even wilder night spots, but this puts most of them to shame."

Chien-Chu shifted mental gears. He'd forgotten that Mosby had spent the last two years on Algeron and was therefore unused to the debauchery currently in fashion.

"No, it's rather recent, actually. It started about six months ago when the Emperor made love to Senator Watanabe during the opening performance of the Imperial Opera. The whole thing took place in his box, but the cheaper seats could see in, and half the people present had opera glasses. The critics said he was marvelous. It's been like this ever since."

Mosby laughed. She was having a good time. Chien-Chu was charming and, if the Emperor lived up to even half of his reputation, would be interesting as well. She couldn't wait to meet him.

"Where *is* the Emperor anyway? Will he arrive soon?"

Chien-Chu shrugged and guided her towards the far end of an enormous buffet table. Mosby had presented him with a choice. He could be honest, and tell her that the Emperor spent a lot of his time conversing with people no one else could see, or he could play it safe, and say something less risky. The second choice seemed better.

"The Emperor's a busy man... it's hard to say when he'll arrive. Here... try some of this lab-grown beef... it looks quite good."

Mosby liked food and was quickly overcome by both the quality and the quantity of the feast spread before her. Lights had been positioned to illuminate the Emperor's offerings and they were generous indeed. She saw the beef that Chien-Chu had mentioned, ham, two or three kinds of fowl, alien flesh from something called a "snooter," several varieties of fish, vegetables, great bowls of fresh hydroponically grown fruit, and enough baked goods to feed a company of legionnaires for a week.

Mosby's plate was quite full by the time that she reached the far end of the table and required both hands to hold it. Chien-Chu brushed her elbow.

"Shall we find a place to sit?"

"Let's," Mosby agreed. "How about that side room over there?"

Chien-Chu looked in the direction of her nod. "Are you sure? The blue room gets pretty raunchy sometimes."

Mosby smiled. "Excellent. After two years on Algeron 'raunchy' sounds good."

Chien-Chu shrugged and followed her across the floor. The door was open and a servant found them seats towards the back of a packed room. It was dark, and that plus some carefully placed spotlights served to keep all eyes focused on the impromptu stage.

Standing towards the center of the stage, just removing the last of her clothing, was a beautiful woman. She was twenty-five or thirty, with black kinky hair and the body of an athlete, or a dancer, for there was discipline in the way that she moved. Her breasts were small and firm, her waist was narrow, and her legs were long and slender.

But there was something else, something Chien-Chu couldn't quite put a finger on, something that disturbed him. What was it? A pallor about her face? A tremor in her hands?

Yes, in spite of her attempts to appear serene, the woman was frightened. Why?

The woman stepped into a shower stall. It gleamed under the lights. Everything, even the plumbing, was transparent, allowing the audience to see every move she made.

The woman started the water, allowed it to cascade over her head, and began a long, leisurely shower.

Water splashed against the sides of the enclosure and provided its own symphony of sounds. The woman smeared bath gel over her breasts, rubbed it to a lather, and rinsed it off.

Chien-Chu felt a familiar stirring between his legs and looked at Mosby to see her reaction. She was eating, her eyes focused on the stage, entranced by the performance.

A spot came on. A man appeared. He was grossly fat, in an obvious state of arousal, and armed with a crude-looking knife. The crowd gave a collective gasp.

Chien-Chu felt an emptiness in the pit of his stomach. Beauty and the Beast. The story was as old as mankind itself... but science had enabled them to tell it in a brand-new way. The scenario was blindingly obvious.

No wonder the woman was afraid. For reasons known only to herself, an incurable disease, perhaps, or a desperate need for money, she had agreed to die. In ten or fifteen minutes, after the shower had been dragged out to the nth degree, the man would hack her to death with the knife.

The screams, like the blood, would be real. For an audience

bored with simulated violence, the real thing would be exciting. Then, just as she slumped to the floor, the lights would snap out. Under the cover of darkness medical technicians would rush in, recover the body, and convey it to a specially equipped surgical suite, where the woman would be snatched from the brink of death to live out the rest of her life in a cybernetic body. Nothing as grotesque as a Trooper II, perhaps, but a good deal less than what she had sold and the audience had psychically consumed.

It wasn't murder, but whatever it was made Chien-Chu sick, and caused him to slide the food under his chair. A hand touched his shoulder. The servant was dimly seen.

"Mr. Chien-Chu? General Mosby?"

"Yes?"

"Admiral Scolari asks that you join her outside."

Chien-Chu was eager for any sort of excuse to leave the room. He rose and headed for the door. Mosby did likewise. Admiral Scolari was waiting. The expression on her face was even more grim than usual.

"The Emperor has convened a meeting of his advisory council. Both of you are instructed to come."

Chien-Chu raised an eyebrow. The Emperor held meetings whenever the fancy took him... and many were a waste of time.

"What's the meeting about?" he asked.

"The Hudatha attacked a human-colonized planet called 'Worber's World.' Initial reports suggest that they eradicated the entire population. The Emperor would value your opinions."

4

Radu are rather torpid and completely harmless if left alone. Once disturbed, however, they are quite vicious, and the entire nest must be destroyed.
SCREEN 376, PARAGRAPH 4
SURVIVAL ON THE SUBCONTINENT HUDATHAN MILITARY CUBE

With the Hudathan fleet on the fringe of the Human Empire
Poseen-Ka selected a pair of long slender tweezers from the array
of instruments laid out in front of him, reached down into the
bubble-shaped terrarium, and took hold of a miniaturized bridge.
Lifting the structure ever so gently, he moved it downstream.

There. Much better. The new location would force him
to recurve the road and bring it in from the south, but the
improvement made the additional effort worthwhile. The
bridge, the village, and the surrounding farmland were an
idealized version of the place where he'd grown up.

He put the bubble on the worktable and sat back to examine
his handiwork. Terrariums were quite popular among space-
faring Hudatha. They took up very little space, formed a link
with home, and gave the owner a sense of control. The latest
models, like his, offered everything from computer-controlled
weather to microbotic birds and animals.

He turned the bubble and admired the display from

another angle. Ah, if only the real world were so malleable, so responsive to his hand. But such was not the case. Each change, each accomplishment, must be planned, implemented, and then secured. And now, with the most challenging task that he'd ever undertaken ahead of him, Poseen-Ka was filled with doubt.

He leaned back in his chair and gloried in the command center's complete emptiness. There were no holograms to demand his attention, no superiors to flatter, and no subordinates to coddle. Just him, and an almost overwhelming angst that nothing seemed to ease.

The victory over the humans had been too easy. Even though the human traitor maintained that his kind were frequently lazy, cowardly, and slow to reach agreement, the humans should have responded by now.

How could they fail to recognize the situation for what it was? A life-and-death struggle in which no quarter would be asked or given. Yet they *had* failed to recognize the situation for what it was, and he should feel happy.

But the same attitudes and beliefs that caused his race to attack every potential threat raised doubts as well. Doubts that a war commander could ill afford to have. What if the human race was like a sleeping giant? A giant that once awakened would rise up to destroy those who had disturbed it?

The pilot was a good example. Crews were still working to repair the damage it had caused. Twelve members of the crew had been killed. What if the vast majority of humans were more like the pilot than the treacherous Baldwin? What if each one of them killed twelve Hudathans? The war to protect his race could become the war that destroyed it.

Worber's World had been caught by surprise. The next planet would be ready. Unless Baldwin was correct and the humans decided to pull back from the rim. There were too many questions and not enough answers.

Poseen-Ka made a decision. He would talk to the female soldier. She had shown every sign of possessing some of the qualities that Baldwin lacked. By speaking with her, he would better understand the human race. A large gray finger touched a button.

* * *

Norwood braced herself as the door hissed open. She'd been lying on top of the ductwork for an hour and a half waiting for this moment.

Keem-So, the Hudathan assigned to guard her, stumped in and looked around. The door hissed closed.

"Hu-man?"

The standard was heavily accented but not bad for someone who'd been studying it for less than a week. The attempt to speak Norwood's language removed Keem-So from the category of "disgusting alien thing" and made her task that much harder.

Norwood steeled herself, rolled off the ductwork, and fell feetfirst towards the deck. The garrote had been fashioned from a length of insulation-stripped wire, acquired during one of her daily walks. The noose passed over the Hudathan's head and tightened as Norwood's feet hit the deck and she pulled on the makeshift handles.

Her stylus provided one handle while the Hudathan equivalent of a toothbrush filled in for the other.

Being shorter than Keem-So, and with the inertia of her fall to help her, Norwood was able to pull the Hudathan back and off his feet. This seemed like a victory until the huge alien landed on her chest and drove the air from her lungs.

Now it became a competition to see who could breathe first: Keem-So, who made gargling sounds and clawed at his throat, or Norwood, who was trapped beneath a mountain of alien flesh.

But the wire was thin, and Norwood was strong, so the Hudathan was the first to pass out. His body went limp but still pinned her down.

Her head swimming, Norwood pushed the alien up and away, creating sufficient room to roll out from under. She felt a moment of remorse as Keem-So lay there, fingers trapped under the wire, blood trickling from his throat. His sphincter had loosened and the stench of alien feces filled the compartment.

Still, his death was nothing compared to the millions who had died on Worber's World, and *would* die over coming weeks and months.

Norwood made it to her knees, sucked air into her lungs, and knew that whatever amount of time she had left could be counted in minutes, or seconds. Keem-So had been sent to fetch or check on her. His failure to return would be noticed and acted upon.

A weapon. She needed a weapon. Duck-walking her way around to the other side of the Hudathan's body, she found his sidearm and removed it from his holster. She was barely able to get her hand around the grip. The handgun traveled about three feet and then stopped, held in place by a cable-cum-lanyard, useless without the power pak that it was connected to. Norwood considered trying to remove the alien's utility belt and the power pak that was part of it, but remembered how heavy Keem-So was. So much for a weapon.

The hatch was still unlocked and opened to her touch. The corridor was empty. Good. Norwood headed for the power section. She knew very little about spaceships but figured the engineering spaces would be a good place to perform some sabotage.

Norwood straightened her clothes, held her head up high, and prepared herself to make eye contact with the first Hudathan she met. If she *looked* confident and *acted* confident passersby would assume that she *was* confident and therefore okay.

That's the way humans would react anyway... but how about aliens? And blood... what about blood? Did she have Keem-So's blood all over her clothes?

She wanted to stop, wanted to look, but it was too late. A pair of Hudathans had turned into the corridor and were coming towards her.

Norwood smiled, remembered that it didn't mean anything to the Hudathans, but left it in place anyway. She nodded as the aliens drew near. Neither one seemed familiar.

"Hello there... does either one of you speak standard? No? Good. Eat shit and die."

The Hudathans gestured politely, made hissing sounds, and continued on their way.

It worked! Norwood felt a sense of grim satisfaction.

The hallway was long, oversized by human standards, and slightly curved as it followed the contour of the ship. Norwood encountered about a dozen Hudathans during the next ten minutes and bluffed them all. Or so she assumed anyway.

Internally lit pictograms appeared at regular intervals and pointed the way to various departments and sections. Keem-So had taught her what many of them meant, including the fact that the circle-within-a-triangle symbol represented the power of the sun, harnessed by a Hudathan-made mechanical structure. Or, put in human terms, a fusion-based power plant.

Norwood came to a T-shaped intersection, saw that the power-plant symbol had shifted to the right, and turned that way. She had traveled less than ten feet when Baldwin and Imbala-Sa stepped out to block her path. A pair of Hudathans grabbed her arms.

Baldwin crossed his arms and raised an eyebrow. "Well, look who we have here. Out for a little stroll, Colonel?"

Norwood tried to free an arm and found that it was locked in place. "Traitor."

Baldwin shook his head in mock concern. "Traitor... hero... words mean so little. Results are what counts." He made a show of looking around. "What happened to Keem-So? An accident, perhaps?"

"Frax you."

"I'd enjoy that... but some other time. Poseen-Ka has requested the rather dubious pleasure of your company." Baldwin gestured towards the power section. "This was stupid, you know. Your movements were reported by twelve or fifteen members of the crew. They would've detained you but weren't sure of your status."

Norwood swore silently. So much for the bluff.

Baldwin hissed at the guards. One said something into a hand-held communicator. The other turned Norwood around and pointed her in the opposite direction.

Baldwin and Imbala-Sa led the way. That was the ironic part, Norwood thought to herself. Baldwin was as much a prisoner as she was. What was wrong with him anyway? What about the court-martial? Had Baldwin been railroaded like some people said?

Norwood pushed the thought away. It didn't matter. Nothing could justify what he'd done. Nothing.

The journey to the command center was a blur. It seemed as if seconds had passed when the hatch slid upwards and she was ushered inside. The holo tank that had dominated the center of the room during her previous visit had disappeared. In its place was an oval-shaped riser. She was told to stand on it... as was a surprised Baldwin.

"Uh-oh," Norwood said conversationally. "You're in trouble again. I wonder how long they'll fry you this time."

Baldwin did his best to look unconcerned, but little beads of sweat had popped out all over his forehead.

Poseen-Ka watched the humans enter the compartment. He felt mixed emotions. A part of him was furious about Keem-So's death, while another part was almost serenely detached, thinking about Norwood's escape and the fact that it was symbolic of his dilemma.

The humans were dangerous, all right, that much was clear, but what to do? Attack the center of the alien empire as his superiors had ordered him to do, or stall, waiting to see how his adversaries would react?

Both courses of action were fraught with hidden dangers. To attack inwards, towards the center of the Human Empire, was to risk his entire fleet.

What if the humans undertook a massive response? Based on the intelligence supplied by Baldwin, the aliens possessed military forces nearly equal to his. The human claimed that they were divided, poorly led, and subject to Imperial whim. But what if he was wrong? Or worse yet, intentionally misleading those with whom he had supposedly aligned himself?

The other course was equally dangerous, if not more dangerous still. To stall, after the attack on Worber's World, was to sacrifice the value of the surprise attack. The humans could, and probably would, use the time to prepare... leading to higher casualties later on. That, plus the political risk involved, suggested that he ignore his fears and follow orders. The problem was that his fears were so strong, so deep-seated, that they were impossible to ignore. That was the unstated purpose of the meeting. To face those fears and make a decision.

Norwood looked around. Poseen-Ka was a brooding presence off to her right, looking straight through her, towards the bulkhead beyond. There were two equally inscrutable aliens to his left, and three to the right, hissing among themselves, speaking into hand-held communicators and, in at least one case, toying with a long, wicked-looking knife. The remaining positions were empty, suggesting that some of Poseen-Ka's staff were on duty elsewhere.

There was the crackle of static, and a long curvilinear screen popped into existence on the bulkhead to Norwood's left. It was filled with thousands of colored squares. They rippled, rearranged themselves, and formed five distinct images. The Hudathans looked different, yet similar, variations on a theme. All wore cross-straps and a single red gem. The backgrounds varied, suggesting they were on different ships. They announced themselves in a ritualized manner.

"Hisep Rula-Ka, Commander Spear One."

"Ruwat Ifana-So, Commander Spear Two."

"Ikor Niber-Ba, Commander Spear Three."

"Niman Qual-Do, Commander Spear Four."

"Suko Pula-Ka, Commander Spear Five."

Poseen-Ka sat up straight. Side conversations ended, communicators disappeared, and the long, wicked-looking knife was returned to its sheath. The war commander spoke Hudathan, but his words were translated into standard and projected to the humans.

"Welcome. We have much to discuss. Before we begin, however, I would like to hear from Colonel Natalie Norwood and Colonel Alex Baldwin. While our cultures are different, there are similarities as well, including a belief that warriors should know their enemies. With that in mind the first question goes to Colonel Norwood.

"You killed one of my crew and escaped from your cell. Why?"

Norwood felt her heart beat faster and did her best to stand tall. "We are at war."

Poseen-Ka made a gesture with his hand. "This is so. Tell me, human... what will your race do now?"

The room was quiet. The question seemed to hang in the air.

The answer seemed so obvious that Norwood saw no harm in giving it. "They will assemble a fleet, defend the empire, and strike at your homeworld."

Poseen-Ka made a gesture of understanding. He looked around the room and up at his spear commanders. The human seemed truthful. He could see the thoughts start to churn. The Hudathan military had enjoyed a long string of victories, so many that the officer corps had become somewhat arrogant. Few took the humans seriously, and of those who did, many felt that the victory over Worber's World had put the matter to rest.

But the possibility, no matter how remote, of an attack on their homeworld served to trigger the deep-seated anxieties that lay near every Hudathan's heart.

Well, *most* Hudathans anyway, because Poseen-Ka's chief of staff, Lance Commander Moder-Ta, looked singularly unconcerned, an attitude that Poseen-Ka would have to take into account, or risk conflict with Moder-Ta's mentor, Grand Marshal Pem-Da, who not only designed the strategy that Poseen-Ka questioned but functioned as his direct superior too. He turned his attention to Baldwin.

"What about you, Colonel? Norwood says we are at war. I agree. Yet you make no attempts to escape. Why?"

Baldwin felt the desire to produce an ingratiating smile and managed to repress it. A smile meant nothing to the Hudathans and would serve to distract them.

"I consider myself a friend to the Hudathan race and have no desire to escape from their hospitality."

Poseen-Ka fingered the gem that symbolized his rank. "Colonel Norwood believes that the humans will launch an immediate counterattack. What is your opinion?"

Baldwin cleared his throat. He felt the sweat on his forehead and left it alone. What the hell was Poseen-Ka up to? The Hudathan knew damned well what Baldwin thought. So it was a put-up job. A way of getting both views in front of his staff without taking a position himself. But why?

Wait a minute... Norwood had expressed an opinion directly opposite to his own. That was it, then! Poseen-Ka, or someone on his staff, had doubts. Who? Moder-Ta? Not very damned likely. Moder-Ta was a fanatic. No, it must be Poseen-Ka himself, and that represented a real threat to Baldwin's plans. He must eliminate such doubts and convince the alien leader to press the attack. Baldwin chose his words carefully.

"Our military forces spend most of their time bickering with each other. As a result of that, poor leadership, and an insane Emperor, my fellow humans will react by pulling their forces in towards the center of the empire. By doing so they will cede most, if not all, of the rim worlds to you, and concentrate their forces for what they hope will be a climactic battle."

Baldwin liked the sound of what he'd said and paused to look around. He was still in the process of learning the nuances of Hudathan body language and facial expression but saw signs of approval. Thus encouraged, he resumed his speech.

"Unweakened by more than token resistance, and having had more time to prepare, the Hudathan fleet will crush the human fleet and reduce them to servitude."

The last part was more hopeful than certain, since it was the Hudathan tendency to annihilate other races rather than subjugate them. But Baldwin could hope. It would be rather enjoyable to sit on the dead Emperor's throne while the same officers who had court-martialed him groveled at his feet.

Norwood had listened to Baldwin's words with an increasing sense of dread. His arguments fit the facts and made a great deal more sense than hers did. Her comments had been more along the lines of wishful thinking than reasoned analysis. In fact, the more she thought about it, the more Norwood believed Baldwin was correct. The empire *would* retreat and cede all but the inner worlds to the Hudatha. That's why they had allowed the torpedoes through—to precipitate a retreat Baldwin felt sure would happen. She felt dizzy and sick to her stomach.

"So," Poseen-Ka said, "we have two humans, and two views of how their race will react. I think you'll agree that their comments were interesting if not especially instructive." He turned to a guard. "Take them away. You know what to do."

The guard made a gesture of assent, motioned for Baldwin and Norwood to leave the riser, and herded them towards the hatch. Poseen-Ka waited until the humans were gone, accepted operational reports from the spear commanders, then opened the meeting to discussion.

The ostensible subject of conversation was strategy, but there were undercurrents as well, most of which centered around the possibility that Norwood was correct.

But each time those sentiments were voiced, Moder-Ta or one of the more conservative spear commanders would ridicule the officer who had put the opinion forth, gradually freezing all such commentary.

Seeing that, and knowing that Moder-Ta, along with those that agreed with him, had the weight of Hudathan authority, tradition, and psychology on their side, Poseen-Ka brought the discussion to a close and issued orders to attack.

It was the right decision. He knew that. But he still couldn't allay the fear that gnawed from within.

Their clothes were stripped off and they were strapped to side-by-side tables. The logic was irrefutable. Norwood had misbehaved and must be punished, while Baldwin had brought her aboard and must share in the blame.

Norwood had expected to die, had *wanted* to die, and was disappointed. There was no way to know why Poseen-Ka had spared her life, only that he had, and that the price would be high.

Baldwin struggled to look brave, to be nonchalant, but started to shake the moment that they entered the room. Norwood felt goosebumps pop out as bare flesh came into contact with cold metal.

Baldwin had a Hudathan-supplied implant, but Norwood didn't, so wires were connected to her head, arms, breasts, legs, and feet. She wanted to cry, and would have if she'd been alone, but bit her lip instead.

Neither said anything until the pain started and both were forced to scream. It went on for a long, long time, until Norwood knew nothing but pain, and could no longer tell her screams from his.

5

Let your plans be dark and impenetrable as night, and when you move, fall like a thunderbolt.

SUN TZU
THE ART OF WAR
Standard year circa 500 B.C.

Planet Algeron, the Human Empire

Wayfar Hardman low-crawled to the edge of the cliff, found a gap between two pieces of shale, and looked down onto the plain below. The humans were little more than dots, spread out to lessen the impact of an ambush, moving forward at a good clip. The wind came from behind the aliens and brought their scent to his super-sensitive nostrils.

First came the plastic-metal-lubricant odor of the cyborgs. It was as strong and brutal as they were. Hardman made a face and wrinkled his nose. But there were more subtle flavorings as well. The tart, rather pleasant scent of the bio bods, the slightly corrupt odor of the corpse they were about to discover, and the clean-crisp flavor of the air itself.

Hardman gave a satisfied grunt. The humans would find the body, jump to the proper conclusion, and follow the carefully prepared trail. All the planning, all the work, would soon pay off.

He watched an airborne scavenger circle the corpse and

land. The body was that of Quickhands Metalworker, his first cousin's oldest son. The unfortunate youngster had died in a climbing accident, and with permission from his family, had been mutilated to resemble a murder victim.

"If," as his father had put it, "our son can fight from the grave, then let it be so."

And so it was that Metalworker had been left in the middle of a carefully prepared stage. A stage that begged the audience to become part of the play and in so doing, led them towards their own destruction.

Hardman realized that his thoughts had become somewhat pompous and smiled. Perhaps his daughter was right. Perhaps his sense of drama *did* get in the way at times. Still, the idea was new and therefore likely to succeed.

Hardman made a note to bury whatever was left of the body with high honors. He scooted backwards and stood. The Naa chieftain was about six feet tall. Hard muscle rippled under his white chest fur as he made his way through the rocks that littered the top of the low, flat-topped hill. The rest of his body was black with gold highlights and occasional flecks of white.

He wore a breechcloth, a weapons harness, and a headset copied from those used by the Legion. Thanks to it, and others like it, he had known when the patrol left Fort Cameroue, and been informed of every move that it had made since then.

Hardman grinned. The humans might have machines that looked down from the sky, but he had eyes in the desert, and they missed very little.

Hardman was able to smell his warriors long before he saw them. The rich amalgam of dooth dung, self-scents, and gun oil hung over the ravine like a cloud. He made a note to thank the mother-father creator for the fact that humans had such a piss-poor sense of smell.

The war party seemed to pop out of the background as he scrambled down a shale-covered slope. The battle mounts surged slightly as they caught his scent. The length of their shadows signaled the end of another one-hour-and-twenty-one-minute day.

The six-legged dooths were shaggy with winter hair and

eager to leave. They were plains animals and disliked the ravine and the dangers that lurked there.

Hardman waved to his second-in-command, Easymove Nightwalker, picked a path through some boulders, and followed it with a series of graceful leaps. He knew the younger warriors were watching, hoping for a misstep that would signal the onset of old age, but his broad toeless feet found firm purchase among the rocks and landed him in the saddle with a satisfying thump. Challengers, if any, would have to wait for a while.

Wedgefoot, Hardman's war mount, stirred uneasily and made the grunting sounds that were typical of its kind. Hardman patted the animal's massive neck and activated his radio. The cyborgs would be scanning for traffic, so Hardman kept the transmission short.

"The humans are coming. We will have one cycle of darkness in which to reach our positions. Let's move."

The brief snatch of sound served to jerk Villain up out of the trance-like state induced by the monotony of patrol. It was encrypted, and therefore unintelligible, but important nonetheless. A low-power transmission on that particular band meant someone or something was within a fifty-mile radius of the patrol. She triggered her radio.

"Roamer Two to Roamer Patrol. I heard traffic on freq four. Confirm."

"That's a negative, Roamer Two," Gunner replied.

"Roamer Three didn't hear it either," Rossif added.

"Ditto Roamer Four," Jones put in.

Roller's voice was hard and sarcastic. "What's the problem, Roamer Two? Getting nervous?"

Villain was about to reply when Booly's voice boomed through the interface.

"Roamer One to Roamer Patrol. Cut the crap. We have some brellas feeding on something off to the right. Let's take a look, Roamer Two."

Servos whined as Villain moved her head to the right. She saw the cluster of carrion eaters and swore silently. *She* was the one with the electro-optics, *she* had the point, and *she* had missed it. Damn Roller anyway. The bastard had a way of getting under her armor.

Villain started to jog, scanning the countryside as she did so, determined not to make the same mistake twice. With each step her metal feet broke through the crust of frozen sand and made a loud crunching sound. Booly clung to her back in the same way that her little brother had so long ago. The memory brought pain and she pushed it away.

Focus, she had to focus, had to see what was around her.

Little tufts of vegetation dotted the plain, then disappeared as the ground rose, and funneled itself into a canyon. The sky had grown dark and started the transition into night.

Villain called up a satellite map, zoomed into the section she wanted, and saw that the canyon cut through the foothills to communicate with the desert beyond. The place was custom-made for an ambush. Exactly the sort of route to avoid if at all possible.

The brellas saw the Trooper II coming but were so gorged with meat that they had difficulty taking off.

"Slow down and stop fifty feet out."

The command came from Booly via intercom rather than radio. It was a kindness on Booly's part. A recognition that she was green and still learning. Other noncoms, like Roller, for example, would've put the order on-air just to humiliate her.

Villain slowed and came to a halt. The last brella drew air in, pushed it explosively outwards, and lumbered into the air. The body it had been feeding on was that of a Naa, only slightly decomposed, but badly disfigured by scavengers.

"The body could be booby-trapped," Booly said calmly, "or surrounded by mines. That's why you stop to scope things out."

Villain knew this was a valuable lesson and was careful to file it away. The sergeant major switched to radio.

"Roamer One to Roamer Seven... I need a trooper on the double."

Booly climbed down from his perch on Villain's back and circled the body. He felt stiff and sore but was careful to conceal it. There was no sign of booby traps, but he did see dooth dung, scuff marks, and some empty shell casings. All pointed to a fight of some kind, and based on the way they were spread around, the legionnaire suspected a one-sided battle.

Wismer had been forced to run from the depression in which Gunner was crouched and arrived slightly out of breath.

"Yes, Sergeant Major?"

The noncom pointed towards the corpse. "Probe the ground. Don't hit the body."

A less experienced soldier might have wondered why the sergeant major had given the assignment to a bio bod when a Trooper II stood ten feet away. But Wismer understood. Booly was afraid the newbie would make a mistake and didn't want to say so. Some said the sergeant major was a borg lover. This sort of thing proved it.

Wismer brought his energy weapon up to his shoulder and fired. There was a stutter of blue light, followed by a puff of steam and the glow of molten rock. Nothing happened, so he repeated the procedure, until the area around the body was pockmarked with shallow black holes.

Booly moved in for a closer look. He used the newly made depressions like stepping-stones, avoiding the unmarked ground and the possibility of an undiscovered mine. Heat seeped up through the bottom of his boots to warm his feet. The body was a mess and the smell made him gag.

Villain decided that Booly was a cut above other noncoms. She knew, as her peers did, that officers and noncoms were taught to sacrifice cyborgs rather than expose themselves to danger.

It made sense in theory. Given their armor, and considerable weaponry, the cyborgs were much more likely to survive than bio bods were. The only problem was that many officers and noncoms tended to ignore the fact that the destruction of cyborg limbs, armor, and sensors was experienced as pain. Pain equal to that felt by embodied brains.

The techies had designed borgs that way on purpose, to make sure that they took care of their expensive bodies, and as a means of discipline. Trooper IIs were heavily armed, after all, and more than a match for a squad of bio bods, so some sort of control mechanism was a must. Or so it seemed to the bio bods.

Villain remembered the zappers the DIs had used on her

in boot camp and shuddered. She knew bio-bod officers were authorized to carry them but hadn't seen one used since basic. She hoped she never would.

A host of tiny black insects acknowledged Booly's presence by taking to the air, buzzing around in a seemingly random pattern, then settling down again. Booly knew that he should have sent Villain to examine the body but wanted to see it with his own eyes. What he saw, and more than that, what he smelled, made him sick. The brellas had gone for the eyes first. Then, following the path of least resistance, they had used the bullet holes to open the abdominal cavity and feast on the victim's entrails.

The Naa's clothing was tattered and stained with blood but told a story nonetheless. The braided armband, worn just above the right elbow, signified membership in the northern tribe. Not unusual in and of itself, since the members of the southern tribe stayed below the equator and didn't venture north except for war and trade.

No, the significance of the armband lay in the fact that this particular Naa had been a member of a tribe, rather than a group of outlaws. That, plus the ceremonial beads that had been ripped from his neck and lay scattered on the ground, suggested an initiate.

Yes, Booly decided, chances were that the body belonged to a young male, undergoing the final rites of passage into adulthood, and unlucky enough to be caught in the open by outlaws.

His expression hardened. Naa outlaws were the scourge of both the tribes *and* the Legion. They took females, stole anything that wasn't nailed down, and took great pleasure in torturing legionnaires. Some took days or even weeks to die.

Booly stood and eyed the gathering darkness. If he could catch them and put them six feet under, Algeron would be a better place to live. But it would be risky, very risky, since the trail led straight into the canyon, and the canyon would make an excellent place for an ambush.

But if outlaws *had* killed the Naa, there was no reason for them to expect a patrol to come along at this particular time, and therefore little or no reason for an ambush. That, combined with the fact that the patrol packed enough firepower to deal with anything short of a full-scale tribal attack, led to his final decision. They would risk the canyon, catch the outlaws, and send them to the Naa equivalent of hell.

Booly walked back to where Villain waited, climbed into position, and activated his radio.

"Roamer One to Roamer Patrol. It looks like some outlaws caught the poor slob, canceled his ticket, and took off through that canyon. We're going after them. Same order as before, condition five, blast anything that moves."

Villain felt emptiness where her stomach had been. She was about to enter what could be a trap. Not only that, but she'd be the first one in and the first one to take fire.

Villain remembered the impact as bullets hit her flesh, the wave of darkness, and the brutal awakening that had followed. Anger rose to displace the fear. No matter what waited in the darkness, and no matter what happened beyond, she would live. Because then, and only then, could she hope to find the person responsible for her death. Find him and kill him.

Villain brought her weapons systems to condition five readiness, cranked her infrared sensors to high-gain, and moved forward. God help any Naa who got in her way.

Gunner waited for Rossif and Jones to move out, checked to make sure that Wutu was covering his ass, and stood up. His sensors probed ahead. The canyon looked dark and ominous. Booly was out of his fraxing mind. Good. This was the patrol he'd been waiting for. The one where he took a missile right between the shoulder blades. The armor was thinner there and more likely to buckle under the force of an explosion.

He'd have to unload the bio bods, but that was SOP and would happen shortly after the first few rounds were fired.

Gunner wondered what death would be like. His wife had believed in paradise, complete with angels, saints, and streets of gold. That would be nice, he guessed, especially if he could see her again, but darkness would be fine. An eternal darkness unlit by the flames that consumed his family's flesh and empty of his children's screams. Yes, he decided, this would be an excellent place to die.

Satisfied that the others had a sufficient lead, Gunner moved forward, his scanners running at maximum sensitivity and his weapons ready to fire. Wutu followed along behind, walking backwards half the time, watching to be sure that nothing approached the patrol from the rear. It was a shit detail but no worse than a hundred others he'd pulled.

It was times like this that Booly wished he was a cyborg, with a cyborg's armor and a cyborg's capacity to see in the dark. He wore night-vision goggles, and they were better than nothing, but hardly equivalent to the images that Villain saw, which were little different from those that she received during the day.

By taking the data provided by Villain's infrared sensors, and combining it with the information provided by her light-amplification equipment, the Trooper II's on-board battle computer could "guess" how the missing information would look, fill the gaps, and feed the composite to her brain.

As a result, Villain could see their surroundings a lot better than Booly could, and had she been more seasoned, that would've been fine. But she wasn't, and one slip, one mistake, could cost all of their lives. Still, this was exactly the kind of experience she needed, so Booly was reluctant to switch her with another cyborg.

The canyon rose around them. Everything had a greenish glow. The canyon's right wall had received the full strength of the "afternoon" sun and was a good deal brighter than the left wall. Banks of still-warm dirt and shale skirted the cliffs, shimmered like luminescent fish scales, and twisted with the canyon itself.

A creek would appear when summer came but was presently trapped in the frozen ground. It formed a highway of darkness down the center of Booly's vision and a background against which the slightly warmer dooth droppings glowed softly green. The outlaws had passed that way, all right, and were up ahead somewhere.

Booly felt the tension start to build. Where were the bastards anyway? Hiding around the next bend? Or out on the desert beyond… huddled around a dooth-dung fire? There was no way to tell.

Booly shrugged with the fatalism of soldiers everywhere. What would be, would be. He stretched. His muscles ached and he was tired of riding Villain. He imagined Roller and the rest of the troopers lolling about inside Gunner's cargo bay and felt a surge of resentment. He pushed the feeling back and clamped a lid on it. Rank hath privilege, but it comes with responsibility too, and this was his.

Villain was careful to scan rather than stare. Scanning made it easier to concentrate, was more likely to pick up movement, and covered a larger area. So her instructors had claimed.

A ghostly blue grid overlaid everything Villain saw. The point of focus was represented by a red X that traveled across the grid in concert with her electronic vision. Numbers shifted in the grid's lower right-hand corner as range, wind speed, and various kinds of threat factors were computed and fed to the interface.

Villain saw movement to the right. Her left arm traveled upwards, as the bright green glow emerged from the rocks and turned its triangular head in her direction. The red X floated over the target and flashed on and off. Flame stabbed the night as the .50-caliber slugs drew a line between her and the small hexapod. It jerked under the impact, tumbled end over end, and exploded into green slush.

Villain stopped firing. She was surprised to find that she had enjoyed the feeling of power the moment brought her. The realization bothered her but there was no time to think about it. Not while they were in the canyon, not while lives were at stake, not while an ambush could wait around the next bend.

"Nice work," Roller said sarcastically. "That should let 'em know where we are. Send up a signal flare next time. It'll make their jobs even easier."

Booly remained silent, which meant that he agreed. Villain cursed her own stupidity. Of course! Why use the machine gun when the laser cannon would do just as well? It made relatively little noise. And why fire at all? It had been a pook, for god's sake, about as dangerous as a wild dog.

She told herself that Booly had ordered the patrol to "blast anything that moved," that she'd never asked to be a soldier, but rejected the excuses as quickly as they came. She had screwed up. It was as simple as that.

* * *

Wayfar Hardman saw the first glimmerings of dawn off to the east. The view was somewhat proscribed by the homemade periscope that stuck up through the sand but was adequate nonetheless. At this point the new day was little more than a vague pinkness that separated earth from sky. Good. The humans would enter the kill zone at first light, time when eyes played tricks and minds made mistakes.

He swiveled the periscope to examine the point where the canyon emptied into the desert. There were no signs of the trip wires, weapons pits, and warriors who hid there. All were underground, sheltered from IR detectors by a layer of uniformly cold sand, waiting for his signal.

His body gave an involuntary jerk as his ears picked up the dull *thump-thump-thump* of heavy machine-gun fire. Had they been discovered? No, the sound was muffled, indicating that the legionnaires were at least a half-kak away.

So what was going on? Had the humans stumbled across some *real* outlaws? No, that was impossible. His scouts would have found and dealt with them hours ago. It was an error, then, a mistake of the sort that youngsters make, and nothing to do with him or his warriors.

Thus reassured, Hardman closed his eyes, tried to ignore the insect that had taken up residence behind his right ear, and settled down to wait. Judging from the sound of machine-gun fire, it wouldn't be long.

Villain felt her spirits soar as she rounded the last bend and saw the desert beyond. It, unlike the dark confines of the canyon, was beautiful to look at. The rising sun had glazed the top of things with a pinkish-gold light and infused the air with a magical softness. The distant foothills seemed to float on an ocean of nearly transparent ground fog and the air hummed with the sound of newly aroused insects.

Villain gloried in the moment and left fear behind as she entered the desert. She was still enjoying it when Wutu emerged from the canyon, took one last look to the rear, and backed into the kill zone.

A warrior named Joketeller Nosmell peered through his periscope, waited for the cyborg to arrive at exactly the right spot and flicked a switch.

The twenty-five pounds of carefully hoarded cyplex explosives went off with a tremendous roar. The force of the explosion removed Wutu's right leg and arm. What remained of his body tumbled high in the air, fell straight down, and hit the ground with a distinct thump.

Nosmell pushed himself up and out of the depression. He had won a great victory and sought to enjoy it. He was smiling happily when Wutu rolled onto his damaged side, activated his machine gun, and pumped a five-round burst through the warrior's chest. Then, hosing the area with suppressive fire, Wutu used his remaining leg to inch himself forward. Chemical inhibitors had blocked the pain, but that wouldn't last forever.

A lot of things went through Booly's mind. The realization that he'd been suckered, the fact that this was a full-scale tribal attack, and the knowledge that he was about to die. The plan was obvious: kill the last cyborg, kill the first cyborg, and trap the rest of the patrol in between.

Booly had leaped away from Villain, and was falling towards the ground, when the shoulder-launched missile struck her chest and exploded.

The noncom never saw the tiny piece of metal that spun away from the explosion, glanced off the side of his skull, and buried itself in the sand. Darkness pulled him under.

Villain felt herself fall. Pain filled her chest. Something hard hit between her shoulder blades. She sent orders to her legs. They twitched in response. Damn. Something moved to the left. She brought an arm up. Light burped. A Naa ceased to exist. Villain felt it again. The power, the joy, the satisfaction. And why not? She was damned near immortal, wasn't she? Villain saw another figure emerge from the ground, made the necessary computations, and killed it.

Gunner understood the situation immediately and lowered his body to the sand. By doing so he protected his vulnerable legs and allowed the bio bods to low-crawl out of his cargo bay, a rather wise decision since the air was full of flying lead and sizzling energy beams.

Gunner felt someone slap a ready button inside his cargo bay, released the hatch, and fired his main armament. The results were spectacular.

Like all quads, Gunner was equipped with four gang-mounted energy cannons. These fired in alternating sequence, but so rapidly that they appeared to be one. Sand melted, rocks exploded, vegetation burst into flame. Naa warriors stood, fired their shoulder-launched missiles, and vanished as blue death cut them down.

There was return fire as well. Explosions rippled across the surface of Gunner's armor. Many hit the bull's-eyes painted on both of his flanks, but none did any real damage. Once down, with weapons activated, an assault quadruped was like a combination tank and pillbox. Absolutely indestructible to anything less than heavy artillery, another quad, or attack aircraft.

Gunner sent a mental command. A hatch opened just aft of his weapons turret. An electronically driven gatling gun emerged, shot upwards on its heavily armored arm, and opened fire. Dirt fountained fifty yards away as a group of four Naa tried to position an antitank gun and failed. The gatling gun fired more than six thousand rounds a minute and simply erased them from the surface of the planet.

Roller edged his way around Gunner's bow and took a look. Booly was down and probably out, Wutu was about 20 percent effective, and the newbie wasn't much better. Both continued to fire but couldn't move. Rossif had tripped on a cable but had escaped without damage and was kicking some serious ass. Jones had taken three missile hits, all within the space of about three seconds, and exploded. Sheltered by Gunner's metal bulk and dug in around his sides, the bio bods were okay.

Roller sighed. Air support would have been nice, but the Navy was supposed to supply that, and they weren't around. It seemed that the brass refused to provide them with security on the ground. It was all part of the eternal pissing match between the Navy, the Marine Corps, and the Legion. He had damned little choice but to save what he could and haul ass.

"This is Roamer Seven. I have assumed command. Roamers Eight and Ten... work your way over to Five and pull his module. Roamers Nine and Eleven ditto the newbie."

Kato swore silently and eyed the distance between Gunner and Wutu. It was fifty yards or so and looked twice that. She looked at Imai, he nodded, and they ran.

Wutu continued to fire, covering them as best he could, but the Naa were determined to bring him down.

O'Brian and Yankolovich had worked their way around to the opposite side of the quad. Villain lay on her back, firing when the Naa made a run at her, but otherwise inactive. Successive missiles had destroyed both of her legs, and a small electrical fire was burning in the vicinity of what had been her right knee. O'Brian could see the sparks. Yankolovich looked his way, nodded, and they ran.

Villain looked up. She had damned little choice. The sun had cleared the horizon and was directing all of its strength into the vid cams that served as her eyes. She ordered them to iris down but nothing happened.

Bullets hit her torso, spanged off, and screamed away. They were annoying but no more harmful than insects. No, it was the missiles she feared, and one more should do the job. She wondered where it was. Did the Naa want her to suffer? Or were they running short of ordnance?

There was movement to the left. She raised a listless arm and fired. A Naa threw up his arms and fell backwards out of sight. Asshole. How much longer could this go on?

Suddenly O'Brian was there and Yankolovich too. It was O'Brian who spoke.

"We're jerking your module number two... have a nice rest."

Villain tried to nod but found that her head didn't work. Blue fire burped overhead as Gunner provided covering fire. Villain's surroundings jerked, swayed, and moved as they pushed her over. The last thing she saw was stones. Each had its own shadow. A bug ran from one to the next.

Yankolovich flipped a protective cover out of the way, grabbed the red T-shaped handle, and gave it one full turn to the right. Then, using the same handle, he pulled Villain's biological support module out the back of her massive head. Injectors pumped sedatives into her brain and the world faded to black.

A massive form materialized next to the bio bods. O'Brian gave mental thanks. Having Rossif there to provide additional cover would make the trip to the quad a lot safer.

Roller was waiting when O'Brian and Yankolovich returned. They ran full speed, dived, and slid the last few feet. Dirt geysered around them as bullets hit.

Gunner redirected the gatling gun towards the source of the fire, triggered a long burst, and watched a boulder disintegrate. Once revealed, the Naa lasted a quarter of a second. Fur, flesh, and blood sprayed outwards as the bullets hit.

Rossif and Jones stalked forward, fired missiles into the rocks, and followed up with machine-gun fire.

O'Brian pushed the biological support module in Roller's direction. Except for the T-shaped handle and the six-pronged connector located on one side, the olive-drab case looked like a .50-ammo box. Roller grabbed it and motioned towards the hatch.

"Get the hell inside! We're pulling out."

O'Brian and Yankolovich dropped into their padded seats and strapped themselves in. Roller entered and the hatch slid closed. Bullets clanged against the quad's armor.

Roller dropped into a seat. His helmet was cracked where a piece of shrapnel had hit it. Blood streamed down the side of his face.

O'Brian's voice was strained. "Where's Wismer, Kato, and Imai?"

Roller wiped his forehead with an arm. "Dead. Along with Wutu."

"And the sergeant major?"

"Dead."

"Shit."

"Yeah."

Roller activated his radio. "All right, Gunner… get us the hell out of here."

Gunner had anticipated the order and rose in one smooth motion. Explosive shells and shoulder-launched missiles sparkled across the surface of his armor. He staggered under the impact, damned the luck that had kept him alive, and followed Rossif out of the kill zone. This was the moment to unleash his massive firepower and the cyborg did so.

All four of his energy cannons spit coherent light, the gatling gun roared defiance, missiles lashed out in every direction, grenades popped skywards, and smoke poured from heavy-duty generators.

Hardman recognized what was happening and gave the necessary orders. "The humans are attempting to withdraw. Allow them to leave. It's impossible to defeat the four-legged cyborg. Enough blood has stained the sand."

A few die-hard warriors unleashed their remaining missiles anyway, but they missed, or exploded harmlessly on Gunner's armor. Minutes later and the humans were gone, with only the wreckage of their cyborgs and a handful of bodies to mark their passage.

Hardman forced himself up out of his hiding place and out into the open. He searched his emotions for elation, for happiness, and found nothing but pain.

Dead warriors littered the ground around him. Blood dripped down the side of a rock. A hand lay palm-up as if asking for friendship. A piece of metal skittered away from his foot. The air smelled of smoke, explosives, perspiration, urine, and feces. Healers moved among the wounded, aiding those that they could, granting eternal rest to those that they couldn't.

It was a victory, a great victory, but Hardman found no pleasure in the pain and death. A hand touched his arm. The chieftain turned to find Deathtricker Healtouch by his side. He was a small male with gray fur and streaks of black.

"Yes?"

"A human lives."

Hardman made a gesture of surprise. "Where?"

"Over there."

Hardman followed the healer back to the point where the battle had begun. A human lay crumpled on the ground, blood running down to pool around his head, his eyes empty of awareness.

"Will he live?"

80

Healtouch looked doubtful. "It is difficult to say. Would you like me to give aid… or release him to the next world?"

The chieftain gave the Naa equivalent of a shrug. "Treat our wounded first. Then, if the human continues to live, see what you can do."

Healtouch made a sign of respect, stepped over Booly's unconscious body, and headed for the makeshift aid station. Hardman watched him go, then transferred his attention back to the body. Like most humans, this one looked soft and as helpless as a newborn infant. If only that were true.

6

*For on men in general this observation may be made: they are ungrateful,
fickle, and deceitful, eager to avoid dangers, and avid for gain, and while
you are useful to them they are all with you, offering you their blood, their
property, their lives, and their sons so long as danger is remote… but when
it approaches they turn on you. Any prince, trusting only in their words and
having no other preparations made, will fall to his ruin…*

NICCOLO MACHIAVELLI
The Prince
Standard year 1513

Planet Earth, the Human Empire

Angel Perez stepped out of the troop carrier and fell towards the
planet below. Others were all around him. Some were cyborgs,
some were bio bods, all were soldiers.

It was night, but that made little difference, because the
objective was radiating enough heat to cook breakfast for a
brigade. Heat that his electronics could detect, sort, and integrate
with surveillance photos taken days and weeks before. The result
was an image similar to what he'd see during the day, except that
a blue grid overlaid everything, and a bright red X floated across
the landscape. Altitude, rate of fall, and a variety of threat factors
appeared in the lower right-hand corner of his vision.

The aliens had been working on their stronghold for more
than a thousand years. The fortress rambled all over the place,
a maze of walls, streets, and buildings. And now, as Perez fell

towards it, the structure grew larger with each passing second.

Perez waited for the chute to open but nothing happened. His chute would deploy when the auto timer told it to do so and not a moment before. It was for his own safety. The longer he fell, the harder it would be for the computer-controlled AA batteries to hit him.

Perez didn't know *how* he knew these things, only that he did. His chute opened, jerked him upwards, and formed a rectangular canopy over his head. It was black like the sky above it, and steerable, like the parasails you could rent at resorts. He looked down, saw a darkened area that might be an open field, and banked in that direction.

Lights snapped on, tracers ripped the night into a thousand abstract shapes, and energy beams stuttered towards space. Some of the legionnaires fired back, but Perez concentrated on the chute and ignored the ground fire. Or tried to anyway.

Tracers drifted past, seemingly harmless but very deadly. The ground rushed up to meet him. He saw a building. It boasted three spires. There was a surface-to-air missile battery located between them. A radar-seeking rocket roared past Perez and homed on a troop carrier. A spire lurched up at him. He tried to avoid it, failed, and gritted his nonexistent teeth.

The impact was horrible. A metal rod hit the lower part of his abdomen, passed up through his reserve ammo bin, power storage module, and on-board processor. He screamed and the world went black.

The voice came from nowhere and everywhere all at once.

"Welcome to the Legion, scumbags. My name is Sir."

The night, the battle, and the pain faded away. Perez found himself at the center of a huge parade ground. He occupied a body similar to the one in the dream. A small but dapper man stood before him. The man had beady little eyes, an oversized nose, and sun-reddened skin. His arms were decorated with colorful tattoos. His white kepi sat square on his head, his khakis had razor-sharp creases, and his boots boasted a high-gloss shine. His eyes moved from right to left and Perez realized that others were present as well. The man spoke in a conversational tone, but his words carried across the parade ground nonetheless.

"Each and every one of you was tried for a crime, sentenced to death, and executed. This is your last chance. *If* you follow orders, *if* you learn what we teach you, and *if* you are very, very lucky, you could become legionnaires. With that honor comes a new name, a better life, and the opportunity to make something of yourselves."

Perez remembered the stainless-steel room, the red dot on his chest, and the certain knowledge that he was going to die. *Had* died, and wound up here, wherever he was.

The man smiled. "Some of you will die in training accidents. Some will commit suicide rather than face another day. And I'll kill three or four of you just for the fun of it."

The man scanned the ranks. His eyes were like lasers, seeming to pass right through whatever they saw.

"Many of you don't believe that. You think the rights you once had still apply. Wrong. You are legally dead, and until such time as you are formally listed on the Legion's rolls, you have no existence other than the one that I grant you."

The man clasped his hands behind his back.

"There was a time when it took months to train a good soldier. Well, not anymore. You are cyborgs. Little more than brains encased in machines. The hair, eyes, noses, arms, hands, tits, ovaries, cunts, cocks, balls, legs, and feet by which you knew yourselves are gone. You won't have to eat, breathe, sleep, shit, or fuck. All you *will* have to do is train. Twenty-four hours of each day, seven days of each week, until you either learn or die.

"If you learn, the Emperor is one legionnaire better off. If you fail, and I pull your plug, it doesn't matter, because you were dead to begin with, and in most cases deservedly so. The empire benefits either way."

Sir looked around to make sure that he had their undivided attention and nodded.

"Most of your learning will take place through a neural interface. The battle that you just experienced was the first of hundreds. By experiencing *real* battles and *real* deaths, you will learn very quickly. Does anyone have any questions?"

Perez found that peripheral vision was better than it used to be and saw a cyborg raise an arm. A distant part of his brain noticed that the arm had a pincer-like hand.

The noncom smiled, pointed a black box in the recruit's direction, and pressed a button. The cyborg screamed, convulsed, and fell to the ground.

Sir looked from right to left. "Lesson number one. I don't like questions. Questions imply thought. Thought implies intelligence. And intelligent recruits are a contradiction in terms. Would anyone like to discuss that? No? Good.

"Here's lesson number two. I am a sergeant. That means I am god. I can walk on water, piss whiskey, shit explosives, and speak with officers. Are there any questions?"

Incredibly enough, Perez saw an arm go up off to his right. He winced as the sergeant pointed the black box in that direction and pressed the button. The cyborg screamed and fell writing to the ground.

The sergeant shook his head in amazement. "They get dumber every day. All right, enough screwing around, company... attenshun!"

Perez had seen troops come to attention on the news and in countless holo dramas. He did his best to comply. The result was more parody than the real thing. The others were little better. Perez expected the sergeant to lash out to punish them for their clumsiness, but he seemed unaware of transgression.

"Company... take three paces forward."

Perez lifted his right foot, moved it forward, and fell on his face. The rest of the recruits did likewise.

The sergeant laughed. "That's right, scumbags. You can't even walk, much less march. Now, get up and try it again."

Perez struggled to obey, and as he did so, wondered if death would have been better.

The Emperor was lost in reverie. The voices squabbled amongst themselves. Some favored an immediate response to the Hudathan attack and others didn't. They wanted to pull back, retrench, and defend the empire's core.

The Emperor knew that he should listen to them, should make some sort of decision, but found it hard to care. Caring involved an expenditure of energy and a certain amount of risk. People who cared got hurt. No, it was better to remain separate from the process, to float along the surface of things, bobbing and twisting while the current carried you along.

And that's where the voices came in. *They* cared, *they* argued with each other, and *they* did all the things he sought to avoid. They enjoyed it, and more than that, *thrived* on it.

The Emperor couldn't remember a time when they hadn't been there, urging him to do what they wanted, arguing amongst themselves.

They had been real people once, with flesh-and-blood bodies, until his mother had selected them as his advisors. Some were scientists, some were military officers, and the others were politicians. There were no artists, philosophers, or religionists, since his mother felt they were little more than gilt on the carriage of state.

He'd been six months old when the advisors arrived. All felt honored to be among those selected, were cheered by the prospect of lifelong employment, and had no idea what they had let themselves in for.

The technology was experimental and was eventually abandoned as too dangerous for use with humans.

But that was *after* the advisors had been digitized, edited, and downloaded into a six-month-old brain.

It was, the Emperor reflected, a miracle that he had grown at all, surrounded as he was by eight contentious minds. The fact that his mother had each and every one of them murdered so they couldn't scheme against him didn't help either. The copies, as they referred to themselves, felt a kinship with the originals, and looked for opportunities to make him feel guilty about it.

But they did like to work, which left him free to do what he did best: enjoy himself. Something he had done less and less frequently since his mother's death.

The voice interrupted and dragged him back to reality.

"Your Highness?"

The Emperor opened his eyes. Four people stood before him: Admiral Scolari, dressed in an absurd set of medieval armor; General Worthington, wearing little more than a G-string; the merchant, Sergi Chien-Chu, swathed in a Roman toga; and the recently arrived General Marianne Mosby, her breasts seeking to escape the almost nonexistent confines of her gown.

The Emperor brightened and motioned the group forward. He'd been present as Mosby had accepted command of her troops but had little chance to talk with her. The meeting would be tiresome, but her presence would serve to brighten it. The copies faded into the background.

"I hope you will accept my apologies for calling you away from the festivities. It seems as though the affairs of state are almost always inconvenient. May I summon refreshments? Some food perhaps? Or wine?"

The foursome looked at each other and shook their heads. It was Chien-Chu who spoke.

"I think not, Your Highness. We have already had benefit of your considerable hospitality and are quite full."

The Emperor gestured towards some ornate chairs. "I'm glad to hear it... Please... sit down."

It was a small room by palatial standards and decorated in masculine style. There were high arched windows, entire walls full of old-fashioned books, a real log fire burning in an open fireplace, and a massive desk that served as a barrier between the Emperor and his guests. Their chairs were arranged in a semicircle and fronted the desk.

Mosby chose a chair, sat down, and subjected the Emperor to a lightning-fast evaluation. She'd seen thousands of pictures, ranging from holo vids to stills, and glimpsed him from a distance. But this was the first time that she had met the man face-to-face and had the chance to size him up.

The Emperor was handsome and very athletic. It was common knowledge that some of his good looks were real, and the rest were the result of surgery, but it made little difference. His hair was dark, parted on the right side, and swept back to touch the top of his shoulders. His eyes were brown and very intense. He had a high forehead, a well-shaped nose, and a strong chin. The weakness, if any, was around the mouth. Mosby thought his lips were a shade too sensual and likely to pout. His mouth was acceptable, though, very acceptable, and worth further consideration.

Mosby decided that the Emperor's chair must be resting on some sort of platform, because he was higher than she was, and had already used that advantage to peer down the front of her dress. Far from disconcerted, she was pleased, and shifted slightly to give him a better view. Their eyes met, electricity jumped the gap, and an unspoken agreement was reached. Later, when the affairs of state had been resolved, they would have an affair of their own. And it would be anything but boring.

The Emperor smiled, leaned back in his chair, and threw a pair of highly polished boots onto the corner of his desk. He nodded towards the right and said, "Watch this."

The air shimmered, filled with motes of multicolored light, and coalesced into a picture. The picture was of a planet called "Worber's World," and the narration was supplied by a militia colonel named Natalie Norwood. What followed was some of the most disturbing footage any of the group had ever seen.

The Hudathan fleet, the waves of assault craft, the swathes of destruction, the millions of casualties, and the seemingly pointless attacks that followed made Chien-Chu sick. They made him afraid as well, because his son, Leonid, was out on the rim and quite possibly in harm's way. He pushed the thought away and forced his mind to the task at hand.

Norwood ended the report with a plea for help and her intention to surrender. The merchant admired Norwood's cool, dispassionate narration and the control required to record it. The empire needed officers of her caliber and he hoped that she'd survive.

"So," the Emperor said, making a steeple with his fingers, "we have a problem. I'd be interested in your reactions. Admiral Scolari, you're senior, I look forward to hearing your thoughts."

Scolari did her best to keep the eagerness off her face. She felt sorry for the people on Worber's World but was eager to use the attack for her own ends. The fact was that the empire had grown too large, too fat to protect, and she favored a smaller, tighter grouping of systems that would make the Navy's job easier. If colonists wanted to live out on the rim, then let them do so, but at their own risk. That a retrenchment would force the Legion off Algeron was frosting on the cake. The Emperor had been out of his mind to grant the Legion its own planet, and this was a chance to right that wrong.

Scolari had other reasons as well. The stronger the military was, the higher taxes were, and there were some very powerful organizations that disliked high taxes. Organizations that would help those who helped them, and with only five years left to retirement, it was time for Scolari to consider the future. She chose her words with care.

"Thank you, Your Highness. I'll start by saying that all of your forces are on Level Five Alert, or will be, as soon as the message torps have had time to reach the most distant outposts."

The Emperor nodded gravely. "Excellent. We must be ready for whatever the Hudathans do next."

"Which raises a question," Scolari said smoothly. "What *will* the Hudathans do next?"

"Push their way towards the center of the empire," Mosby predicted confidently, "destroying everything in their path."

Scolari frowned. Her question had been rhetorical rather than real, and Mosby's response had caught her by surprise. She forced a smile.

"Thank you for your opinion, General, but I would like to offer mine first."

Mosby saw what she thought was a sympathetic look from the Emperor and inclined her head. "My apologies. I was thinking out loud."

Chien-Chu's respect for Mosby went up a notch. The woman might be a bit liberal for his tastes, but she was nobody's fool, and knew her stuff. The Hudathans had created an advantage. Of course they'd follow up. To do otherwise would be stupid.

"So," Scolari continued, "I have dispatched scouts to find the Hudathan fleet and report on its activities. Intelligence is critical to a well-reasoned response. We know very little about this race and their motivations."

"And in the meantime?" Chien-Chu asked softly.

"And in the meantime," Scolari answered irritably, "we can discuss some of the more obvious alternatives."

Mosby sensed the merchant's approach, saw the twinkle in his eye, and joined in.

"What alternatives are those?" the general inquired.

Scolari had lost control of the situation and knew it. She hurried into the alternatives in hopes of regaining the upper hand.

"The first alternative is to do nothing beyond what we've done already. Our forces are on the highest level of alert, our scouts are gathering intelligence, and the argument could be made that a reactive posture is best."

Scolari looked at the Emperor, hoping for some sign of agreement, but found little more than polite interest.

"The second alternative is to assume that the aliens have ambitions beyond Worber's World, and based on that to pull our outlying forces back into a defensive posture. That would give us more strength with which to defend the empire's more populated and industrialized systems."

"It would also leave the rim worlds open to the kind of destruction we saw in Colonel Norwood's report," Mosby said grimly.

Scolari looked to Worthington for support, found him staring at the expensive carpet, and decided to press on.

"Last, and in my opinion least, we could locate the Hudathan fleet and launch all-out attack."

The Emperor raised a well-plucked eyebrow. The voices in his head had grown louder again, echoing the disagreement in the room, and vying for his attention. It was hard to think.

"Why do you consider an all-out attack to be the least desirable option? It's the kind of advice that I'd expect from some of my more timid citizens. A great deal of blood was shed when my mother created this empire. Are you afraid to shed a little more?"

Scolari felt an emptiness in the pit of her stomach. The Emperor was more lucid than usual. It was a direct question and demanded a direct answer. An answer in which she would be forced to commit herself. Scolari took a deep breath.

"It is the empire that concerns me. It has grown since your mother pieced it together from the ruins of the Second Confederacy. Grown and prospered. But how large can the empire grow before its own weight pulls it down? That which expands must eventually contract."

The Emperor nodded. He pressed fingertips against his temples. Many of his internal advisors agreed with Scolari and urged him to support her. But the Emperor sensed that to do so would severely lessen his chances of having sex with General Mosby. And that was something he looked forward to. No, it was better to say something sympathetic and let the debate continue.

"Thank you, Admiral. It's refreshing to hear a military advisor propose something other than massive retaliation. However, duty requires that I hear all sides of an issue prior to a final decision, and I suspect that General Mosby has other views. General?"

For the first time that evening Mosby wished that she was wearing something less revealing. Scolari looked silly in her armor, but it did lend a martial air, and that served to support her arguments. Still, the Emperor had been careful to seek out her opinion, and that boded well. She made an effort to minimize her cleavage and summoned her most serious expression.

"With all respect to the admiral, I disagree with her recommendation. To pull our forces back, and abandon the frontier, would signal weakness and encourage the aliens to attack. We have other enemies as well, like the Clone Worlds, the Itathian Hegemony, and the Empire of Daath. One sign of hesitancy, one sign of weakness, and they could join forces against us."

"The operant word is 'could,'" Scolari interjected. "There's no certainty that they actually would."

Mosby shrugged her rather plump shoulders. "Nor is there any certainty that they wouldn't. Why take the chance? Let's find the Hudathans, hit 'em with everything we have, and settle the question once and for all."

Worthington spoke for the first time, and in doing so, earned Scolari's eternal gratitude. "I like your spirit, General, and am sympathetic to your basic instincts, but what makes you so sure that we can win? Wouldn't it make more sense to see what the scouts are able to find out? And make a decision at that time?"

"No," Mosby said stubbornly, "it wouldn't. Weeks could pass by then, reducing the possibility of an effective counterattack, giving the enemy what they're trying to take."

"I think General Mosby has a point," Chien-Chu said carefully. "Time could be critical."

"Yes," the Emperor replied, "but so is information. And I want more of it before making a final decision. Thank you for taking the time to visit with me... and I trust you will return to the ball. The evening is still young."

The Emperor's comments were an obvious dismissal. The advisors rose, made their way to the door, and turned to bow. Mosby had made her curtsey, and was about to back out of the room, when the Emperor lifted a hand.

"General Mosby..."

"Yes, Your Highness?"

"Stay for a moment. I wish to discuss your forces and their readiness for battle."

Scolari had already made her exit but was close enough to hear the Emperor's words and see Mosby reenter the room. Damn! It was her body that the Emperor wanted—there was little doubt of that—but would Mosby find a way to use the situation? She would certainly try.

Scolari, with Worthington at her side, and Chien-Chu trudging along behind, headed for the ballroom. Their thoughts were very different. Scolari's seethed as she plotted a course through the obstacles before her. Worthington's were more measured, considering, analyzing, and evaluating. Chien-Chu's were uncharacteristically dark as he remembered what he had seen and worried about his son.

The marines who stood to either side of the Emperor's door looked straight ahead. As with all such assignments, it was important to know what to acknowledge and what to ignore.

Mosby closed the door behind her. The Emperor got up, came around his desk, and crossed the room. He was a little shorter than she'd thought he'd be, but still over six feet, and slim. He was dressed in a high-collared jacket, a pair of bloused trousers, and the knee-high boots that she'd noticed before. He brought an aura of expensive soap and cologne with him. He stopped only inches away.

"You are very beautiful."

Mosby smiled. "Thank you, Highness. You're rather attractive yourself. And you waste very little time."

The Emperor laughed. It was a deep throaty chuckle that Mosby found to be very sexy.

"You must call me Nicolai, and yes, there is little time to waste. I sense that you and I are alike in that respect. We know what we want and are not afraid to grasp it."

So saying, the Emperor brought his hands up to cup Mosby's breasts and brushed her lips with his.

Mosby stood on tiptoe, placed her hands behind his head, and kissed him. It was soft at first and grew steadily more passionate, until both were short of breath. Mosby allowed a hand to slide down and rest between his legs. What she found was more than satisfactory. Their lips parted and their eyes met.

"You're far from shy."

Mosby smiled. "Why? Does the Emperor have a preference for shy generals?"

"Apparently not," the Emperor responded dryly. "Come, let's retire to my bedroom. We can be more comfortable there."

The Emperor took Mosby's hand and she followed him across the room. A sensor detected their approach, a section of bookcase slid aside, and a doorway was revealed.

"How sneaky."

"Yes," the Emperor agreed. "Sneakiness is an extremely important prerequisite for the throne... as my mother would have been happy to tell you."

As with the Emperor's study, one wall of his bedroom was taken up with high arched windows, but that's where the similarity ended.

The walls, the carpet, and the enormous bed were white. The windows were open, it was raining outside, and the curtains billowed into the room. Music came from somewhere and blended with the sound of the rain to make new harmonies.

Mosby looked around but was unable to find any of the accouterments that she might have expected. No mirrored ceilings, specially crafted furniture, or camera arrays. She felt reassured and disappointed at the same time.

The Emperor raised an eyebrow. "You approve? Shall I close the windows?"

Mosby smiled. "I approve, and leave the windows open. I love the rain."

The Emperor was very gentle, almost surprisingly so, given the fact that he could take whatever he wanted. His hands were warm, slow, and patient. They removed her gown, panties, and stockings. And then, when she lay naked on the bed, he touched her hair.

"Shall I remove this? Or would you prefer to wear it?"

Mosby looked up into his eyes. "That's entirely up to you, Nicolai. Do you want me? Or the woman I chose to impersonate?"

The Emperor smiled and removed the wig. Her real hair was short, so short that it was little more than fuzz, and he ran a hand across it.

"You are very beautiful."

She held up her arms, and he took a moment to enjoy what he saw, before accepting her embrace.

It took time to undress himself, to kiss her from head to toe, and to make long, slow love. And, when the climax finally came, it was like the first act of a two-act play. Satisfying, but lacking in finality, as though more could be said, done, and felt.

That was when the Emperor kissed her nose and ran the palm of his hand over the stubble on her head.

"Did you like it?"

Mosby grinned. "And if I didn't? Would you change my opinion by Imperial decree?"

The Emperor nodded solemnly. "Of course. More than that. I would declare your opinion a state secret and swear you to silence."

Mosby giggled. "Save yourself the trouble, Nicolai. It was good."

"So you liked it?"

"Yes, I liked it."

"Enough to try it again?"

Mosby made a purring sound deep in her throat. "Definitely."

"Good, and that being the case, I took the liberty of inviting a friend to join us."

Mosby felt a momentary sense of alarm as another hidden door slid open and a second man entered the room. She didn't recognize him at first, but that changed when he stepped into the light. The Emperor? Or an exact replica... right down to the erection that jutted out in front of him.

The emperor ran a hand down her arm. "There's no need to be alarmed. He's a clone. You have no idea how many boring ceremonies he attends on my behalf."

Mosby knew about clones, and had fought a brigade of them during a border dispute five years before, but had never interacted with any. She forced herself to sound blasé. "He looks good... but does he share your taste in women?"

"Oh, he most assuredly does," the Emperor replied. "Now relax, while I show you that if one emperor is good, two are even better."

Mosby did as she was told and found that the Emperor was absolutely right.

7

You legionnaires are soldiers in order to die and I am sending you where you can die.

FRENCH GENERAL FRANÇOIS DE NEGRIER
Standard year 1883

Legion Outpost NA-45-16/R, aka "Spindle," the Human Empire
The Hudathan assault ships came out of the sun. The light, heat, and radiation that emanated from the brown dwarf covered their approach at first, but the legionnaires had excellent detection gear and picked them up.

"Here they come, Captain, right on time."

The electronics tech had bright red hair, freckles, and the inevitable nickname of Red. He wore a brightly colored floral shirt and sat before a large console. It boasted hundreds of red, green, and amber indicator lights, a multiplicity of screens, displays, and readouts, plus a multilevel keyboard similar in appearance to those that had controlled pipe organs hundreds of years before. The keyboard, and the alternative voice-recognition system, linked Red with "Spinhead," the planetoid's central computer.

Though intended for scientific and commercial purposes, Spinhead, along with a few million imperials' worth of ancillary equipment, had been pressed into military service after the attack two days before. And Red, though still a civilian, had become an honorary member of the Legion.

Captain Omar Narbakov was a tall thin man with black skin and quick brown eyes. His head was shaved and gleamed when he moved. The officer looked at his watch and swore. Red had bet him that the next attack would come at exactly fifteen minutes after the hour and it had. He reached into a pants pocket, found a wad of crumpled currency, and removed a ten-spot.

"Here. Buy yourself a decent shirt. That one makes my eyes water."

"You were suckered, Omar."

Graceful after nine months of near weightlessness, Narbakov turned towards the sound of Leonid Chien-Chu's voice. "Oh, yeah? How's that?"

Those who knew both men said that Leonid Chien-Chu resembled his father, though the son was a good bit taller and as slim as a commando knife. There were laugh lines around Leonid's eyes and mouth. They grew deeper when he spoke.

"Red took all the data from the last seven attacks, ran it through Spinhead, and came up with an estimated time of attack."

Narbakov turned on Red. His expression would have turned many people to stone. "Is that true?"

"Of course," Red answered cheerfully. "What? Do I look stupid?"

"Yes," Narbakov replied. "Thanks to that shirt. I want my money back."

Red grinned as the officer snatched the money out of his hand.

"So," Leonid said, doing his best to sound unconcerned, "are you going to do something about the incoming ships?"

Narbakov looked surprised, as if unable to understand why the merchant would ask such a silly question.

"Sure… they should be in range about a minute from now. That's when operation boomerang goes into effect. Then, after the geeks sort that out, my cyborgs will open fire."

"And the combination will be sufficient to hold them off?"

Narbakov glanced at the screens. "Yeah… for the moment. But who knows? Hell, there's a miniature fleet out there. They have enough firepower to open this roid like a can of baked beans. It might be different if we had some ships, or fighters, or some idea of when help might arrive. But we don't, so if the geeks really want this chunk of real estate, they're gonna take it."

Leonid thought about that. The Hudathans had the power... but would they use it? The planetoid called "Spindle," and the equipment on it were critical to obtaining the substance known as "stardust." An all-out battle might destroy the very thing they wanted, which would explain why the aliens had held some of their forces back.

But what if he was wrong? Or the Hudathans grew tired of the prolonged battle and moved to end it? What then?

The lights dimmed as power was drained away from the main fusion plant and Narbakov spoke into his mike. Every legionnaire on Spindle heard what the officer said and knew what he meant.

"Remember Camerone."

Rulon Mylook-Ra watched the asteroid fill more and more of his heads-up wraparound visual display. The planetoid was more than three hundred units long and half that at its widest point. One end was larger than the other and permanently pointed towards the sun. This was rather convenient from Mylook-Ra's point of view, since the closest end boasted some of the best targets and put the sun behind him.

The boat had its own navcomp, but to avoid any possibility that their assault craft could be used against them, generations of Hudathan war commanders had placed most of the processing capacity on board their larger ships. This approach had a number of negative implications, including a heightened susceptibility to electronic countermeasures, and a potentially disastrous effect should one or more of the mother ships be destroyed.

But none of these problems confronted Mylook-Ra as he vectored in on the asteroid, chose a high-priority target and gave the necessary order.

The ship jerked as a flight of missiles raced away. Each missile had its own guidance system, so the Hudathan was free to activate his secondary weapons. They consisted of two energy cannons mounted under each of the assault boat's stubby wings.

Energy stuttered out, drew red-hot lines across the planetoid's rocky surface, and intersected at an antenna array. Pieces of metal spun free, supports collapsed, and what was left glowed cherry red. The Hudathan pulled up and looped around.

Mylook-Ra felt a sense of satisfaction. It turned to concern when he realized that his missiles were unaccounted for. They should have hit the target by now, or failing that, destroyed themselves. And there was another anomaly as well. He had encountered almost no defensive fire. Why was that? Previous flights had experienced stiff resistance.

The Hudathan triggered the com link and was just about to ask the flagship for more information when an entire array of alarms went off. Mylook-Ra was still thinking his way through the problem when the missiles he had fired moments before hit his ship and blew up.

Leonid weighed less than three earth pounds and held onto an air duct for additional stability. A series of monitors carried the action. The Hudathan assault craft exploded, Red whooped, and Narbakov nodded approvingly.

"Nice going, Red, but it won't work next time."

Leonid knew what the officer meant. Stardust, the almost magical stuff that had brought them there in the first place, was gathered by remotely controlled spacecraft called star divers.

It takes a lot of sophisticated equipment to guide a spaceship through a sun's corona and bring it home again. Equipment that Red had used to subvert and redirect the Hudathan missiles. A total of four ships had been destroyed.

It was a neat trick but it would only work once. There were any number of things the Hudathans could do to protect against similar attempts in the future.

Narbakov eyed the screens and activated his mike. "Another flight is on its way. Let's show them what it means to attack the Legion."

* * *

I'll tell you what it means, a cyborg named Seeger thought to himself. It means that some poor bastard will get his ass blown off. Never mind that it's made of plastic and metal... it hurts just the same.

An entire platoon of Trooper IIs was assigned to Narbakov's company. Some had been killed by now, but the remainder were located on Spindle's rocky surface, hiding behind low-lying ridges or in the craters that dotted the planetoid's surface. Hiding, and waiting for the next flight of fighters, at which point they would become sentient antiaircraft batteries.

Seeger had taken the name of the Legion's best known poet, considered himself to be something of an intellectual, and felt sure that Narbakov's novel use of cyborgs would wind up in the textbooks. Assuming anyone survived to tell the story.

Seeger stood, scanned the input relayed to him from Spinhead, and counted the incoming ships. There were thirteen... fourteen... fifteen of the no-good homicidal sonsofbitches. The cyborg tracked the fighters with the intensity of a person whose life depended on the outcome. Which it did.

Around Seeger, and behind him, the other members of the platoon did likewise. There were thirty-two in all, down from thirty-seven when the attacks had begun, and spread thin to minimize casualties.

The best target on Spindle consisted of the huge ramp-shaped railgun. It was used to launch the star divers and had been constructed within a V-shaped valley, a fact that had forced the aliens to fly a predictable path during low-level attacks and had enabled Narbakov to prepare a novel strategy.

Though not on a par with the heavily armored surface installations the aliens had destroyed during previous attacks, the cyborgs were highly mobile and could fire twelve mini-missiles without reloading. By lining both sides of the valley with Trooper IIs, Narbakov had created a veritable gauntlet of defensive fire.

Thirty-two cyborgs, launching two missiles a second, could fire 384 independently targeted weapons in roughly twelve seconds.

So, lulled into a false sense of security caused by the lack of ground fire during their first pass, and angered by the casualties inflicted by their own missiles, the Hudathans came in fast and low. Command swore that their missiles would track properly this time, but the pilots didn't believe it and stuck to their secondaries. Lines of blue energy plowed red-hot furrows across the asteroid's rocky surface.

Seeger had little more than a fraction of a second in which to see an incoming fighter, run a solution, and fire. By slaving his computer to Spinhead, and by working as part of a cybernetic network, his accuracy was greatly enhanced. Death lashed out from both his launchers and sped towards the assault boats.

Unlike their mother ships, the fighters were too small to mount defensive energy fields, so a hit was a hit.

A ship filled Seeger's targeting grid, floated under the red X, and came apart as five or six missiles struck it. The resulting wreckage hit the ground about five miles away and, unrestrained by gravity, cartwheeled his way. The fighter was no more than a mile off when it exploded and sent chunks of metal flying in every direction.

"Move! Move! Move!"

The order came from Seeger's platoon leader, a bio bod named Umai, and didn't need repeating. The second wave of Hudathans had plotted their positions by now and were on their way.

Seeger turned and ran-shuffled towards his next position. It was important to move quickly but to do so without breaking surface contact. Sure, the asteroid's anemic gravity would pull him back down five or ten minutes later, but he'd be dead by then.

A pair of fighters swooped overhead, and a line of explosions rippled along the ground behind him. Seeger dived into a crater, rolled, and bounced to his feet. It was a mistake and he knew it. His boots had already broken contact with the ground, and he was soaring upwards when someone wrapped their arms around his knees.

"Whoa, big fella... keep that up and you'll be in orbit."

Seeger mumbled words of appreciation as the man pulled him down.

The civilians wore brightly decorated space armor. One featured a jungle motif and the other was covered with self-referential sayings that Seeger managed to ignore. They had learned their duties less than twelve hours before but carried them out with efficiency and a certain amount of panache.

One took his right side and the other his left. Missile magazines floated away and new ones were snapped into place. A hand slapped Seeger's arm. The voice was female this time and originated from the suit with the jungle motif.

"Good luck, soldier. We'll meet you at position number three."

Seeger nodded his gratitude and turned his attention to Spinhead's feed. A dozen globe-shaped things had appeared over the foreshortened horizon and were gliding towards him.

Sunlight hit one side of the objects and left the other dark. They looked a lot like the airborne float pods that drifted across the surface of his native Elexor each spring. Except that the float pods were harmless.

Death stuttered down, caught a pair of civilians shuffling towards cover, and popped them like organic balloons. Were they the ones who had rearmed him? He couldn't tell.

Seeger swore, launched two missiles, and fired his gas-jacketed machine gun. The recoil pushed him backwards and threatened to dump him on his can, but the results were worth it. The pod was well within range and the lack of an atmosphere allowed the bullets to gain even more inertia. They drew a beautiful red line between his arm and the globe.

Seeger had no way of knowing what had destroyed the thing—the missiles or the bullets—but it blew up and showered him with slow-motion debris.

Umai came on-line.

"L-One to L-Troop. Here's some scoop from Spinhead. The pods are *unmanned*. Repeat, unmanned."

Seeger gave a grunt of disgust as he left the crater for position number three. The pods were unmanned. So fraxing what? They could kill you just as dead, couldn't they? Officers. Dumb shits one and all.

The civilians were waiting behind an outcropping of rock. They were uninjured, which made Seeger glad. The man spoke first.

"Good shooting, soldier... you nailed that pod but good."

"Damned straight," the woman added. "How's your ammo?"

Seeger ran a reflexive check. He still had ten missiles, 82 percent of his machine-gun ammo, and enough power to run his energy cannon full bore for five minutes and twenty-seven seconds.

"I'm in good shape. Haul butt and I'll meet you at position four."

The civilians signaled their agreement and were about to depart when Narbakov came on-line. Seeger held up a restraining hand. The civilians waited.

"N-One to L-Troop. You did a nice job. Go to condition three, repeat, condition three."

Condition three translated to "standby." Seeger motioned for the civilians to return and scanned the horizon. Nothing. For the moment anyway.

The legionnaire sat down, wished that he had lungs to smoke a cigarette with, and waited for Lieutenant Umai to say something stupid. It didn't take long.

Red stood and stretched. "That's all, folks. Spinhead predicts another major attack in about four hours with assorted harassment missions in between."

Leonid forced himself to release the air duct and found that his fingers hurt. They'd survived another attack. He thought about the empire, about the Emperor, and about his father.

What were they doing anyway? Where was the Navy? The Marine Corps? And all the other government types who were paid to handle this sort of thing? Surely the message torps had arrived by now.

What about his wife, Natasha? She'd be worried—that much was certain—but what was she doing? Was she running a comb through her long black hair? Humming softly as she wrote a letter? Laughing at something his mother had said? She had a wonderful laugh that sounded like bells tinkling.

Narbakov's voice jerked him back to reality.

"Come on, Leo… it's time for the daily damage assessment."

Leonid nodded and followed the officer out of the control center and into an emergency lock. A hatch slid closed behind them. A message had been printed on the wall. It was overlaid with graffiti but still readable. "We hope that you enjoyed your visit to Fatside Control. Please come again."

Spindle had a prolate shape, similar to that of an eggplant, or spindle, hence the name. The blunt end, commonly referred to as "Fatside," was eternally pointed towards the sun, while the other end, "Thinside," was pointed away.

So the names made sense even if the sign didn't.

The forward hatch hissed open and Narbakov stepped out. Leonid followed.

Fatside had been chosen to house the primary habitat, since it was larger, and thanks to its exposure to the sun, a good deal warmer. So warm, in fact, that air-conditioning was a must. An additional advantage was that Fatside's considerable metallic content served to protect residents from radiation.

The administrative and living spaces had been excavated rather than built, so the walls were of rough-hewn stone, still marked where the robotic mining machines had eaten their way through the rock.

The corridor ended at what looked like an alcove but was actually a shaft. Narbakov stepped inside, flexed his knees, and jumped upwards. Leonid did likewise. The next landing was ten feet up, but thanks to his almost nonexistent body weight, the merchant had little difficulty making the jump. He waited for the hand bar, grabbed it, and was spared the indignity of crashing headfirst into the padded ceiling.

A technician nodded, stepped into midair, and floated downwards.

Leonid pushed himself out into the main corridor. There was another vertical shaft to his immediate right. The simplicity and efficiency of the system pleased him.

The corridor was crowded with miners, technicians, and the occasional legionnaire, all of whom were forced to vie for space with robots, automated transporters, piles of supplies, broken-down mining equipment, and the mess caused by the never-ending construction. That plus the poor lighting made for a crowded and almost oppressive atmosphere.

Passersby could have been gloomy and depressed, and

probably should have been. After all, they were under constant attack and cut off from help. But Leonid was struck by, and somewhat proud of, the fact that they weren't. The jokes, smiles, and routine greetings were much as they had been prior to the Hudathan attacks, with only tired eyes, and in some cases fresh bandages, to show the pressure they were under.

It was as if Narbakov could read his mind. "Morale is surprisingly good."

Leonid nodded his agreement.

Both men grinned, knowing they were likely to disagree about everything else.

The staging area in front of the main lock was a madhouse. The smell of stale sweat hung over the crowd like a cloud, only slightly diluted by the sharp tang of ozone and the all-pervasive odor of chemical sealants.

Thirty or forty men and women were in various stages of undress as they either donned or removed their space armor. Six of them were legionnaires and came to attention when Narbakov appeared. He returned their salutes and slapped a woman on the back.

"Nice work, Sergeant. Your team did well."

Leonid had no idea what the officer was referring to, but smiled, and nodded his agreement. It was important to show civilian support.

"Stand aside! Get away from the hatch!"

The voice was amplified and originated from within the lock. A klaxon sounded, a beacon flashed, and doors slid open. The first thing to emerge was a blast of cold air. That was followed by a transporter, which, like most equipment on Spindle, was extremely light and powered by a small electric motor. It lurched slightly as its balloon-style tires hit the uneven floor.

The machine carried a heavy load, though, including a pair of wounded bio bods, a badly mangled Trooper II, and three medics. All, with the exception of the cyborg, wore space suits with the helmets off. One of them caught sight of a med tech and yelled instructions.

"We've got a borg with a jammed life support module, a

leaky pressure system, and more holes than a Swiss cheese! Tell surgery to prepare suite four, rig a number three laser, and stand by. We're on the way."

Leonid stepped aside to make room for the transporter. Held aloft by the lack of gravity, and pulled by the vehicle's suction, a cloud of vaporized blood followed behind. The wounded bio bods were conscious, but the Trooper II just lay there, like a giant among Lilliputians. The merchant wished him or her the best.

Some miners were slow to move out of the transporter's way and Narbakov gave one of them a shove.

"What the hell's wrong with you? Get the hell out of the way!"

The miner turned, raised his fists, and paused.

Narbakov was frustrated, worried about the cyborg, and ready to take it out on someone. It must have shown, because the miner made a face and waved the officer off.

Narbakov pressed an angry thumb against the pressure plate on his locker. It opened with a pop.

"Civilian asshole!"

Leonid thought about the men and women on Spindle's surface, risking their lives to rearm cyborgs like the one on the transporter, but decided to let it pass.

They stepped into their suits, checked each other's seals, and entered the lock. It was crammed to capacity with repair crews, legionnaires, and supplies. In spite of the fact that their helmets were on, most had open visors and were still talking to each other.

"Good to see you doing some work."

"Work? What the hell would *you* know about work?"

"Screw off, toolhead. I do more work in one shift than you do in two."

"... his head right off. Couldn't find the damned thing afterwards. Must be in orbit."

"So where's the Navy? That's what I wanta know... where's the fraxing Navy?"

"So she says, 'Hey, dude, wanta get it on?' And I say..."

"... an entry in my file. Can you believe that shit?"

A klaxon went off. The voice belonged to a woman who had never been off planet Earth.

"Seal your suits. Seal your suits. Seal your suits."

The chatter stopped instantly. Visors were sealed, checks were made, and silence prevailed. The regulations regarding radio discipline were strictly enforced. Unnecessary conversation could cost a civilian a week's pay or put a legionnaire on report.

No one resented the rules, or tried to flout them, because to do so was to risk lives. Their own and others as well. There were a lot of ways to die on Spindle, and good clear communications were critical to keeping the death rate as low as possible.

The hatch opened and people spilled out onto the asteroid's surface. This was the moment that Leonid always looked forward to, the time when he stepped out of the lock and was bathed in dull red sunlight.

The sun was huge and filled a quarter of the merchant's vision. His visor darkened slightly, but not much, since the dwarf produced only 0.4 percent as much energy as the same area of the sun seen from Earth's surface. It was one of the things that he missed the most, the warmth of sunshine on his skin and the interplay of sun and clouds. Pleasures that disappeared when you lived inside an asteroid.

This sun was different. It had a mass twenty-five times that of Jupiter, or about one-fortieth that of Earth's sun. But despite its large mass, the dwarf had a radius of only 76,900 kilometers, giving it an average density of 26, a statistic that took on additional significance when compared to the density of lead (11), gold (19), and osmium (22).

The dwarf had begun to contract from a gas cloud about 154 million years previously, and its deuterium-burning phase had been over for 79 million years. It was still cooling, with a surface temperature of 1,460 K, as compared to the sun's 5,780 K, and was hotter inside than out. Material near the core would heat up, expand, and rise towards the surface. There it would cool, become more dense, and sink towards the interior.

The atmosphere was cool enough to contain a variety of molecules including corundum, perovskite, melilite, spinel, fosterite, enstatite, and more mundane things like titanium oxide, iron-nickel alloys, and sodium, aluminum, magnesium, and calcium silicates. Most existed in the form of condensates about fifty to one hundred micrometers across and dust particles of the same size.

Chien-Chu knew that the different types of condensates and dust particles liquefied, evaporated, and solidified at different temperatures and pressures, producing the fogs, mists, clouds, and similar structures that swirled across the dwarf's surface. And somewhere in that seething caldron of activity, tiny particles of stardust were being formed, strange stuff that had the unique ability to produce lasing of wavelengths all across the visible spectrum.

The result was brilliant scintillations in a rainbow of colors, sometimes simultaneously, sometimes in pure monochromatic gleams. The effect was completely chaotic and therefore endlessly fascinating to watch, and if there was one thing that people were willing to pay for, it was personal significance. They'd pay large amounts of money for the thing, substance, or condition that set them apart from their peers and made them seem special.

Wait a minute… A terrible heaviness settled into the pit of his stomach. Given the fact that stardust had no established military or industrial applications, and that the Hudathans were unlikely to define "beauty" the same way that humans did, there was little doubt as to what they would do. Having failed to take Spindle with a minimum amount of force, they would gradually escalate, until victory was theirs. Narbakov's voice intruded on the merchant's thoughts.

"Come on, Leo… we've got work to do."

Leonid turned his back towards the sun. "Yes, Omar, we certainly do."

Ikor Niber-Ba, commander of Spear Three, looked out through armored plastic. The sun, and the grotesquely shaped asteroid that attended it, filled the view port.

The humans had no long-range weapons, a fact that had allowed him to bring his command ship in rather close, lessening the distance that his fighters had to travel.

Niber-Ba was tiny by the standards of his race, little more

than 250 pounds, a condition that had plagued him all of his life. In a society based on strength he had been weak. A punching bag for stronger males and the object of derision by females.

But the blows and insults had both strengthened and hardened Niber-Ba, pushing him in on himself, making him harder and smarter than those around him.

Eventually his nickname, "The Dwarf," had been transformed from insult to honorific and struck fear into the hearts of many. And the fact that the Dwarf was confronting another sort of dwarf was not lost on Niber-Ba, for he had spent many years comparing himself against the societal ideal and had a highly developed sense of irony.

It was this ability to look within, to see his own failings, that came to his rescue now. Spear Three had been delayed, kept from rejoining the rest of War Commander Poseen-Ka's fleet, and it was his fault. He had been too cautious, too paranoid, holding back when he should have launched an all-out attack. The substance that the humans worked so hard to scoop out of the sun's atmosphere had no strategic value, after all, and was, from a Hudathan point of view, completely worthless.

There was no reason to delay the attack that an officer like Poseen-Ka would have launched by now, no reason except his own timidity and fear of failure.

Niber-Ba drew himself up to his full height of five foot six, did an about-face, and headed for the ship's command center. The humans were about to die.

8

Before one can perceive beauty one must first open his eyes.
NAA FOLK SAYING (SOUTHERN TRIBE)
Circa 150 B.C.

Planet Algeron, the Human Empire

Booly awoke slowly, almost grudgingly, accepting his surroundings in small hazy increments. The first thing he felt was a delicious sense of warmth. It made a nice contrast to the cool air around his face.

He could smell the odor of cooking and something that could only be described as perfume. Not just *any* perfume, but a heady concoction that reminded him of summer meadows and the most beautiful women that he'd ever known. Booly felt the air stir in the vicinity of his face and fingers probe the side of his skull. It hurt a little, so he opened his eyes and found himself looking at a pair of shapely breasts.

The breasts were different somehow, and given the befuddled state of his mind, it took the legionnaire a moment to figure out why.

Then he had it. They were covered with a pelt of short sleek fur, like that of a mink or a Siamese cat.

The female completed her inspection of his scalp and straightened up. Her breasts disappeared down inside a modestly cut blouse. Her eyes slid past his, paused, and came back. They were charcoal gray like the fur that surrounded her delicately shaped face.

"You're awake."

The words were Naa rather than standard, a fact that registered on Booly's brain but made no difference. He understood the language well, thanks to the chemically enhanced fast-learn mnemonics that he and every other legionnaire on Algeron had been subjected to.

The language was simple in many respects, having lots of words with only one syllable and no final consonant. The simplicity was deceptive, though, because Naa was a tonal language, relying on pitch to determine which of many possible meanings a particular syllable had. There were four recognized pitches: high, medium, low, and very low. The language was further complicated in that the pitch could be rising, falling, or constant.

The net result was a language that seemed simple at first, but like ancient Chinese, was actually quite complex, a complexity made more difficult by the fact that the original tongue had been divided into two major dialects. One was spoken in the northern hemisphere, and a different one was used south of the great mountain range. Booly knew both.

"Yes, I'm awake."

The female smiled. Her lips were full and reminded him of little pillows. If his ability to speak her language surprised her, she gave no sign of it.

"You looked down my blouse."

Booly blushed and shook his head. "You're mistaken."

She raised a well-shaped eyebrow. It was more pronounced than its human equivalents and had a feline aspect to it. "Really? Then explain this."

He hadn't known about the erection until she touched the blanket that it supported. The offending member wilted and disappeared.

"Windsweet?"

The voice was deep, distinctly male, and came from somewhere nearby.

The female placed two fingers over her lips in the Naa sign for silence. Her voice was a whisper. "It's my father. Close your eyes and pretend to be asleep."

Booly started to ask why, but something about the way that she spoke changed his mind. The legionnaire closed his eyes. There was a scraping sound, followed by the jingle of metal on metal and a rustling next to the legionnaire's bed. The same voice spoke again, only louder this time.

"How is he?"

"Better, or at least I think he is, but still asleep."

"Asleep or unconscious?"

"Asleep. He was awake for a minute or two," Windsweet said calmly.

Booly opened his eyes the tiniest bit. He saw a male, about six feet tall, with white chest fur and a mostly black body. Wayfar Hardman gave a satisfied grunt. "Excellent. Let me know the moment that he awakes. We'll kill him and send his head to General St. James."

Windsweet did something to the covers. "It's up to you. Father, but it has been a long time since we had a prisoner, and the council meeting is only a week away."

Hardman thought it over. The legionnaire would make an excellent display during the upcoming council meeting. A little something to remind everyone of the successful ambush. Not a bad idea with young subchiefs like Ridelong Surekill nipping at his heels. Besides, he had little stomach for cold-blooded murder, and only said such things because they were expected of him. Hardman gave his daughter a respectful look.

"You inherited your mother's brains as well as her beauty. It shall be as you suggest. One thing, though…"

"Yes?" Windsweet said patiently.

"The human would look a lot more impressive if he were on his feet and dressed in full battle gear."

Windsweet nodded agreeably. "I'll see what I can do."

Hardman touched his daughter's cheek and left. Windsweet sat on the edge of Booly's bed.

"You can open your eyes now."

The legionnaire did as he was told.

"You heard?"

"Yes." His voice came out as a croak. "You saved my life. But why?"

Windsweet looked at him. He saw a variety of emotions flicker through her cool gray eyes but couldn't identify any of them.

"Tell me, human… why does the wind blow?"

The question took him by surprise. He considered a pseudoscientific answer but rejected it as inappropriate. "Because it does?"

Windsweet smiled. "Exactly. Now go to sleep. You need your rest."

General Ian St. James raised his right arm, pointed the remote towards the ceiling, and pressed a button. The white plaster disappeared and was replaced by a large holo screen. The picture showed the same bed that he lay on now, except that the electronic version of himself was naked, as was Marianne Mosby.

It had been her idea, of course, since St. James was far too self-conscious to do something of that sort on his own, but she'd insisted, and, as with everything else, Marianne got her way.

But St. James was glad, because the holo was one of the few remembrances he had of her, and the only one in which she was naked.

There was a price to be paid, however, including the sight of his own naked posterior and the realization that she had maintained eye contact with the camera throughout the entire thing. The officer watched sadly as Mosby smiled at him over his own shoulder, repositioned her body for a more intimate shot and came to a rather loud climax.

It was somewhat disturbing to realize that her pleasure stemmed more from the fact that their passion had been taped than from the act itself.

St. James touched a button and the image disappeared. Darkness filled the room. The holo should have angered him, should have caused him to reject her, but it didn't. For the thousandth time he wondered where she was and what she was doing. It would have something to do with the attack on Worber's World, that was for sure. But what? A message torp had arrived two cycles before, but instead of answering questions, it had raised even more.

The empire had been attacked. Worber's World had fallen. Millions of citizens and a thousand legionnaires had been killed. Some had been classmates, friends, or enemies. All would be missed, remembered, and added to rolls of those who had died in battle. It was, St. James reflected, a kind of immortality, since the Legion honored its dead above all else.

But he was alive and faced with the problems that went with living. His orders were clear: intensify training, maintain a high state of alert, and prepare to evacuate his troops. Not "deploy," which would make sense given the Hudathan attack, but "evacuate," as in run. Not too surprising, since the orders had been signed by Admiral Scolari, the gutless wonder herself, but worrisome nonetheless.

What if the Emperor's advisors agreed? What if Marianne caved in? But that was unthinkable. Marianne was an extremely aggressive leader. She would never shirk her duty... or do anything to compromise the Legion's base on Algeron.

No, she'd fight for what she believed in, as Scolari would soon learn. He looked forward to hearing from her. Although official communications were routed through Scolari's office, the Legion had a long-standing system of its own, and Marianne would use it.

St. James clasped his hands behind his head. It was unfortunate that the Naa had picked this particular moment to launch an offensive... but such was life.

A heavily armed force had been sent back to the ambush site. It had recovered all of the bodies except for that belonging to Sergeant Major Bill Booly. Patrols were looking for the noncom, but St. James had little hope of actually finding him.

That was a real loss, since legionnaires like Booly didn't come along every day. He'd been a true volunteer, a man who had joined looking for adventure, and stayed because he was good at what he did.

St. James rolled over, sat up, and put his feet on the floor. Like it or not, the empire was at war. The dirtiest, riskiest, and stupidest chores would go to the Legion. It was his job to get them ready. He stood and headed for the shower.

Gunner stepped off one of the smaller personnel elevators, directed a vid pickup towards the sky, and saw that it was momentarily night. A meaningless distinction on Algeron, but comforting nonetheless, since darkness was traditionally associated with free time.

The spider-form body felt light and maneuverable after days spent as a quad. The light eight-legged construct was in many respects his *real* body, since it took care of his life support functions and would serve as his escape vehicle in the unlikely event that the larger quad body was severely damaged. Assuming that he *wanted* to escape, that is… which was damned unlikely.

Gunner made his way towards the main gate, waved his electronic pass at a sensor, and waited for the personnel port to slide open. It made a humming sound as it did so.

A sentry waved. Gunner waved back, and picked his way through scattered debris towards the dubious delights of Naa town. The dome-like roofs were nearly invisible in the darkness, but light showed through rectangular windows and spilled from open doors. Laughter, both human and Naa, floated up towards higher ground.

Gunner moved away from the noise and the establishments that it came from. Almost without exception the bars, whorehouses, and restaurants that occupied the domes closest to the fort were the exclusive domain of the bio bods. After all, what self-respecting cyborg would waste his or her time on entertainments that could no longer be enjoyed? That would be stupid, especially when an enterprising human named Otis Foss had created a sanctuary that catered to cyborgs.

Foss was one of the small group of humans who had been on Algeron prior to the Imperial decree that ceded the planet to the Legion, and had taken advantage of that fact to create a thriving, albeit semi-illegal business.

Gravel crunched as Gunner's disc-shaped pods made contact with the ground. A half-starved pook saw him, growled, and slinked away. Bio bods, both human and Naa alike, saw the spider-shaped body and pretended they didn't. That's how it was in Naa town. Get horribly wasted, screw your brains out and mind your own business.

Foss had named his establishment "The Cyborg's Rest" and hung out a sign to that effect. No one had ever actually called it that. The sign had been destroyed in a storm, people had taken to calling it "Fossy's Place," and the name had stuck.

Fossy's Place was larger than those that served bio bods, and had to be, since his clientele took up a lot more space.

Like most of the habitats on Naa, most of Fossy's Place was underground, safe from winter storms, insulated against both heat and cold. Gunner made his way down a well-used ramp and stopped in front of a durasteel door. There were outlaws to consider, and raids by the military police, so it paid to be careful.

A hidden scale weighed Gunner, scanners confirmed that he was a cyborg, and a computer opened the door.

The public room occupied a large circular area. It was dimly lit, interrupted here and there by supporting beams, and had a dirt floor. There was a wall-sized holo system, but most of the customers had little use for bio-bod dramas, porno, sports, or dance, so Foss ran outdated news cubes, documentaries on the Legion's history, and scenics from a variety of Imperial planets. Quite a few of the cyborgs liked music, though, and the sound system was on, broadcasting to those who chose to receive it.

Cyborgs have little need of things to sit on, so, other than some unusually tall card tables, the room was bare of furniture. There were decorations, though, including a wall-sized rendering of the 1st REC's insignia, an amazing array of captured weapons, and a stuffed Naa known as "Chiefy." Though variously represented as a Naa chieftain, outlaw, and philosopher, the unfortunate carcass actually belonged to a day laborer who'd been hit by a truck during the construction of Fort Camerone, and preserved by members of the Legion's Pioneers. How Foss had obtained it, and why, were shrouded in mystery.

The place was packed. There were lots of Trooper IIs, a couple of Trooper Is, a scattering of spider-forms, and a pair of off-duty fly-forms. They had stork-like legs, sleek bodies, and extendable wings in case they were forced to punch out of whatever aircraft they happened to be flying at the moment.

Most of the clientele were interfaced with virtual-reality gambling scenarios, were playing old-fashioned card games, or just shooting the shit. The war with the Hudathans was the main topic of conversation. Everyone figured the Legion would see action; the question was when, and most of all, where.

Some of the conversation could be heard, but a good deal of it took place on channel 3. All of it stopped momentarily when the door opened, then started again as Gunner made his entrance. He was well known at Fossy's Place, an accepted, if somewhat eccentric, member of the crowd.

There were the usual number of greetings, insults, and non sequiturs. Gunner made the appropriate responses, wove his way between the widely separated tables, and headed for the alcove where Foss traditionally sat.

Foss was a medium-sized man of indeterminate age. He was mostly bald and had an unlit cigar clenched between his teeth. He looked up from his comp. The initial interchange never varied.

"Hi, Gunner. How're things goin'?"

"Shitty. How 'bout you?"

"Shitty, but that's life. You want the usual?"

"Yeah."

Foss looked down at the console and used his index fingers to peck at the keys. "I heard about the ambush... sorry you survived."

"Yeah," Gunner responded, "it's gettin' so a guy can't even get killed in this borg's army."

Foss grinned. "Well, it seems that we're at war with some kinda geeks. Maybe they'll cancel your ticket."

"Here's hoping," Gunner said matter-of-factly. "Which room?"

"Number six... and that'll be fifty imperials."

"Put it on my tab."

Foss sighed. "You don't have a tab. What you have is a massive debt."

"I'm good for it."

Foss sighed again. "Okay, but make a payment soon, promise?"

"You got it."

"Good. Have a nice time."

Foss watched the cyborg make his way down a darkened ramp. He shook his head in amazement. Gunner was strange, even by cyborg standards, and kind of sad.

Gunner paused in front of room 6, waited for the door to hiss open, and glided inside. The room was dimly lit and empty of all furniture.

"Hello," the voice said, "and welcome to the Dream Master 4000. The Dream Master represents the culmination of a thousand years of scientific achievement. You are about to relive the happiest, saddest, most exciting, or most peaceful moments of your life. Now, listen carefully, and follow these easy…"

The control panel glowed softly. Gunner extended a leg, bypassed the first few steps of the computerized sequence, and jacked a cable into the side of his triangular head. Light exploded inside his brain, color swirled, disintegrated, and coalesced into abstract shapes. They drifted on a field of black. The voice returned.

"… you are ready to choose a memory. You may do so by recalling those images or sensations that most typify that particular experience."

Gunner knew that many, if not most, of his peers would have chosen a sex act, a drug-induced high, or the excitement of battle. But he chose the memory that he'd always chosen before and would always choose in the future.

Gunner remembered the zoo, packed with animals from a dozen earth-type worlds, and thick with their native foliages. He remembered the smell of animal dung, the warmth of the sun on his neck, and what it felt like to hold his wife's hand. He remembered how the birds made strange belching sounds, how his children had screamed with laughter and his wife had told them to quiet down.

And Gunner was gone, transported back to the happiest moment he'd ever experienced and a life that had ceased to exist.

* * *

Cissy Conners checked to make sure that the store was empty, locked the till, and made her way to the storeroom. It was dark inside and deliciously cool.

She selected a case of soft drinks and picked it up. It was hot outside and the cold stuff was really moving. Cissy envied them, the ones that were out in the sun, and looked forward to joining them. Her relief would come in an hour or so, and she'd be free, until night school, that is, and another evening of classes. A degree in business, that was her dream, and in two, three years at the most, she'd have it.

Her expression brightened. Mark had made a point of sitting next to her the night before. Would he do it again? The thought filled her with delicious anticipation.

The cool-case was heavy and took all of Cissy's strength. She carried it to the front of the store and noticed that two customers had entered during her absence. She put the case on the floor and slid behind the counter.

One of the customers, a woman, stood at the rear of the store and was scanning that morning's printout of a popular newsmagazine. The other customer, a man, stood a few feet away, and judging from the way that he looked around, was nervous about something. Not only that, but he wore a ball cap and wraparound sunglasses, as if he were trying to look cool or conceal his identity. Cissy felt her heart beat a little bit faster. She forced a smile.

"May I help you?"

"Yeah," the man said, doing his best to sound tough. "Keep your hands where I can see 'em and give me everything in the till."

The gun looked huge. It wavered slightly.

Cissy knew what she was supposed to do. Give the man the money, wait until he was gone, and call the police. She moved her hand towards the till, remembered that she had locked it, and reached for her purse.

The first slug hit her arm, tore its way through, and punctured a coffee urn on the shelf behind her. Blood pumped and Cissy screamed.

The second slug punched its way through Cissy's shoulder, threw her backwards, and smashed her into the wall.

The third slug struck her chest, and she wanted to scream, but dead people can't scream. Can they?

"Hey... give us a break, Villain. What the hell is that anyway? Your idea of a joke?"

Villain awoke, looked around, and found that she was in bay 4, slot 7, of Fort Cameron's cybernetic maintenance facility. There was a shortage of Trooper II bodies, so they had installed her in an antiquated bi-form and attached her to the 1st RE.

The Trooper II across from her had lost an arm and was looking in her direction.

"Sorry, I had a bad dream."

The Trooper II leaned back, allowed the supportive cradle to accept its weight, and let its vid cams go out of focus.

"All right, then. But have the decency to kill your transmitter."

Villain checked, found that her transmitter was on, and turned it off.

She remembered the face that had killed her and wondered where he was. The Legion was careful about that sort of thing... about making sure that you didn't know. It was part of the process, of leaving the past behind, of starting over. They wanted her to let go of what had happened, to place herself in their hands, to live in the present.

So the man could be serving time in prison, or dead, having been executed for her death, or in the streets killing for the pure pleasure of doing so. That was what she felt deep inside, that the man was alive somewhere, untouched by what he'd done.

Villain had nine years, two months, and four days left before her enlistment was up. And the moment that it was, she'd find the man who had stolen her life, and deprive him of his.

Booly donned his uniform, minus weapons, of course, and stepped through the beadwork curtain that separated the underground sleeping chamber from the dwelling's main room. The living-dining-cooking area was circular, with a combination fireplace-furnace at its center and a walkway all around. Odors filled the room, carefully blended to please Naa noses, and heavy with meaning.

The room *smelled* warm and cozy, and looked the same way, which took Booly by surprise. It was nothing like the interspecies whorehouses of Naa town or the hovels that he'd searched during sweeps.

He saw two males and a female, all in their teens, preparing food in the area immediately around the fireplace-furnace. Their curiosity was plain to see, along with a tiny bit of fear and a certain amount of revulsion.

Booly understood. He was the enemy, after all, the boogey man come to visit, and the youngsters weren't sure how to react. He smiled at them, thankful that the expression meant the same thing in both cultures, and made his way towards a vertical ladder.

The ladder was made of wood, was well constructed, and creaked slightly under his weight. The legionnaire noticed that the structure had been built double wide, a design that permitted one Naa to go up while another came down, or in the case of an emergency, would allow the entire family to exit in a hurry. It was smart, a word that he'd never thought to apply to the Naa before, but seemed increasingly appropriate.

The ladder terminated at a broad platform, about six feet short of the surface, and off to one side from a second ladder.

The human didn't understand the design at first, until he considered it from a military point of view, and realized how hard it would be to fight an invader from the top of a ladder.

A nice sturdy platform would be much better, allowing more space from which defenders could fight, and providing them with a natural rallying point. Not only that, but a heavy curtain made from tanned dooth hide would serve to screen the second ladder off from interior light and keep the heat in. It was rolled at the moment and secured to the ceiling via two Legion standard pulleys.

Booly made his way up the second ladder and stepped out into bright sunlight. It was cold and his breath fogged the air around him.

A single glance told him why Naa villages were so hard to find without the help of a spy sat. Unlike the adobe domes of Naa town and the hovels that the outlaws threw together, there was nothing to see except for some holes in the ground. And there weren't very many of those. Twenty-five or thirty at most, widely separated from each other, so they looked natural, especially when surrounded by jagged foothills already full of holes, crevices, caves, and the like. A fire pit occupied the exact center of the village but looked largely unused. It would be barely visible from the air.

Still, good as things were, they could have been better. Booly frowned as he saw the well-beaten path that led away from the immediate vicinity, towards a narrow passageway. The damned thing was like a gigantic arrow that pointed where? Towards water? A food source? Whatever it was offended his sense of military propriety and made him angry at someone's stupidity.

Booly caught himself and laughed. Since when was it his responsibility to protect the enemy? If the Naa were stupid enough to reveal their position to satellite photography, then so much the better. He'd like nothing more than to see some members of the 2nd REP fall out of the sky.

"You laugh, human. Does that mean you are brave? Or just very, very foolish?"

Booly turned to find himself face-to-face with a Naa warrior. It wasn't Windsweet's father, but a younger male, with orange fur and the beads of an initiate. A warrior, then, and well armed, including a .50-caliber recoilless pistol that had formerly belonged to one of the Legion's NCOs. That, plus some baggy pants, a leather harness, and a quilted vest completed the outfit.

Booly shrugged. "Doesn't one presuppose the other? Would a sensible male be brave?"

The Naa laughed. "Spoken like a true warrior. I am Movefast Shootstraight, Windsweet's brother and Hardman's son."

They touched palms in the traditional Naa greeting. Booly gestured towards his surroundings.

"Tell me something, Movefast. Where am I allowed to go? And where's my guard?"

The Naa laughed and his eyes twinkled. "You may go wherever you please, human, as long as you return within two settings of the sun. As for guards... they are all around you. What's more, they never sleep, can't be bribed, and are eternally loyal."

The human looked around, saw nothing but craggy ridges, and understood what the warrior meant. The hills were like guards, hemming him in, limiting his movements. Not only that, but the Naa had walked every ridge, every canyon, and would have little difficulty catching him. And, judging from Movefast's expression, would enjoy the chase.

Booly grinned. "I see what you mean."

Movefast smiled. He had nice teeth. "Good. I'll see you at main-meal, two settings from now."

The human nodded and watched the warrior walk away. There was pride in the way that he held himself, grace in the way that he moved, and strength in the way that he leaped to the top of a boulder and scrambled up a scree-covered slope.

It suddenly occurred to Booly that the Naa would make damned fine troops.

He filed the thought away, followed the well-beaten path to a fissure in the rocks, and mounted a series of well-placed stepping-stones. By leaping from one to another, the Naa were able to avoid the thick layer of dooth dung that covered the floor of the passageway below.

The path zigged and zagged for a bit, each angle creating a natural defensive point, before emerging into a large open area. It was beautiful in its own way, covered with knee-high yellow-gray grass that sparkled with frost.

A herd of shaggy-looking dooth could be seen in the distance, heads down, grazing on the winter grass. Warriors ambled along beside them, guarding the animals from carnivores and outlaws.

Booly shook his head in frustration. The path, the field, and the dooth would all show up in a satellite photo, *had* shown up and been filed away under some sort of code name. That was the silly part, that the Legion *knew* where most of the villages were and left them alone. Just as the Naa knew where Fort Camerone was but never tried to destroy it.

It was all part of the strange relationship that existed between the Legion and the Naa, a relationship built on a curious mix of respect, hatred, trust, and fear. It was, Booly suspected, a measure of how alike the two races were and how stupid the continual warfare was.

The main path spilled out onto the plain, separated into numerous trails, and disappeared into the grass. Booly stayed left, chose a path that cut across the face of a scree-covered slope, and set out to get the lay of land. Rugged foothills or no, it was his duty to escape, and he had every intention of doing so. Not today, but soon. *After* he had recovered, *after* he had acquired some supplies, and *after* he knew his way around.

The trail had been created by countless generations of wild animals and improved by the Naa. Why was not exactly clear, since the path had no particular military value and was too high off the valley floor to be connected with food. But a path generally has a destination and Booly had nothing better to do.

He had walked for thirty minutes or so and worked up a good sweat when he saw the archway. It was a natural feature, left when softer material had separated from hard, and then enhanced with some judicious pick work. Voices could be heard and the tunnel served to funnel them in his direction.

"Why not? It's not as though you're a virgin or something. The entire tribe knows that you had sex with Keenmind Wordwriter."

"Because I don't love you. It's as simple as that."

"Don't love me?" the first voice asked incredulously. "Don't love me? And you loved Wordwriter? Is that what you're trying to say?"

"That's exactly what I'm trying to say," the female voice said firmly. "Now, get your hands off me."

"What if I don't? What then?"

Booly frowned. The female voice belonged to Windsweet. There was no doubt about that or the perfume that drifted his way. He stepped through the archway and out onto a sun-splashed ledge. He saw a spectacular view, a carefully spread doothskin robe, and a picnic lunch. His arrival caused quite a reaction.

A warrior, larger than average and heavily armed, scrambled to his feet. He wore a breechcloth, weapons harness, and lace-up sandals. His otherwise handsome features were contorted with rage. "Explain your presence here!"

Booly felt adrenaline enter his bloodstream and struggled to control it. The Naa was armed and sure to win a fight. The noncom smiled blankly and waved towards the panoramic view. "I came to look around. Wonderful place for a picnic. I can see why you chose it."

"Yes," Windsweet said, getting to her feet. "It is pretty, isn't it? We were just about to leave. Would you like to accompany us? The sun will set soon and the trail can be dangerous."

Booly had no difficulty reading the gratitude in her voice, or the anger on the warrior's face.

"Enough of this nonsense. I have work to do." The Naa grabbed the blast rifle that had been propped up next to a rock, stomped through the archway, and hurried down the trail. Both the dooth hide and picnic lunch were left behind for Windsweet to handle. She started to pack and Booly hurried to help.

"Thank you."

"For what? Interrupting your picnic?"

Windsweet paused and looked him in the eye. "How much did you hear?"

Booly did his best to look innocent "Hear? I didn't hear anything."

Windsweet shook her head sadly. "Why do you lie so much? Ridelong is obnoxious, but he tells the truth."

Booly shrugged. "I'm sorry. I wasn't sure what you wanted to hear."

"The truth," Windsweet said softly. "I want to hear the truth. Lies have little value."

Booly looked at her kneeling there in front of him, with the vast sweep of wilderness behind her, and decided that he'd never seen anyone so beautiful. The words came of their own accord.

"The truth is that you are the most beautiful female that I've ever seen."

She reacted with pleasure that quickly turned to concern. "You mustn't say things like that."

"You told me to tell the truth."

"It *isn't* true, and besides, we are of different races."

"Not so different that we can't see beauty in each other," Booly replied.

"No more," Windsweet said sternly. "I forbid it. My father would kill you if he knew what you just said. And mark this, human: Ridelong doesn't dare bring me harm, but he wouldn't hesitate to hurt you."

"All right," Booly replied, "on one condition."

"What's that?"

"I have a name, not as pretty as yours, but a name nonetheless. It was taken from an ancient song. My name is Bill. Say it."

"Bill."

"Good. Let's have an agreement. I won't refer to you as 'Naa,' and you won't address me as 'human.'"

Windsweet laughed. The legionnaire loved the way that her eyes danced and was nearly overwhelmed by the smell of her perfume.

"It shall be as you say, Bill. Now, let's go. It will be dark soon and the trail is difficult."

Booly helped her pack, shouldered the dooth hide, and followed her through the archway. There was grace in the way that she moved down the trail. His eyes were drawn to the movement of her well-shaped head, the sway of her narrow hips, and the flash of down-covered legs.

Part of what he felt was a sexual desire so strong that it almost hurt.

Most of his friends had made use of the prostitutes in Naa town and told extravagant stories about how attractive they were, but Booly had listened with little interest. The very idea of having sex with an alien had seemed wrong and twisted somehow.

But Windsweet had changed all that. He could not only imagine having sex with her, he *wanted* to have sex with her, a fact that surprised him to no end.

Of equal interest, however, was the tenderness he felt towards her, an emotion he'd never felt for the female legionnaires that he'd slept with.

All of which was extremely troubling, since it was Booly's duty to escape, and his desire to stay.

9

The currents carry us where they will, and we are grateful, for life is motion.
THE SAY'LYNT GROUP MIND KNOWN AS "RAFT ONE"
As dictated to Dr. Valerie Reeman
Standard year 2836

Planet IH-4762-ASX41, the Human Empire

The cobalt-blue sky hung over the ocean like a huge umbrella. It was marbled here and there with streaks of white. Some of the streaks were made by cirrostratus clouds, but others had been left by Hudathan attack ships, and it was these to which the Say'lynt had turned their collective consciousness.

There were three main rafts, plus two lesser bodies, not sufficiently mature to take part in the decision-making process. Each raft incorporated billions of individual phytoplankton and covered more than a thousand square miles of softly undulating ocean. The rafts were three feet thick, acquired most of their energy from the sun, and dominated the oceanic food chain.

It had taken millions of years for the parent raft to develop the thousands of brain nodules that, when linked together by endless miles of thin, almost translucent fiber, constituted a group mind. And it had taken millions more to create two additional beings and attain full mastery of the seas. For everything in the

127

world-spanning ocean lived in harmony with the Say'lynt and depended on them for existence.

There were the lesser plants that fed off the more highly developed plankton's waste products, the zooplankton that fed on them, the larger zooplankton that ate their smaller cousins, and so forth, all the way up to some large but relatively mindless vertebrates that swam the depths of the Say'lynt's watery domain.

But the air was a different matter, lying outside of the Say'lynt's native element, impervious to their direct control.

Yes, the phytoplankton had made significant progress towards the control of the water cycle, aided by the fact that land occupied less than 2 percent of the planet's surface, but control of the atmosphere lay thousands, if not hundreds of thousands, of years in the future.

Not so for the humans, and more recently the Hudatha. They had machines that allowed them to command the skies in ways that the Say'lynt had never imagined.

The humans had arrived first, their aircraft screaming across the heretofore undisturbed sky, spewing poison into the air.

It was, the Say'lynt soon learned, typical of the way that the aliens behaved. They moved quickly, acted on impulse, and could accomplish many things in a short period of time.

It took the humans less than five planetary rotations to map the world's surface, analyze its composition, occupy one eighth of the existing landmass, and discover the Say'lynt.

The discovery, if "discovery" was the right word, occurred when a biologist named Reeman attempted to take a sample from Raft Two in the northern hemisphere. Understandably annoyed, Raft Two had struck back by seizing control of the biologist's higher thought processes. Though not especially unusual from a Say'lynt point of view, the seizure, and subsequent release, had proved fascinating to the humans, and an agreement had been struck.

A limited number of humans would be allowed to stay on the planet and study the Say'lynt, if they agreed to leave the environment exactly as they had found it and were willing to be studied in return. Though clearly unused to being the object of study themselves, the humans had agreed, and kept their part of the bargain.

So the subsequent arrival of the Hudathans, the ceasing-to-exist of their human friends, and the related damage to the environment had angered Rafts One, Two, and Three, causing them to seize control of a low-orbit space machine and take a position in a war they didn't fully understand.

Raft Two adjusted to a storm that had disturbed the southern portion of its enormous anatomy, formulated a question, and sent it towards the others. Both were thousands of miles away.

"The ones who call themselves 'Hudathans' say we must release the ship or suffer massive damage to ourselves and the environment."

"It could be true," Raft Three added slowly. "You saw how quickly the humans were destroyed."

"Yes," Raft Three put in, "but Dr. Valerie and the others were what the humans call 'scientists.' The outcome might have been far different if some of the specialists they call 'soldiers' had been present."

"And that was our fault," Raft Two thought. "The humans offered us a contingent of soldiers but we refused."

"Yes," Raft Three agreed. "That was an error. The humans are strange but preferable to the Hudathans. But what can we do?"

Although the question was not addressed to Raft One, all three of them knew that by virtue of its age and greater experience, it was most qualified to answer.

"I have given this matter some consideration," Raft One answered. "Given the fact that this situation lies outside the realm of our experience and involves a conflict that we do not fully understand, we could use some expert advice. A human soldier seems best, but failing that, one of the experts that Dr. Valerie referred to as 'slimeball politicians.' "

"Yes," Raft Two agreed, "but can we obtain such advice? We are unable to leave the environment and the Hudathans have surrounded the planet with their war machines."

"Which," Raft One thought calmly, "is why it will be necessary to make the Hudathans get one for us."

"But how can we do that?" Raft Three asked.

"By threatening to seize more of their ships," Raft One answered easily. "Like the humans, the Hudathans find our ability to control their brain nodules to be very frightening."

"True," Raft Two responded, "but we are unable to reach further than the ship already under control. It was in what the humans call 'low orbit' when we struck. The rest are beyond the extent of our influence."

"I am aware of that," Raft One replied patiently, "but the Hudathans are not."

"Ah," Raft Three thought. "You propose to use the strategy that Technician Henza referred to as a 'bluff.'"

"Exactly," Raft One responded smugly. "Skills gained through the game called 'poker' have many applications. The humans lacked the strength to defend us, but they gave us weapons, and it is our responsibility to use them."

War Commander Niman Poseen-Ka held the terrarium up to the light, gave a grunt of satisfaction, and admired his latest handiwork.

The original kit had not included mountains, or the materials necessary to make them, but some malleable plastic requisitioned from the engineering department, plus some other odds and ends, had been sufficient for the task.

The mountains were gray, like the ones near his native village, and tipped with white.

Poseen-Ka put the terrarium down with an audible sigh. He had put the moment off as long as he dared. There was work to do and decisions to be made.

The war commander stood and approached the holo tank. A likeness of the planet that the humans had designated as IH-4762-ASX41 hung in midair, rotated before his eyes, and challenged him to make a decision. It was blue, with wisps of white, and relatively unimportant in and of itself.

True, the Say'lynt had demonstrated some unprecedented mental powers, but weren't much of a threat. Yes, they had taken control of a Hudathan cruiser, but he could lose the ship and still brag of a casualty rate that was 82 percent lower than predicted.

As for the Say'lynt's threat to take over the rest of his fleet, well, he doubted their capacity to do so. After all, why threaten that which you can actually do? No, it was a strategy intended to force compliance with their request. And a strange request it was.

The Say'lynt wanted a human soldier. Or, failing that, a politician, although the war commander wasn't sure that he understood the difference. They hadn't said why, but Poseen-Ka assumed that the phytoplankton wanted military advice and had chosen this method to obtain it. It was a request that he would deny under normal circumstances, but was now tempted to grant, since doing so would take a day and maybe more. He had time to burn.

With the exception of the Say'lynt, and some rather stubborn humans on an asteroid called "Spindle," the campaign had been a tremendous success. His ships had laid waste to seven systems, destroyed hundreds of ships, and taken so many outposts, research stations, fuel depots, and other installations that he'd lost count. There had been little more than scattered unorganized resistance. When would the humans finally respond?

The question filled his thoughts while on duty and his dreams while asleep. He should have been happy, joyful even, riding the wave of a great victory. But nothing was sufficient to rid himself of the constant angst that rode in the pit of his stomach. The feeling that terrible tragedy lay somewhere up ahead, that they were moving too fast, bypassing too many planets, overreaching their supply lines.

There were others, though, like Lance Commander Moder-Ta and his mentor, Grand Marshal Pem-Da, who thought things were going well. Extremely well if the congratulatory message torps were any indication.

It was clear that Pem-Da and the others felt the joy that had evaded him, relished the victories that left him feeling hollow, and lusted for more. They opposed a delay of any sort and, had they been aware of his true feelings, would have held them up to ridicule.

But Poseen-Ka believed in his instincts, believed that the basic fears that had guided his race for so long were a blessing rather than a curse, and he was determined to take them into account.

So a strategy was in order. Something that would seem legitimate and buy some time. The Say'lynt were the perfect answer.

Poseen-Ka turned, lumbered across the command center, and sat in his chair. He touched a button and a noncom hurried to respond.

Norwood was doing push-ups when the guard arrived. She did them every day at exactly 0900 and had been able to increase the total number of reps from twenty to twenty-five.

It was all she had to show for the last few weeks. The exercise had started out as a discipline, a way to restore strength to her tortured body, but had become something more important. The push-ups were a statement of optimism, of progress, of hope for the future. The hatch opened without warning and she forced herself to ignore it.

"… twenty-two… twenty-three… twenty-four and twenty-five."

Norwood made a show of jumping to her feet. If the Hudathan was impressed, his face didn't show it. Another guard stood right behind him.

Norwood was naked from the waist up, which meant nothing to the guards, but bothered her. She reached for one of the olive-drab T-shirts she had requisitioned from Baldwin's supplies and pulled it over her head.

"Yes?"

The Hudathan blinked. His voice was a sibilant hiss. "You will don whatever equipment you deem necessary for a trip to the surface and accompany me to the launching bay."

"Trip to the surface? Why?"

"Because the war commander has ordered it," the Hudathan said simply. "You have five units of time in which to prepare."

The Hudathans left the compartment, the hatch hissed closed, and Norwood finished dressing.

She knew very little about the planet below, except that it was inhabited by some sort of intelligent plankton and had been home to a small group of human scientists. They, like all the humans encountered so far, had been ruthlessly exterminated.

So what the hell was going on? There was no way to know,

but one thing was for sure: after weeks spent cooped up in her tiny compartment any sort of outing would be welcome.

Norwood checked her wrist chrono, made sure that she had exceeded the time limit by at least two minutes, and left the compartment. There were four guards, SOP since the death of Keem-So, and at least two more than was really necessary. Two marched in front of her and two behind. It made an impressive sight and everyone below the rank of lance commander hurried to get out of the way.

The hallway was a lot like the other passageways on the ship. There were the usual pictograms, including one that consisted of an oval with a delta-shaped ship passing through its center. A symbolic representation of the launch bay, no doubt, and judging from the increasing number of Hudathans dressed in flight suits, it lay just ahead.

The hallway narrowed in a manner that would force boarders to attack single file, broadened out again, and ended in front of a lock. It was open and Baldwin was waiting.

Norwood hadn't seen him since the torture session. He looked tired, tense, but otherwise unchanged.

"Colonel Norwood."

"Baldwin."

Baldwin noticed the omission of his rank but chose to ignore it. "You're looking well."

"Thanks. I work at it. What's going on?"

Baldwin shrugged. "It seems that the Say'lynt have some unused mental powers. They took control of a ship and refuse to release it until the Hudathans allow them to speak with a human soldier."

Norwood raised an eyebrow. "Yeah? So where do *you* fit in?"

Baldwin shook his head sadly and stepped into the lock. A guard motioned for Norwood to do likewise. She obeyed. The hatch closed and another slid open.

The launch bay had been pressurized. It was a huge space, full of ships, technicians, robots, and heavy equipment. The air was warm, as if it had been in there for a while, and heavily laced with ozone, a fact that didn't bother the Hudathans since they had an almost nonexistent sense of smell.

A guard gestured towards a heavily armored shuttle and the humans headed in that direction. Norwood was the first to speak.

"So what do phytoplankton want with a soldier? Human or otherwise."

Baldwin frowned. "Advice seems like the best bet. The Say'lynt liked the scientists, came to rely on them, and took possession of the Hudathan ship after they were killed. The result is a trump card they don't know how to play."

"And you'll help them solve the problem," Norwood said sarcastically.

"I'll offer some advice," Baldwin said calmly.

"Like what? Surrender and commit suicide?"

"No," Baldwin said stoically. "I'll suggest that they release the ship, limit the use of their mental powers, and form an alliance with the Hudatha."

"And if they refuse?"

Baldwin shrugged. "I'll cross that bridge when I come to it. War Commander Poseen-Ka had a suggestion, though."

"Really? What was that?"

"He suggested that I shoot you as an example of what happens to those that resist Hudathan rule." Baldwin pulled his jacket open.

Norwood looked and saw that the other officer had been entrusted with a sidearm. It was of human design. Fear rose to constrict her lungs. She forced it back down. "I see. Is that what you plan to do?"

They had reached the shuttle. Baldwin stopped and turned in her direction. He looked pained. "No, of course not. What do you take me for?"

Norwood looked him in the eye. "I take you for a man who has willingly, knowingly, participated in the mass murder of millions of human beings. What possible difference would one more make?"

Anger filled Baldwin's eyes. "Don't push your luck, Norwood. I could change my mind."

A guard motioned with his blast rifle and the humans entered the shuttle.

No effort had been made to hide the conduit that ran along

the bulkheads or to cushion the metal decks. The seats were of the tubular variety favored by military minds everywhere and large enough for two average-sized humans.

Norwood sat down, pulled the harness as tight as it would go, and found it was still loose.

The trip to the surface was completely uneventful. The Hudathans talked among themselves, Baldwin stared at the seat in front of him, and Norwood contemplated ways to get her hands on his gun, none of which seemed practical.

Just prior to touchdown, Norwood would have sworn that she felt something feathery touch her mind. It was a strange sensation, unlike anything she'd experienced before, and gone so quickly that she wasn't sure it had actually happened.

The shuttle landed with a gentle thump and the entry port hissed open. Air flooded into the passenger compartment and Norwood drew it deep into her lungs. It was clean and cool. She liked it and needed no urging to release the harness and make her way outside.

The shuttle had landed on a tropical island, replete with lush foliage and a crystal-clear lagoon. Not even the lumps of heat-fused sand, the slagged dwellings, or the freshly dug graves were sufficient to ruin the beauty. It was quiet—so quiet that she could hear each wavelet lap on the immaculate beach, a sound so peaceful, so soothing, that she wanted to take a nap.

The others must have felt the same way, because the Hudatha had decided to lie down in the shuttle's shade, and Baldwin had made a place for himself in the warm sand. It felt perfectly natural to settle down beside him, snuggle into a more comfortable position, and drift off to sleep.

The dream was flooded with light: beautiful, warm, life-giving light that streamed down from the sky to bathe her body in its yellow-orange goodness. Her body was a huge undulating mass. It covered thousands of square miles, was constantly mending itself, and was linked to the life around it.

Norwood found that her intelligence was everywhere yet nowhere at all. It felt strange because she was used to having her thoughts centered in one single place rather than dispersed over an area the size of a small country. But she liked it and found the sensation to be quite comfortable.

"So you like the Say'lynt and would like to live as we do?" The voice came from nowhere and everywhere at once. It seemed to roll and reverberate through her consciousness.

"Yes, if this is how you live, I would love to be like you." A feeling similar to gentle laughter eddied around her. "Dr. Valerie felt that way too. She wanted to know if we could take her in, make her part of ourselves, and leave her other body behind."

"And could you?"

Norwood felt a deep sadness sweep over her.

"No, unfortunately not. Not even when the Hudathans came to kill her."

"I'm sorry."

"Yes, the Hudathans have brought us much sorrow, an emotion we've only rarely felt before. Still, each experience brings a lesson, and this one is no exception. Teach us that we might learn."

Norwood remembered Baldwin and wondered if he was having the same dream. She started to speak, started to ask that very question, but the voice interrupted before she could do so.

"No, the other soldier has different dreams. Here, we will show you."

Before Norwood could object, she became part of a nightmare.

Baldwin had been asleep for about thirty minutes when the hand shook his shoulder. It belonged to his aide, Lieutenant List, a darkly seen form that stood next to his cot.

Baldwin swung his still-booted feet over the side and felt them sink into the mud under his bunk. A steaming cup of hot coffee was thrust his way and he took it.

"Yeah? What the hell does he want now?"

The "he" referred to General Nathan Kopek, the Emperor's twenty-five-year-old nephew, a major pain in the ass. List understood and responded accordingly.

"The general has a plan and would like your opinion."

Baldwin chuckled softly. "That'll be the day. Still, your tact is appreciated and will come in handy someday. Assuming you survive, that is."

List smiled, nodded, and slipped out through an opening in the curtain.

Baldwin stood, sipped the cup dry, and relished the warmth that spread through his stomach. He thought about a shave, rejected the idea as a waste of time, and pushed the curtain to one side.

Mud squished under his boots as he circled some ammo cases and entered the ops center. A computer beeped softly, the radios murmured, and Staff Sergeant Maria Gomez swore as she dropped a stylus and was forced to fish it out of the goo. They had tried to keep the mud out, but found it was damned near impossible and had finally given up.

"Damn this pus ball anyway!"

Baldwin removed his combat harness from the back of a chair and buckled it on. "I'll second that motion."

"Oh, sorry, sir. I didn't know you were there."

"That's quite all right, Sergeant. You can swear at this planet all you want. And give it a few licks for me."

Gomez smiled. The colonel was all right, more than all right, damned good-looking. Too bad she wasn't an officer. She'd screw his brains out.

"Would you like something to eat, sir? I've got some heavily modified X-rats on the stove."

Baldwin sniffed. Gomez could make anything taste good—everyone knew that—and the smell was tempting. But Kopek would throw a fit if he took more than five or ten minutes to reach the command bunker.

"Thanks, but no thanks. The general awaits."

Gomez wanted to say something comforting but knew that she couldn't. That would mean lifting the veil of pretense that hung over the brigade, violating the charade in which they pretended that the general deserved his comets and was a rational being. No, that would never do, so she held her tongue.

Baldwin selected a poncho from the three or four that hung near the entrance to the bunker and pulled it over his head. He opened the door to the alcove, waited for the bunker's computer to clear him through, and made his way up the ramp to ground level.

It was night and miserable as hell. The rain tapped against

Baldwin's head, his breath fogged the air, and his boots sank into the mire. It took a conscious effort to pull them free, step forward, and let them sink again.

A sentry started to salute, remembered that he shouldn't, and tried to hide what he'd done.

Baldwin smiled. "Thanks, Private. The geeks have enough advantages. No point in picking targets for them."

"Yes, sir, I mean no, sir, sorry, sir."

"That's all right. I hope your relief comes soon."

The sentry was silent but felt a little warmer as the officer trudged away.

The command bunker was on the far side of the compound, intentionally separated from his in case of an attack, which meant that he had a long ways to go.

A flare soared into the air, went off with a loud pop, and bathed the fire base in a hard white glare. It was followed by the *thump-thump-thump* of a heavy machine gun and the cloth-ripping sound of lighter weapons, as the geeks probed the outer wire. Energy beams flashed, robot spots hummed into position, and a section of radio-controlled mines was detonated.

It was a harassment raid, intended to keep the humans awake and scared shitless. It was working, because morale had already started to slide and was taking efficiency along with it.

A balloon-tired APV, all rigged out for desert warfare and shipped to Agua IV by mistake, rounded the side of a sandbagged tent and lost traction. The engine raced and the tires whined. Semi-liquid crud flew in every direction.

Mud spattered across the front of Baldwin's poncho and dripped onto his boots. He turned away, chose an alternate path, and kept on going.

The APV was a good example of how hosed things were. The indigs, a stubborn group of sentient quadrupeds, had taken exception to annexation and were fighting an effective guerrilla action against the "Imperial warmongers."

Incensed by this obvious act of treason, the head warmonger himself had dispatched a brigade of army troops to Agua IV under the command of his favorite nephew, all the better to season the lad and prepare him for mayhem on a truly massive scale.

Never mind that the boy was fresh out of the Imperial Military Academy, arrogant as hell and addicted to Gar weed. And never mind that the supply idiots had continued to send them Class III desert gear or that the geeks outnumbered them thousands to one or that the terrain was damned near impassable. The brigade had to win or forever tarnish the empire's nonexistent honor.

Still, as screwed up as things were, Baldwin felt sure they *could* win if he were allowed to lead his own troops. But that was impossible, since General Nathan Kopek had refused the role of figurehead and insisted on making the decisions himself, no matter how stupid, irrational, or suicidal those decisions might be.

There was a roar of sound as a black-on-black troop carrier passed overhead and dropped toward the well-defended LZ. Another followed it, and another, in a steady stream of heavily armored aircraft.

The rain forced Baldwin to blink. It ran back along his face and trickled down his neck. Something, the rain or something else, sent a shiver down his spine.

What the...? There was no exercise, no mission, slated for tonight. Then it came to him. Kopek! The miserable bastard was up to something!

Baldwin ran towards the command tent. The mud sucked at his boots as if trying to hold him back. He was conscious of movement around him, of heavily armed troops emerging from their underground bunkers and moving towards the LZ.

Damn! Damn! Damn! What was the silly sonofabitch up to now?

A momentary flash of light came from the direction of the command bunker and Baldwin hurried towards it. A sentry moved to block his way, saw who it was, and stepped aside.

The ramp was slick with rain, but free of mud, thanks to the efforts of the poor slobs assigned to that day's shit detail. Baldwin palmed the door lock, was recognized by the bunker's computer, and stepped inside.

The alcove was full of neatly arranged boots and carefully hung ponchos. Kopek might be a dope addict, but he was a tidy one, and lord help the poor slob who tracked mud into the general's personal domain.

But Baldwin was in a hurry and seething with anger. He palmed the second door, waited for it to hiss aside, and stepped through. His boots left big muddy prints on the spotless red carpet. He took ten paces forward, put hands on hips, and looked around.

There were ten or fifteen people present. Some were toadies, some were members of the general's personal bodyguard, and the rest were duty grunts, stuck with operating the com gear or providing administrative support. All of them looked his way.

"What the hell's going on here?"

General Nathan Kopek was a slim young man with hooded eyes and pouty lips. He was in the process of donning an ornate set of battle armor with the help of his batman.

"I believe it is customary to address superior officers as 'sir' or 'madam.' Please do so."

"Yes, *sir.* So what the hell's going on here, sir?"

Kopek saw the muddy bootprints and frowned disapprovingly.

"We are in the process of preparing a surprise attack. Something you would be well aware of if you spent more time attending to your duties and less time in the sack."

Baldwin searched the other man's eyes, looked for the dilated pupils typical of Gar weed users, and found them. They looked like lakes of darkness. Kopek was using, and subject therefore to all the drug's effects, including delusions of grandeur, a false sense of omnipotence, and occasional hallucinations. Baldwin fought the desire to yell and scream. It was extremely important to remain rational and in control.

"I see. And the target of this attack?"

The batman fumbled a closure and Kopek pushed him away. He buttoned the flap himself. His eyes gleamed with enthusiasm. "Geek central, the nursing complex at Alpha Three, Zebra Seven."

Baldwin considered what Kopek had said. The humans had known about the nursing complex for some time. Almost all of the indig's offspring were born there, entering the world in one of the many birthing caves, where they were warmed by natural hot springs and blessed by the priesthood. It was a holy place, and a poor one to attack, since doing so would earn the humans a level of hatred that no amount of diplomacy would ever erase.

But there were other reasons to avoid the place as well. Military reasons that the general had chosen to ignore. The nursing complex was located deep inside a mesa-shaped mountain. The mountain had sheer walls and was surrounded by an impenetrable rain forest on one side and a rushing river on the other. The only practical way to get into the place would be to land on top of the mountain and fight down through a veritable maze of tunnels and caves. Each foot of the way would be contested by fanatical warriors, defending not just their freedom but the very existence of their race. Such an attack would be more than suicidal, it would be unbelievably stupid and would lead to disastrous results.

Baldwin swallowed hard. "Sir, I beg you to reconsider. It will be extremely difficult to penetrate the tunnel complex. The indigs will defend every foot of tunnel to the death and hate us forever if we win."

Kopek nodded as if he had expected those very arguments. "Just the sort of rationalizations one would expect from a slacker and a coward. Your request to reconsider is denied."

Baldwin came to attention. "In that case I request the general's permission to lead the assault."

Kopek waved the words away and allowed his batman to hand him a gold-tipped swagger stick. "Don't be silly. I have no intention of granting you a position from which you can sabotage my efforts. No, you'll be where cowards should be, safe and sound. Guards! Place Colonel Baldwin under arrest and throw him in the stockade."

Baldwin was still screaming his objections when the guards threw him into the muddy stockade, still pleading when the troop carriers lifted off, and still crying long after the sound of their engines had disappeared.

The subsequent massacre, in which Kopek was one of the first to die, had made headlines clear across the empire. It was dramatic stuff.

Never mind that the attack had been poorly conceived, never mind that more than two thousand soldiers had died, and never mind that the indigs had pushed the humans back onto their isolated fire bases. Kopek's incompetence would reflect poorly on his uncle, so the truth was twisted into something new and delivered all over the empire.

Kopek was transformed from incompetent to hero. The Emperor himself had laid a wreath on the young warrior's coffin. Statues had been erected on every world that wanted an Imperial favor, three different and wildly inaccurate holo vids had been shot, and Colonel Alexander Baldwin had been court-martialed.

He was completely excoriated, labeled as a coward, and stripped of his rank. Someone had to take the fall, someone had to pay the price, and he was the logical choice.

It was the bitterness generated by this injustice that had burned its way to the core of Baldwin's soul, had cut the threads of his humanity and set him on the path towards revenge.

Norwood felt a momentary sense of confusion as she floated free of Baldwin's memories and became herself once more. Raft One sent soothing thoughts.

"The one called Baldwin sleeps now. He will feel better when he awakes."

"What about his mission? You wanted to speak with a soldier."

"I *am* speaking with a soldier," Raft One replied easily. "A *sane* soldier. We would value your advice."

Norwood thought out loud. "My guess is that the Hudathans would like to recover their ship but are willing to sacrifice it if need be."

"Yes," Raft One agreed, "Baldwin's thoughts confirm what you say. There's something else as well. It's his belief that the one called Poseen-Ka is, how do you say, 'stalling for time.' Deliberately avoiding combat while he waits for your race to react."

"How very interesting," Norwood mused. "I wonder what Poseen-Ka really thinks. Well, regardless of that, the fact remains that the Hudatha have the means to destroy your planet without coming in range of your mental powers."

"That is correct," Raft One confirmed. "We acted without consideration of the consequences."

"Then you have very little choice," Norwood thought. "You must negotiate the best terms you can."

"What about the human soldiers?" Raft Three asked. "Will they come to our aid?"

Norwood gave the mental equivalent of a shrug. "A few weeks ago I would have said yes, but I'm no longer certain. I hope so, but Baldwin's memories reveal how flawed our leadership can be, so there's no guarantee. All you can do is make a deal and hope for the best."

"They could destroy us the moment that we release their ship," Raft Three said suspiciously.

"Maybe," Norwood agreed, "but I doubt it. To destroy you would be to destroy your abilities, and it's my guess that the Hudatha would like to study you, something they won't have time to do until the war is over."

"It's risky," Raft Two put in, "but we don't have much choice."

Norwood delighted in the sunlight, the gentle movement of the ocean, and the presence of the Say'lynt.

"No, my friends. The truth of the matter is that you have no choice at all."

10

Again, in basic training, we had been forbidden to say please or thank you as such words implied the existence of gratitude, charity, and benevolence.

EX-LEGIONNAIRE CHRISTIAN JENNINGS
Mouthful of Rocks
Standard year 1989

Planet Earth, the Human Empire

Angel Perez stopped just inside the tree line where the combination of the shadows and his camouflage would make him difficult to see. He swept the area for electronic activity, came up empty, and dumped his detectors. The principle was second nature by now. Instructors had screamed it while he was awake and machines had whispered it during his sleep.

"Detection equipment is a two-edged sword. It can find the enemy or reveal your presence. Use it sparingly."

The meadow appeared to be empty, but appearances can be deceiving, so Perez knew better than to take the situation at face value. He boosted his vid cams to high mag and searched the area for any of a hundred possible signs—dead grass that could indicate the roof of an underground installation, loose soil that could conceal a minefield, tire tracks, tread marks, old campfires—but the meadow gave no hint of those or any other threats. It was lush with green grass, dotted with yellow and blue wildflowers, and broken here and there by weathered boulders. They were large enough to conceal a few bio bods or a small vehicle, but it didn't seem likely.

The rest of his company, a mixed force of cyborgs, bio bods, and native troops, was coming up fast. Perez had the point. The transmission was short and scrambled.

"Red Dog One to Pointer Six. Report. Over."

"Pointer Six to Red Dog One. I have a visual all-clear tree line to ridge line. Over."

"Roger that. Uplink authorized. Scope the reverse side of the ridge. Over."

"Roger."

Perez selected the appropriate frequency, made contact with one of three sky-eyes assigned to that particular area, and took a peek through its vid cam. Shit! There was armor on the other side of the ridge! Big stuff just waiting for his company to emerge from the tree line.

The cyborg activated the command channel just as the enemy identified the sky-eye and blew the device out of the sky.

"Pointer Six to Red Dog One. Over."

"This is Red Dog One. Go, Pointer Six."

"There are fifteen to twenty heavies dug in on the reverse side of the slope. I have a ninety-six percent match with indig armor. Over."

"Roger, Red Dog One. Sit tight. Over."

Perez allowed himself a brief moment of relaxation. The training exercise was just that, a virtual-reality scenario created to test recruits like Perez.

Which explained why he couldn't remember what the company CO looked like, where the outfit had been the day before yesterday, or what planet he was on. Perez knew that the instructors could have filled those gaps had they chosen to but saw no need.

After all, why bother? The meadow *looked* real, the breeze *felt* real, and the situation *was* real for all practical purposes, since his life depended on the outcome. Unlike bio bods, cyborgs were subjected to something called the "graduation exercise," or GE, which they either passed or failed. The GE was the culmination of basic training, the final test of all that the recruits had learned, and so close to actual combat that the two were virtually indistinguishable. If Perez passed, he'd be admitted to the ranks of the Legion, and if he failed, his life would be forfeit just as it would be in actual combat.

The GE was a brutal uncompromising test designed to separate the weak from the strong and the dull from the bright. It stemmed from simple economics. It cost very little to train and equip a bio bod. But the technologically sophisticated bodies provided to cyborgs were expensive, a fact that made it worth the Legion's while to identify the most durable and agile minds. The rest were destroyed, as they would have been anyway, had they been executed or allowed to die of natural causes. No one knew how or when that death would come, only that it would, and that no exceptions were made. Perez pushed the thought away.

He'd come a long way since first awakening. He'd endured the insults, the zappers, and the endless mind-numbing drill. He'd learned new skills, overcome bad habits, and survived where Morales, Sibley, Lisano, Ho, and Contas had died. Yes, the very thing that had destroyed some of his fellow recruits had strengthened Perez and made him better.

The critical moment had arrived during a field exercise. The squad had done well for once and earned a ten-minute break. It takes effort to keep a trainer on its feet, so the recruits had lowered themselves to the ground, and discussed the relative merits of bestiality.

Most of the stories were lies, but the conversation caused the recruit to look around and realize what jerks his companions were. It was a moment of epiphany, of sudden realization, when Perez accepted the fact that he was no better than they were, and probably worse. The decision to change that, to make himself a better person, had seemed like the logical thing to do.

During the days that followed he dealt with the loss of his body, accepted the fact that it was his own fault, and decided to make amends. Assuming such a thing was possible, that is.

"Red Dog One to Pointer Six. Heads up. We're on your tail. Over."

Perez checked his forward-looking sensors again and came up

empty. He triggered his radio. "Roger that, Red Dog One. Over."

Then they were all around him, quads, the earth shaking under their pod-shaped feet, Trooper IIs like himself, trees swaying where massive shoulders had brushed them, and bio bods, slipping from one shadow to the next like evil spirits.

The quads would cross the open space first, followed by a mix of Trooper IIs and bio bods, with the lightly armored support vehicles and native troops bringing up the rear.

The enemy armor would get in some licks, but the vacuum jockeys would keep the bastards pinned until the quads could finish them off. Some of the legionnaires, members of the 2nd REP, would go straight up the scree-covered slope, but most of the force had been divided into two groups and ordered to sweep around opposite ends of the hill.

Perez was impatient and eager to get the whole thing over with. He welcomed the order when it came.

"Red Dog One to Red Dog Force. Let's kick some ass. Over."

The quads stepped out into the open and a trio of heavily armored ground support aircraft screamed out of the sky. Fingers of white appeared along their wings and pointed towards the enemy. The missiles made dull thumping sounds as they hit, and smoke boiled up from the other side of the ridge.

A barrage of SAMs rose to greet the planes. They rolled, split formation, and dumped chaff. Some of the missiles went for it and some didn't. Of those that didn't, most were destroyed by antimissile missiles, but at least two made it through. Both hit the same aircraft. It exploded in midair and rained debris on the enemy. Perez waited for a chute but didn't see one.

The recruit followed the quads out onto the field, checked to make sure there was plenty of space between himself and the others, and brought his sensors on-line. The battle had started and there was no point in stealth.

The enemy armor opened fire, lobbing shells up and over the ridge line, while remaining hidden from view. The barrage was computer-controlled and designed to fall in a neat checkerboard pattern. It turned the meadow into a hell of exploding shells and flying metal.

Perez moved forward, waiting for the range to close, waiting to kill. What? Why? He didn't know. The simulations never said. It was as if it didn't matter, as if Perez had no need to know *why* he fought, so long as he did. And, remembering all that they'd taught him about the Legion's traditions and history, the cyborg knew it was true. The Legion always went where it was ordered to go, did what it was ordered to do, and, with the exception of Algeria in the 1960s, had never objected.

The CO was brisk and matter-of-fact.

"Red Dog One to Red Dog Force. Remember the plan. Break left and break right. Get a move on. The longer we stay in the middle of this meadow, the longer they shoot at us. Over."

Perez turned left, saw movement, and zoomed in. Armor! The enemy had guessed the Legion's plan and were coming out to fight! He activated his radio.

"Pointer Six to Red Dog One. We have enemy armor preparing to engage our left flank. Over."

"Red Dog One to Pointer Six. Roger that. Hold as long as you can. Red Dog Seven and Eight are on the way. Over."

"That's a roger, Red Dog One."

Perez saw that two of the light tanks were heading straight for him. He glanced left then right. He was all alone! The incoming shells had destroyed the nearest quad and three Trooper IIs. The quads designated as Red Dog Seven and Eight were nowhere in sight.

An energy beam sizzled by his head. Another scorched the earth in front of him. A line of explosions marched across the field behind him. Shrapnel rattled off his armor. Perez took two quick steps, felt his right foot sink into a hole, and fell face-downwards on the ground. Damn, damn, damn!

Would the instructors pull the plug on him right now? Send him plunging into the blackness of death? Or give him another chance?

Nothing happened, so Perez assumed the best, rolled onto his right side, and fired a smoke grenade from the launcher located on the inside surface of his left arm. It hit the ground about ten feet away. Gray-black smoke boiled up around him just as the tanks arrived.

The tankers must have lost track of him, or assumed that he'd been hit, because both had redirected their fire to the soft-skinned vehicles toward the tree line.

The tanks were huge things, their tracks reaching as high as the cyborg's head, crushing everything they encountered. Not thinking of the consequences, not sure of what he was doing, Perez stood and jogged along between them.

Each vehicle was equipped with a tri-barrel energy cannon. The air crackled, hissed, and popped as they fired. A canvas-covered truck exploded; bodies flew through the air and fell into the resulting fire. The screams were horrible.

Perez considered his missiles, rejected them because of the short range, and chose his laser cannon instead. It would never penetrate the tank's armor-plated sides, but the tracks were more vulnerable and offered an acceptable target.

Still jogging, Perez aimed his cannon at the tank on the right and fired. Blue light flared, hit a drive wheel, and held. Nothing happened at first, and it was difficult to run and stay on target at the same time, but he kept on.

The laser had never been intended for sustained fire and started to overheat. Specially designed feedback circuits fed pain to the cyborg's brain. He fought the pain, saw the drive wheel turn cherry red and fuse with the track. The result was both sudden and completely unexpected. The track seized up, the tank turned left, and its energy cannon burped blue light. The resulting beam struck the other tank's turret, bored its way inside, and hit an ammo bin. The resulting explosion destroyed both of the tanks and Perez as well.

The blackness faded along with the neural interface. The support rack whined, delivered Perez to a standing position, and went silent. The sergeant known as "Sir" stepped out of the control room, grinned, and delivered a mock salute.

"Congratulations, Perez. You were stupid but brave. Just the sort of borg the Emperor wants most! Welcome to the Legion."

His internal advisors were especially strident that morning and the Emperor found it difficult to concentrate. Some were telling him how to deal with the Hudathans, others were urging him to have sex with the specially designed android that Governor

Amira had shipped him, and at least two were arguing the merits of Bach versus an alien composer named Uranthu.

The Emperor frowned, pressed fingers to his temples, and willed them to be quiet. Some obeyed and some didn't.

The Emperor nodded to his herald, waited through the usual announcement, and slipped through the curtains.

The palace boasted two throne rooms, one for ceremonial occasions and a smaller, more intimate version reserved for the day-to-day business of running the empire. This was the smaller chamber, painted white and finished with gold trim. Heavy red curtains hung along one wall, made a fitting backdrop for the throne, and hid the passageway from which the Emperor emerged.

The throne was simple rather than ornate and was quite comfortable. It sat on a well-carpeted riser and faced a semicircle of now empty chairs. All of his most trusted advisors were there, bowing, curtseying, and in some cases, sending him what they hoped were significant looks. The Emperor had no idea what the looks meant, but nodded anyway, and was rewarded with a number of self-satisfied smiles.

The Emperor sat on his throne and looked around. This was the third such meeting since the Hudathan incursion had begun, and his advisors had arrayed themselves along both sides of the issue.

Admiral Scolari was still intent on a withdrawal. By gathering all of their forces in one place, she planned to create a shield on which the Hudathan spear would almost certainly break. Or so she claimed. The fact that she was on friendly terms with the corporations that referred to themselves as "The Consortium of Inner Planets" had not escaped the Emperor's attention.

Governor Zahn was a clever politician whose system was located well within the boundaries that Scolari was willing to defend, and he sided with her.

General Worthington was pretending to be neutral but would almost certainly cave in to Scolari when neutrality was no longer possible.

Like Chien-Chu, the formidable Madam Dasser had financial interests in the rim worlds and was determined to sway the council towards a vigorous defense.

Professor Singh was mostly brain and very little emotion. He alone had pointed out that due to the tremendous distances involved, the conflict would take place over months, and possibly years. He saw the whole thing as a game, not unlike chess, and believed in preserving all of the empire's options until the very last moment. It was Singh's advice that the Emperor had used to delay a final decision. Not because he necessarily agreed with the academic, but because he found it difficult to decide, and didn't want to offend the ever-so-delicious General Marianne Mosby.

She was resplendent in her general's uniform and confident that he'd see things her way. They'd been seeing each other for about three weeks now, and her attempts to influence him had been just as vigorous as her lovemaking, and a lot more predictable. A bit boring actually, which meant that he'd have to do something about it soon, but not quite yet. No, he'd enjoy the general for another week or so, after which he'd be forced to make a decision about the Hudatha, a decision that might or might not be to Mosby's liking. He smiled.

"Please be seated."

Expensive fabrics rustled and swished as his advisors took their seats.

"Bach was a great composer, but Uranthu *is* a great composer, and we have yet to understand the full scope of his work."

All of them had heard such non sequiturs before and had become quite adept at hiding their reactions. Scolari frowned, and Madam Dasser shifted her weight from one side of the chair to the other, but the rest of them showed no reaction.

Governor Zahn sought to get the conversation on track. He was a wiry little man with a dome-shaped head and big hands. The shoulders of his cape were covered with stardust, a medallion in the shape of his planetary crest hung around his shoulders, and his pants were fashionably baggy.

"An interesting observation, Your Highness. I'm sure that all of us look forward to hearing more of citizen Uranthu's music. In the meantime, however, there are some other items of business that demand our attention, and, in light of your busy schedule, I suggest that we discuss them now."

Part of the Emperor was annoyed to have his comment dismissed so lightly, but another aspect of his personality was pleased with the way that Zahn had saved him from the possibility of embarrassment, and played along.

"You're quite right, Governor Zahn. We must keep our noses to the grindstone. How about it, then? What are the Hudathans up to now? Admiral Scolari? General Worthington? General Mosby? A report, please."

Scolari was jealous of such opportunities and had made it quite clear to both Worthington and Mosby that she was senior and would therefore speak for all three of them when that was appropriate. She made a production of checking her notes.

"The Hudatha have continued to advance since the attack on Worber's World. They have taken possession of at least seven of our outlying systems, destroyed hundreds of ships, and either captured or neutralized a long list of other assets as well."

Chien-Chu grimaced at the admiral's choice of words. His son, and the others unfortunate enough to be on Spindle, were fighting for their very lives. To refer to them as "assets" was to relegate them to the status of things rather than people. He struggled to control his frustration and found his eyes drawn to Madam Dasser's. She smiled grimly and gave a little shrug, as if to say she was sorry.

The Emperor made a steeple with his fingers. It reminded him of the pyramid that he'd erected over his mother's grave. It was huge, and completely transparent, so that sunlight could dance across the surface of her tomb. The words came of their own accord.

"Mommy liked a lot of sunlight. That's why the palace has so many windows."

"Yes," Admiral Scolari agreed smoothly, "your mother was a wonderful woman. We all miss her. I wonder how she would have dealt with the current crisis."

"Crisis?" The Emperor fought for control. The last comment had been his and couldn't be blamed on the copies. Scolari was smooth.

"Seven systems have been lost to Hudathan aggression. We must formulate some sort of response. I recommend that we withdraw all of our forces from the outlying sectors, use them to reinforce the inner planets, and meet the aliens with our full strength."

"And I respectfully disagree," Mosby said calmly. "I recommend that we use the home fleets to reinforce the rim worlds, fight for every square mile of vacuum, and wear the bastards down. Failure to do so will result in a casualty rate that is higher than necessary and lend encouragement to our other enemies as well."

"Well said," Madam Dasser said pointedly. "Wouldn't you agree, Sergi?"

Chien-Chu smiled and nodded dutifully. "Yes, I would. I find the general's arguments to be most persuasive."

"Persuasive, but not necessarily convincing," Governor Zahn said smoothly. "I believe that there's a good deal to be said for Admiral Scolari's point of view."

The Emperor let his hand stray down to the side of his throne. It shook slightly. He pressed what looked like an upholstery tack but was actually a button. His herald appeared as if by magic, hurried to his side, and whispered gobbledegook into his ear. The Emperor nodded wisely, dismissed the man with a wave of his hand, and stood. His advisors hurried to do likewise.

"My apologies. Pressing though the matter under discussion is, the empire is a complicated organism, and other matters vie for my attention as well. I shall consider all that's been said and render a decision soon. Thank you."

The advisors were silent for a moment after the curtains closed. Silent, and with the possible exception of Professor Singh, frustrated, since no decisions had been made.

But all of them were aware that the throne room could be bugged, and probably was, so they reserved their comments until out in the hall. There they paused, said their goodbyes, and went their separate ways.

Chien-Chu found himself walking by Madam Dasser. She was at least seventy years old, but looked a good deal younger and walked with the ebullience of a teenage girl. She had short, carefully kept gray hair, pretty features, and almost flawless skin. Her clothes were expensive but simple. She spoke first.

"There's a precedent, you know."

"Really? And what's that?"

"Nero. They say he fiddled while Rome burned."

"They also say he set the fire himself, in order to clear ground for his new palace."

"And you think the Emperor is capable of such manipulations?"

Chien-Chu smiled and shrugged. "Who's to say?"

Madam Dasser looked at him critically. Her bright blue eyes gleamed with intelligence. "You're an interesting man, Sergi. Your words lead in interesting directions but never arrive anywhere."

"What would you have me do?"

"Anything, for god's sake. We must react before the Hudathans destroy all that we've built."

"You think it's that serious?"

Madam Dasser stopped and caused Chien-Chu to do likewise. They were at the center of an inner plaza, a place where the noise generated by the central fountain would make eavesdropping difficult. They were of the same height and her eyes looked directly into his.

"Of course I think it's that serious. And you do too. The difference is that I'm ready to act and you're waiting for a miracle to happen. Well, it isn't going to happen. The Emperor is only semi-rational at best, and even during his better moments, heavily influenced by his personal desires. You know it, I know it, and the others know it too."

Chien-Chu looked around. Water splattered the edge of the fountain, birds twittered as they flew inside the transparent dome, and people clustered here and there. Dasser's eyes looked as intense as they had to begin with. The merchant forced his voice to remain calm.

"Treason is punishable by death and forfeiture of all family holdings."

"What?" Madam Dasser demanded. "You think that my family and I failed to consider that? But consider the alternative as well. Death at the hands of the Hudatha. Is that any better?"

Chien-Chu thought of his son again, isolated on an asteroid where he had sent him, cut off from help and fighting against tremendous odds. Fighting? Or dead? There was no way to know. The answer came of its own accord.

"No, I guess it isn't."

"Then you'll help? You'll oppose the Emperor?"

"The decision is not mine alone. I must speak to my wife. Together we will think about it."

Dasser nodded. "Good. But don't deliberate too long. As time passes, so does the opportunity to act."

"There are others who think as you do?"

"Yes, and all want you to join. We need your intelligence, wisdom, and strength."

Chien-Chu felt anything but wise and strong. But he smiled at the compliment, bent at the waist, and said, "Thank you, Madam Dasser. You have given me much to think about. We shall meet again soon."

Admiral Scolari had asked for and been granted an audience with the Emperor, although the circumstances were a bit unusual. The Emperor was something of a physical fitness buff, had his own personal gym, and, duties allowing, worked out at 3 P.M. each day.

This afternoon was no exception, so Scolari found herself talking to a man who wore only a jockstrap.

While sex had never been an especially important aspect of Scolari's life, she found the Emperor's lack of clothes to be more than a little distracting, a discovery that bothered her almost as much as the distraction itself and made it that much harder to speak coherently.

The Emperor favored a vast array of computer-controlled machines for his workouts and was presently caged inside a device designed to enhance his shoulder muscles. Each movement was accompanied by a loud grunting noise, which forced Scolari to speak more loudly than she would have liked.

"Thank you for the audience, Your Highness."

"You're quite... *grunt*... welcome... *grunt*... Admiral. What's on your mind? *Grunt.* The Hadathans again?"

"Indirectly, yes," Scolari said. "I am, however, mindful of the fact that Your Highness has taken the matter under consideration and will deliver a decision in due time."

The Emperor stopped, released himself from the machine,

and struck a pose. Muscles bulged, veins throbbed, and sweat glistened on his skin. Scolari experienced some almost forgotten sensations and pushed them away.

"So what do you think?" the Emperor asked, clearly expecting some sort of compliment.

"Very impressive, Your Highness. No wonder the ladies fight each other for your attentions."

"Money and power help too," the Emperor said pragmatically. He lay down on a well-padded bench, punched some instructions into the console that hung over his head, and took hold of a T-bar.

"Now, where were we? Something about the Hudathans?"

"Yes, Highness. The possibility that the Hudathans might attack the very center of the empire has various sectors of the citizenry concerned. Most have reacted appropriately, knowing that you and our armed forces will protect them, but some have allowed fear to cloud their judgment."

"Thirteen... fourteen... fifteen... there."

Metal clanged as the Emperor let go of the T-bar and a hundred and fifty pounds of weights hit the pile below. He sat up and wiped his forehead with a towel.

"Treason? Is that what you're talking about?"

Scolari was on dangerous ground here and chose her words with care. "Possibly, Highness, though treason is a strong word and should never be used without sufficient proof."

The Emperor stood. "And you lack that proof?"

"Yes, Highness, which is why my words take the form of a warning, rather than an accusation."

The Emperor jumped, grabbed hold of a horizontal bar, and started his pull-ups.

"Who... *grunt*... would you warn me against?"

Scolari swallowed. This was the moment that she had dreaded. The moment when she blended truth with a carefully fabricated lie and hoped that the Emperor would accept it.

"General Mosby, Highness."

The Emperor's feet made a thumping sound as they hit the floor. She saw anger in his eyes as he turned to confront her. "If this is political, an attempt to discredit the general because she disagrees with your strategy, I will hang you from the flagpole in front of your headquarters."

Scolari fought to control the fear that bubbled up from deep inside. "No, Highness, never! I admitted that I had no proof, but I have suspicions, and a duty to report them."

"Good. Liquids are important, you know. You should drink at least three or four glasses of water every day."

Scolari blinked in surprise, recovered, and guided the Emperor back to the subject at hand. "Thank you, Highness. Although we lack evidence against General Mosby, we know she's sympathetic to the Cabal's point of view, and likely to support them."

The Emperor selected a staff about six feet long, placed it across the top of his shoulders, and rotated his torso. "Cabal?"

Scolari repressed a sigh. "The secret group that favors all-out action against the Hudatha, Your Highness."

"Yes, of course," the Emperor said thoughtfully, "and who else belongs to this Cabal?"

"Madam Dasser does, Your Highness."

"You have proof?"

"Yes, Highness. We managed to introduce a number of transmitter-equipped microbots into her mansion. One of them was designed to look like her favorite brooch. She wore it yesterday. Her conversations left no doubt as to the Cabal's existence and her membership in it."

"She said nothing about General Mosby?"

"No, Highness."

"And Chien-Chu?"

"Nothing, insofar as we know. Madam Dasser did not elect to wear the brooch today, but left the council meeting with Chien-Chu and spoke with him by the fountain."

"And?"

Scolari shrugged. "And nothing, Highness. The fountain made it impossible to hear what they said."

A full minute passed before the Emperor spoke. Scolari was afraid that he'd gone off the rails again and was relieved to discover that he hadn't. The Emperor removed the staff from his shoulders and used it to lean on. "My mother gave me some advice about situations like this. She said that it's best to let people talk, since that's where most of them will leave it, but to be ready for action. So, tell me... are we ready for action?"

Scolari nodded grimly. "Yes, Highness, we are."

The Emperor smiled. "Good. Then there's nothing to worry about, is there?"

11

Legion Outpost NA-45-16/R, aka "Spindle," the Human Empire

"I say it'll work," Leonid Chien-Chu said stubbornly.

"And I say you're full of shit," Captain Omar Narbakov replied calmly.

The men stood on Spindle's rocky surface and looked up at the electromagnetic launcher more commonly referred to as "the railgun." It was huge and the far end was lost in the blackness of space.

The idea had been around for a long time. The concept required a pair of conductive rails, a power source, and a projectile that rested on the rails and completed the circuit. Then, by providing a powerful pulse of electric current, like that available from Spindle's massive accumulators, it would be possible to push the projectile forward. Once in motion, the object would accelerate for the entire length of the rails, gain a great deal of velocity in the process, and fly off in whatever direction it had been aimed.

Initial research had focused on the possibility of a "super cannon" capable of lobbing artillery shells at targets hundreds or even thousands of miles away. There were difficulties, though, and other more cost-effective ways to kill people, so scientists turned their attention to the possibility of payload launching systems. After all, they reasoned, why use expensive chemical rockets to launch satellites when a railgun could accomplish the same thing for a fraction of the cost?

The idea looked good on a CRT but there were problems, the most difficult of which was that anything small enough, and rugged enough to withstand the stress of a railgun launch, would cost more than the chemical rocket that it had replaced.

But time passed, man colonized space, and electromagnetic launchers came into their own. Space was the perfect place to use a railgun. With no atmosphere to overcome, railguns consumed less power and subjected their payloads to less stress. Besides, who cared how much stress a chunk of rock endured on its way from an asteroid to a pickup barge?

So, when stardust was discovered, and the decision had been made to gather the stuff in commercial quantities, railgun-launched scoops had been the obvious solution. The scoops, also called "star divers," were fully automated spaceships. The railgun provided a highly efficient, low-cost way to get them started, but conventional drives carried them the rest of the way.

A typical mission would carry a star diver around the sun, in through the sector of the atmosphere that looked the most promising at that particular moment, and back by a carefully calculated deceleration curve. Once the ship had slowed sufficiently, tugs took over and guided the star diver into Spindle's docking facility, where it was unloaded, fueled, and prepared for the next launch.

What Leonid proposed to do was turn the railgun back to its original purpose. He wanted to convert the device into a cannon, use the star divers as the high-tech equivalent of cannonballs, and launch them at the Hudathan fleet. It would, he'd pointed out, give them the means to strike back and possibly win. Narbakov had been quick to disagree. The merchant found it hard to be patient.

"Why, Omar? Why are you so opposed to the idea?"

"Because you don't have the means to launch *enough* star divers to do any good."

Narbakov had a point. The railgun was similar to the single-shot rifle Leonid had received on his twelfth birthday. In order to reload, it had been necessary to open the bolt, eject the empty casing, and insert a fresh cartridge. Only then could Leonid close the bolt, aim at the target, and squeeze the trigger. The gift had been his father's way of teaching finesse over force. After all, why use ten bullets when one would do the job? Which was fine then… and useless now.

"All right, Omar, you have a point. But you're forgetting one important factor. The Hudathan fighters rely on their mother ships for fire control, attack linkage, and electronic countermeasures. So if we kill the mother ships, we'll kill the fighters too."

"True," the legionnaire said grudgingly, "but the Hudathans have three battleships. The first star diver might catch one of them by surprise. The rest won't."

"Unless we find a way to launch all of our surviving star divers within seconds of each other," Leonid countered, "in which case it might work."

"Maybe," Narbakov admitted, sunlight gleaming off his visor. "But the effort to do so will siphon effort away from the rest of our defensive preparations."

Leonid shrugged. The suit barely moved. "So what? You've done an incredible job, Omar, more than anyone could rightfully expect, but we're going to lose. We might survive the next attack, or the one after that, but the geeks will eventually win."

Narbakov stood tall. His voice was stern. "Then we will die as they died at Camerone, at Dien Bien Phu, and at the Battle of Four Moons."

Leonid sighed. "Suit yourself, Omar. But I plan to live."

Ikor Niber-Ba stood on the platform and looked the length of the launch bay. It had been sealed and pressurized for this occasion. Rank after rank of pilots, crew, technicians, and soldiers stood at attention. Beyond them, towards the rear of the enormous compartment, rows of battle-scarred fighters waited to rejoin the fray. A trio of robotic vid cams stood poised around him, their insectoid bodies still, their lenses ready to feed to the other ships whatever ensued.

This was it, the moment when he inspired them with visions of victory, when he struck the sympathetic chords of racial fear, when he motivated them to win. But the words had fled to places unknown and taken his surety with them.

The Hudathan cleared his throat. The sound was small in the cavernous space. The problem lay not with those who stood before him, but with those who had died, their bodies preserved within their suits, forever drifting through the blackness of space.

Not to overcome a fortress, or to subdue a planet, but to deny the humans a substance that glittered when exposed to light.

The situation made no sense, had no meaning, yet held him in its ice-cold grip. A grip that was all the stronger now that morale had started to sag, now that his fighter pilots had grown unduly cautious, now that the myth of Hudathan invincibility had been shattered. The seemingly endless assaults and the ensuing casualties had planted seeds of fear in the hearts of his crew, and it was his job to root them out before they could grow and flower.

Niber-Ba clasped his hands behind his back and swept the audience with his eyes.

"You have done well. Time and time again you have looked death in the eye and stared it down. And thus it shall be one more time. Not two, three, or four more times, for there is no need. One overwhelming blow will be sufficient to crush all resistance, to seal the humans in their rocky tomb, to eradicate the menace that they represent. With that in mind I will commit *all* of our ships, and *all* of our fighters, to the next attack. Our robo-spies are cruising the surface of the asteroid even now, and the moment that their reports have been analyzed and cross-checked, we will attack."

A sharp-eyed psych officer felt the confidence flow back into those around him, saw them swell with pride, and seized the moment. "A cheer for Ikor Niber-Ba! Long may he command!"

The cheer was part shout, part war cry, and it shook the ship's hull metal with its power. Niber-Ba felt it, was lifted by it and was immeasurably cheered. No one could stand in the way of warriors like these. No one.

Seeger waited for the other cyborg to get into position, grabbed his end of the steel I-beam, and lifted. It, like the fifteen others before it, would be used to reinforce the railgun's basic structure. In order to launch six star divers, and do so in a relatively short period of time, all would have to be positioned and ready to go. That was why Leonid Chien-Chu had ordered his workers to build a complicated framework over the point where the ramp met the asteroid's rocky surface, and why Seeger, along with three more of the Legion's cyborgs, was lending a servo-assisted hand.

If the launcher was about to become a cannon, then the framework was a magazine, feeding full-sized spaceships into the chamber like bullets into a gun—spaceships that would put a lot of stress on the ramp as they were fired in quick succession.

Seeger followed the other borg down the side of the railgun's support structure and paused when she did.

"Are you ready?" Her name was Marie and she'd spent more than a thousand imperials to have her voice synthesizer reprogrammed to sound like that of a famous pop singer, which allowed her to pick up the odd credit or two singing in bars. Lots of guys had hit on her, hoping to score through a dream box, but none had succeeded. None that he knew about anyway.

"Yeah," Seeger replied. "That's a roger."

"Okay."

Marie looked upwards towards the point where the bio bods were working to weld the steel supports into place. Laser torches burped blue-white energy, headlamps bobbed up and down, and a latticework of crisscrossed I-beams divided the star field into a maze of squares and rectangles. She switched from the Legion's utility channel to the frequency used by everybody else.

"Ground here. You guys ready for some steel?"

A male voice answered. "That's a roger, babe. Send it up."

Marie's voice was sweet but ice cold. "My name isn't 'babe,' butt hole, and here comes your steel."

Marie bent at the knees, Seeger did likewise, and both straightened together. Unrestrained by gravity or an atmosphere, the I-beam soared upwards.

Someone—Seeger wasn't sure who—grabbed the beam and pulled it in. At that exact moment, as a laser torch lit the scene with a whitish-blue glare, something round drifted by. It moved slowly, deliberately, as if it had every right to be there, which it might, for all he knew. Yet something bothered him. A similarity between the object and what? Then he had it. Float pods! Like those on his native Elexor! Like those the Hudathans used during their attacks. Seeger tracked the device while keeping his voice light and casual.

"Marie, meet me on F-5."

Marie turned his way, curious as to the reason for his request, and switched to F-5. It was a combat frequency, scrambled both ways, and theoretically secure.

"What's up?"

"Remember the float pods? The ones the geeks use every once in a while?"

"Who could forget? I was there when one of those things cooked Salan in his own brain box."

"Well, it's payback time. Look upwards, to the left of the railgun, drifting right."

Marie looked. A bio bod would have seen little more than laser torches and headlamps, but the cyborg was equipped with sensors, and once she knew where to look, had little difficulty separating the globe from the metal around it. Thanks to her infrared sensors, light-amplification equipment, and on-board processing capacity, the globe looked much as it would have in broad daylight. With one small exception, Seeger was right.

The target was a killer pod, all right, except that it had a lot of what looked like sensor housings rather than weapons turrets, and had a flat-black finish.

That suggested a spy-eye, or the geek equivalent, and meant the device was capable of blowing the whole plan out of the water. One look at the information it would bring back would be enough to let the Hudathan commander know what the humans were up to.

"You were right, Seeg. It's a robo-spy sure enough."

"We need to grease that thing... and do it quick."

"How 'bout Lieutenant Umai?"

"Get serious. It'd take the loot a full hour just to pull his thumb out of his ass. Let's nail the little sonofabitch while the nailin's good."

"That's a roger," Marie agreed. "But we can't shoot at it from down here without hitting the railgun or a bio bod. Let's climb."

Seeger nodded. "You take the right... I'll take the left."

"Roger that."

Both of the cyborgs began to climb. Seeger made good time. The combination of handholds, light gravity, and his own strength made the task relatively easy. Light flared from above as the welders continued their work. The cyborg felt his body temp start to soar as sunlight hit his back.

It was a trade-off—one of many the tech types had made while designing the Trooper IIs—cooling capacity for weight. The result was a cybernetic body that had the capacity to move a little faster than it otherwise would have, but a marked tendency to overheat during prolonged combat or exposure to direct sunlight. Cooling systems had been developed to deal with the conditions found on hell worlds, but Seeger didn't have one.

A readout began to blink in the corner of his video-generated, computer-enhanced vision, and then, to make sure that he got the point, pain was fed directly into his brain. Pain that was little more than a throb to begin with, but would soon grow and transform itself into a red-hot poker that seared its way to the center of his mind and forced him to respond.

It was a safety system, a built-in way to make sure that cyborgs took care of their expensive bodies and conserved the empire's valuable resources. The only trouble was that it might keep him from reaching the robo-spy, from killing it, and that would cost a great deal more.

But those that had designed the system were elsewhere, working in the safety of their laboratories or eating lunch in their subsidized dining rooms, unaware and uninterested in the impact that their decisions had on people millions of light-years away.

Seeger grabbed the I-beam above his head, pulled himself up, climbed to his feet, and looked around. Marie was at the same height about seventy feet away. She pointed upwards and between them.

The robo-spy slipped into a shadow and rose along a vertical beam—a beam that supported the recently built structure that would feed star divers down onto the rails, where they would be launched like missiles towards the enemy fleet. The situation had just gone from bad to worse.

The cyborgs climbed with renewed energy. They had to get a clear shot at the robo-spy, had to destroy the device before it could escape and report to its masters.

A pair of bio bods were welding a joint directly above him. They turned, sunlight gleaming off their visors, as Seeger swung a leg over the crossbeam and pulled himself up. He nodded, jumped for the next crosspiece, and did a chin-up.

Pain lanced through Seeger's brain as the temp reading on the rear portion of his armor hit 150° F. The techies were trying to defend the body they'd given him, trying to control him from their nice safe laboratories, trying to kill Marie and all the rest. That was the price of failure, the price that thousands of legionnaires had paid before him, the price known as death.

Seeger gritted his nonexistent teeth and pulled. Pain did its best to roll him under, servos did what they were told, and he gained the topmost piece of steel. Light bounced off metal and tried to spear his vid cams as the massive shape of a star diver moved his way. A pair of yellow strobe lights marked the positions of the small one-person tugs that had attached themselves to the spaceship like so many leeches and were pushing it into place.

"Seeger! Look!"

The voice belonged to Marie. She too had made it to the top of the structure and was pointing to her left. The robo-eye had seen the star diver and was lurking in the shadow cast by a vertical I-beam while it watched the proceedings. It was roughly halfway between them, and neither one needed any prompting to move towards it.

There was no response at first, as if the robo-spy was so

engaged in gathering intelligence that it had ignored everything else. But that was not the case.

The mini-missile caught Marie in the abdomen, exploded, and blew her in half. Though lightly armed compared to the float pods the cyborgs had encountered before, the robo-spy still had teeth.

Seeger responded with missiles of his own and a blast from his energy cannon. The resulting explosion lit the entire railgun for a fraction of a second and was extremely satisfying. Marie's voice jerked him back to reality. Although her body had been blown in two, her braincase was intact, slowly falling towards the asteroid's surface.

"Look! The robo-spy launched something!"

Seeger swore. The other borg was right. A small container, the size and shape of a standard tennis ball, had been flung free of the explosion and was accelerating away. There was little doubt that the globe contained the robo-spy's memory, headed for home.

Seeger brought his laser cannon up, switched his sensors to full mag, and tried to see what they showed him. His temperature reading had soared to 163° F by now. At about 170°, major systems would start to fail. The pain was so intense that it felt as if his head would explode.

Lieutenant Umai was yammering in his ears. "Seeger? What the hell are you doing up there? No one authorized you to fire. Get your ass down here so the old man can boil it in oil."

The ball soared, sunlight glinted off its polished skin, and the cyborg adjusted his aim. Lead it… lead it… lead it… fire!

A line of blue light reached for the memory module, touched it, and caused it to explode.

Seeger saw the hit, gave thanks, and allowed the pain to roll him under.

12

The wheels of war turn slowly and grind many lives beneath their weight.

MYLO NURLON-DA
The Life of a Warrior
Standard year 1703

Planet Algeron, the Human Empire

Another one-hour-and-twenty-one-minute period of darkness had begun. Two warriors, one of whom was Windsweet's brother, marched in front of Booly, while two more brought up the rear. The guards were there to make sure that Booly showed up for the council meeting. It would be embarrassing if he didn't and Hardman was in no mood to take chances.

The warriors held torches aloft. They made a circle of light and produced a pungent smoke. The legionnaire inhaled some of it and was forced to cough.

An opening loomed ahead. Booly saw that the rock around the tunnel's entrance had been carved to resemble the mouth of a mythical beast. What looked like razor-sharp teeth ran across the top, fangs curved down along both sides, and a tongue bulged out into the ravine. It looked real in the flickering light produced by the torches.

The legionnaire had never come across this spot during his

wanderings and wondered how that was possible. Did the Naa cover the tunnel with some sort of camouflage netting during the day? There was no way to tell.

Shootstraight and his companion mounted a series of stone steps, stood on the beast's tongue, and waited for Booly to join them. A warrior shoved him from behind and he stumbled forward.

The tunnel was oval in shape and the floor was smooth from use. Vertical grooves had been cut into the walls to simulate the inside of the beast's throat. The temperature dropped as they moved inwards and water slid down along the stone walls.

Booly saw that the reddish-brown liquid was captured by the grooves, channeled into gutters, and drained through holes drilled for that purpose. Holes made with primitive hand tools and a lot of sweat. The system was careful, logical, and, like most plumbing, completely nonthreatening.

So why did fear come bubbling up from some primordial source? Why was his throat so dry? And why did he have an almost overwhelming desire to look over his shoulder?

The answer was simple. The beings who had enlarged and perfected the tunnel so long ago had imbued the stone with a part of themselves. Booly felt as if they were all around him, their eyes peering from dark crevices, their work-thickened fingers ready to close around his throat.

Shootstraight turned. The torchlight reflected in his eyes. "Watch your step."

The warning came just in time. Booly shifted his weight and stepped downwards. The stairs were broad, cut from solid rock, and worn towards the center.

The legionnaire wondered how long the steps had been there and how many feet had trod them. The tunnel felt old, very old, and might have been there for a thousand years.

A current of warmer air touched Booly's face. There was a deep booming sound reminiscent of the Legion's kettledrums. It came at evenly spaced intervals, like the beating of an enormous heart, and added an even more ominous note to his surroundings.

Booly pushed the fear away, assured himself that it was only one more element in an elaborately staged play, but felt his heart beat a little faster nonetheless. A layer of sweat had formed on the legionnaire's forehead. He wiped it away.

The staircase turned to the right, light filtered up from below, and the booming sound grew louder. The smell of incense filled his nostrils, and an oval-shaped doorway appeared ahead. The first pair of guards passed through and Booly followed.

Shootstraight stopped just beyond the entryway, motioned for the human to do likewise, and signaled for silence.

The cavern was huge. The roof arched upwards and disappeared into darkness. It was supported by thick pillars of ornately carved rock. Torches had been set into slots cut for that purpose and served to illuminate the artwork.

Booly saw packs of wild pooks, snowcapped mountains, herds of woolly dooth beasts, clouds, intertwined serpents, rushing rivers, and much, much more, each image joined with the rest, all interconnected to support the ceiling or sky.

The carvings seemed to suggest an understanding of how ecosystems are structured, of the underlying unity that makes life possible, but that was Booly's human interpretation. The artists had been Naa, and given that fact, might have imbued the carvings with other meanings. Or none at all.

The floor of the cave sloped down and away from the point of entry towards a stage more than a hundred yards away. The surface under the legionnaire's boots was too even, too smooth, to be natural, and had taken an enormous amount of work to excavate and finish.

Hundreds and hundreds of sleek-headed Naa sat cross-legged on the floor. Most came from beyond the confines of the village, were leaders in their own right, and had come together in order to set policy and make decisions. Their attention was focused on the platform and Booly could see why.

First there were the council seats. They had been chipped from solid stone and looked very uncomfortable. There were three to a side, with another, slightly raised chair located at the center. It was occupied by Wayfar Hardman. He, like the council members around him, wore colorful robes. A ceremony was under way, some sort of blessing perhaps, in which an ancient crone dribbled powder into a brazier and chanted incantations.

But the chairs, the council members, and the ceremony were

nothing compared to the massive and now antiquated Trooper I that stood to the left side of the stage, and the equally impressive Trooper II that stood on the right. Both were at rigid attention. Their vid-cam eyes glowed like rubies and stared out at the audience.

For one brief moment, Booly thought the Naa had captured the cyborgs and found a way to hold them against their will. Then he realized that the bodies were little more than empty suits of armor, placed there as evidence of Naa valor, similar to the trophies that filled the regimental museums at Fort Cameron. Their joints had been welded in place and their eyes had been lit from within.

The Trooper I was old and stained, as if dug out of the ground somewhere, but the Trooper II looked relatively new. New, but slightly disjointed, as though it had been ripped apart and pieced back together again. Booly took a closer look. The newness of the paint, the absence of the supplementary cooling fins that veteran borgs mounted along the outer surface of their upper arms, suggested the same thing. The body was Trooper Villain's, or had been, depending on whether or not she'd been rescued.

The legionnaire felt a lump form in his throat. Damn it anyway! If only he'd been more careful, more cautious about leaving the ravine, more of his people might have lived. He'd been unconscious during most of the battle, but the Naa had given him their version of what had happened, and Booly knew that casualties had been heavy. It seemed clear that a pair of bio bods, and at least one borg, had tried to pull Villain's braincase. But there was no way to know if they'd succeeded, and if they had, whether the newbie had survived.

The drumbeats died away. Hardman stood and looked about him. An expectant hush fell over the room. Booly turned to Shootstraight and whispered in the warrior's ear. "What now?"

The Naa grinned. "My father will open the meeting by reminding the audience that the harvest was successful, and then, having taken credit for their full stomachs, he'll give them a detailed account of the trade agreement that he negotiated with the southern tribe. Most will be bored. Knowing that, Father will call for you and describe the battle. Don't be surprised if the number of legionnaires has doubled during the intervening period of time."

Booly smiled. "So this is a political speech… designed to keep everyone happy."

"Exactly. You have them as well?"

"Yes, we do, although there are a great many things that most politicians are afraid to say."

The warrior made a face. "I understand. Look over there… towards the far pillar. Do you see my sister?"

Booly looked and had little difficulty picking Windsweet out of the crowd. She had a beautiful profile. The sight of her made his pulse pound. A frown came to his face when he saw that Ridelong Surekill sat next to her.

"I see her."

"And the warrior who sits next to her?"

"Ridelong Surekill."

"Exactly. He's a chief in his own right and would like to succeed my father as chief of chiefs."

"How likely is that?"

Shootstraight looked out across the cave as if considering his answer. "Today? Not very. Tomorrow? Who knows? The people are fickle. All it takes is one poor harvest, one loss to the Legion, and they will turn on him like a diseased pook."

"And you? Will you follow in your father's footsteps?"

Shootstraight chuckled. "Not on your life, human. I would rather throw myself from the Towers of Algeron than do what my father does."

The crone completed her ritual, made gestures towards the audience, and left the stage.

Hardman thanked the woman and started his speech. The next thirty minutes passed slowly. Booly had very little interest in the amount of wild grain harvested that year, the condition of the dooth herds, or the rate of exchange that Hardman had negotiated with the south. But the topic changed after that and so did Booly's pulse. The legionnaire heard his name mentioned, felt someone push him forward, and stumbled down the corridor towards the stage. Hundreds of heads turned to watch, and seeing that, the human started to march. He was a legionnaire, by god, and no matter what came next, he'd look like what he was.

Windsweet watched Booly make his way towards the stage, saw the change in his step, and recognized his courage. To be alone in enemy hands, to be paraded in front of them, yet maintain your poise. That was bravery, that was strength, and that was a man to admire.

Admire and what? Love? Did she dare think it? Or worse yet, feel it? For to do so was to take the first step of a long and difficult journey, one that would cost her dearly, that would bring her untold pain, that would take her places that she'd never dreamed.

Was there a choice? Did love really work that way? Could you choose to fall in love? Or, if it didn't seem practical, decide against it?

Windsweet looked at Surekill and saw that the warrior's eyes were on Booly. She saw hatred there, a feeling that she'd never seen on the human's face, or smelled in his emotions, in spite of what the humans had taught him about her people, in spite of the ambush, and in spite of his captivity.

No, Windsweet decided. Love had a mind of its own, and once that mind was made up, went where it liked.

Wayfar Hardman watched the human approach. He made a striking figure in his uniform and battle armor. A trophy came to life. Hardman could tell that the chiefs were impressed. As well as they should be, given the extent of his victory. Still, it had been his daughter who had suggested that he use the human in this fashion, so some of the credit was hers.

Yes, he suspected that Windsweet's desire to spare a life had entered into the calculation, but the advice had been sound nonetheless.

Hardman's eyes found her sitting next to Surekill, watching the human walk towards the stage. They made a handsome couple, everyone said so—except Windsweet. She never stopped her prattle about love, respect, and all that other silliness.

The chieftain thought about his own mate, how beautiful she'd been on the day of their marriage, and of the life they'd lived together. Though driven by politics, the marriage had grown to be something more, something neither had reason to regret.

That was how it would be for Windsweet. Yes, Surekill was

impatient for power, yes, he was headstrong, but such is the strength of youth. A strength that would stand his daughter in good stead during the coming years. And by giving Surekill his daughter, Hardman could buy one, maybe two years of additional power. The younger warrior could use the additional time to mature. He would learn the arts of peace, as he had learned the arts of war, and build a home for his wife.

The plan made sense. He'd speak to Surekill in the morning. A feeling of peace and tranquility flooded Hardman's soul. It felt good to solve such a troubling problem. He stood, welcomed Booly to the stage, and swept the audience with his eyes.

"An enemy stands before us, but he fought bravely and deserves our respect. He, like the wind, the rain, and the snow, was sent to strengthen us, to make us hard. And we *are* hard. Hard enough to survive where other creatures die, hard enough to fight the Legion, hard enough to win our planet back!"

The strange undulating cry came from deep within a thousand throats, echoed back and forth off cavern walls, and sent a chill down Booly's spine.

General Ian St. James raised his wineglass. The man on the other side of the snowy-white tablecloth did the same. His name was Alexander Dasser, eldest son to the famous Madam Dasser, and formerly a lieutenant in the 3rd REI. He still wore his hair high and tight, kept his body trim, and knew how to drink.

"*Vive la Légion!*"

"*Vive la Légion!*"

The men drained their glasses, put them down, and grinned at each over the dinner table. They had been friends since entering the Legion together many, many years before. Dasser had served his time and resigned his commission to run part of the family's far-flung business empire.

St. James had stayed, risen steadily through the ranks, and become a general. He smiled.

"You look well, Alex."

"And you, Ian."

"And your family?"

The merchant shrugged. "We live in troubled times, my friend. We are extremely concerned about the Hudathan menace."

St. James nodded soberly. "So are we. I have orders to prepare for a possible withdrawal."

Dasser smiled grimly. "Yes, I know. General Mosby has fought against it, as has my mother. But Admiral Scolari keeps pounding away, and the Emperor is weak, if not entirely out of his mind."

St. James felt his heart beat just a little bit faster at the mention of Mosby's name. His eyes narrowed. He looked around the candlelit room. There were about thirty tables and half were occupied. No one seemed especially interested in the general or his guest, but it paid to be careful.

"Careful, Alex. The empire has many eyes and ears. Even here."

Dasser nodded noncommittally and poured some more wine.

The officer struggled to keep his voice neutral. "How is General Mosby doing with her new assignment?"

The other man chuckled. "Well, that depends on how you measure success. The general is bright, and an extremely capable officer, but I'm afraid that it's her body that the Emperor likes best."

St. James felt himself drawn like a moth to the flame. Sensing the danger, feeling the heat, but unable to resist.

"General Mosby and the Emperor?"

Dasser nodded. "That's what they say. My mother hopes that it's true. The Emperor's bed is one battlefield on which Mosby should be able to defeat Scolari hands down. Or bottoms up, as the case may be."

St. James fought for control. Dasser didn't know, couldn't know, about his affair with Mosby, and hadn't meant to hurt his feelings. But the pain was just as intense as if he had.

"In any case," Dasser said, "here's a little something from the general herself." He pushed a data cube across the table.

St. James was far from surprised. The Legion had long maintained channels of communication separate from those provided by government. Some of those channels were electronic in nature, some were robotic, but the most useful tended to be living, breathing human beings, ex-legionnaires mostly, but others as well, which taken together were part of a vast interlocking network, built on loyalty, trust, and a thousand years of tradition.

The officer reached out, took the cube, and slipped it into a pocket.

The rest of the meal was pure hell. St. James wanted to leave the table, wanted to rush to his quarters, wanted to see Mosby's face on his ceiling. But that would be unseemly, and more than that, downright rude, so he forced himself to stay.

The conversation went on and on, the courses came and went with maddening slowness, and the cube seemed to press against his skin. Taunting him, teasing him, robbing him of all reason.

St. James knew it was stupid, knew that the contents would leave him disappointed, but couldn't help himself. Fantasies flooded his mind. He had visions of an apologetic Mosby, contrite after her fling with the Emperor, begging his forgiveness. He saw the two of them coming together, getting married, and having children. Even if it meant their careers, meant leaving the Legion, meant living as civilians.

Dasser droned at him all the while, talking about the Hudatha, walking the thin edge of treason. He didn't say so in as many words, but hinted at a secret cabal, a group with plans to overthrow the Emperor.

The message was clear. The Legion should align itself with the Cabal, should oppose Admiral Scolari, or plan on dying with the rest of the empire. The Hudatha were strong. The Hudatha were ruthless. And the Hudatha were coming. Any sign of weakness, any sign of retreat, would serve to bring them on that much faster.

St. James believed the other man, and agreed with him, but couldn't wait for the conversation to end. The fantasies were too strong, too compelling to ignore.

The meal was finally over.

The men rose, embraced each other, said the traditional goodbyes, and headed for their separate quarters, Dasser to add to the encrypted notes in his minicomp, St. James to play the data cube.

The officer forced himself to be patient, to walk slowly, to return the salutes, to enter his quarters as if there was nothing on his mind, nothing burning a hole through his pocket, nothing urging him to run and cram the cube into the player.

Then he was in his room, lying back on his bed, staring upwards as the ceiling blurred, divided itself into a million bits of light, and coalesced into a likeness of Marianne Mosby.

She was as beautiful as ever, but all business, and not the least bit apologetic. What she said echoed what he'd heard at dinner. Conditions had become steadily worse. The Hudathans had taken more of the outlying planets. Scolari continued to recommend a retreat. A retreat that would leave even more frontier worlds vulnerable to attack, that would force the Legion to abandon Algeron, that would centralize power in the admiral's hands. No one knew what the Emperor thought, or would finally decide, but it didn't look good.

When the recording was over, and the ceiling had returned to its normal appearance, St. James allowed himself to cry. Not for the empire, not for the Legion, but for himself.

They woke Angel Perez, now known by his *nom de guerre*, Sal Salazar, with little or no ceremony. One moment he was nothing, a mindless, shapeless, colorless mote floating in a sea of darkness, and the next moment he was himself again, a cyborg, conscious of the systems that were coming up all around him, racking focus to see the med tech's face. She was middle-aged, had a scar across her face, and the words "cut here" tattooed around her neck. She looked into his vid cams as if aware that he was looking at her.

"Welcome to Algeron, home of the Legion, and all that other crap."

Then it came to him, his graduation from boot camp, acceptance into the Legion, and departure for Advanced Combat School on Algeron. A departure made simple by adding his brain box to a fifty-borg rack, hooking him to a computer-controlled life support system, and sending him to la-la land on a tidal wave of drugs.

After all, why ship big bulky Trooper II bodies all over the place when you didn't have to? It was cheaper and easier to ship brain boxes separately and plug them in when they arrived.

Salazar was about to reply to the med tech's greeting when he realized that something was wrong. *Very* wrong.

The feedback, the readouts, the sensors, none of them were right. He ordered his left arm to move, looked for the air-cooled, link-fed .50 caliber machine gun that should have been there and saw a Class Three, Model IV, cyber hand with tactile feedback and opposable thumb instead.

"What the hell?"

The med tech shook her head sympathetically. "Don't panic, big boy. We're running a bit short on Trooper IIs, that's all. Should get a shipment any day now." The woman straightened and put hands on her hips. "Hey, big boy, you tell me. Which is better? A bi-form or a whole lotta shelf time?"

The idea of sitting helpless in his brain box, listening to neuro-fed music or playing electro-games made Salazar's nonexistent skin crawl.

"I'll take the bi-form."

The med tech nodded. "That's what I thought. Now, take a break while I check your systems."

The systems check was over fifteen minutes later. Salazar received a temporary assignment to the 1st RE and headed for admin.

It wasn't difficult to find his way through Fort Camerone's labyrinthine passageways thanks to the schematics available from the bi-form's data base. No, the hard part was getting used to his insubstantial body.

Intended for light utility chores, and completely unarmed, the bi-form weighed about 250 pounds, one-quarter the weight of a fully armed Trooper II, and was therefore a good deal more maneuverable. Salazar felt like a truck driver in a sports car.

He was a bit clumsy at first and had a tendency to overreact, but soon got over it. He missed the Trooper II's bulk, however, and the sense of power that went with wearing one, especially when he saw veteran borgs swaggering down the corridors.

He knew that most of them were jerks, like the men and women he'd known in boot camp, but that didn't stop him from admiring their style. The worn armor, the carefully maintained body art, the equipment mods, all the little things that set them aside and marked them for what they were—survivors.

Something Salazar wanted to be as well, which meant that he'd have to separate the substance from the swagger and keep the part that had value.

Of equal interest were the khaki-clad bio bods, the camo-painted robots, the murals depicting glorious death, the holo pix of dead heroes and heroines, the animated dioramas of battles past, the E-boards listing that day's events, a heavily armed patrol clumping towards an elevator, and in one hallway, the sight of two handcuffed Naa warriors, heads up, eyes bright, being led towards the intelligence section.

Yes, the hallways were fascinating, which made the admin section all the more boring. It was huge, and divided into subsections with names like "Logistics," "Supplies," "Intelligence," "Budget," and "Personnel."

The latter seemed like one of the *most* boring places to work, so it was only natural that a bio-bod noncom named Dister would assign him there and place him under the direct supervision of a borg named Villain.

Dister was a stumpy little man with protruding ears and a huge nose. His uniform was wrinkled and strained where a sizable potbelly pressed against it. His voice was loud and easily heard over the humming noises made by the computers that surrounded them. Everything was white, blue, or gray, and shaped like a box. The noncom spoke and Salazar listened.

"The work is relatively easy—hell, *real* easy after boot camp—and certainly won't overload your circuits. You'll find that Villain is competent enough, though crabby as hell and a bit short-tempered. She was hit first time out and hasn't recovered yet."

Salazar wanted to know more, wanted to hear about the battle, but Dister turned a corner and another bi-form appeared. Except for an ID plate that read "Villain," it looked exactly like he did.

Her bi-form stood six feet tall, had an ovoid head, side-mounted vid cams, a lightly armored chest cage, skeletal arms, equally skeletal legs, and a pair of four-toed feet. They were encased in rubber and squeaked when she moved. She nodded towards Dister.

"Corporal."

Dister gestured towards Salazar. "Meet your new assistant. Name's Salazar. Straight from boot camp. Show him the ropes."

Salazar noticed that Villain didn't even glance in his direction. Her vid cams whirred as she zoomed in on Dister. "Thanks, but no thanks. I don't want an assistant."

The bio bod's eyes narrowed. His voice grew softer instead of louder. "Oh, really? Well, I don't give a shit what you *want*. Salazar is your assistant, so get used to it."

There was a moment of silence, and for one brief second Salazar felt sure that Villain would object, but the moment passed. Her voice was dead, empty of all emotion. "Yes, Corporal. Sorry, Corporal."

Dister nodded. "Good. Now, get your chrome-plated butt back to work. Good luck. Salazar. Let me know if she gets out of line."

So saying, the little legionnaire did a neat about-face and marched down the hall.

It was, Salazar decided, just about the worst possible thing that the noncom could have said, almost guaranteed to piss Villain off. He wished he could smile disarmingly, knew he couldn't, and chose his words with care.

"Sorry about that."

Villain shrugged noncommittally. Her reply came via radio. "It doesn't matter. Just do what I say, keep your mouth shut, and we'll do fine."

Salazar started to reply, made the decision to nod instead, and waited for Villain to give him some orders. This, he decided, was only marginally better than boot camp, and in some ways worse. He made a note to find out when the Trooper II bodies would arrive and see if there was a way to get the first one they activated.

Ryber Hysook-Da gloried in the life-threatening plunge down through Algeron's atmosphere, a plunge carefully calculated to simulate a meteor shower and fool the human detection systems. His insertion pod was equipped with a specially designed ceramic skin. It glowed where air molecules rubbed against its surface. Some of the heat found its way inside and turned the Hudathan's skin white.

Hysook-Da activated the mind-link and checked his detectors. There were no signs of pursuit. Not that they had much to pursue him with. Maybe the humans were as stupid as everyone said. After going to the trouble and expense of building a military base on Algeron's surface, they had neglected to surround the planet with warships.

What were they thinking of anyway? Intelligence claimed that the problem stemmed from some sort of political rift between the Navy and a force called "the Legion." But that was too silly, too fanciful to believe, so there must be another more credible explanation. Well, no matter, the humans deserved to die, so he'd help them on their way.

The pod bucked, rolled, and righted itself. The Hudathan checked the progress of his team, saw that all five of the entry pods were tracking along behind his, and gave a grunt of satisfaction.

This was a glorious moment, the first step in what Hysook-Da felt sure would be a rapid ascent to power, followed by a long and successful life.

First would come the completion of his mission on Algeron, followed by at least three celebrations of valor and rapid promotion to spear commander.

But that would be only the beginning. With the human empire in ashes, and his military record as a springboard, Hysook-Da would enter the dark and labyrinthine world of Hudathan politics. Then, through a combination of cunning and absolute ruthlessness, he would rise to the very top!

Just the thought of it left the young warrior nearly dizzy with lust.

A buzzer buzzed, a warning light flashed, and a tingling sensation ran the length of his left arm. Had the humans detected their presence? Were missiles rising to intercept them?

Fear flushed the dreams of glory from his head. A naturally produced stimulant entered his circulatory system. Training took over, readouts snapped into focus, and he scanned them for danger. It was there but not in the form of incoming missiles.

The outer surface of the pod's ceramic skin had started to overheat. A minute correction in the angle of attack was sufficient to silence the buzzer, darken the light, and rid himself of the tingling sensation.

The overheating persisted, however, and held just below the critical level as the pod smashed its way through two layers of air and entered a third.

Algeron filled his mind-screen. An artist might have gloried in the way that the sun washed the clouds with pink, and a geologist might have marveled at the mountaintops that reached up to touch space itself, but Hysook-Da saw none of that.

What he saw was a target, a military objective, swarming with life-forms that threatened his kind. Not through anything they'd done, or were likely to do anytime in the near future, but what they *could* do, *might* do, *would* do, if given enough time and freedom. Yes, as with any potential enemy, the time to stop them was now.

Clouds whipped up around him, a crosswind pushed the pod sideways, and the outermost layer of ceramic skin flaked away. The pod's on-board computer sent a tingling sensation down his arm and put a message in his brain.

"PREPARE FOR INSERTION STAGE THREE."

Hysook-Da checked the other pods, saw they were still in place, and ran a hand-check on his gear. Webbing... check. Main chute... check. Reserve chute... check. Weapons... check. And so on, until each piece of gear had been touched, and where possible, verified. He sent a message back.

"Ready for insertion stage three."

"STANDBY... THREE UNITS AND COUNTING..." A digital readout appeared in the corner of Hysook-Da's vision. He felt his stomach muscles tighten as the numbers became steadily smaller. Five... four... three... two... one.

Bolts exploded. Large sections of what had been the pod's skin were blown outwards, fell, and exploded yet again.

Nothing larger than a rivet would survive to reach the ground. Hysook-Da extended his arms and legs, felt air rush by his neck, and hoped he was on target. The still-functioning computer claimed that he was—not that it made a great deal of difference, since it was too late to correct his course anyway.

The seal around his visor broke. Air rushed by his face. Tears were torn from the corners of his eyes. The clouds vanished and a wasteland appeared below him, blurred by the tears but identifiable nonetheless.

Good… that corresponded with what was supposed to be down there… and meant that the mission was still intact.

The Hudathan checked his readouts, confirmed the fact that he was still high enough to appear on radar, and scanned for his team. Each was equipped with a low-powered locator beacon, and assuming everything was all right, would appear on his mind-screen.

He looked and looked again. One… two… three… four… Where was number five? The worthless piece of dat feces had disappeared. It figured. Marla-Sa had always been jealous of him and would do anything to ruin his chances. "STAND BY TO RELEASE MAIN CHUTE… FIVE, FOUR, THREE…"

Hysook-Da waited for "ONE," sent the appropriate signal, and felt the fabric spill from its pack.

The chute opened with a powerful jerk, the world stabilized around him, and a sense of relief flooded his mind. He had survived, up to this point anyway, and stood a good chance of making it to the ground.

It seemed like only seconds had passed when the boulder-strewn ground rushed up to greet him, smacked the bottom of his boots, and sent a shock through his legs. He rolled, recovered, and pushed himself away from the frost-glazed dirt. He was alive!

There was very little wind. The chute collapsed around the Hudathan and draped itself over some nearby boulders. Hysook-Da reeled the fabric in, gathered it together, and shoved the bundle under some rocks.

The team maintained strict radio silence while they homed in on their leader's beacon and gathered around him.

Hysook-Da checked to make sure they were uninjured, swore when he heard that Marla-Sa's pod had failed to separate, and used a carefully placed micro-sat to verify his position. The results confirmed what his eyes had already told him.

It would take the better part of a Hudathan day to reach the hills, and who knew how many more to find the indigents and buy their loyalty. A difficult task, but not impossible, given the fact that the Naa had reason to hate the humans and were fighting against them.

Confidence filled the Hudathan's mind. The day would come when Hudathan children would study his exploits in school. He would help by making sure that the Naa granted him some sort of dramatic name. "The Warrior Ghost of Algeron" would be nice, or something very similar. He'd give it some thought during the march.

There wasn't a lot of cover but the Hudathans were well trained and used what there was. The team maintained patrol formation, kept their sensors tuned to maximum sensitivity, and paid close attention to their surroundings. Their heads swiveled right and left, their breath fogged the air, and their feet made prints in the frosty soil.

Some distance away, small, almost invisible animals scurried in front of them, sun glinted off a visor, and light speared distant eyes, eyes that had been turned to the south when the team landed. They blinked, brought the Legion-issue glasses back a hair, and narrowed. Someone was coming. Not Naa, not human, but similar in appearance.

The warrior zoomed in, recorded twelve carefully selected images, and tucked the device into his pack. Then, having checked to make sure the dots were still coming his way, the warrior lowered himself to the ground and started to run. It was a graceful lope that ate distance and conserved energy.

It looked as if trouble was on the way and Surekill would want to know.

13

Planet Earth, the Human Empire

The Emperor stood with his back to the room. A tiny insect buzzed around his head. Sunlight streamed in through the high arched window and threw his shadow across the floor.

Admiral Scolari stood just beyond it, her heart beating like a drum. This was the moment that she'd been waiting for, when the Emperor made his decision and the tide turned her way. Like his mother before him, the Emperor had done a masterful job of playing each branch of the military off against all the rest, preventing any of them from growing too strong.

After all, why grant the Legion their own planet, if not to balance the influence of the Navy and Marine Corps?

But the Hudatha threatened the entire empire, and in order to counter that threat the Emperor would have to place all of his forces under a single command or risk the possibility of defeat. There was no substitute for a single vision, a single strategy, and a single leader.

And there was little doubt that she should be that leader, since it was the Navy that tied the empire together and would bear the brunt of any attack—an attack she'd meet with the largest fleet ever assembled. Then, by dealing the enemy a single decisive blow, she'd join the short list of military leaders who through a single engagement had changed the course of history.

And then? Well, who knew? But it would be stupid to let all that power go. Besides, there was the Consortium of Inner Planets to consider. They had sponsored her and would expect a say. Would they decide to leave the Emperor in place? It seemed unlikely at best. The Emperor interrupted her thoughts.

"My decision is made."

"Yes, Highness."

"All of my forces will withdraw to the inner planets and prepare to defend them."

"Including the Legion, Highness?"

The Emperor spun on his heel. Sunbeams rayed around him. His voice was hard and unyielding. "I said *all* of my forces, did I not?"

Scolari bowed her head. "Yes, Highness. Sorry, Highness."

The Emperor waved the apology away. The copies argued in his head. Some favored his decision while others opposed it. Damn them anyway, eternally squabbling, making his life miserable.

"There's no need to apologize. You have your orders. Carry them out."

Scolari bowed low. "Yes, Highness. Immediately, Highness."

The Emperor nodded and turned his back. Scolari did an about-face and her cloak swirled around her as she headed for the door. An insect was perched on her left shoulder but it was far too light for the admiral to notice.

A pair of Trooper IIs stood guard as General Marianne Mosby closed the front door to what had been her house and hurried down the walkway. It was dark and the streetlamps threw circles onto the street.

The hover limo was long, black, and heavily armed. The engine hummed, the vehicle floated just off the pavement, and a blast of fan-driven air hit her ankles.

A door opened and she slid inside. The interior smelled of leather and expensive cologne. The cologne belonged to her XO, a handsome colonel named Jennings. Light came from the ceiling and left half of his face dark. He smiled sardonically.

"The general travels light."

Mosby smiled in return. "That's one of the many advantages of a career in the military. Uniforms can be obtained almost anywhere."

Jennings chuckled and turned towards the driver. "Subport seventeen and step on it."

"Yes, sir."

The officers were pushed backwards as the limo accelerated away from the curb. Jennings looked out through the window, saw the main gate flash by, and watched for signs of pursuit. There were none. He turned to Mosby.

"So far, so good."

Mosby nodded. "If mutiny can be described as 'good.' There's no possibility of error?"

Jennings shook his head. "None. Madam Dasser's people managed to get a microbot in through the Emperor's security. He gave the orders himself."

Mosby felt an emptiness settle where the bottom of her stomach should have been. She'd been confident of her ability to seduce the Emperor, to turn his opinions around, to guide him to the right direction. But she'd failed, and because of that, the entire Legion was in danger. Scolari would be more than happy to throw their lives away in battle, or failing that, to disband the Legion altogether and merge its personnel with the Marine Corps.

Mosby scratched the expensive leather with her fingernails. No! It mustn't happen! The preparations had been put in place some time ago and the orders had gone out. 64 percent of the Legion's personnel on Earth were about to take part in what would look like an elaborate war game but was actually a mass escape. An escape that would free them to fight the Hudatha on the rim worlds, where victory could still be won and lives could still be saved.

Mosby felt bad about those left behind, but knew there was nothing she could do, since a larger force would almost certainly raise suspicions. Once free of Earth's gravity well, she'd give orders to head for Algeron and worry about the consequences later.

The driver merged with traffic on the Imperial Expressway, changed to the VIP lane, and activated the strobes mounted behind the limo's grille. Other vehicles, those driven by Imperial bureaucrats and the like, hurried to get out of the way. The limo accelerated, followed the freeway through the center of an office complex, then down between government buildings and out towards the suburbs beyond.

Lights sparkled for as far as the eye could see. They glittered white, blue, and amber, like semiprecious stones thrown on black velvet, lighting the way for citizens only barely aware of the danger they were in. For the empire's losses had been systematically understated until now, a strategy that had given the Emperor some additional time, but wasted most of it as well.

A suspicion entered Mosby's mind and was followed by the conviction that it was true. The Emperor had used her, grown tired of her, and tossed her away! Stalling all the while.

The shame of it brought blood to her face and she turned towards the window. Damn the man! His mind had been made up from the start.

It took the better part of fifteen minutes to reach the outskirts of the metroplex and exit towards subport 17. Though fairly sizable, the spaceport was only one of thirty that ringed the Imperial City and handled the tremendous amount of traffic it generated.

Mosby watched as repellers flared and a large transport, outlined by its navigation lights, moved off the apron and onto a launch zone. She hoped it was one of hers, packed with legionnaires, only seconds from relative safety.

The limo turned, threw her against the door, and accelerated up a side street. Warehouses stood side by side on the left and right. Mosby saw a checkpoint up ahead, felt the nose rise as the driver adjusted the fans, and braced her feet as the limo slowed. Scanners read the barcodes engraved on both fenders, a computer confirmed the VIP license plates, and activated a variety of automatic weapons systems. Safeties switched on, lights flashed green, and Mosby heaved a sigh of relief.

If Madam Dasser's security forces could infiltrate a microbotic snooping device into the Imperial Palace, then the Emperor's secret police could easily do likewise. Mosby had prepared herself for the very real possibility of a trap, but the checkpoint had been the logical place to spring one, and their failure to do so was a burden lifted.

The limo swung wide of the terminal, made its way onto the apron, and headed towards the north end of the field. Auto loaders, maintenance bots, and support vehicles flashed by to either side. Lights could be seen through the windshield as a line of transports ran through their preflight checks and prepared to lift.

Jennings said something into his pocket phone and put it away.

"We're looking good, General. I made arrangements for you to board the *Enduro*. She's the biggest and, if it comes to a chase, the fastest."

Mosby felt mixed emotions and put them aside. Though normally disdainful of officers who used rank to ensure their own safety, it was imperative that she reach Algeron.

Assuming the escape was successful, Scolari would call it "mutiny" and move against the Legion. It was Mosby's duty to give St. James as much warning as possible. The fact that she'd be welcome in his bed was nice but entirely beside the point.

A transport loomed out of the night, its shape streamlined to deal with planetary atmospheres, but only slightly so, relying on brute strength to overcome the shortcomings of its boxy design.

The door hissed open and Mosby stepped out. She looked around. Where was her adjutant? A noncom to guide her aboard?

The questions were still coming when night turned to day and a spotlight pinned her to the concrete. The voice came from nowhere and everywhere at once.

"Freeze! You are under arrest! Any attempt to move or to communicate with others will result in death!"

Four APCs swept in around the limo, aimed their weapons in her direction, and hovered in place.

Mosby froze. There was little or no point in doing anything else. Scolari had known all along, had waited for the perfect moment, and nailed her in the act. That would make a difference later on, the difference between a conspiracy to commit mutiny and the real thing, which should be sufficient for a death sentence.

She heard Scolari before the admiral actually appeared. There were inserts built into the soles of the other officer's combat boots and they made a clicking sound as she walked.

The admiral's face was gaunt but alight with pleasure. The words had been rehearsed and flowed smoothly from her tongue.

"Well, what have we here? The much-vaunted Legion slinking away in the night? Heading for home? How sad that such a famous organization should die such an ignominious death."

Mosby shrugged. "I may die but the Legion will live on."

Scolari shook her head in mock sympathy. "I think not, my dear. You see, I know that the Legion lives not in the trophies displayed on Algeron, or in the uniforms you wear, but in the hearts and minds of the great unwashed horde. Yes, the Legion lives in the stories they've heard, and when the myth has been destroyed, the organization will follow. Think about how the story will play in the media, how the people will feel, and you'll understand what I mean."

Mosby didn't have to think about it. She knew Scolari was right. The Legion was about to die.

Metal glowed cherry red, radiated heat, and caused Sergi Chien-Chu to sweat. He thumbed the torch to a finer setting, finished the weld, and removed the protective facemask.

The sculpture, one of many that dotted the grounds around his mansion, was a fanciful mélange of rusty metal plates, all flying in different directions. Each plane, each angle, was in conflict with all the others, challenging their positions and making a statement of its own.

Or so it seemed to Chien-Chu. But others perceived things differently. His wife was a case in point. Where he saw angles in conflict, she saw pieces of rusty metal, and where she saw a rainbow of color, he saw flowers dying in a vase. But such is marriage, and a happy one too, though strained by the situation on Spindle.

Each dawn brought the hope that a message torp would arrive, that the news would be good, that Leonid was alive. But each sunset made such a message less and less likely, and their spirits would spiral downwards.

Chien-Chu had taken refuge in his work, and in his hobbies, but Nola spent long hours knitting on the veranda, thinking about her son or comforting their daughter-in-law.

Natasha was a lovely young woman with huge eyes, a long oval face, and a slender bird-like body. Chien-Chu adored her almost as much as he did his son, and feared that the news of Leonid's death would be very, very hard on her. No, he mustn't think like that, for to do so was to tempt fate. Or so his mother had always said.

"Uncle Sergi! Uncle Sergi! Auntie Nola wants you!"

The voice belonged to a five-year-old boy. He was a chubby little thing, like the puppy that gamboled at his heels, and long overdue for a bath. Mud, his favorite substance next to chocolate cake, covered his face, hands, and playsuit.

Chien-Chu lifted the boy in his arms. "She does? And what does Auntie Nola want?"

A pair of serious brown eyes met his. "She wants you to come to the house, that's what. There's a woman to see you."

Chien-Chu hung the laser torch on the sculpture and started for the house. It was a long, low one-story affair and seemed part of the ground that it stood on. Ivy climbed here and there, brick peeked out between neatly trimmed shrubs, and windows winked in the sun.

"And does this woman have a name?"

The boy shrugged. "I made mud pies."

"I made a sculpture."

"I'll bet Aunt Nola will like my mud pies better than your sculpture."

Chien-Chu shook his head. "No sucker bets. I'm getting too old."

"How old are you?"

"None of your business."

Chien-Chu was huffing and puffing by the time he reached the veranda but too stubborn and too proud to put the boy down. They entered the living room together.

It was huge, with high ceilings, dark beams, and a massive

fireplace. An eclectic mix of modern and traditional furniture was scattered about.

Nola Chien-Chu and Madam Valerie Dasser sat on opposite ends of a comfortable couch. They held teacups in their hands. Madam Chien-Chu took one look at her husband and frowned.

"Sergi! Look at you! Overalls. Filthy ones at that. And Toby! Shame on you!"

The little boy smiled happily. "I made mud pies."

"You look like a mud pie. Now, run upstairs and take a bath. Your piano instructor will be here in half an hour."

"But I don't like him!"

"I don't want to hear any more. Now, scoot."

The little boy took one look at his aunt's face, saw that she meant it, and ran towards a hallway.

Chien-Chu dropped into his favorite chair, ignored his wife's pained look, and smiled at Madam Dasser.

"Good afternoon, Madam Dasser. What a pleasant surprise."

"A surprise perhaps," Madam Dasser replied, "but not especially pleasant. I bring bad news."

Madam Chien-Chu's teacup clattered as a hand flew to her mouth. The Eurasian eyes that had fascinated Chien-Chu these many years were wide with fright.

Dasser shook her head. "That was thoughtless of me. Can you forgive me, Nola? The news has nothing to do with Leonid. Not directly anyway."

Chien-Chu sighed, opened the brass box next to his elbow, and selected a cigarette. He wasn't supposed to smoke but it didn't seem to matter anymore. He sucked on the filter, felt the tip ignite, and sucked the smoke into his lungs. It came out in a long thin stream.

"And?"

Dasser took a sip of tea. "The Emperor ordered his forces to withdraw from the rim. That was yesterday afternoon. Most of the 3rd REI, along with elements of the 4th, and the 1st REC tried to lift seven hours later. They were caught and placed under arrest."

"And General Mosby?"

"The general and her staff have been charged with treason."

Madam Chien-Chu turned pale. A withdrawal meant almost certain death for those on Spindle. Her hand shook slightly as she gestured towards a darkened holo tank. "There was nothing on the news."

Dasser smiled grimly. "There will be. Scolari threw the whole thing to the media about thirty minutes ago. The explanation was rather one-sided, to say the least."

Chien-Chu thought about his son, about his daughter-in-law, and the millions of other human beings spread along the rim. All had been sacrificed. He took a drag off his cigarette. His voice was low but tight with anger.

"Scolari's an idiot... but I had hopes for the Emperor."

Dasser wanted to state the obvious, wanted to push him, but played it cool instead.

"Yes, the whole thing is most regrettable."

He looked her in the eyes and chose his words with care. "The poetry group that you told me about."

"Yes?"

"Could I come to a meeting?"

Dasser smiled as she set the hook. "We'd love to have you."

Chien-Chu nodded, stubbed his cigarette out, and swore when it burned his finger.

14

God knows 'twere better to be deep
Pillowed in silk and scented down,
Where Love throbs out in blissful sleep,
Pulse nigh to pulse, and breath to breath,
Where hushed awakenings are dear.

But I've a rendezvous with Death
At midnight in some flaming town,
When Spring trips north again this year,
And I to my pledged word am true,
I shall not fail that rendezvous.
LEGIONNAIRE ALAN SEEGER
KIA the Somme
Standard year 1916

Legion Outpost NA-45-16/R, aka "Spindle," the Human Empire
Spear Commander Ikor Niber-Ba felt his heart swell with pride
as the task force's entire complement of fighters and troop
carriers formed up and headed for the strangely shaped asteroid.
All three of his battleships had moved in close, shortening the
distance the smaller vessels had to travel, and bringing their
mighty armament to bear. He could actually see the surface,
mark the spots where metal and molten rock glowed cherry red,
and glory in what the spear had accomplished.

They had pounded the asteroid for the better part of a Hudathan day, laying waste to every surface installation they could find, preparing the way for the final ground assault. And what an assault it would be. Every soldier not required to operate the ships would be involved.

Light reflected off fighters as they went in for one last strafing run. The troop carriers moved more slowly, dark silhouettes against the sun's bright corona, staying in formation, mindful of their assigned landing areas. Only fifteen or twenty units of time would pass before the last of them had landed, discharged their troops, and lifted again.

The humans had been clever, very clever, but no amount of cleverness would protect them from the "Intaka," or "blow of death." Originally part of the lexicon that had grown up around Gunu, a highly disciplined form of personal combat, the concept of Intaka had been adopted by the Hudathan military and used to describe the use of overwhelming force.

Though favored by most of his peers, almost all of whom had grown up big and strong, Niber-Ba had a tendency to withhold the Intaka, using it only as a last resort. This stemmed from the fact that opponents had always been larger than he was, from a natural sense of thrift, and from a healthy dose of Hudathan paranoia. After all, why use more resources than necessary to overwhelm an opponent? Especially in a universe where more enemies were almost certainly waiting to attack.

But this situation was different. Niber-Ba knew that now, and knew that he should have recognized the enemy's weakness from the start and used the strategy of Intaka to defeat them.

The knowledge of that failure, and the deaths that it had caused, had left him sleepless for three cycles running. Nothing could bring dead warriors back to life or cleanse the shame from his soul. But victory could advance his people's cause. Yes, victory would go a long ways towards easing the pain, and victory would be his.

Niber-Ba turned his attention to the command center's holo tank and committed himself to battle.

* * *

Red eyed his screens, confirmed Spinhead's analysis, and spoke into the mike.

"Time to serve the hors d'oeuvres… our guests have arrived."

The electronics tech's words were heard all over Spindle. By Captain Omar Narbakov, who was supervising the last-minute reinforcement of a weapons pit, by Leonid Chien-Chu, who was struggling to make a splice, by Legionnaire Seeger, who placed a rock in front of something he wanted to hide, and by all the others who waited by their posts, stomachs hollow with fear, palms slick with sweat. This was it, the moment they'd been dreading, when their lives would depend on skills that most of them had never tried to acquire, and on luck, which observed no loyalties and belonged as much to the enemy as to them.

The exception was Narbakov. He had dreamed of this moment as a boy, trained for it as a man, and waited these many years for it to arrive. He savored the taste of peppermint as a piece of candy dissolved in his mouth, the hiss of oxygen as it blew against the side of his face, and the hard unyielding landscape beyond his visor. The dwarf hung like a searchlight in the sky, throwing hard black shadows down across Spindle's surface, many of which concealed his troops.

Yes, this was *his* moment, his Camerone, his place to die. The thought brought no fear, no dread, just a mounting sense of excitement. For a legionnaire *will* not die, *cannot* die, as long as others live to remember him.

Narbakov stood in the open, disdainful of the Hudathan fighters that crisscrossed the asteroid's surface, and chinned more magnification into his visor.

The Hudathan troopships had started to land, dropping onto their preassigned LZs with the delicacy of bees landing on flowers, dropping their troops like so much pollen. There was no response, no defensive fire, because Narbakov *wanted* the Hudathans on the ground. He was tired of being pounded from space, tired of fighting the aliens on their terms, and eager to strike back.

A Hudathan tripped, lost contact with the ground, and floated away. The alien looked like a large balloon, a plaything waiting to be popped, and the image made Narbakov laugh—a sound that made its way onto the command channel and caused his subordinates to look at each other and shake their heads in amazement. The old man was terminally gung ho—everyone knew that—but the laugh was bizarre even for him. Still, if the cap could laugh at the geeks, how tough could the assholes be?

They grinned, checked their weapons one last time, and waited for the order to fire.

Narbakov switched to freq 4. The civilians had military-style code names but rarely remembered to use them. Leonid was known as "Boss One."

"N-One to Boss One."

Leonid swore at the interruption, completed the cable splice, and wound tape around the repair. "Chien-Chu here... go ahead."

Narbakov looked heavenwards, hoped god had provided a separate reward for civilians, and did his best to sound normal.

"Sorry to bother you, Leo... but the place is crawling with geeks. I'll be forced to open fire in a moment or two. How are things going?"

Leonid dropped the cable and looked up at the launcher. Although some quick-thinking legionnaires had prevented the Hudathans from finding out how important the linear accelerator was, they had still done their best to destroy it. Not from any particular concern about the device, but as part of their general effort to destroy everything on Spindle's surface and prepare the way for their troops.

A battleship-mounted laser cannon had sliced through a section of gridwork, slagged the small ops center located to one side of the ramp, and severed a major cable run. Leonid had repaired the last of the cables himself, and the ops center had been bypassed, but the intermittent flash of laser torches signaled that repairs were still under way.

Leonid looked out towards the area where Narbakov should be, saw sticks of light lance downwards, then disappear as a fighter completed its run. The silence made the daggers of light seem less dangerous, like the laser shows held on Empire Day, but the civilian knew they were different. People died wherever the light touched.

"Omar? You okay?"

The officer had started to lose his patience. "Come on, Leo.

Quit screwing around and answer my question."

"I need time, Omar. Thirty minutes."

"Get fraxing real, Leo. We'll be ass-deep in geeks thirty minutes from now."

"Twenty."

"Ten and not a goddamned minute more. You tell those toolheads of yours to get their shit together. Out."

Leonid looked up towards the glow of laser torches. How long till the Hudathans saw the lights and came to investigate?

The civilian began to climb. His breath came in short angry puffs. Damn. Damn. Damn. A series of explosions marched across the horizon and terminated near lock 4. Shit. Shit. Shit. They *had* to complete the repairs, *had* to launch the star divers, *had* to hit the battleships. He chinned a button.

"Cody... Hecox... Gutierrez... how much longer?"

"Twenty, twenty-five minutes, boss." The voice belonged to Cody.

"Make it five."

"No can do, boss. One launch maybe, two if you're lucky, three, forget it. The stress will tear the ramp apart."

"We're out of time, Cody. Spot-weld as many joints as you can and then jump."

Cody was silent for a moment. "Okay. You're the boss. Five and counting."

Torches flared as the construction workers made their welds, leapfrogged each other, and started over again.

Leonid ignored them, stepped onto a side platform, and eyed the star diver's long oval shape. It was huge, almost the size of a destroyer escort, and packed with sophisticated technology. It pained him to treat the ship like this, to use it as a high-tech cannonball, but there was no other choice.

Leonid looked upwards. Five additional ships hung over his head, stacked on top of each other like bullets in a magazine, held there by a hastily built framework of steel. Would the jury-rigged conveyor mechanism feed the ships down onto the ramp quickly enough? Would the accelerator hang together long enough to fire them?

He looked down at the simplified control panel. Wires

squirmed in and out of it like worms feeding on a corpse. The device had six ready lights, all of them green, and a box-shaped switch protector. Leonid flipped the cover out of the way. The button was red and pulsed to the beat of his heart.

The hatch disappeared, the twelve troopers who constituted Dagger Two of Arrow Five ran-shuffled down the ramp, while Arrow Commander Imbom Dakna-Ba felt his legs turn to jelly. He willed them to move, *commanded* them to do so, but they refused. His aide, a tough old veteran named Forma-Sa, was tactful.

"Is there a problem with your equipment, sir?"

Dakna-Ba *wanted* to answer, wanted to say yes, wanted to come up with an equipment malfunction that would keep him aboard the troop carrier, but the words froze in his throat. Dagger Three made their way down the ramp, angled left, and took cover in a crater. The officer waited for the almost inevitable hail of defensive fire and was even more frightened when it didn't come. The humans had fought like Stath Beasts up till now... something was wrong.

"Sir?"

Dakna-Ba tried to speak but succeeded in producing little more than a squeak.

Forma-Sa nodded understanding, deactivated his implant, and placed his helmet next to the officer's. "It's time to disembark, sir. Make your way down the ramp or I'll be forced to put a bullet through the back of your head."

Dakna-Ba found himself in motion. The humans frightened him, but Dagger Commander Forma-Sa scared him even more. There were stories about the things he'd done, terrible stories, and the officer believed them. The ramp shook slightly beneath his boots.

He looked around. Now it would come, the searing light, followed by complete and total darkness. But it didn't. What *were* the humans doing? Somewhere down below the level of the fear there was tranquillity, and within that tranquillity the ability to think, and the thoughts seemed to express themselves of their own volition.

"It's a trap, Dag. Instruct our troops to keep their heads down."

The noncom nodded his satisfaction and relayed Dakna-Ba's orders to the troops. No sooner had he done so than all hell broke loose. There was no sound in the silent world of space, but the stutter of energy beams and the subsequent radio chatter told their own story.

He'd been right! Not only that, but he'd survived the first few seconds of battle and hadn't lost control of his bowels!

Dakna-Ba felt strength seep into his legs. They were steady once more and responded when he ordered them to move. The officer activated his implant.

"Daggers Two, Three, Four, and Five advance. You know the objective… let's show the Dwarf what the fighting fifth can do!"

Crew-served automatic weapons began to fire as troopers emerged from the shadows, from craters, and from rocks to advance on their objective.

Light stuttered blue as the incoming fire intensified and tracers flickered around them. Forma-Sa watched approvingly as Dakna-Ba ran-shuffled along with the rest, shouting words of encouragement, his head swiveling right and left. The youngster would make a halfway decent officer one day *if* he learned quickly enough, *if* he managed to survive.

Dakna-Ba considered the task ahead. His orders were clear: force the air lock that intelligence had labeled as "0-12," make his way into the heart of the human habitat, and destroy the computer located there. The computer had already played a key role in the asteroid's defense and might otherwise continue to do so.

It was either an extremely important endeavor, entrusted to Dakna-Ba as a sign of respect, or a suicide mission assigned to him because he was the most junior officer around, and therefore expendable. Dakna-Ba wanted to believe the former but knew the latter was a good deal more likely.

The humans had dug in around the lock. Light flashed back and forth as both sides exchanged fire.

A scream ripped through Dakna-Ba's mind as a trooper started to say something and was literally cut in half. Dakna-Ba saw him off to the left, the top half of his suit spinning away while the bottom half remained where it was. Blood and entrails shot straight upwards, stabilized, and floated away.

The officer turned back, began to issue an order, and stopped when something grotesque appeared. It was taller than a Hudathan, heavier, and equipped with weapons where its arms should have been. Energy beams seemed to have little effect on the thing and tracers bounced off it. A cyborg! Intelligence had warned him that such things existed, had told him that the humans had an entire army comprised of cyborgs, but he was surprised nonetheless. Though sufficiently advanced to field cyborgs of their own, the Hudathans had a deep-seated aversion to the concept involved, and didn't use anything more complicated than nerve-spliced artificial limbs.

"Hit the dirt!"

The order came from Dag Forma-Sa, and Dakna-Ba obeyed. He hit hard, bounced, and nearly broke free. Light flickered, tracers sectioned the darkness, and the Hudathans started to die.

The thing was hunting his troopers the way a Namba Bak hunts gorgs, probing between the rocks, driving them out into the open. Shocked by the cyborg's apparent invulnerability, and unsure of how to deal with it, some of the troopers ran. The cyborg liked that and picked them off with the precision of a marksman at the range.

Dakna-Ba activated his implant.

"Fight the cyborg as you would a tank... fire your SLMs!"

The response was spectacular. The cyborg staggered under the explosive impact of at least six shoulder-launched missiles, continued to fire even as it fell to its knees, and didn't stop until an explosion took its head clean off.

Shaken but victorious, the Hudathans fought their way through an amalgamation of civilians and legionnaires to reach the lock. It was made of thick steel, reinforced with concrete, but yielded to some carefully placed explosives.

The violent decompression that followed came as no surprise to those within. They had expected it and were prepared to fight the aliens for every inch of the habitat's hallway.

* * *

Red swung his boots down from the console and took a sip from the mug at his elbow. The coffee was fresh-brewed and tasted good. He had climbed into his suit as a precautionary measure, but the control area was equipped with its own lock, so it would be a while before he needed the helmet. He shook his head in dismay. The environmental display left no doubt as to the situation and the radio traffic confirmed it. The geeks were inside the habitat and headed his way. They wanted Spinhead and he couldn't really blame them, the computer had played a key role in the asteroid's defense and was about to defeat them. Red smiled, selected a frequency, and spoke into his mike.

"Hey, boss… this is Red."

Leonid checked the watch built into the left arm of his space suit. "Shoot."

"They're inside and headed my way."

"That's a roger. Shoot me the latest and bail out."

Red touched a button. It took a fraction of a second for the accumulated data to make its way through a maze of cables, leap through the repairs, and enter the ship's on-board computers.

"Sent."

Leonid nodded, thankful that the star divers would have the latest data on the speed, position, and orientation of the Hudathan ships, and realized the technicians couldn't see him.

"Thanks, Red. Now take a hike. Boss out."

The technician chinned his mike and said, "Yes, sir," but stayed right where he was. The Hudathans had done a pretty good job of sterilizing the asteroid's surface but had missed a jury-rigged antenna or two. And those, plus Red's skill, meant that the star divers could be steered for up to five or ten seconds after they were launched. The chance was too good to miss. Besides, the coffee was hot and tasted damned good. Red took another sip. He looked around. The control center was empty and would make a lonely place to die.

Seeger waited for the Hudathan patrol to pass, stepped out of his hiding place, and shot the last of them right between the shoulder blades. It wasn't nice, it wasn't fair, and Seeger didn't give a shit. Vapor out-gassed and pushed the already dead alien away.

Still moving forward, the rest of the patrol remained blissfully ignorant while Seeger killed them one at a time, until their leader was the only one left. In fact, Seeger was taking aim, getting ready to fire, when the noncom turned. The cyborg would never know if it was a routine check or a sudden premonition of danger that caused the alien to turn, but the outcome was the same. The Hudathan turned, registered an expression that looked very similar to human fear, and died as Seeger burned a hole through his visor.

Seeger felt a grim sense of satisfaction. Six geeks down and a gazillion to go.

Leonid swallowed. His throat felt dry. "Cody, Hecox, Gutierrez, time's up. Finish the weld you're on and jump."

The laser torches flared, then disappeared one after the other. The voice belonged to Gutierrez.

"Are you sure, boss? There's some geeks headed this way."

Leonid was anything but sure. He kept his voice steady nonetheless. "Yeah, I'm sure. Now, get the hell off this rig before I dock you a day's pay."

The toolheads laughed in spite of themselves, jumped free of the ramp, and drifted away. It was scary, but gravity would eventually prevail, and the further away the better.

Gutierrez thought of Leonid standing there, his finger poised above the big red button, and said what came to mind.

"Vaya con dios, boss. Hasta la vista."

Leonid heard the words, swallowed his fear, and brought his finger down. The results were instantaneous.

Energy was drawn from Spindle's massive accumulators, channeled into the linear accelerator, and translated to forward motion. It seemed as if the ship was there one moment and gone the next. Steering jets winked red as the star diver broke free of the asteroid's gravity and the drives kicked in.

The ramp shook with the force of the ship's departure and Leonid braced himself against a rail. How long would the ramp continue to hang together? Leonid looked upwards and saw that the next star diver had already begun its descent.

* * *

The words arrived via the Hudathan's implant and were said so calmly, so routinely, that it took him a moment to appreciate their full significance.

"The humans have launched a ship. Initial analysis indicates the vessel is analogous in size and shape to one of our Class IV freighters."

A launch? Analogous to a Class IV freighter? Niber-Ba's mind hurried to catch up. Were some humans trying to escape? Hoping to avoid his battleships? No, they were smarter than that, so...

The spear commander stared into the holo tank, sought the new spark of light, and gave a grunt of satisfaction when he found it.

The same voice, a bit more intense now, interrupted his thoughts. "The human ship is headed for the *Light of Hudatha.*"

A thousand words lined up and waited to be said but not a single one passed his lips. The *Light of Hudatha's* shields were down in order to allow the returning troop carriers to enter her bays. Not only that, but the battleship was extremely close to the asteroid, which left no time to maneuver. A new sun was born, lived for a few seconds, and died. Fully one third of the Dwarf's offensive power went with it.

Niber-Ba was still struggling to understand what had happened, to accept what it meant, when the voice spoke again. It was pitched a little higher this time and barely under control.

"The humans have launched a second ship. Initial analysis indicates that it will collide with the *World Taker* one unit from now."

The Dwarf resisted the temptation to hurl orders towards the *World Taker,* knowing the ship's commanding officer had heard the same information he had and was doing what he could to avoid the attack. No, his task lay elsewhere.

"Target primary weapons batteries on the point of launch. Fire!"

Red waited for the Hudathans with the patience of a spider sitting on its web. Most of the corridors boasted surveillance cameras and about 70 percent of them were still operable. That allowed the technician to watch as the aliens fought their way through the halls, stumbled into a variety of booby traps, and stood outside his lock. The moment had arrived.

The remote consisted of little more than a switch and some wires that disappeared into a dark corner of the control room. He picked it up, pushed the button, and heard the distant thump of explosives.

Dakna-Ba swore as the explosion brought tons of rock crashing down around them. The humans had extinguished all of the habitat's lights. Dust swirled through the beam projected by his helmet. Bodies moved, headlamps danced, and casualties were counted. The news was anything but good. Three of Dakna-Ba's troopers had been crushed. Three added to the what? Sixteen or seventeen killed so far? It made little difference. The debris blocked the hallway and left only one direction he could go. Forward. He motioned toward the lock.

"Blow it."

A demolitions expert hurried to obey.

Dakna-Ba looked around. Forma-Sa? Where was Forma-Sa? Then he remembered. A human had stepped out of a hidden alcove, shoved a drill bit against the noncom's chest, and pulled the trigger. Dakna-Ba had killed the human at the same exact moment that the sudden decompression had turned Forma-Sa inside out. It would have been horrible, except that it came during a day filled with horror, and seemed ordinary by comparison.

The lock blew. Dakna-Ba felt concrete spatter against his armor. He went through the door low, his weapon spitting death, knowing the defenders had the advantage. And they did, or more accurately Red did, because the grenade blew the Hudathan's left leg off. Death followed a fraction of a second later.

The ensuing battle was bloody but relatively short-lived, since Spinhead had orders to blow the control center the moment that Red went down. There were no survivors.

Leonid ground his teeth in frustration as the third ship dropped into place. The ramp was shaky and the Hudathans could retaliate at any moment. He had seconds, minutes at most, to launch the ship and jump clear. Star divers four, five, and six would go unused. The button made the transition from amber to red. Leonid brought his fist down. The ship sped down the ramp, fired its drives, and headed for the last of the Hudathan ships. The second star diver hit its target, blew up, and bathed Spindle in white light.

Leonid waved his fist at them. "Take that, you bastards!" It was then that the ship-mounted energy cannons turned Leonid, the ramp, and the remaining star divers into a lake of molten metal.

"Target destroyed."

The words barely registered on Niber-Ba as he fought to save his command. There was no time to move the ship, no time to regret the decisions he'd made, and no time to lose. A third star diver was on the way and it was aimed at him.

"Target primary, secondary, and tertiary weapons systems on the human ship. Fire!"

The primary and secondary weapons systems were computer-controlled and responded immediately. Missiles slipped out of their launch tubes, energy beams leaped through the darkness, and the Dwarf bit his lip. The ship was close and still accelerating...

Missiles hit, exploded, and cut the star diver in two. One half tumbled off towards the sun, but the other turned end over end and headed straight for the Hudathan battleship.

A klaxon went off somewhere in the background and Niber-Ba heard himself screaming over the interface. "Raise the screens! Fire! Fire! Fire!"

But there was no time to raise the screens, and even though the main batteries continued to fire, the wreckage absorbed the additional damage and kept on coming. It hit the Hudathan ship broadside, triggered a massive explosion, and disappeared along with its target.

Captain Omar Narbakov shielded his eyes from the momentary glare. "Well, I'll be goddamned. Three for three." He chinned his radio.

"N-One to Boss One."

Silence.

"Hey, Leo, it's me, Omar. You did it, you miserable sonofabitch, you did it!"

Nothing.

Narbakov shook his head sadly and looked around. There was still some scattered fighting but the humans had won. His ragtag force of legionnaires and civilian irregulars had won on the ground, and whatever fighters and troop carriers the aliens had left would be forced to surrender. Deprived of their mother ships, they had neither the fuel nor computer capacity to travel through deep space.

Then it occurred to him. In spite of his determination to die a glorious death, he was inexplicably alive. Not only that, but his duties had prevented him from getting involved in the fighting, and he'd never been in any real danger. And now, thanks to the fact that he'd survived, there was an enormous amount of work to do. Launch message torps toward Earth, repair the habitat, tend to the wounded, the list went on and on. Shoulders slumped beneath the weight of his responsibilities, Narbakov trudged off towards his makeshift command post.

Seeger checked to make sure that his area was secure and headed for a distant spire. It looked like a finger pointing towards space. Given the length of his legs and the near absence of gravity, it was easy to cover lots of ground in a short period of time.

The signs of battle were everywhere. Sunlight winked off a half-slagged antenna, the wreckage of a Hudathan troop carrier drifted past, a blast-darkened crater marked a cyborg's last stand, and a helmet bounced off the legionnaire's shoulder.

But Seeger's eyes were on the spire and the jumble of debris around its base, for that was the place where he had hidden Marie. There'd been no backup body to put her in, and no surety that the habitat would remain secure, so he'd rigged an oxygen supply, a nutrient drip, and a solar array, and left Marie where she'd be safe. Or should be anyway, barring accidents or plain bad luck.

"Marie? Can you hear me?"

Her reply was reassuringly acerbic. "Damned right I can hear you. As can anyone else within a hundred klicks!"

Seeger felt warm inside. "So who gives a shit? We kicked their butts."

He stepped between a couple of boulders, lifted one out of the way, and remembered what it felt like to smile. She was there, all right, a head, shoulders, and torso that would have looked grotesque to anyone else, but meant everything to him.

"Hi, baby."

"Hi, ya big lug."

"You ready to haul ass?"

"I would be, except that I seem to have misplaced it somewhere."

"No problem. Help will arrive soon, and we'll submit a req for a brand-new ass."

"I love you, Seeg."

"Yeah, I love you too. Come on, let's get the hell outta here."

And with that the cyborg freed Marie from the jury-rigged life support systems, tucked her under his right arm, and stepped out into the sunlight. It felt good to be alive.

15

Legio patria nostra, or *"The Legion Is Our Country."*
MOTTO OF THE FRENCH FOREIGN LEGION
STANDARD YEAR (APPROXIMATE) 1835

This motto was established after the Legion was "ceded" to the Spanish government as an act of political convenience. Forced to take part in a Spanish civil war, the Legion fought bravely, often without pay, rations, or uniforms. Of the 4,000 Legionnaires who took part, roughly 500 survived. Almost totally decimated, the Legion was reinvented on December 16, 1835.

Planet Algeron, the Human Empire

General Ian St. James knew what the orders were long before they appeared on the screen. It was a moment he had dreaded, and put off as long as he dared, knowing he'd be forced to make a terrible decision. He touched a key. Words flooded the screen.

IMPNAVCOM/EARTH

Date: 6/26/2846 Standard
From: Admiral Paula Scolari IMPNAV
Authorization Code: IMPERSEC/6786-HK-8648
To: General Ian St. James IMPLEG

The Navy, Marine Corps, and Legion have been placed under a single command subject to my orders. (Ref. Imperial Decree HM-

6791 dated 6/25/2846 Standard.)

You are hereby directed to withdraw all forces from Algeron, and having done so, to redeploy them according to subsequent orders.

All military weapons, supplies, equipment fortifications, and emplacements are to be destroyed prior to withdrawal.

Transports sufficient to your needs will arrive on 6/30/2846 Standard.

Any deviation from these orders will be dealt with in the most severe possible way.

St. James read the last paragraph again. He'd never seen anything like it. Rather than assume the blind obedience that human military tradition called for, Scolari had threatened him. A fact that could mean nothing or a great deal.

Where was Marianne in all this? Why did the orders originate from Scolari rather than her? There were a lot of potential answers and none of them pleasant.

St. James frowned, sent the orders to his printer, and waited for six sets of hard copy to whir out.

Then, with the frown firmly in place, and his eyes on the floor, he left his quarters for the situation room. It was located a hundred feet down the main corridor and was guarded by a Trooper II. The cyborg crashed to attention as St. James entered.

The situation room was huge, large enough to house a hundred people if necessary, and very spartan. The walls were opaque at the moment, but had the capacity to transform themselves into a multiplicity of screens, all of which were linked to a powerful battle computer located twelve stories underground.

His staff rose as the door hissed closed. They stood around a circular table made of native hardwood, cut from the forests that bordered the Towers of Algeron and handcrafted by members of the Legion's Pioneers. The wood came in a variety of hues, including red, brown, and a light, almost blond color, that had been worked into the table mosaic-style to form a star.

St. James forced a smile. "Take your seats. You'll be glad you did."

So saying, the officer walked the circumference of the table and handed hard copy to each member of his staff.

There was Colonel Alice Goodwin, commanding officer of the 1st Foreign Infantry Regiment, or 1st RE. Forty-five or so, she had a badly scarred face and a determined mouth. She, and the legionnaires under her command, had responsibility for the Legion's administrative affairs.

Goodwin had been a line officer once, and a damned good one, having earned the sobriquet "Crazy Alice" when she attacked an enemy machine-gun nest single-handed. The resulting wounds had taken her out of the field but not out of the Legion. St. James could count on her anytime and anyplace.

There was the dark and volatile Colonel Pierre Legaux. He commanded the 1st Foreign Cavalry Regiment, or 1st REC, 90 percent of which were cyborgs. Light gleamed off the officer's metal parts and caused St. James to wonder if the rumors were true.

The Legion had a long-standing rule that bodies more than 51 percent artificial were classified as cyborgs... and cyborgs were not qualified for command. So how did Legaux, who looked like he was at least 70 percent artificial, manage to retain bio-bod status? There were plenty of theories, most of which centered around corrupt medical personnel, but no one knew for sure. Except Legaux, that is, and he wasn't talking. But one thing was for sure: the cyborgs had a profound trust for their commanding officer and would follow him through the gates of hell. Yes, Legaux was an asset.

If Legaux was an asset, then the next officer, Lieutenant Colonel Andre Vial, was a question mark. Though possessed of a good record, and competent enough, there was something about the man that St. James didn't trust. Was it the slick ingratiating personality? The preening good looks? The innuendos aimed at his peers? Whatever it was annoyed St. James and caused him to wonder about the officer's loyalty. But as luck would have it, Vial commanded Algeron's contingent of the 5th Foreign Infantry Regiment, or 5th REI, most of which was spread out across a dozen rim worlds. He'd have a role in what came next, but a small one.

Then came Lieutenant Colonel Jennifer Jozan, a tiny little thing with black hair, snub nose, and a perpetual twinkle in her eye. She loved practical jokes, and was forever playing them on her superiors and subordinates alike, a habit that did nothing to lessen everyone's affection for her. But she was tough, and commanded the 13th Demi-Brigade de Légion Étrangère, or 13th DBLE, with an iron hand, which accounted for the nickname "Iron Jenny."

Next was Lieutenant Colonel Tam Tran, a diminutive man with an extremely keen mind and a whipcord body. He commanded the famed 2nd Foreign Parachute Regiment, or 2nd REP, and his green beret lay on the table in front of him. Known for leading from the front, Tran was an asset indeed, and would play a key role in the difficult days ahead.

Last but certainly not least was his XO and personal friend, Colonel Edwina Augusta Jefferson, better known to her friends as just plain "Ed," the real power behind his throne. She had an excellent mind, a robust sense of humor, coal-black skin, and a body that weighed more than 250 pounds. Most of the weight came in the form of muscle, and god help anyone who got in her way. She commanded the 2nd Foreign Infantry Regiment, or 2nd REI, and had just returned from the rim. Her report would help lay the groundwork for a decision.

St. James rounded the table, found his chair, and sat down.

"All right... you've seen the orders. What do you think?"

There was silence for a moment as the officers glanced at each other across the table. Forthright as always, Legaux went first. Light reflected off the metal plate that had replaced the left side of his face. A servo whined as he held the hard copy aloft. His vocal cords had been replaced by a synthesizer and his voice sounded hoarse.

"The orders are a travesty. Algeron will be forfeit if we obey them, and worse than that, the entire rim as well. Scolari is an idiot."

"Scolari is *anything* but an idiot," Jozan said softly. "She cares more about the Navy, and about her own career, than the good of her empire."

"Yes," Tran agreed. "This is the first step of many. Scolari intends to sacrifice the rim worlds and gain control of the Legion in the process."

"If we let her," Legaux muttered darkly.

"What choice do we have?" Goodwin asked. "Orders are orders."

There was silence for a moment as the officers thought about that.

It was then that St. James turned to Vial. "What about you, Andre? What do you think?"

Vial had been dreading this moment, dreading the necessity to take sides, knowing the others would settle for nothing less. It was the worst situation he could think of, one in which his commanding officer had allowed subordinates to tread the thin ice of insubordination, and was inviting him to do likewise. Whatever he said, whatever he did, could come back to haunt him. Vial summoned his most serious expression and chose his words with extreme care.

"Our orders have frequently been difficult... but the Legion has followed them in the past."

It was a good answer, an answer acceptable to the others, and perfect for use during a mass court-martial. Many of those around the table nodded, acknowledging the truth of Vial's words and reevaluating their opinions.

"Except for Algeria," Tran said evenly, and everyone nodded to this as well, because Algeria was as much a part of the Legion's history as Camerone.

It had occurred in the late 1950s, when the Legion had allowed itself to become embroiled in French politics and had wound up holding the short end of the stick. A significant portion of the Legion had mutinied, been defeated, and subsequently punished. Some of the mutineers had been executed.

"Which brings us to the last paragraph of these orders," Jefferson said, pointing a huge finger at her printout. "It seems as if Scolari doubts our loyalty."

"For good reason," Legaux said darkly.

Maybe," St. James said carefully, "and maybe not. Let's hear what Ed has to say. She just returned from the rim... and may shed some light on the strategic situation."

Jefferson shrugged massive shoulders. "The situation can be summarized with a single word: 'chaos.' I hit dirt on seven different planets, visited four of our outposts, made courtesy calls at two naval stations, and talked to a variety of diplomatic types.

"Everyone I spoke with agreed. The Hudathans are sweeping inwards, destroying everything in their path, driving waves of refugees towards the center of the empire. They arrive in yachts, clapped-out freighters, tugboats, speedsters, garbage scows, anything that could make it into hyperspace and out again. There were thousands of them in orbit around the planets I visited, begging for food, fuel, and medical care. All screaming their heads off, looking for handouts, and spreading panic. 'The Hudathans are coming,' 'The Hudathans are unstoppable.' 'The Hudathans are merciless.' There were so many of them that orbital collisions had become commonplace and hundreds of people died every day."

"But what about the swabbies?" Goodwin asked. "Did they bring it under control?"

Jefferson grimaced. "No, just the opposite. They had orders to pull out. They were in the process of destroying the Imperial naval base on the day I left Frio II."

Jozan shook her head sadly. "No wonder the people have panicked. What about our folks?"

"Holding firm," Jefferson said grimly, "and doing what they can to prepare for the Hudathans. But they're alone, vulnerable to space, and will soon be cut off."

The room was silent as the officers considered what those words meant. Not one, but dozens of Camerones, as the Legion died one outpost at a time.

St. James stood and brought his fist down on the table. "No! I won't allow it! The Legion will hold! And more than that, win! Are you with me?"

Vial watched his peers answer one by one.

Tran: "Of course."

Goodwin: "Count me in."

Legaux: "Damned right."

Jozan: "We have little choice, sir."

Jefferson: "The Legion is our country."

All eyes turned to Vial. He swallowed, forced a smile, and nodded his head. *"Vive la Légion!"*

He listened to their voices echo his and knew it was the right thing to say. But was it the right thing to do? What if the Legion lost? What if Scolari emerged triumphant? Only a fool cuts himself off from all possibility of retreat. No, Vial would consider the facts, make a plan, and put it to work.

"So," Tran said. "Now what?"

"Yes," Jozan agreed. "We need a plan. The transports are on the way. What shall we do when they arrive?"

General Ian St. James smiled wolfishly and looked around the table. "I suggest that we take the transports and use them to reinforce as many outposts as we can."

There was a brief moment of silence followed by delighted applause. St. James heard it and knew that the thousands who had gone before him had heard it too. The battle had begun.

The cyber tech pulled the last of the leads. "All right, give it a try."

Villain did as instructed. She sat up, swung her feet over the side of the rack, and stood. The Trooper II was brand-new. The interface felt crisp and responsive. All of the primary, secondary, and tertiary power systems worked, along with the feedback circuits and weapons systems.

"Take a few steps. Tell me if you detect any problems."

Villain walked over to a power-assisted workbench. The cyber tech wore an orange exoskeleton and paced along beside her.

"So? Whaddya think?"

Villain felt the power surge into and around her, gloried in the knowledge that she could destroy anything less than another cyborg, and gave the tech a massive thumbs-up. "It feels good. Very good."

The tech nodded his satisfaction. "You take care of that bod or answer to me."

Villain grinned inside, knowing she could kill the bio bod with one swipe of her hand, and chuckled. "Don't worry, corp. I'll treat this body as if my life depends on it."

The tech laughed, waved her off, and turned towards the long row of cyborgs that awaited his attention. Priority one, Priority one, Priority one, hell, the whole fraxin' bunch of them were classified Priority one. Damn the brass anyway. Always playin' games, screwin' things up, and passin' the blame. Bullshit, that's what it was, bullshit pure 'n' simple.

The hallways seemed busier than usual, and Villain thought that she detected some sort of underlying tension, as if trouble was on the way. An inspection? A Naa uprising? The Hudathans everyone talked about? There was no way to tell.

Well, it didn't matter a helluva lot, since soldiers do what they're told, and she'd been ordered to rejoin her unit. To do so, however, it would be necessary to kiss Dister's bio-bod ass and obtain his thumbprint. Assuming he could pull it out of his ass long enough to get the job done. Still, it would feel good to get clear of admin and back to the line, especially since that meant getting rid of Salazar, who, for reasons Villain couldn't quite put a finger on, never ceased to piss her off.

Maybe it was the straight-arrow way that he did things, the way he deferred to her over the smallest issues, or just his puppy-dog personality. But whatever it was would be left behind and that made her happy. Villain was humming by the time she reached the admin section.

It was busier than usual, with bio bods and cyborgs alike running in every direction. Something big was about to happen, that was for sure.

Villain wound her way through the computer section back to Dister's office. The diminutive noncom was on his way out the door. He had a printout clutched in his hand.

"Villain! Nice-looking bod. Congratulations." He waved the printout. "The loot wants this stuff and wants it now. Park your butt in my office. I'll be right back."

Villain stepped into Dister's office, ignored the bio-bod-sized furniture, and looked for something to do. The corporal's computer terminal had been activated. The words "Personnel Files" blinked on and off. Villain glanced around. Dister liked his privacy and kept the walls slightly opaque. She would look like little more than a smear to those outside.

The Trooper II's enormous digits made it difficult to type, but the cyborg corrected her mistakes as she made them and managed to enter her name. Information flooded the screen. Her real name, the way she had died, and her performance rating. All of it was there. The "highly competent" rating both surprised and pleased her.

She looked around. There was no sign of Dister and the people outside were little more than shadows. Working quickly, Villain pecked the name "Sal Salazar" into the computer. This time she was both shocked and amazed.

Sal Salazar had originally been known as Angel Perez, and it was *he* who had walked into the convenience store that day and pumped three bullets into her body. A host of conflicting emotions fought each other for dominance. Grief, rage, and an almost consuming need for revenge collided with each other, bounced away, and collided again.

A com line started to buzz. Dister! He would return any moment now. The thought jerked Villain back to reality, cleared the conflicting emotions from her head, and caused her to focus.

The com set continued to buzz as the Trooper II's sausage-like fingers moved from key to key. Salazar would be reassigned as well... but to which outfit? It was slow, agonizing work, but she found his next assignment. His body had arrived, and yes, he was slated to join the 1st REC, but as part of another company. That, Villain decided, would never do.

Hoping that Dister wouldn't choose that particular moment to appear, the cyborg changed the newbie's assignment to match her own. The error would be discovered, Villain knew, but not before Salazar had spent a week or two in the wrong outfit. By then, with the pragmatism of noncoms everywhere, Roller would arrange to keep him, since doing so would be easier all the way around.

The cyborg had just completed her work and stepped away from the terminal when Dister reappeared.

"Goddamned officers... sorry, Villain... you know the loot. Crazy Alice gave him some orders and the silly sonofabitch is running around like we're going to war or something. Now, let's put your transfer through and get your miserable butt outta here."

Villain heard the noncom ask her a series of questions and heard herself give the appropriate answers, but her attention was elsewhere. She imagined what it would feel like to get Salazar where she wanted him, to put a hole through his braincase. The thought pleased the cyborg and she smiled deep inside.

Ryber Hysook-Da stumbled as a Naa warrior jerked on the rope that had been tied around his neck. He caught himself, struggled to break the cord that bound his wrists behind his back, and was rewarded with a kick. The physical pain was negligible, but the psychological discomfort was so intense that the Hudathan feared he would pass out, and barely avoided doing so.

To be ambushed by barbarians and lose his entire command, that was bad enough. But to be dragged along the mountain path like a mind-wiped zook, that was an indignity beyond all imagining, and something he'd never forgive. No matter how hard the Naa begged, no matter what they offered to do, he'd never forgive them. Oh, they'd be sorry, all right, extremely sorry, when the Hudathan attack ships came down out of the sky.

The path passed between two pinnacles of rock, each topped by a heavily armed sentry, then widened out as it entered the village. Hysook-Da saw the dark circular shafts and remembered that the Naa lived underground, like ibble grubs, a fact that served to reinforce his contempt for them.

The furry bipeds were everywhere, boiling up out of the ground and appearing from between the rocks. They were pointing and gabbling in their native tongue. He knew the language rather well, thanks to the spy-eyes that had been insinuated into their villages months before, but he couldn't keep up with their speed. One thing was clear, however, and that was the fact that at least some of the barbarians said that he smelled bad, so bad that he shouldn't be admitted to the village. Those comments came mostly from juveniles, who were shushed by their parents and admonished to be more polite.

Then one of their leaders appeared, or Hysook-Da assumed the barbarian was a leader, because of the manner in which other adults hurried to get out of his way. He was large for his kind, had orange fur streaked with white, and wore a breech-cloth. A weapons harness crisscrossed the chieftain's chest and seemed barely capable of containing the muscles that rippled just under the surface of his skin. He approached the Hudathan without the slightest sign of fear and stood an arm's length away. His nose wrinkled slightly and twitched as his nostrils sealed themselves shut.

"My name is Ridelong Surekill. They tell me that you speak our language."

Hysook-Da felt his spirits lift. Finally! A leader with whom he could negotiate. He chose his words with care. Diplomacy must rule the moment. Revenge would come later.

"Yes, Excellency. I was sent to meet with you, to discuss the war now being fought, and to seek your support."

Surekill looked thoughtful. "I see. Well, come along, then. I will listen to what you say."

So saying, the Naa turned his back and walked away. A shove encouraged Hysook-Da to follow. The chieftain's words should have reassured him, should have put his fears to rest, but suddenly, for no reason that he could be sure of, the Hudathan was very much afraid.

Though curious about his destination, Booly was enjoying himself. It was dark and the next one-hour-and-twenty-one-minute day was more than an hour away.

But the sky was full of stars, Hardman led the way with a torch, and Windsweet walked by his side. The sight of her, the smell of her perfume, and the occasional touch of her arm were intoxicating.

The fact that her brother, Movefast Shootstraight, followed along behind did nothing to lessen the legionnaire's pleasure. No, the presence of a guard served to take him off the hook, to make escape impossible. That possibility had grown in importance as he had regained most of his strength and learned the lay of the land. Booly felt certain he could escape, had chosen to stay, and felt guilty about it. It was a problem that he'd have to face in the very near future. But that was tomorrow, or the day after, or given the multiplicity of days on Algeron, next week.

This was now and the legionnaire was determined to enjoy every moment of it.

The trail turned to the right and started upwards. Windsweet brushed against his shoulder. "What are you thinking?"

The words came in standard and carried very little accent. Windsweet had acquired a command of his language in a surprisingly short period of time. Booly appreciated both the effort she'd gone to and the privacy that his language afforded them.

"I was thinking about you, how beautiful you are, and how much I love you."

Her head jerked his way. "You mustn't say such things. They are—how do you say?—inappropriate."

"Why? They fill my heart and beg to be said."

"You are surprisingly expressive for a warrior. Are all humans so?"

Booly followed her through a narrow place in the trail and caught up again. "No, and neither am I. Not until I met you, that is."

Windsweet was silent for a moment. "I know it is wrong, and I will regret saying it, but I love you as well."

Booly felt his heart soar towards the stars that twinkled above and come crashing to the ground. She loved him and he could not stay. Both things were true and in conflict with each other. He wanted to talk to her about it, wanted to explain, but just then the path opened into a small valley.

The legionnaire saw the entry shafts typical of a Naa village, but realized that this one was smaller than Hardman's and a little more exposed. Flames leaped upwards from the ceremonial fire pit located at the village's center and backlit the fifty or sixty Naa who had gathered around its warmth. Before the flames died down again, the legionnaire saw something that made his blood run cold. A tripod had been erected over the fire pit, and something hung from that tripod, something that jerked and twisted in an effort to avoid the flames below it. He spoke and the words were Naa.

"Where are we? What are they doing?"

Windsweet looked at her father. He gestured with the torch. "Go ahead. Tell him."

Windsweet's expression was wooden, as if she had strong feelings but was struggling to hold them back. "They call this village 'Windswept,' because of the way that the wind swoops down from the hills, and Ridelong Surekill rules here as chief."

Booly absorbed that, knowing that Surekill had no affection for him, wondering as to the purpose of the visit.

"And the thing that hangs over the fire?"

Windsweet looked away. "There are ways, ancient ways, mostly forgotten. Many think they should be left to the past but some would bring them back."

The legionnaire started to speak, but stopped when Windsweet brought her hand to her mouth and touched her lips.

Warriors appeared from the dark and shouted greetings to Hardman, Windsweet, and Shootstraight. Surekill appeared, striding out of the darkness, placing an arm around Windsweet's shoulders. She frowned but allowed the arm to remain where it was.

The chieftain was in fine form, relishing his role as host and determined to make the most of it. "Wayfar! Movefast! Windsweet! Welcome to our village. Come, refreshments are waiting, and a dance performance like none you've seen before!"

Booly found himself swept along in the crowd, and while not treated to refreshments, occupied a place next to Surekill in front of the fire. Windsweet sat to the chieftain's left. Dooth-skin rugs had been spread for their comfort, incense hung heavy in the air, and firelight flickered in a dozen sets of eyes.

The thing, still suspended over the fire, squirmed and whimpered pitifully as the fire reached up to lick at the lowest portions of its anatomy.

"You see?" Surekill asked. "Just as I promised. A dance performance like none you've seen before!" The chieftain laughed, as did many of his warriors, but Hardman and Windsweet were silent.

The legionnaire had been allowed to keep some of the more harmless items of his gear. He felt for the flashlight, pulled it from a pocket, and turned it on. The thing was suspended in a wire net. It was doubled over, and therefore difficult to see, but Booly was able to make out leathery gray skin, a sauroid face, and a pair of fear-filled eyes. They blinked then closed as the smoke slid around them. Words hissed out of the thing's frog-like mouth and Booly realized that it was sentient. He spoke without thinking and realized that the others had been waiting for him to do so.

"What is it?"

"It calls itself a 'Hudathan,'" Surekill answered pleasantly. "A warrior named Ryber Hysook-Da, to be exact. He claims the status of subchief and came seeking an alliance with the Naa."

Booly looked up to where the Hudathan emissary swung over the fire. He'd met some aliens, and seen pictures of many more, but never one like this. "And you said no."

"Of course," Surekill replied matter-of-factly. "We have no need for allies. The Legion will fall to us... and to us alone."

The legionnaire looked Surekill in the eye and gestured towards the Hudathan. There was a void where his stomach should have been. "It wanted you to join an alliance against the human empire?"

Surekill spoke as to a cub. "Yes, human. That's what I said. The Hudathan claims that his race attacked yours, destroyed one of your most important planets, and will consume your entire empire. You were unaware of this?"

Booly forgot where he was and shook his head. A planet destroyed? What the hell was going on? The Emperor would fight—that went without saying—and the Legion would lead the way. He had to escape, had to make it back, had to join his unit. Surekill was waiting, and anger had gathered behind his eyes.

"This is news to me. I have never heard of the Hudathans, much less a war. It must have started very recently."

"Yes," Surekill said. "That agrees with what the smelly one told us. Now, seeing that the Hudathan is an enemy of your people, perhaps you would like the honor of lowering him into the pit?"

Hardman had been silent up until now. He cleared his throat, knowing that Surekill was likely to resent his words and take issue with them. He looked for and found encouragement in his daughter's eyes.

"Are you sure this is a good idea? The question of an alliance should rightfully go before the council of chiefs, and if you take it upon yourself to kill the alien, they will resent it."

Surekill wanted to hurl words at Hardman, wanted to say, "They? Or you? Which is it, old man? Which would resent my leadership more?" But he didn't. Nor was there a need to do so. He had anticipated the situation and made a plan to deal with it. He smiled disarmingly and did his best to sound reasonable.

"An excellent point, Wayfar. I admit to being a bit hasty at times, and…"

It was at that point that one of Surekill's most trusted warriors, Nevermiss Rockthrow, cut the rope that held the net aloft. Ryber Hysook-Da screamed as he fell into the pit, and screamed, and screamed, and screamed. His last thoughts were of how things should have been. This was not the way he had planned to die.

16

Words can be as lethal as bullets. Choose them carefully, aim them well, and use them sparingly.
IRULU BODA-SA
Hudathan mystic
Standard year 1414

With the Hudathan fleet off the Planet Frio ll, the Human Empire

The courier was little more than a pile of twisted metal. Bullet holes made a dotted line across a stubby wing. A gash, large enough for War Commander Niman Poseen-Ka to stick his arm through, marked the place where a piece of free-floating debris had hit the fuselage. Another hole, still plugged by a defective missile, signaled what should have been a death blow. The weapon had been disarmed and torches flared as technicians worked to remove it.

Once assigned to the battleship *World Taker*, the courier had survived the destruction of its mother ship and made its way to the main fleet, because, unlike fighters and troop carriers, couriers were equipped with hyperspace drives and were capable of interstellar travel.

Poseen-Ka circled the vessel, careful to step over a multiplicity of tools, hoses, and loose parts. His hands were clasped behind his back, his head was tilted back as far as it would go, and his eyes probed the wreck like lasers.

His aide, a junior officer named Ikna Kona-Sa, did likewise, walking the same way that his superior did, mimicking his mannerisms. Poseen-Ka was unaware of this, just as he was largely unaware of the landing bay itself or the ship that it was part of. His attention was on the scout and the news that had arrived with it.

The fact that the pilot had managed to ram the crippled ship through hyperspace, find the fleet, and land was absolutely amazing. Yes, the flight officer would receive the highest honors that the Hudathan military could bestow upon him, in spite of the fact that he had brought bad news rather than good.

It seemed that Spear Three, under the command of Ikor Niber-Ba, had been attacked and completely destroyed. It was terrible news. He should have been sad, angry, anything but satisfied. Yet the word "satisfaction" best described the way he felt.

The war against the humans had been *too* pat, *too* easy. Where others had seen victory he had seen the threat of defeat. There is, after all, a difference between *winning* a victory and gaining one through default. That was what the Hudathan forces had managed to accomplish so far. Because in spite of the often heroic resistance offered by military units left behind, and civilians as well, their navy had refused to engage in anything more than a skirmish or two. Why?

It could mean that the humans were weaker than they appeared, and would surrender their empire one system at a time, or, and Poseen-Ka considered this possibility more likely, that they had sacrificed some of their less important holdings in order to buy time. Time that would allow them to consolidate their forces and prepare their own Intaka, which, coming as a surprise, would be all the more powerful. That was the source of Poseen-Ka's satisfaction. The loss of Spear Three had clearly demonstrated that the humans *could* fight, *would* fight, if given the right situation, and were extremely dangerous when they did so. Especially considering that Niber-Ba had attacked what was primarily a civilian target and lost his entire command.

But that was *his* interpretation of the facts, *his* analysis of the situation, and others would sit in judgment of him: individuals such as his superior, Grand Marshal Pem-Da, his chief of staff, Lance Commander Moder-Ta, and yes, the human known as Baldwin, who in spite of his nonexistent rank had the power to influence minds by virtue of who and what he was.

All had their own hopes, fears, and motivations, motivations not necessarily aligned with his and therefore threatening. The destruction of Spear Three would present them with the perfect opportunity to replace him with someone more to their liking, since a loss of that magnitude necessitated a court of inquiry.

They were routine affairs for the most part... but not always. No, there were the cases of incompetence that such investigations had been designed to ferret out, the situations in which bad luck and the friction of war had conspired to ruin someone's career, or worse, times when politics entered the picture, and routine investigations were used to remove officers with unpopular opinions.

Given the fact that Poseen-Ka had counseled patience and stalled for time, when many wanted to leap down the enemy's throat, he was vulnerable to criticism.

The court would point out that Niber-Ba had failed to administer the Intaka, and by not doing so, had given the humans the opportunity to prepare a counterattack. The similarity between the Dwarf's approach and his own was too clear to deny. Had his subordinate knowingly followed his example? And picked the wrong moment to do so? Or had *he* erred by giving command of Spear Three to an officer so much like himself? Had he made other mistakes as well? Mistakes that were waiting to make themselves known.

Poseen-Ka felt himself start the slide down towards depression. No! He pushed the feelings away. To doubt, to fear, to become entangled in all the possibilities, would lead to his defeat as surely as a bullet through the head.

No, he must do something positive, find evidence that his strategy was correct, and present that evidence to his superiors. Poseen-Ka tore his eyes off the wreck, waved to his aide, and headed for the lock. The human female had proven herself useful once before. She might again.

* * *

Colonel Natalie Norwood had just finished doing her thirty push-ups and was about to do some deep knee bends when the door to her cell vanished into the overhead. A Hudathan filled the entryway. Bodyguards stood behind him. There was no mistaking the fact that the visitor was War Commander Niman Poseen-Ka himself.

Alarmed but determined not to show it, Norwood folded her arms. She was dressed, thank god, but something less than presentable. Not that it mattered, since Poseen-Ka had no way to know if she was presentable or not.

"Don't you people ever knock?"

Words formed on the Hudathan's tongue and waited to be said. They were stern and would put the prisoner in her place. He held them back. He needed the human's cooperation, and interpersonal conflict was an unlikely way to achieve it.

"I am sorry. Your norms are strange to me and I forgot."

Surprised by the war commander's apology, and a bit taken aback, Norwood gestured for him to enter. The Hudathan's bodyguards started to follow but he waved them back.

Poseen-Ka looked around, saw the wire mesh that had been installed to keep the human out of the ductwork, and sat on the fold-down bunk. It creaked under his considerable weight.

"You know where we are?" he asked.

"In orbit around a planet called Frio II."

"That is correct. And what, if anything, do you know about the fighting here?"

Norwood shrugged. Her voice was tight with emotion. "You arrived, found the place largely undefended, and went to work on exterminating the population. There were thousands of ships in orbit, refugees from planets you had already taken, and they were easy meat for your fighters. Your pilots used them for target practice, popping them like inflatable toys, laughing while they died.

"Then, with nothing left in orbit, you went to the ground. Frio II was only lightly populated, so there was no need to use overlapping swathes of destruction as you did on Worber's World, so you attacked individual towns and cities instead.

These proved more difficult than anticipated, however, due to the harsh surface conditions and the fact that the habitats were largely underground."

If Norwood expected some sign of sorrow, some sign of remorse, she was sadly disappointed.

"A military installation still exists."

Norwood brightened a little. "Really? That's wonderful. I hope they kick your oversized butts."

Poseen-Ka seemed oblivious to the insult and made a gesture she didn't understand. "There is little possibility of that. We control the system, the space around the planet, and for all practical purposes the planet itself."

Norwood's hands started to shake. She shoved them into her pockets. "Well, goody for you. So why the visit?"

Poseen-Ka stood. He towered over her, but there was something in his eyes, something she couldn't quite put a finger on. Understanding? Compassion? Fear? Whatever it was made him less intimidating.

"I need your help."

Norwood looked up at the alien trying to see if he was serious. "You've got to be kidding."

"No, I am absolutely serious."

"Never."

"You helped with the phytoplankton."

"That was different."

"As is this."

Norwood searched Poseen-Ka's face, looked for some sign of what the alien was thinking, and found nothing. "What would you have me do?"

"Convince some humans to surrender."

"So you can murder them? Never!"

"I will allow them to live."

"So you say."

"I give you my word."

"Screw your word. Have Baldwin do it. That's what you pay him for."

"I don't trust Baldwin."

The words were so honest, and so unexpected, that it took a

moment to understand and absorb them. Poseen-Ka was truly asking her for a favor, taking her into his confidence, offering some sort of friendship. But why? Was it real? Or a trick? She looked up into his eyes. "Why?"

"Because he is a traitor and cares only for himself."

Norwood sensed he was telling the truth. She also sensed that there was more truth to tell. "And?"

"And he sides against me."

"In what way?"

The alien made a motion with his hands. "He, like many of my superiors, feels that I should bypass planets like the one below and strike at the heart of the human empire."

Norwood felt a sense of excitement, as if she was close to learning something very important, and worked to keep her face impassive. "And you?"

"I think that your superiors could be preparing a trap for us, and even if they aren't, could find a way to take advantage of the unsecured systems that we left behind."

Norwood nodded. "So you want to take more time, secure planets like Frio II, and attack the inner planets after that."

"Exactly."

Norwood frowned. "I still don't understand. How would I help? And why should I do so?"

The alien was silent for a moment as if choosing his words with care. "I need evidence that your superiors are preparing a trap for us. Evidence I can use to defend my strategy. But your soldiers have orders to destroy such information before they die."

"Really?" Norwood asked sarcastically. "How rude. And you expect me to help? Well, forget it. That would be treasonous."

"Would it?" Poseen-Ka asked. "Would it be treasonous to save human lives? Especially in light of the fact that they have already been sacrificed? Left behind to delay us, or worse yet, because no one cares? Surely you have wondered. Where is your navy? Why do they run before us? When will they fight? All I ask is a chance to examine some records. I am willing to give hundreds of lives in return."

Norwood struggled to deal with her emotions. She *had* asked herself those questions, not once, but hundreds of times.

It was clear that something was wrong, terribly wrong, but what? Why had the Navy withdrawn? Was it part of a plan, or just massive incompetence on an Imperial scale? She wanted to believe the first possibility, but feared the second, and found herself in a terrible position.

Assuming the defenders were willing to surrender and provided her with the information that Poseen-Ka wanted, what then?

If there was a trap, or the likelihood of one, Poseen-Ka would continue his present strategy of destroying the human empire one system at a time. If there was no trap, and Poseen-Ka lost his command, or was forced to adopt a more aggressive strategy, the Hudathans would strike at the heart of the empire, an attack that would almost surely cost millions, if not billions, of lives.

Measured in terms of casualties, it seemed as if Poseen-Ka's strategy of steady attrition would be better for the human race, allowing as it did for some sort of counterattack.

So, by helping Poseen-Ka, she might help the war effort. But what if she was wrong? What if her decision cost billions of innocent lives?

The easy answer was no, because that was the answer that her training had prepared her to give, and she was fundamentally opposed to helping the Hudathans in any way. But what of the lives she could save?

Sweat covered Norwood's forehead as she replied.

"I'll help under the following conditions: that you will accept the surrender of every human on the planet, that you will feed and house them appropriately, and that you will forswear all use of torture."

The Hudathan made a motion with his right hand. "Done. It shall be as you say."

Norwood shook her head. "No, I haven't finished yet. I reserve the right to tell others about our conversation and why I agreed to help you."

Poseen-Ka thought for a moment. "Humans, yes... but Hudathans, no... and that includes Baldwin."

Norwood nodded. "Fair enough... and one other thing."

The Hudathan looked stern. "I warn you, human. I grow weary of your demands."

Norwood shrugged. "Promise you won't connect me to your machines. Sex is nice… but the session after my visit with the phytoplankton damned near killed me. A sincere 'thanks' is reward enough."

"It shall be as you say. Prepare for a trip to the surface. We depart one subperiod from now."

The Hudathan left, the hatch hissed downwards, and Norwood was left to contemplate what she'd done.

The cabin was large by shipboard standards, befitting someone of Lance Commander Moder-Ta's rank, and Baldwin felt his heart thump against his chest. Why had he been summoned? What did the Hudathan want? A hundred questions jostled each other looking for answers. He rose as the officer entered the compartment and sat in a fold-down chair.

Moder-Ta was big, but not as large as Poseen-Ka, and wore a large blue gem in his weapons harness. His eyes were like stones, black and unyielding. The skin along one side of his head was furrowed and ridged where a blaster bolt had come within a hairsbreadth of taking his life. His mouth, thin-lipped like a frog's, formed a line across his face.

"You may sit."

Baldwin sat.

"So," Moder-Ta began expressionlessly, "you heard about the courier? About the Dwarf's defeat?"

Baldwin frowned. "The Dwarf?"

"Spear Commander Ikor Niber-Ba."

"Thank you. That is to say yes, I heard about his defeat."

"And your opinion?"

A lump had formed in Baldwin's throat. He forced it down. "Humans can be ingenious when cornered. Had Commander Niber-Ba struck quickly, and done so with overwhelming force, he would've won."

Baldwin held his breath. He had taken the chance and said what he really thought. How would it be received?

There was a long silence while Moder-Ta looked through him to the bulkhead beyond. The answer, when it came, was all Baldwin could have hoped for.

"Yes, human. I agree with you, and more importantly, so does Grand Marshal Pem-Da. Tell me, what do you think of our strategy overall?"

Baldwin felt a sense of joy bubble up from deep within. It could be a trick, could be an attempt to set him up, but he didn't think so. No, the message was clear. Moder-Ta thought that Poseen-Ka was in the process of committing the same error that Niber-Ba had, and wanted Baldwin to confirm that opinion. And, knowing that the Hudathan had Grand Marshal Pem-Da's support, the human would be foolish to do otherwise. He spread his hands before him.

"I fear that the fleet could fall into the same trap that destroyed Spear Three. We should strike for the heart of the empire, and do it now, before they are ready to receive us."

"Well said," Moder-Ta hissed. "Well said indeed. Now, answer me this… Would you be willing to testify to that? Even if it meant going against War Commander Poseen-Ka's interest?"

A sense of caution rose to replace the excitement that Baldwin had previously felt. "Testify?"

"Yes. The loss of Spear Three necessitates an investigation. The war commander will be asked to explain and justify his actions."

A variety of thoughts churned through Baldwin's mind. This amounted to a court-martial. Of course! Moder-Ta opposed his superior, and more than that, wanted his position. Baldwin's testimony, added to whatever else the chief of staff had up his sleeve, could bring Poseen-Ka to his knees. It made perfect sense. But was it in his, Baldwin's, best interests? What if Poseen-Ka was exonerated? What then?

"Well?"

Moder-Ta wanted an answer.

Baldwin steeled himself.

"Yes, I would testify as to my opinion, even if that testimony ran counter to the war commander's interests."

"Excellent," Moder-Ta hissed. "You won't be sorry."

* * *

Some bio bods had built a fire in a corner of what had been the admin offices. The resulting smoke had a tendency to gather near the ceiling before making its way through the makeshift chimney.

There were many schools of thought as to what burned best, but Major Ralph Hoskins favored the nice thick manuals provided by the idiots on Algeron, since they were extremely dry and made violet-colored flames.

He grabbed one, saw that the title had something to do with quarterly fitness reports, and threw it into the fire. Flames licked up and around it, turned the cover brown, and danced upwards. Hoskins removed his gloves and held his hands towards the heat. It was cold, barely above freezing, and had been for days. The bozos who had designed the base had relied on a civilian fusion plant for power and he was paying the price for their stupidity. The plant, like the city it served, had been destroyed during the first few hours of fighting. He heard movement behind him.

"Major Hoskins?"

The voice belonged to Sergeant Ayers.

"Yeah?"

"The geeks sent an emissary with a white flag."

A part of Hoskins's mind wondered how the aliens knew what a white flag signified and another part didn't give a shit. He was tired, very tired, and not in the mood for puzzles.

"So? Shoot the bastard and grab the flag. Doc's running short on bandages."

"This bastard is a woman, sir, a colonel, and she claims to be from Worber's World."

Hoskins turned his back to the fire. Ayers was almost unrecognizable under multiple layers of clothes. The winter-white outer shell wasn't so white anymore. A red splotch marked the spot where she had taken a round through her left biceps.

"That's impossible. Worber's got waxed early on. There were no survivors."

Ayers shrugged. Her clothing barely moved. "Yes, sir."

Hoskins groaned. The situation was bad enough without stray colonels wandering around. "She got any geeks with her?"

"No, sir. Not close by anyhow."

"I'm coming. Jeez. Can't a guy take a break around here?"

Ayers shook her head sympathetically. "That's the Legion for you, sir. If it ain't one thing it's another."

Hoskins zipped his jacket to the neck, shoved his partially warmed hands into his pockets, and made for the emergency exit. The power lifts had gone belly-up along with everything else.

Hoskins opened the steel fire door, waited for an in-bound patrol to clatter past, and started upwards. The stairs were thick with half-frozen mud, trash, and empty shell casings, leftovers from the night the geek commandos had penetrated the perimeter and made their way inside. Something of a mistake since they had ran right smack-dab into a pair of Trooper IIs.

He hadn't slept for two rotations and had four flights of stairs to climb, so Hoskins was puffing by the time he reached the surface. Plumes of lung-warmed air jetted out to meld with colder stuff around him. He paused by the main doors, nodded to the cyborgs on duty, and received their salutes in reply.

"Going for a stroll, sir?"

"Yeah, I thought I'd slip out for a nice cold beer."

The borgs laughed and opened the blastproof door. It made a screeching noise as it slid out of the way. Bitterly cold air and driving snowflakes bit at the officer's face as he stepped outside.

The base had been dug into a low hill, one of the few things the engineers had done right, and commanded a 360-degree view of the fields that surrounded it. They were white with new-fallen snow. It hid the bodies that no one had the energy to bury and granted the base a beauty it didn't deserve. The city of Loport appeared and disappeared through the snow, its blackened spires pointing accusingly towards the sky, its citizens buried under heat-fused concrete. The horror of it was so immense, so appalling, that Hoskins couldn't get his mind around it.

Lieutenant Marvin Matatu materialized out of the snow. The hood, goggles, and scarf obscured everything but a narrow band of brown skin that ran from one cheek to the other.

"Major."

"Lieutenant."

"Did Ayers find you?"

"Yeah. What's this flag of truce crap?"

"Beats me, sir. Shall we bring her in?"

"Can we see her from here?"

"Yes, sir. Straight out and about thirty feet to the left. Next to the burned-out APC."

Hoskins accepted the binoculars, felt the cold bite his hands, and zoomed in. The APC had been destroyed on day one. Less than four days ago but it seemed like a month. He panned left, found a snowsuit, and stopped. The woman stood at parade rest with a staff in her right hand. The flag was white and snapped in the breeze. Her hood had been thrown back to expose her face, and he was struck by the fact that she looked pretty, and very, very cold. Hoskins handed the glasses to Matatu and jammed his hands into his pockets.

"How did she contact us?"

"On freq four, sir. She knows radio procedure backwards and forwards."

"And she claims to be from Worber's World?"

"That's affirmative, sir."

"All right, Marv. Run a body scan on her, bring her in, and tell Ayers to strip-search her. If she's bent, blow her head off."

"Yes, sir."

Norwood had just about decided to give up, to turn around and hike back to the waiting Hudathans, when the transmission came over freq 4.

"Stay where you are. An escort will bring you in."

The snowflakes were falling more thickly now, circling her like butterflies trying to land, pulling the sky down to the ground. That was good because the less she saw of Frio's tortured surface, the better.

The legionnaires seemed to materialize out of the ground in front of her. They wore snow-white parkas, green berets, and the winged-hand-and-dagger emblem of the famed 2nd REP. Four of them faced outwards, guarding against attack, while a fifth ran a scanner over her entire body.

Norwood stood completely still, controlling the words that wanted to come pouring out, filled with pride. These men and women had held, and held, and held, and were still holding against impossible odds. Stripped of the support they were entitled to, standing against an entire spear, they had held. Oh, how she longed to grab a gun, to stand beside them, to fight a battle she could understand.

The legionnaire with the scanner nodded to the others and made the device disappear.

"All right," a corporal said. "You're clean. Follow Baji and be damned sure to put your feet exactly where he does. There are mines all around us."

Norwood did as she was told, pausing for a second as they passed a Trooper II, its gigantic form spreadeagle in the snow. A shoulder-launched missile had taken the cyborg's head off. Time had passed, and the heat from the Trooper II's body had melted the surrounding snow and lowered the creature into a temporary grave. A thin crust of snow had already formed on the cyborg's chest and would eventually hide it from view.

She was still thinking about the cyborg as they led her past a hastily built barricade, through a maze of sandbags, and up to the installation's main entrance.

There a sergeant named Ayers took over. She was pleasant but firm and had some legionnaires to back her up. Both were women. They took Norwood into an unheated storage room where she was ordered to strip and grab her ankles. The cavity search was far more humiliating than anything the Hudathans had done to her.

When it was over, Ayers pulled the rubber gloves off, nodded towards her clothing, and said, "Sorry, Colonel. You can get dressed now."

Norwood struggled to keep her composure, but knew she was blushing, and hated the legionnaires with every fiber of her being.

They led her down some muddy stairs, through a fire door, and into an office. Smoke swirled above her head, drifted towards a makeshift chimney, and disappeared. A fire burned in one corner of the room. She saw a tall, somewhat stooped officer throw a binder on the blaze, stand, and turn her way. He had a long homely face and inquisitive eyes. Stubble covered his cheeks and he looked tired.

"Colonel Norwood, I believe? My name's Hoskins. Major Ralph Hoskins, Imperial Legion, 5th REI. Welcome to IMPLEG

Outpost 479. Sorry I can't offer something more in the way of hospitality, but the O club is temporarily closed."

Norwood grinned in spite of herself. It felt good to be in the presence of a regular human being again. His hand was at least a couple of degrees warmer than hers and guided her towards the fire.

"Sorry about the search, but the geeks are clever, and try new things on us all the time."

Norwood started to reply but stopped when Hoskins waved a .50 recoilless in her direction.

"One more thing, Colonel. I haven't got a lot of time to screw around, so tell the truth, or I'll blow your brains all over the fraxing wall."

The smile had never left Hoskins's face, and while Norwood believed every word the officer had said, she liked him nonetheless. She nodded, accepted a seat in front of the fire, and started her story. It took the better part of an hour to tell. All the while Hoskins listened attentively, asked intelligent questions, and stoked the fire.

Norwood told Hoskins everything, right down to the doubts she had about what she was doing, and the possibility that she was a well-intentioned traitor.

Both were silent for a long time afterwards. The legionnaire spoke first.

"Well, I'll say this much for you, colonel: you're either one helluva liar or one of the most amazing officers it's been my pleasure to meet."

"Thanks, I think."

Hoskins smiled. "So, here's a sitrep. I have fifty-six effectives, seven of whom are Trooper IIs, which nearly doubles our firepower but doesn't make much difference in the long run. The Hudathans can clean our clock anytime they want to, and if it wasn't for this Poseen-Ka fella, would've done so by now. I know it and you know it. Ever hear of a battle called 'Camerone'?"

Norwood shook her head.

"No? Well, it's a big deal in the Legion. Sort of Masada, the Alamo, and the Battle of Four Moons all rolled into one. What it boils down to is that this guy named Danjou stumbled into some

Mexicans, was outnumbered thousands to one, and refused to surrender. He was killed, as were most of his men, and that's the way legionnaires are supposed to go."

Norwood frowned. "Surely there was more. A purpose, a reason, an objective."

Hoskins shook his head. "Nope. Nothing more than pride, glory, and honor. Danjou and his men died for nothing. And that, my friend, is both the horror and the beauty of it."

Norwood nodded slowly. "So what are you telling me? That you'll hold to the end? Die rather than surrender?"

Hoskins shrugged. "I don't know. You say the Hudathans will accept our surrender. Do you believe them?"

"Yes, I believe Poseen-Ka."

"But what if he loses his command? What then?"

Norwood looked him in the eye. "I don't know."

Hoskins was silent for a moment.

"I have what he wants, or something very close to it."

Norwood felt her heart beat a tiny bit faster. "You do?"

"Yes. I have a set of orders from IMPNAV Earth, ordering me to withdraw, and another set from Legion headquarters on Algeron, ordering me to stay. The second set arrived just before the Navy pulled out. I kept them in case I live long enough to get court-martialed."

"So," Norwood said slowly, "we can't be absolutely sure, but it sounds as if Poseen-Ka is correct and they're laying a trap for him. More than that it sounds as if the Legion disagrees with that strategy, and has mutinied."

"Exactly," Hoskins agreed, throwing the remains of his coffee against an already stained picture of the Emperor. "Which leaves me in a rather interesting position."

"You can die a glorious death, or surrender and hope that Poseen-Ka remains in command."

"Knowing that he'll kill thousands, if not millions, of people."

"Better millions than billions."

"Shit."

"Yeah."

Hoskins stuck out his hand. "I'm with you, Colonel. Here's hoping that we're right... and god help us if we aren't."

17

There is no retreat, but in submission and slavery. Our chains are forged.
Their clanking may be heard on the plains of Boston! The war is inevitable—
and let it come! I repeat it, sir, let it come!

PATRICK HENRY, AMERICAN PATRIOT

Standard year 1775

Planet Earth, the Human Empire

Sergi Chien-Chu was naked. The bright lights nearly blinded him. He tried to suck his stomach in but couldn't. He started to say something, but the technician, an attractive young lady in her twenties, motioned for silence. She was naked too, a fact that threatened to cause an involuntary reaction, and made him blush.

The merchant closed his eyes as the woman dropped to her knees, pulled a pair of IR-sensitive goggles down over her eyes, and aimed a pair of tweezers at his pubic hair.

Had Chien-Chu known, or even dreamed, that participation in the Cabal would require this level of personal sacrifice, he would have refused to join. But it was too late now.

Even microbots generate warmth and this one appeared as a luminescent yellow dot against the light green of Chien-Chu's body heat. The technician held the merchant's penis out of the way, closed her electronic forceps around the tiny machine, and removed it from the forest of gray and black pubic hair. She stood and held the offending machine up to the light.

In spite of the fact that the robot was smaller than a piece of lint and almost invisible to the naked eye, it was capable of recording and retransmitting conversations up to fifty feet away. How it had found its way into his pubic hair he had no idea. There was little doubt about *who* had put it there, however. The Emperor's security apparatus was legendary, and given the evidence now before his eyes, could literally reach anywhere.

"You can talk now. The forceps and the equipment they're connected to function as a transducer. The bug thinks you're watching a routine biz vid on changes in the precious metals markets."

"Great," Chien-Chu said, fighting to keep his belly in. "May I dress now?"

The technician placed the microbot, one of three she had found on and about Chien-Chu's person, into a specially designed black box and sealed the lid. She had a rather nicely proportioned posterior and the merchant found it hard to ignore.

"Yes, a robe has been provided for your comfort. But there's no point in putting your clothes on, since I will reintroduce the microbots as you leave. The people who put them there would be suspicious otherwise and double their efforts to keep an eye on your activities."

Chien-Chu sighed and reached for the robe. There had been a time when he looked forward to getting naked with attractive young women but the circumstances had been considerably different.

The robe was white, with dusty blue vertical stripes, and fit as though it had been made just for him, which knowing Madam Dasser it probably had. This was no gathering of wild-eyed revolutionaries, but a meeting of influential people, all of whom expected and were used to having the very best. The merchant pulled the robe on, tied the belt around his considerable waist, and turned towards the young woman. She had a wonderful pair of breasts.

"Thank you for the help."

The woman smiled brightly as if nothing could be more normal. "Think nothing of it. It was my pleasure."

Chien-Chu doubted that, but felt no desire to debate the point, and headed for the door. He was almost there when she spoke again.

"Mr. Chien-Chu?"

He turned. "Yes?"

"You might want to shave your pubic hair. Especially if you plan to do this sort of thing on a frequent basis. It makes the bugs easier to find."

The merchant nodded, offered what he hoped was an appreciative smile, and left the room.

The country villa, for that was what it appeared to be, was beautiful, if somewhat improbable. Though brought by limo, and unable to see out through darkened windows, the merchant had been allowed to keep his wrist term and knew that the ride had been far too short to reach the city limits, much less the country. Still, the whitewashed walls, earthen-tile floors, luxuriant plants, and high-vaulted ceilings were everything that a villa should be and more. The fact that the windows were fake, and looked out on scenery that was thousands of miles away, did nothing to lessen the effect. The hall carried him to a short flight of stairs and down into a sitting area, filled with people. The bamboo furniture had overstuffed cushions and a floral motif. He was the last person to arrive and the others rose to greet him. All wore robes similar to his. Madam Dasser performed the introductions.

"Hello, Sergi, I'm so glad you could make it! You know Ari Goss? Of Goss Shipping? And Zorana Zikos, of Zikos Manufacturing?"

The list went on and on, until Chien-Chu had met or been reintroduced to about thirty people, all of whom were movers and shakers, and many of whom came as a complete surprise.

Seeing his coconspirators, and knowing the risks they had taken to be there, did a great deal to improve the merchant's morale. Like him, most of them had made a pretty penny from the status quo and were unlikely to support change for change's sake. No, these were hardheaded business people, out to protect their own interests, yes, but capable of looking to the greater good as well. Or so he hoped.

With the introductions complete they all took their seats. Madam Dasser allowed her eyes to roam the room.

"Before we begin, I'd like to take a moment to tell Sergi how sorry I was to hear about the death of his son. The price of victory was terribly high, but it's the only one we have so far, and it shines like a beacon in a sea of darkness. Sergi, I'm sure that everyone here shares in your grief and is willing to help. You have only to ask."

The words demanded a speech, or a comment of some kind, and Chien-Chu had nothing prepared. That Leonid was really dead, blown to atoms while defending what amounted to expensive glitter, had changed his outlook on life. Money seemed less important now, as did the things that it could buy and the possessions that he had accumulated.

Chien-Chu had already been committed to a meeting with the Cabal when the news of his son's death had spurred him on. He felt a desperate need to give the tragedy some sort of meaning, to transmute the loss into a gain, if not for him then for others.

Chien-Chu found his grief and used it to empower his words. He stood to tell them what he felt, and more than that, what he hoped.

"Thank you, Madam Dasser. I will convey your condolences to my wife and daughter-in-law. My son's untimely death makes me all the more determined to fight the Hudatha *before* they reach the center of our empire. I salute each and every one of you for having the vision to see… and the courage to act. The Hudathans represent a very real danger.

"But as I look around this room I see an even greater danger. The danger that we will create still another government by the few, for the few. The danger is inherent in our wealth, positions, power, and yes, the nature of our race. We are a selfish lot, much given to our own interests, and careless of others. The only thing that can overcome this danger is a unanimous commitment to something higher.

"I speak of a government that represents the people, that protects them from harm, that opposes rather than fosters evil. It is *that* goal to which I am drawn, *that* ideal to which I pledge my fortune, and *that* possibility for which I would sacrifice my life."

There was a brief moment of silence followed by enthusiastic applause. Madam Dasser beamed her happiness, stood, and held up a hand.

"I think you can see why I wanted Sergi to join our group. Now, recognizing that each group needs a leader, I would like to nominate Sergi Chien-Chu. Is there a second?"

There was, and the proposal was approved by a unanimous vote. The merchant knew he'd been set up, knew that Madam Dasser had lined up most of the votes ahead of time, but didn't mind. He wanted to take action against the Hudatha and was willing to do whatever it took to get the job done.

So when the voting was over, and all eyes rested on him, Chien-Chu took control of the meeting. He knew it was a significant moment in his life, this transformation from merchant to politician, but it felt no different from the hundreds of business meetings that he'd chaired as head of Chien-Chu Enterprises.

"Thanks for the vote of confidence... although you may decide to rescind it before this meeting is over."

There were the proper number of "nevers," "oh nos," and amused chuckles, but the merchant was quite serious. He knew talk was cheap, and that some of them would balk, or actually rebel, when it came time to make a personal sacrifice.

But that problem lay ahead. The first task was to devise a strategy, build support for it, and identify tactics by which he could make it happen.

The next four hours were spent in sometimes heated discussion from which a strategy eventually emerged. The approach they agreed on was almost identical to the one that Chien-Chu had visualized from the very beginning, but served to take everyone through the logic involved, and resulted in a much higher level of buy-in.

"So," Chien-Chu summarized, "we're agreed that the Hudathans must be stopped, and that to accomplish that, it will first be necessary to remove the Emperor."

His words brought nods of agreement and long solemn looks, for this was the stuff of treason, and one traitor in their midst, or one undiscovered bug, could result in imprisonment or even death for all of them. Chien-Chu continued.

"Given the fact that we are not an especially bloodthirsty

group, and lack the means to get an assassin past the Emperor's security apparatus, it seems better to overthrow rather than assassinate him."

"That's just great," Zikos replied, her artificially tight skin furrowed with uncharacteristic wrinkles, "but how?"

Chien-Chu smiled. "How indeed? Remember what I said? That you might want to replace me with someone else? Well, now you learn why. Unlike revolutionaries of the past, we already have a highly disciplined, well-equipped army at our disposal."

"The Legion," Madam Dasser said thoughtfully.

"Exactly," Chien-Chu replied.

"But they're in prison," Goss objected, crossing and recrossing his long hairy legs.

"Some are," Chien-Chu agreed, "but some aren't. What about the legionnaires on Algeron? Will they board Admiral Scolari's transports? Knowing that they'll be sacrificed, or worse from their point of view, absorbed into the Marine Corps? I think not. As for those on Earth, the answer's simple: we'll free them."

"But how?" Senator Chang Yu asked.

"By force of arms," Chien-Chu replied. "Except for you, and one or two others in the room, the rest of us control companies with highly trained paramilitary security forces. Properly armed, coordinated, and led, they will free General Mosby's forces from prison."

"What about the possibility that some of them might inform on us?" Susan Rothenberg, of A-roid Mining, inquired.

Chien-Chu shrugged. "We'll invent a cover story to explain the need for special training and coordination between our companies. In the meantime I suggest that all of you sift your personnel for government agents. That process has already begun within Chien-Chu Enterprises."

"Excellent," Madam Dasser said approvingly. "Just excellent."

"And then?" Zikos asked.

"And then we strike at the palace, seize control, and replace Admiral Scolari with a more aggressive officer. The Navy will head for the rim, find the enemy, and engage them."

Goss flicked an imaginary piece of lint off the sleeve of his burgundy-striped robe.

"But what happens in the meantime? It will take time to accomplish what you propose… and millions could die. To say nothing of our holdings along the rim."

"That's very true," Chien-Chu said calmly. "Which is why we must mobilize our ships, load them with supplies, and reinforce those worlds that still have a chance."

"That would cost billions!" Rothenberg exploded. "We'd be bankrupt long before it was over!"

"Possibly," Chien-Chu replied calmly. "But what happens if we don't reinforce them? What of A-roid's holdings along the rim? What of your employees? What of your family should the Hudathans make it this far? What are they worth?"

There was silence for a moment. Madam Dasser was the next to speak.

"Sergi's right. Dasser Industries makes roughly twenty percent of the munitions used by both the Marine Corps and the Legion. Every ship we have will load and lift as soon as possible."

Chien-Chu nodded his agreement. "My company will do the same." He turned towards Susan Rothenberg. The robe made her look like a frumpy housewife. "But you raise a good point, Susan. Someone should track the expense involved, and assuming that we win, petition the next government for compensation. Would you be willing to take charge of that effort?"

It was apparent from the emphatic nodding of the industrialist's head that she would.

Chien-Chu looked around the room. They were with him and the time had come to deal with tactics.

"Good. Now that we have a strategy in place, let's get down to brass tacks."

The succeeding eight hours were some of the most difficult in the merchant's long and varied life.

The commandant didn't like the Legion and never had. Maybe it was their snobby nose-in-the-air-my-shit-don't-stink ways, or maybe it was the fact that he'd spent twenty-three years in the Marine Corps, or maybe he was just a mean old bastard like his wife claimed.

Whatever the reason, Commandant Wendell T. "for tough shit" Gavin loved to see legionnaires sweat. And, since it was their day to "walk the wall," there'd be enough sweat to plant crops on the parade ground, or "grinder" as the prisoners called it.

Grinning with anticipation, Gavin stepped out of his air-conditioned office into the noonday heat. The thermometer by the door read 115°F and would climb at least five degrees in the next hour. That was the beauty of locating the military prison in the middle of Death Valley. The name fit and the temperature was part of the punishment.

The balcony was a small affair, similar to the one that the Pope used in the Vatican, except that the pontiff tried to comfort her flock, and Gavin liked to torture his.

The commandant took two steps forward, made sure that his brass belt buckle was centered over the railing, and clasped his hands behind his back. The grinder was exactly one mile long and one mile wide. A cube of what looked like solid rock stood at the west end of the space. It was located almost directly under Gavin's boots. Nearly six thousand khaki-clad men and women were arrayed in front of it. They stood at parade rest, eyes forward, kepis gleaming in the sun.

Guards were visible here and there, towering over the legionnaires on their bright orange exoskeletons, watching for signs of rebellion.

Staff and prisoners alike looked up through the heat-induced haze, saw the commandant appear, and waited for the signal. A minute passed. Another followed. Heat rose from the pavement in waves. Gavin seemed to waver, disappear, and come back again.

Finally they saw it, the tiny nod that brought a corporal through the door and put an iced lemonade in Gavin's right hand. He raised it like an ironic salute, held it there until their throats ached, and took a long, slow drink.

Gavin was a tall man, with a long skinny neck, and his Adam's apple seemed to bob up and down for an eternity. Then, when about a third of the drink had been consumed, he held it up, let them imagine how good it would taste trickling down their parched throats, and dumped it over the railing. The liquid hissed as it hit the pavement below.

Gavin performed the ritual the same way every day, and Mosby didn't know which was worse—the act itself or how predictable it had become.

The heat, short rations, and hard physical exercise had conspired to take fifteen pounds off her frame. She felt the difference and took a grim pleasure in it. Gavin was hardening her, preparing her for the conflict to come, sowing the seeds of his own destruction. Because Mosby was waiting, waiting for her troops to reach the very peak of physical fitness, and then, before they started the long slide down, she would strike.

Hundreds, maybe even thousands, of her troops would die, but the prison would fall. And then, using vehicles taken from the prison, they would head for the nearest spaceport, seize a ship, and lift for Algeron.

It was a desperate plan, an insane plan, but better than no plan at all. Better than dying a meaningless death, giving up, or giving in.

Mosby did an about-face. Sweat ran in rivulets down her face, neck, and arms. She ignored it. They stood before her, rank after rank of men and women with faces of stone. They knew what today was about. It was about survival, but more than that, it was about pride, because Gavin wanted them to break and they would refuse to do so.

"Attenhut!"

Six thousand men and women crashed to attention. Mosby let her eyes roam over their ranks. She saw no cyborgs. Since they were dangerous even when disarmed, their brain boxes had been pulled, stashed on racks, and plugged into computer-controlled life support systems. They had no music, no neuro-games, and no communication with each other. It was a punishment far worse than that about to be suffered by the bio bods. Mosby forced herself to the task on hand.

"You know the drill. It's our turn to walk the wall. A combined force of swabbies, grunts, and other assorted riffraff moved it five miles yesterday. We'll move it six. *Vive la Légion!*"

"*Vive la Légion!*"

The answering cry shook Gavin's windows. He looked up from his computer screen, frowned, and made a note to cut the legionnaires' rations by another twenty-five calories a day.

From what had once been a sloppy, unorganized effort similar to what civilians might display under similar circumstances, Mosby's officers and NCOs had evolved a highly efficient, well-ordered process, capable of moving tons of rock from one end of the grinder to the other with a minimum amount of confusion and wasted effort.

Orders were given, bodies started to move, and the wall began to "walk." The huge cube of what looked like solid rock that occupied the exact center of the parade ground was actually made from more than a thousand blocks of carefully cut stone. Each block weighed a deceptively light fifteen pounds, an amount easily lifted by men and women alike, until the heat began to sap their strength, and endless repetition dulled their minds.

Then what had once been easy grew difficult, terribly difficult, to the point that the legionnaires would stagger back and forth, drop blocks of stone on their feet, and collapse from heat prostration. But that would be later in the afternoon, much later, and this was now.

She could have exempted herself from the labor, could have given orders while the others worked, but Mosby refused to do so. And because she refused to do so, her officers and NCOs were forced to refuse as well, a fact that led to no small amount of grumbling.

So General Marianne Mosby seized a block of granite, hugged it to her chest, and marched towards the far end of the grinder. Once there she'd put it down, pass hundreds of legionnaires on her way back to the ever-dwindling pile, and grab another one. As the day progressed, the blocks would become slippery with sweat, would burn her blistered hands, would double, triple, and quadruple in weight, until each one felt as though it weighed a thousand pounds. And she'd do it over, and over, and over again until the wall of granite had been "walked" from one end of the grinder to the other. Mosby ran her tongue over dry lips. It would be a long, long day.

* * *

Mosby frowned as the Emperor, *two* Emperors, caressed her body. It felt good, but it was wrong, terribly wrong, and she couldn't remember why. There was something she should say, something she should do, but the exact nature of it escaped her.

The door clanged open, a light stabbed her eyes, and a baton poked at her leg.

"Rise 'n' shine, General, there's someone ta see ya."

Mosby swung her legs over the side of the bunk, felt cold concrete under her feet, and blinked as light flooded the cell. It was night outside and the cold air raised goosebumps on the surface of her skin.

The guard was a big man, with a big man's gut and a twenty-four-inch shock baton that dangled from a wrist strap. The sun had taken a toll on his skin and it shattered into an endless maze of wrinkles as he spoke.

"Don't know why ya bother, Doc. Who cares if these yardbirds get a blister or two? They're traitors, that's what they are, and lower than snake shit."

Chien-Chu nodded agreeably and did his best to avoid the guard's alcohol-laden breath. "You're right about that, Sarge, but rules are rules, and we're supposed to check 'em once a month."

The merchant put his medical bag on the bunk, withdrew the diagnostic scanner, and fumbled for the switch. It made a humming noise, and a row of indicator lights came on. One had nothing to do with things medical. It glowed amber and assured Chien-Chu that the area was clean, a somewhat surprising but welcome piece of news. He turned to the guard.

"Take a break, Sarge, I'll be fine."

The guard didn't move. "Is she gonna strip? I'd love ta see her tits. The regular doc don't mind."

Chien-Chu frowned. "Oh really? Well, I do. So please step into the hall."

The guard started to bluster, but remembered that doctors hobnob with the likes of lieutenants, captains, and even loftier brass, making it dangerous to piss them off. Besides, the regular doc would be back the next time around, and things would be different.

"Well, hurry it up, Doc. We ain't got all night."

Mosby was furious. To be discussed as if she wasn't there, to be treated like a chunk of meat, was the most humiliating experience she'd ever had. The door clanged shut and she looked up at the doctor. The words "Dasser Medical" had been stitched over the breast pocket of his white lab coat. He looked familiar somehow.

"Thank you."

Chien-Chu smiled. "It was my pleasure. You've lost quite a bit of weight. Are you all right?" The voice triggered her memory.

"Sergi! It's you!"

Chien-Chu chuckled and held a finger to his lips. "Shsssh. Quiet now… Yes, it's me… and we have minutes at most. Listen carefully. The prison will be attacked. I can't say when… so be ready at all times. I may or may not be present. Once you are free, take your troops to the palace, find the Emperor, and lock him up. Do not—I repeat, do not—kill him. We have no wish to build the new government on piles of bodies."

"'We'? 'New government'? There are others?"

"Yes, but there's no need to know their names. Only that they exist and believe that the Hudathans should be stopped *before* they reach the center of the empire."

A baton clanged against the door.

"Come on, Doc! You've got one thousand two hundred and forty-seven more prisoners to go!"

Chien-Chu sighed, turned the scanner off, and placed it back in his bag. Mosby kissed him on the cheek.

"God bless you, Sergi… and the others too. We'll be ready, I promise you that, and follow any orders that you give."

The merchant nodded. "Kick some butt for me."

The throne room was empty except for the Emperor. He'd been there for an hour now, or was it two? Watching the sunlight move across the floor while trying to think. It was difficult with the copies jabbering away, arguing about everything from the Hudathan crisis to the latest fashion trends, but he tried nonetheless.

The thoughts didn't come, however—not the ones he needed anyway—because a memory got in the way. He was down on the sun-splashed floor, playing with a toy truck, when someone said his name. A pair of boots walked by, brown boots gleaming with polish, and he felt a sense of joy. It was his father, he knew it was, the only memory he had of that elusive figure.

What would life have been like if his father had lived? Would he be alive even now? Providing the advice that he so desperately needed? A balance against the entities that battled each other in his head?

"Your Highness?"

The voice was hesitant and belonged to his herald.

"Yes?"

"Admiral Scolari to see you."

The copies clamored for attention. They wanted to talk with Scolari, a desire made dangerous by the different things they wanted to say and results they sought to achieve.

The Emperor forced himself to remain outwardly calm. He reached inside himself, found a reservoir of strength, and used it to demand silence.

Reluctantly, and with no small amount of grumbling, the copies faded into the background. The herald was still waiting, his face expressionless, his eyes focused on a spot over the Emperor's head.

"Thank you. Send the admiral in."

Scolari swept into the room on a wave of self-confidence. Her uniform was immaculate and a long cape swirled around her. Every aspect of her plan had succeeded so far and there was no reason to think that anything would go wrong now. She bowed.

"Greetings, Highness."

The Emperor shifted his weight from one side of the throne to the other. "Greetings, Admiral. You look happy. I could use some good news."

Scolari realized that she'd been smiling and summoned a more serious expression. "I wish that I had some for you, Highness... but such is not the case."

The Emperor allowed himself a sigh. "What now?"

"The Legion will refuse to board the transports I sent to bring them back."

"Will? Or has?"

Scolari shrugged. "My source, an officer in a position to know, said 'will.' But a good deal of time has passed since the message torp was launched, so we must assume that they refused."

The copies tried to speak but the Emperor forced them down. He felt angry. Angry at Mosby for putting the Legion first, angry at the Legion for their traitorous ways, and angry at Scolari for bringing the whole thing to his attention. He struggled to appear impassive.

"And?"

"They must be punished," Scolari said vehemently. "I request permission to attack Algeron."

The Emperor felt inclined to agree, and was about to grant his permission, when a copy managed to assert itself. This particular advisor had been a famous general and her words rang true.

"The Legion seeks to protect itself from the admiral's ambitions. Their motto says it all. 'The Legion is our country.' Let the matter go until *after* the Hudatha have been dealt with. To do otherwise is to risk defeat."

Had that voice been the only one that he'd heard, the Emperor might well have refused Scolari's request. But still another copy, a political strategist this time, weighed in with another opinion.

"The Legion is a highly respected force. Word of their rebellion will spread, infect the colonies, and spark a revolution. You must punish them quickly, *before* the Hudatha arrive, and the war is fought."

Because this argument seemed just as cogent as the first one, and was more emotionally satisfying, the Emperor agreed. He looked Scolari in the eye, wondered how much time had passed during his deliberations, and told her what she wanted to hear.

"You have my permission to attack Algeron."

Scolari beamed. "Thank you, Highness!"

The Emperor bowed an inch. "You're welcome. I'm disappointed in the Legion and will eventually disband them. But proceed with care. The Hudatha are coming and we must be ready."

Scolari nodded eagerly. "The fleet is assembling even now."

"Excellent. Bring me victory and the rewards will be well worth having."

Scolari bowed at the waist, backed away from the throne, and smiled.

"They certainly will," she thought to herself, "they certainly will."

Like the man who owned it, the space yacht was strong rather than sleek, and comfortable rather than fancy. Though well upholstered and nicely equipped, the lounge fell short of opulent. It was circular in shape and boasted six acceleration couches, only two of which were occupied.

Natasha Chien-Chu felt herself pushed down into her couch as the yacht lifted off, blasted its way up through Earth's gravity well, and accelerated away. She looked to the left, saw that her father-in-law's eyes were closed, and realized that he was asleep. The first real sleep he'd had in days. And why not? The merchant was safe now, secure in the knowledge that his crew would handle the ship, and he could relax.

Natasha reached for a dimmer switch, brought the lights down, and thought of her husband. His death seemed unreal, like a story she'd heard but couldn't quite believe. But it *was* real, as were the aliens who had caused it and the ship that carried her towards Algeron.

Someone had to visit Algeron and negotiate an agreement with the Legion. Natasha understood that but had no desire to be part of the process. She knew she should care, knew Leo would want her to fight, but found it hard to do. No, her link with Sergi, with Nola, with the universe itself, had died, and left her drifting like a planet without a star.

Her ostensible purpose, to function as her father-in-law's aide, was little more than Nola's idea of good therapy. "Get her out, get her moving, the activity will do her good."

Natasha could almost hear her mother-in-law's voice. She smiled and felt the tears trickle down her cheeks.

18

… And unto fathers certain rights are granted, and unto mothers likewise,
for they are the source of life…
UNKNOWN AUTHOR
Naa Book of Chants
Standard year circa 1000 B.C.

Planet Algeron, the Human Empire
The cavern was half the size of the one that had served Wayfar
Hardman's village for countless generations, but whatever
it lacked in space was more than made up for by a feeling of
snug warmth, a sensation made all the more enjoyable by the
knowledge that it was snowing outside. The central fire, fueled
by a generous supply of dried dooth dung, burned with a steady
violet-blue flame. Heat radiated outwards like ripples from the
center of a pond. It warmed Hardman's bones and added to the
sense of well-being that went with six mugs of Surekill's ale. It
was powerful stuff of which the younger male was justifiably
proud. Hardman belched softly and looked around.

The cavern was packed almost to capacity. Family units sat in
clumps, bachelors, perfumed to the hilt, watched maidens from
the corners of their eyes, and oldsters, so close to the fire that it
threatened to singe their fur, swapped lies that everyone had
heard before.

There, lit by the fire's cheery glow, sat Windsweet. So lovely, so perfect, so like her mother. The human sat next to her, arms clasped around his knees, staring into the fire, while Surekill sat on the other side, nodding in agreement with something she'd said and poking the fire with a long stick.

The two of them looked so happy, so perfect together, that Hardman was filled with benevolence. He took a sip from his most recent mug of ale, thought about how lucky they were to be in love, and rose to his feet. The cavern swam out of focus and came back again.

"Brothers! Sisters! I ask the right of speech!"

Conversations stopped, heads turned, and a multiplicity of voices responded.

"Granted!"

Hardman smiled and gestured expansively to the crowd.

"Thank you." His eyes made contact with Windsweet's but failed to see the concern reflected there.

"First I would like to thank my host, Ridelong Surekill, for the warmth of his hospitality."

A series of short undulating whistles signaled the villagers' agreement.

Hardman smiled. "And then, responding to Surekill's love for my daughter, and her affection for him, I would like to announce their impending marriage."

There was a moment of shocked silence followed by absolute pandemonium. The cavern was filled with whistles, shouted congratulations, and a host of questions. When would the marriage take place? Where would the ceremony be held? How did the couple feel?

Windsweet looked shocked, Booly looked angry, and Ridelong looked triumphant. But Hardman saw none of it. He held his mug aloft and waved for silence. The noise died away. Hardman smiled benignly.

"Quiet now... there are formalities to be observed... and none shall go unsaid. So, in the words used by my father before me, and his father before him, I do formally give my daughter to Ridelong Surekill, admonishing him to protect her from harm and reminding him of the responsibilities attendant to such a gift. For a warrior must put the needs of his mate before all others, must share his bed with none but her, and must provide for his cubs. So, there being no challengers for my daughter's affections, and…"

"Wait!"

Surprised, and groggy with ale, Hardman stopped. He looked, and looked again. No! It couldn't be true! It was the human who had spoken!

Booly stood and looked at Hardman. He was almost as surprised as the chieftain. He felt Windsweet tug at his pants leg and chose to ignore it. His voice was calm and cut through the silence like a well-sharpened blade.

"I, William Booly, challenge Ridelong Surekill for the affection of this maiden."

The form was wrong, but the meaning was clear, and the villagers made a loud hissing noise as they inhaled all at once. Slowly, surely, like a snake uncoiling from its rest, Surekill stood. His eyes blazed with anger and his hands were clenched at his sides.

"Then prepare to die!"

Stunned, and shocked at the way in which his plan had turned from triumph to disaster, Hardman tried to intervene.

"No, the human could never many my daughter. Therefore…"

"Silence!" Ridelong shouted, causing Hardman's son and the rest of his retainers to reach for their sidearms. "I have been challenged. No one—I repeat, no one—has the right to refuse such a challenge except me."

Hardman looked at his daughter. Where he had hoped to see joy there was anger, sorrow, and pity. He had unintentionally betrayed her, and she would never, ever forgive him. The alcohol-induced warmth was suddenly gone, washed away by the cold icy knowledge of what he'd done, and the chieftain felt tears well up in his eyes. But there were no words that could ameliorate what he'd done or stop the bloodshed that would inevitably follow. He sat on the ground, lowered his head, and cradled it with his arms. His retainers moved in around him but allowed their hands to drop from their guns.

An elder known as Deepwell Gooddig stepped forward. He

had white fur with black spots. His manner was solemn. He looked from Surekill to Booly.

"The challenge has form, and as form master, it is my duty to see that you observe it. The human will choose the time. Surekill will pick the weapons. I will select the place. Human?"

The legionnaire heard himself say "Now," and wondered if it was the right choice. What the hell was he doing anyway? Fighting over a Naa maiden when he should be on his way to Fort Camerone. General St. James would want to know about the Hudathans, and he, Sergeant Major Bill Booly, had a duty to tell him. A duty it would be damned hard to fulfill if he was dead.

The form master turned away. "Surekill?"

The warrior looked the human in the eye, grinned, and said, "Knives."

The way Surekill said it left little doubt as to his expertise with the weapon or his desire to use it on Booly.

The oldster nodded, gave the matter some thought, and announced his choice.

"The fight will take place aboveground at the center of the village. Each combatant is allowed one assistant, who will give such advice as they can, and ensure that the proper forms are observed. Who stands for Surekill?"

A dozen voices rang out, but Surekill nodded towards a warrior named Easymove Quietstalk, a big rugged-looking individual who stepped into the firelight with the confidence of a natural athlete.

Gooddig signaled his approval. "Good. Who stands for the human?"

There was a long silence, finally broken by the rasp of hobnails on stone. Heads turned as Windsweet's brother, Movefast Shootstraight, stepped forward and stood by Booly.

"I stand for Booly."

Pleased by Booly's challenge, yet sorry at the same time, Windsweet was touched by her brother's support. Never, in even her worst nightmares, had she envisioned something like this. Her father had created a situation in which no one could win and everyone would lose. Fear filled the pit of her stomach and gradually turned to lead.

Surekill grabbed her arm. "There's no need to worry, my sweet. I will split the human in half and dump his entrails at your feet."

Windsweet jerked free of his grasp and spit the words out one at a time. "Never—I repeat, never—touch me again."

Anger blazed in Surekill's eyes. "So that's how it is! You'd rather grunt and groan beneath the weight of a furless alien than marry one of your own kind!"

Windsweet's hand made a cracking sound as it hit the side of Surekill's face.

Surekill gave a surprised grunt and the crowd gasped with horror. They had never seen anyone treat Surekill in such a manner and live. The warrior started to say something, spat into the fire instead, and turned away. Backed by his warriors, he stalked towards the surface.

More than a little embarrassed, and unsure of what to do, the assemblage broke up and headed for the main passageway. Maidens tittered over Windsweet's disgrace, warriors discussed the upcoming battle, and cubs ran every which way, shouting their excitement and squealing when cuffed behind the ear.

Booly felt a hand seize his elbow. He turned to find Shootstraight by his side. The warrior's voice was little more than a whisper.

"Listen, human... for there is little time. I have a smoke grenade. I'll throw it the moment we reach the surface. The villagers will scatter and prepare for an attack. Run, make your way into the hills, and hide for three days. It will be safe after that. Head for the place that you call 'Camerone' and don't come back."

The offer was tempting, very tempting, since it would allow him to do the very thing that duty demanded. But to lose Windsweet, to cede her to someone she hated, was more than the legionnaire could stand.

His eyes found Windsweet's. She was waiting there beside the path, her eyes bright with determination, her lip quivering with pent-up emotion. He spoke loudly enough for her to hear.

"Thanks, Movefast. Your sister is fortunate to have a friend and brother such as you. But the challenge stands."

Shootstraight made a gesture with his hands. "I don't know

which one of you is crazier, my sister or you. But there's honor in what you say, and I hope you skewer Surekill like a newly slaughtered dooth. Come, we must head for the surface."

Booly looked at Windsweet, saw her kneel beside her father, and did as he was told. The last of the villagers were heading up the path in front of them. Shootstraight spoke again.

"Tell me, human, are you good with a knife?"

"I taught hand-to-hand combat in the 2nd REP."

Shootstraight gestured his approval. "That's good, very good, because Surekill is an expert. It's our experience that humans prefer to kill at a distance, avoiding personal combat when they can, a fact that influenced Surekill's decision. He assumes that you lack the necessary skills, and more than that, are afraid of cold steel."

Booly produced a twisted grin. "I *am* afraid of cold steel. Aren't you?"

Shootstraight laughed. "Of course! That's why I avoid affairs like this one. Now, listen carefully. Surekill's arms are longer than yours, so stay outside his reach, and watch for tricks. He likes to trip his opponents, slash them as they fall, and finish them on the ground."

The legionnaire nodded. "And if I manage to disarm him? What then?"

Shootstraight looked surprised. "Then kill him. He's not the sort of enemy to leave alive."

Booly was still thinking about that last piece of advice when he pushed the dooth-hide curtain aside and stepped out into the snowstorm. Snowflakes danced, whirled, and performed intricate pirouettes all around him, adding their substance to the shroud of newly fallen snow.

It was cold, and a driving wind made it even colder, causing the legionnaire to shiver. It was dark and the villagers had started a fire. The flames leaped higher as a flammable liquid was poured into the pit. The form master appeared at his elbow.

"Markers have been erected. The combatants must stay within them. Please follow me."

Snow crunched under Booly's boots as he followed the oldster towards the fire. The markers consisted of poles driven into the ground. Each boasted a pennant of red cloth. They pointed towards the east and snapped in the wind.

Surekill stepped out of the storm. He loomed large in front of the fire. "So, alien. You have the courage to face me."

Booly shrugged. "Talk's cheap. Let's get on with it."

The warrior bared his teeth and started to say something in reply, but the form master stepped between them. He held a tray. It supported four knives, all of which were about eighteen inches long.

"Each combatant will choose a weapon."

Booly examined the blades with a critical eye. Each was handmade and therefore different from the others. Some of the knives were double-edged, some had evil-looking serrations, and some came equipped with blood gutters. He looked at Surekill.

The warrior reached out, selected something akin to an ancient bowie knife, and ran the edge along his naked forearm. A thin line of blood appeared.

Booly nodded approvingly. "I'd like to see that again... only deeper this time."

"Choose," the form master said sternly.

The legionnaire chose without looking. The knife felt heavy and cold. "What about rules?"

"There is one rule," the form master replied. "Stay within the area marked by the pennants. Leave it and your life is forfeit."

Snowflakes tickled the legionnaire's face as he looked around. He saw the pennants, the crowd, and Windsweet. She stood next to her father. She raised her right hand and placed it in the center of her chest. The Naa sign for affection. Her father stiffened and looked straight ahead.

A tremendous warmth suffused Booly's body, for he knew what the gesture had cost her, and would cost her far into the future. He smiled, made the same gesture in return, and turned back to his opponent.

"When do we start?"

The form master raised his arm, stepped backwards, and brought it down. "Now."

Booly threw the knife underhanded, aiming upwards at his opponent's chest, hoping to end the contest before it began. But the legionnaire hadn't practiced in a long time, and instead of penetrating Surekill's chest, the weapon struck him between the eyes hilt-first.

The force of the blow might have felled a lesser being, but Surekill shook the pain off and moved forward.

The human swore silently, marked the place where his knife had fallen, and waited for the warrior. Knife attacks can be categorized as high, middle, or low. Surekill held the weapon in his right hand, waist-high and edge-up. He planned to come in close, open Booly's abdomen with a jab, and rip his way upwards.

Light reflected off Surekill's blade as he lunged forward. The human stepped away from the knife and transferred his weight to his right foot. Then, using his left arm to block the thrust, the legionnaire launched a side kick to the warrior's left knee.

Something gave, the chieftain staggered, and Booly aimed a palm-heel strike at his opponent's nose.

It didn't work. Where humans had semi-soft cartilage, the Naa had solid bone, which could take a great deal of punishment.

Surekill recovered, swept the knife in from the right, and was rewarded a thin scarlet line across the legionnaire's abdomen. It didn't hurt but would before long.

Booly backpedaled and Surekill limped forward. A thin layer of snow had settled on the warrior's head and dusted his shoulders.

"Watch the markers!"

The voice belonged to Shootstraight. Booly looked and saw that he was running out of room. Surekill grinned, lifted the knife high, and shuffled in for the kill.

The legionnaire stepped forward, grabbed Surekill's knife arm with his left hand, and reached under the warrior's armpit with his right. The human's hand closed on his opponent's collar, his hip provided a fulcrum, and the chieftain went down. Booly hung on and tried to twist the knife from Surekill's hand. The crowd groaned.

But no sooner had the warrior hit the ground than he kicked upwards, aiming for Booly's groin, but hitting his thigh instead. Forced to let go, the human staggered backwards and felt his feet slip out from under him. The impact knocked the air out of his lungs.

Now it was Surekill's turn to take the offensive. And the situation was exactly the way he liked it. The human was on the ground, unarmed, and vulnerable to attack. He stood, limped forward, and dived.

Booly rolled to the right, felt something hard beneath the snow, and wrapped his fingers around the hilt of his knife. Surekill hit the ground with a loud thump. Pain lanced across the legionnaire's abdomen as he stood. The wound was shallow but long, and had soaked his pants with blood.

The warrior lurched up and out of the snow. His eyes were like slits, his teeth were bared, and a growl rumbled in his throat.

"Come on, pook... it's time to die!"

The human dived into a somersault, kicked himself out of it, and drove the knife upwards. The blade went through the warrior's throat, severed a major artery, and left him choking on his own blood.

Slowly, like a man preparing to pray, Surekill fell to his knees. Blood stained the snow around him. Then, wearing an expression of surprised disbelief, he toppled forward onto his face.

A collective sigh was heard. Windsweet turned and buried her face against her father's chest. The chieftain blinked as a snowflake hit his eye. He put an arm around Windsweet's shoulders and patted her on the back.

Thoughts started to form. Perhaps the situation wasn't so bad, after all, Hardman thought. Surekill was dead, a fact that virtually guaranteed his own continued ascendancy, and his daughter had turned to him for comfort.

Yes, the human was the problem. Get rid of him and everything would be fine. But he'd have to act carefully, very carefully, so his daughter would never suspect. Hardman watched Booly give the bloodstained knife to the form master and smiled.

Snow whirled down past the wall-mounted spotlights, hit the updraft created by the spaceship's repellers, and soared upwards as if returning to its source.

St. James waited for the vessel to settle on pad 7, then hurried out to greet its passengers. Snow squeaked beneath his boots and his breath appeared as jets of steam. The ship was not especially large but looked roomy and comfortable. The hull had a shape similar to that of a Terran crab, minus the legs, of course, and the stalk-mounted eyes. Metal pinged as it started to cool and some auto stairs positioned themselves in front of the lock.

What would Sergi Chien-Chu be like? A self-important businessman full of lofty rhetoric and dedicated to lining his pockets? St. James hoped not, because the message from his friend Alexander Dasser indicated that this man headed the Cabal and was the Legion's best hope for the future.

The lock whirred open and a shaft of light hit the ground. A figure appeared, far too slight to be that of a man, and drew a cape around her shoulders. A hood hid her face, but there was something about the grace with which she descended the stairs that grabbed the legionnaire's attention and held it. Then as the woman stepped off the stairs and the light hit her face, the interest turned to fascination.

The woman had a slender body, a long oval face, and enormous eyes. They looked haunted somehow, as if some horrible tragedy had befallen her, and was never far from her thoughts. Her voice was soft and gentle.

"My name is Natasha Chien-Chu. My father-in-law will be along in a moment."

St. James was surprised by the strength of his own disappointment. If Sergi Chien-Chu was her father-in-law, then she was married, and as unapproachable as the Emperor himself.

"Welcome to Algeron, Madam Chien-Chu. My name is Ian St. James. I command the Legion's free forces."

Natasha frowned. Snow swirled around her face. "Thank you. It saddens me to know that General Mosby and her people are in prison."

St. James raised an eyebrow. "You know the general?"

"No, but my father-in-law does."

A short, rather chubby man appeared from behind her. His eyes were brown and filled with intelligence. "Who do I know?"

Natasha smiled. "General St. James, my father-in-law, Sergi Chien-Chu. We were discussing General Mosby and the fact that she's in prison."

"But not for long," Chien-Chu said cheerfully. "We hope to break her out."

Charmed by the merchant's unassuming ways and startled by his directness, St. James found himself smiling. "Welcome to Algeron, sir. I have a feeling that the Hudathans are in deep trouble."

Nothing remained of the snowstorm except for a few errant flakes that spiraled down from a lead-gray sky. The sun was little more than a dimly seen presence, so heavily shrouded by clouds that only a small portion of its light found its way to the surface. The Towers of Algeron, which would normally draw the eye towards the south, were completely invisible.

Roller knelt beside a pile of still-warm dooth dung and pushed the goggles up onto his forehead. His breath fogged the air around him. He'd known very little about tracking when he'd arrived on Algeron but learned a good deal since.

There had been six animals. The first or second dooth had defecated and the rest of the pack train had ground the feces into the otherwise pristine snow. The depth of their tracks indicated that the animals had been heavily loaded, and judging from the way that the imprints overlaid each other, the caravan had traveled single file.

The absence of Naa tracks reinforced his impression that the dooths had been ridden rather than led. While that made it more difficult to tell how many warriors there were, he could make a fairly accurate guess. There had to be at least six Naa, one per animal, and could be as many as twelve individuals, if they rode doubled up.

As to identity, well, the hoofprints left little doubt as to that. The tribes liked to brand their livestock in two ways: with a symbol burned into their hides, and with marks filed into the circumference of their hooves. The first approach allowed them to pick their animals out of a large herd, and the second permitted them to track their property even when accompanied by dooth belonging to someone else. But these hooves bore no tribal markings, which suggested they had been burned away with acid or filed down. A bandit trick, designed to save them if caught with stolen merchandise, or at least lighten their punishment. Not that the tribes were inclined towards mercy where bandits were concerned. Most of them died head-down in a campfire. Roller stood and looked around.

His unit was substantially understrength, as were all the patrols from Fort Cameron these days. There was Gunner, crazy as ever, hull-down in a gully, scanning the wastelands with his sensors; the Trooper II named Villain, who, in spite of her last performance, showed every sign of developing into a fairly decent soldier; her understudy, a newbie named Salazar, who was so green that it hurt; and a pair of bio bods, both of whom rode in the quad. It was a relatively small force, entirely inadequate for any sort of tribal action, but more than a match for some raggedy-assed bandits. Or so Roller hoped.

The fact was that the Old Man had stripped Algeron in order to reinforce the rim world outposts. Roller understood the theory but wondered if it would work. Could the Legion stop the Hudathans all by themselves? And what about the Navy? What if the Emperor sent them against Algeron? The noncom shook his head in wonderment. Oh well, his job was clear, and that being the case, he'd get on with it.

The snow creaked as he walked towards Villain, circled, and stepped up behind her shoulders. He pulled the goggles down, strapped himself in, and activated his radio.

"Roller One to Roller Patrol. There's bandits up ahead. Let's move it."

The sleeping cubicle was one of many that had been carved from the earthen walls. A generous supply of dooth-wool blankets provided sufficient warmth, and a curtain made from trade fabric supplied the illusion of privacy.

Booly heard movement nearby. His hand slid down to grip the piece of conduit that lay by his side. It was of Terran manufacture and had originally been part of a shuttle that had crashed fifty miles to the north.

Day was fading to night aboveground, which made it just

right for one of the one-hour naps that the Naa took every six hours or so, or an attempt on his life.

Not that anyone had made any threats or actually moved against him. No, it was a feeling, that's all, a sort of simmering resentment that made the human nervous. He'd be glad when they left Surekill's village for Hardman's, or better yet, when he could escape altogether. But what about Windsweet? The thought of leaving her behind, of losing her for all time, made his heart ache.

There was another sound, closer now, and Booly sat up. The pipe wasn't much as weapons go but would be better than nothing. He pushed his back into a corner and prepared to defend himself. The curtain slid aside and a cloud of perfume enveloped him. Windsweet!

The curtain closed as she slipped in beside him. No words were said or required. Lips found lips, bodies came together, and hands slipped along unfamiliar flanks. The attraction was so strong, so powerful, that Booly found himself gasping for breath. The combination of her sleek sensual fur, the hard muscle just under the surface of her skin, and the tongue that explored his mouth brought the human to a state of instant arousal. Even the pain caused by his wound did nothing to lessen his excitement.

Feeling Booly grow hard, and taking pleasure in it, Windsweet wrapped her fingers around his erection and moved her hand up and down. The legionnaire shuddered, made her stop, and started his own gentle exploration.

Time passed, and the intensity of their lovemaking increased, until Windsweet could stand no more. She sought his penis and pulled it inside.

Booly bit his lip against the pleasure of it, forced himself to hold back, and matched the rhythm with which she moved. He didn't know which was better, the physical pleasure or the wonderful intimacy of being with the woman he loved. For that was the way he thought of her, as a woman, rather than an alien.

Slowly, but with the surety of any natural force, the pace quickened until both reached climax together, biting each other's shoulders in an attempt to remain silent, and riding a tidal wave of pleasure. A wave that turned back on itself, became a whirlpool, and sucked Booly down into an ocean of sensation.

There was a long silence when it was over. It felt wonderful to lie there, with Windsweet by his side, kissing his neck and whispering endearments in his ear. He kissed her in return, told her that he loved her, and knew that he meant it. It was that knowledge that made the words so hard to say.

"Windsweet..."

"Yes?"

"I love you."

"You said that."

"And I meant it."

"Good."

Booly did a push-up and looked down into her eyes. "But there's a problem."

"You have to leave."

"Yes. How did you know?"

"I knew from the beginning. The way all females know."

"And yet you came?"

A tear rolled down Windsweet's cheek. She made no attempt to wipe it away. "I came to say goodbye."

"I'll be back."

"It would be better if you stayed away."

"I don't think I could."

"Then what is, shall be."

Booly nodded. "Exactly."

"Then leave now, while we're in a village other than my own, where my father would be duty-bound to follow."

"He'll let me go?"

"I think he'd show you the way if he could. Nothing would please him more."

"What about food? Weapons?"

"Father left both for me to find," Windsweet replied. "I left them right outside."

"So I should leave."

"Yes," Windsweet replied softly, "but only after we make love for a second time."

Her hands pulled his head to her breasts, a nipple found its way into his mouth, and the legionnaire found it easy to oblige.

* * *

The situation room was nearly empty, containing as it did only three people. The lights were dimmed and one large section of wall had transformed itself into a video screen. An officer with a shaved head, black skin, and tired-looking eyes was talking.

"… so the star divers hit just the way Leonid figured they would, blew the battlewagons out of the sky, and saved the outpost. I'm sorry to report that he was killed when the geeks scored a direct hit on the linear accelerator. Leo was a civilian, and drove me crazy sometimes, but he was one helluva man."

St. James touched a button on the armrest of his chair. The screen faded to black.

"I'm terribly sorry."

The words sounded false even as St. James said them, for he knew that he *wasn't* sorry, and was in fact rather happy. Not that a brave man had died, but that his wife existed and was technically free. But he must be careful, very careful, to respect her grief, and take whatever time was needed.

The strange part was that he'd seen Narbakov's report long before the Chien-Chus had arrived, but had failed to connect the two.

Chien-Chu's voice cracked when he spoke.

"Thank you, General, This was very thoughtful of you. I wish he were still alive, but it's gratifying to hear that my son's death meant something to those around him, and cost the enemy dearly."

Tears trickled down Natasha's cheeks and she smiled apologetically. "Yes, General. Thank you. It helps to know the circumstances of my husband's death."

St. James resisted an impulse to take Natasha in his arms and kiss the tears away. He gave an understanding nod, rose, and held her cloak.

Booly's breath came in short angry puffs. He looked back over his shoulder. The trail was so evident, so clear, that a child could have followed it. It crested a rise, dipped out of sight, and reappeared a hundred yards behind him. A dooth appeared while he looked, followed by another, and still another. Not

Surekill's warriors, whom he'd managed to shake during the darkness two cycles before, but bandits who had cut his trail and decided to follow. The lead rider waved a weapon over his head, shouted something unintelligible to the others, and urged his mount down into the gully. The rest followed.

Booly squinted upwards at the sun, adjusted his direction slightly, and started to jog. The map that Windsweet had given him, plus a substantial head start, had enabled him to escape from the mountains. Camerone was fifty, maybe sixty miles away, which meant that the bandits would catch him within the hour.

He had the handgun that Windsweet had given him, the same one they'd captured him with, and two spare magazines. That gave him forty-five rounds, forty-four to use on the Naa and one for himself. The legionnaire remembered the way the Hudathan had died, head-down over the fire pit, and ran a little faster.

What he needed was a natural fortress, a spot where he could make good use of the bullets he had, and hope that the bandits would go away.

Booly skidded down a slope, regained his balance, and braked with his heels. The riverbank was steep, so he took it in a series of long jumps and gave thanks when the ice didn't break. After skate-walking across to the other side, he encountered another steep embankment, used some rocks to pull himself up, and climbed towards the top. The slope was noticeable, but not too tough, and he jogged upwards. The wound had opened and his undershirt felt wet. He heard a shout as he topped the rise. A bullet buzzed by his shoulder and the report followed a quarter second later.

The legionnaire zigzagged towards some freestanding boulders, heard two additional rifle shots, and turned the corner. It felt good to have something solid behind his back.

A flat area lay up ahead, dotted with loose rocks and interrupted by a steep-sided flat-topped hill. The legionnaire remembered that hills of that type were called "kopje" back on Earth and had often served as ready-made forts. He headed for the nearest one, his breath coming in short gasps, his stomach on fire.

Snow crunched under his boots as he circled the kopje, reached the other side, and started to climb. A mixture of loose snow and rocks slid out from under him as he climbed. He swore, grabbed onto some rocks, and heaved himself upwards. More, just a little bit more, and he'd reach the top.

The legionnaire's legs pumped, his arms pulled, and suddenly he was there, crawling over the edge and dropping into a slight depression. A wonderful place where bullets couldn't reach him and air could enter his lungs.

Cold, almost numb fingers felt through his clothing, searched for the first-aid kit that Windsweet had included with his gear, fumbled with a zipper that got in the way.

The antiseptic burned like hell when he sprayed it on the wound, and the butterfly closures did a half-assed job of pulling the wound margins together, but he was in no position to be picky. A fresh ABD pad, followed by some gauze wound over his shirt, and the legionnaire was done. His weapons, or in this case "weapon," was next.

Booly freed his gun belt, checked the spare magazines to make sure they were loaded and free of dirt, and made an interesting discovery. The two pistol-launched flares that he habitually carried on his belt were still there. He gave it some thought, decided that the bandits knew where he was, and thumbed the release. The magazine fell in his lap.

Booly blew on cold stiff fingers, slid two rounds out of the magazine, and replaced them with flares. Having done so, he slapped the magazine into the well, heard it click home, and aimed the pistol towards the sky. He pulled the trigger, saw the flare explode three hundred feet over his head, and did it again. Any patrol leader worth his or her salt would know what that meant. "I'm up to my ass in shit. Come quick."

But would someone see it? Booly shrugged fatalistically, freed the magazine, and replaced both rounds. The bandits were closer now and he'd need every bullet he had.

Villain spotted the energy flash against the upper right-hand corner of her vision grid. Numbers appeared and changed as she zoomed in. She was surprised and pleased by her own professionalism.

"Roller Two to Roller One. I have a hot spot three miles ahead, vector seven, elevation three hundred and falling. Both heat and height correspond with a Legion-issue pistol-launched signal flare. Confirm?"

"That's a roger," Gunner said quickly. "Roller Three has it too."

Salazar had seen the flash as well, but had mistrusted his sensors and remained silent. He swore at himself for being so stupid and gave thanks that they didn't know, especially Villain, who'd done everything within her power to make his life miserable. Why? He didn't have the faintest idea. Roller interrupted his thoughts. The orders were crisp.

"Roller One to Roller Patrol. We have a friendly in trouble. Implement condition five, repeat condition five, and keep your sensors peeled.

"Roller Three, feed the ops center a contact report and request a spy-eye. Not that the bastards will assign us one, but hey, we can ask.

"Roller Two, run the freqs, find the friendly, and make contact. I want an ID, sitrep, and background.

"Roller Four, watch the back door, and if we take one in the ass, make sure that you're dead when the whole thing's over.

"All right, people, move it out."

Booly held the gun in his right hand and stuck the left into his right armpit. It felt good to warm his fingers. Snow had melted under his knees and soaked his pants.

Judging from all the noise they'd made, the bandits had arrived, found the spot where he'd climbed the hill, and were getting ready to come after him. He wondered how they'd go about it. One at a time? All in a rush? From every direction at once? There was no way to tell.

The legionnaire looked around, found a fist-sized rock, and threw it towards the noise. It hit about a third of the way down the slope, bounced, and clattered to the bottom. All hell broke loose as the bandits fired up towards the top of the kopje. The shooting should've stopped after a second or two, but didn't, which meant they were coming after him.

Booly held the pistol in a two-handed grip, waited for the firing to stop, and stood the moment that it did. The bandits were right where he'd expected them to be, about six feet from the top, completely exposed. Not only that, but the need to maintain a firm footing and use their weapons at the same time hampered their ability to fire.

Booly worked from left to right, aimed for their chests, and gave them two rounds apiece. Blood spurted out of their backs, arms flew upwards, and bodies tumbled backwards as the bullets hit.

In the fraction of a second between the time when the legionnaire killed the third Naa and the slug hit him from behind, Booly saw the dooths, the bandits, and something that wasn't supposed to be there, but was. A Legion standard laser cannon, disassembled for transport, now in the process of being put together. How? Why? The questions blended together as the force of the bullet turned him around.

The bandit had a long piece of dirty white linen wrapped around the bottom half of his face. One end hung free and snapped in the wind. He stood on the crater's edge, the assault rifle still at his shoulder, savoring his moment of victory.

The first slug hit him crotch-high, and the next three marched steadily upwards, ending when the fourth went through his heart. He was already in the process of falling when the last bullet hit.

Worried that others might be coming up the same way, Booly hurried to the other side of the depression and looked over the edge. The bandit was still tumbling down the slope, his ragged clothing billowing around him, blood marking the rocks that slowed his fall. There was no sign of others.

Four down and what? Six, eight more to go? The legionnaire was still calculating the odds when movement caught his eye. Someone or something was coming over the last rise. A Trooper II, by god! And a quad! With another Trooper II bringing up the rear! They'd seen his flare and were coming to the rescue.

But wait a minute... what about the laser cannon? Properly handled, it could destroy a Trooper II and damage a quad. And where were the bandits? They should have charged him by now. Then he realized what had happened.

At least one of the bandits was smart, damned smart, and had used Booly to bait a trap. And the plan could work too, because the patrol would never expect a group of ragtag bandits to have a laser cannon and would charge straight into the ambush.

His shoulder ached, as did the wound across his stomach, but Booly jumped onto the kopje's rim and waved his arms back and forth anyway. Blood, his blood, splattered across the tops of his boots. His vision went out of focus, the sky appeared over him, and a rock drove the air out of his lungs. Booly fought the blackness but it pulled him down.

Salazar saw something appear on top of the low-lying hill, move, then disappear? A man? He zoomed in but the image was gone.

"Roller Four to Roller One. I saw a bio bod standing on top of the low-lying hill. It could be our friendly. Confirm?"

"Roller Two, negative," Villain said.

"Roller Three, negative," Gunner added.

Roller was pissed. He shifted his weight from one foot to the other, which caused Villain to lurch unexpectedly.

"Watch the back door, damnit... Rollers Two and Three will handle the rest. Two will go in for the kill while Three provides cover."

Salazar swore silently. He couldn't win for losing. But he *had* seen a figure on top of the hill, a human figure, though he wasn't sure why he thought so, and it meant something. But what? He alternated between walking backwards and looking back over his shoulder, hoping the figure would reappear. It didn't.

Villain savored the ass chewing that Salazar had received, and followed bandit tracks around the side of the hill. Her number three knee servo had started to overheat and sent jolts of pain up through her electronic nervous system. She forced herself to ignore the pain and brought her arms up into firing position. The movement saved her life, since the laser cannon had been sited low, behind a jumble of rocks, and the beam hit the cyborg's right arm instead of her head.

While the impact of a bullet or a cannon shell delivers

hydrostatic shock, the beam had no mass and did nothing to slow her down. Villain's arm melted and drooped downwards, but she was otherwise unaffected.

Villain turned, tried to bring her machine gun into play, but didn't quite make it. The grenade went off in the vicinity of her right ankle, blew part of her foot off, and caused her to come crashing down. Roller leaped clear.

"It's an ambush! Give us some fire support. Three, and Four, take them from behind!"

Eager to die, and hoping that his time had come, Gunner dropped the bio bods and stalked forward. He made no attempt to use the cover that was available, and walked into the ambush as if on parade, his bull's-eyes inviting the bandits to fire.

Fire they did, first with the laser cannon and then with a series of shoulder-launched missiles taken on the same raid that had garnered them the first weapon.

The quad staggered under the impact of multiple missile hits, gave thanks that his day had finally arrived, and slid nose-first into a shallow ravine.

It was only after he'd tried to get up that the cyborg realized that he'd been holed, and taken out of the fight.

They'd never kill him, not with the pop guns they were using but it didn't make much difference. He couldn't move and only 32 percent of his armament could bear on the enemy. He raised the gatling gun, turned it towards the bandits, and opened fire. A mixture of snow and dirt fountained around the rocks where the Naa were hiding, and one of them jerked under the multiple impacts, staggered backwards, and fell.

The bio bods, a man named Hutera and a woman named Briggs, hooked up with Roller and worked their way to the left. If they could flank the bandits and nail the gunner, the battle would be won.

On her chest now, crawling towards the enemy, Villain fired her shoulder-mounted launchers. The missiles hit, went off with a roar, and shook the ground. The explosion should have killed the bandits, should have finished the battle, but didn't.

One of the Naa was still alive and determined to take Villain with him. Snow exploded into vapor and dirt turned to glass as he squeezed the trigger and traversed the weapon to the left.

Villain watched the geyser move her way. Shit! Shit! Shit! She was going to cook, going to die, going to...

Rocks exploded under the weight of his pod-like feet as Salazar rounded the hill and probed for something to kill.

It had taken time to make his way around the kopje from the opposite side, more time than he would have liked, but it couldn't be helped. Wait, what was that? An energy cannon, that's what, concealed behind a pile of shattered boulders, traversing towards Villain.

Salazar fired both arms at once, the bullets hitting the Naa a fraction of a second before the energy beam, cutting him apart while the laser cooked the resulting pieces.

The cyborg skidded to a stop, checked to make sure that the bandits were dead, and made his way over to Villain.

"Are you okay?"

Villain gritted nonexistent teeth. "Shit, no."

Salazar smiled inside. If Villain was pissed, then everything was normal. "Hey, what the hell are you complaining about? The techs will put you right in no time."

Salazar helped the other cyborg to her feet and accepted most of her weight. She looked at him. "You took my life and gave it back."

"I what?"

"Nothing. My arm hurts, that's all."

Roller's voice interrupted their conversation.

"Nice work, Four. Okay. Hutera, Briggs, find the friendly and bring 'im in. Somebody fired that flare. Three, call for a lifter, and Two, sit your butt down. You look like hell."

The vast majority of the Legion's officers were with their units on the rim worlds or out on training exercises, so the O club was relatively empty. As if sensing their superior officer's desires, those who were present had found ways to mind their own business. Music seeped over the sound system, voices murmured, and dishes clinked.

General Ian St. James looked across the snowy-white linen and decided that he was one of the luckiest men alive. Not only had Sergi Chien-Chu fallen ill and retired early, his daughter-in-law had chosen to stay.

While he should have invited his staff to dine with Natasha, he had intentionally failed to do so.

The result had been a marvelous two-hour dinner conversation. He had caused her to laugh on at least two occasions, victories planned as carefully as any battle, and had seen the woman she'd been. A wonderful creature, full of life, given to fun.

During those brief moments, St. James had dedicated himself to restoring her spirits and to winning her affection, for surely life offered no greater prize than the one before him. In fact, St. James was so lost in his thoughts of her that the corporal had to clear his throat twice to gain the officer's attention.

"Yes?"

"A message from the com center, sir. The OOD told me to bring it over."

St. James took the seemingly blank piece of paper, dismissed the messenger, and placed his thumb on the access patch. Words appeared. He read them, blinked, and read them again.

"Well, I'll be damned."

Natasha put her wineglass down. She frowned. "Is something wrong?"

St. James shrugged. "It seems that some Hudathan agents landed on the surface of Algeron."

"That's bad."

"Yes, but a man long thought to be dead has come back to life."

"And that's good."

"Yes," St. James answered, pouring her some wine. "That's very good."

19

Each battle has three parts: the plan, which is forever changed by contact with the enemy, reality, which is never what it seems, and the memory of what took place, which evolves to meet current needs. Successful officers trust none of them.

GRAND MARSHAL NIMU WURLA-KA (RET.)
INSTRUCTOR, HUDATHAN WAR COLLEGE
Standard year 1952

With the Hudathan fleet off the Planet Frio II, the Human Empire
The officers' wardroom had been reconfigured to match traditions and regulations established thousands of years before. The court, comprised of Grand Marshal Pem-Da, War Commander Dal-Ba, and Sector Marshal Isam-Ka, sat behind a ceremonially draped table, with their backs to the steel bulkhead. Translators hung round their necks and looked starkly utilitarian compared to the jewel-encrusted splendor of the ceremonial weapons harnesses that they wore.

Witnesses for the court of inquiry, War Commander Niman Poseen-Ka's own chief of staff, Lance Commander Moder-Ta, Spear Commanders Two and Five, and the alien known as Baldwin, sat along the left wall, while those testifying for Poseen-Ka, including Spear Commanders One and Four, plus the geeks called Norwood and Hoskins, sat along the right.

It was, Grand Marshal Pem-Da reflected, highly unusual to have so many aliens involved, and a bit disturbing as well.

Though not specifically prohibited by Hudathan regulations, the inclusion of aliens seemed in poor taste.

Still, the excessive use of geek testimony could serve to weaken Poseen-Ka's case and strengthen Moder-Ta's. Something Pem-Da would welcome, since he favored a more aggressive strategy and wanted Moder-Ta to win. The truth was that Poseen-Ka had received his current command over Pem-Da's vehement objections, an error that could now be corrected.

Yes, Pem-Da decided, the situation was well under control and should proceed in predictable fashion. That being the case, why was he so frightened? Especially since Poseen-Ka was the one that stood accused.

Yet, who could argue with observable fact? The more he achieved, the more he had to lose and the more afraid he became. It was as natural as one, two, three.

Viewed in that manner, *he* had more to lose than Poseen-Ka did, even though the likelihood of actually doing so was less. Pem-Da watched War Commander Niman Poseen-Ka walk in, take the seat at the center of the room, and stare off into the distance.

It was no accident that the accused had been assigned the only chair *not* backed by a bulkhead. The location was part of the psychology, part of the ritual, and symbolized Poseen-Ka's complete vulnerability.

Pem-Da could imagine how the other officer felt. Cold, vulnerable, and a bit sick to his stomach, as if an animal had crawled into his belly and was eating its way out.

It was sad that such a promising officer should have to be destroyed, sacrificed to the needs of the Hudathan race, but that was the way of war. The fact was that Poseen-Ka's strategy was wrong, and worse than wrong, potentially disastrous. By advancing so slowly and allowing the humans time to prepare, he had paved the way towards defeat. The destruction of Spear Three testified to that. Rather than bypass an unimportant target and hurl his forces towards the center of the geek empire, Poseen-Ka had squandered one fifth of his command on a third-rate objective.

Yes, Pem-Da decided, the time had come to appoint a new leader. Moder-Ta perhaps, or another of the young bucks that looked to him for counsel and deserved a bump.

"Your attention, please."

War Commander Dal-Ba was slightly overweight, and more than a bit cranky, since he'd been recalled from a well-deserved leave to preside over the inquiry. Though not exactly in Pem-Da's pocket, he owed the grand marshal a favor or two and would listen to Moder-Ta's arguments. He scanned the compartment.

"By the authority of the ruling triad, Section 3458 of military regulations, and the authority vested in me, this court of inquiry is now in session. Lance Commander Moder-Ta will read the charges."

With the exception of Poseen-Ka's, which stayed straight ahead, all eyes in the room went to Moder-Ta. He stood, knowing that his career was at stake, and glorying in the risk. Victory meant favor from Pem-Da and the possibility of promotion; failure meant death.

Not figuratively, as in falling from favor, but literally, as in catching a bullet right between the eyes. Because should Poseen-Ka win the ensuing confrontation, he would automatically give Moder-Ta the most dangerous assignments available. Such was Hudathan tradition, and a good one at that, acting as it did to ensure a certain amount of loyalty.

Still, there were always those who were willing to risk everything on the chance that they could trim years, or even decades, off the long, slow journey to the top, and Moder-Ta was one of these.

Moder-Ta cleared his throat, looked at the printout held in his right hand, and spoke.

"Acting on information that Spear Three, of the fleet presently under War Commander Poseen-Ka's command, was committed to action and subsequently destroyed, the court calls upon said officer to answer such questions as seem pertinent, and to justify his actions. Failure to answer these questions, or to cooperate with the court, is punishable by imprisonment or death. Does everyone understand?"

No one replied, so Moder-Ta resumed.

"At the point when the officers of the court are satisfied that the relevant facts have been accumulated, evaluated, and understood, they will adjourn and come to a decision. Their decision shall be binding, final, and implemented within a single cycle. Does everyone understand?"

The humans glanced at each other but remained silent, so Moder-Ta took his seat.

Dal-Ba signaled approval with his left hand.

"Good. Then let's get on with it. Using information provided by Spear Three's lone survivor, data gathered by robo-spies, and the reports submitted by Spear Commander Niber-Ba prior to his death, the intelligence section was able to reconstruct a model of the conflict. However, due to the fact that the model is based on very little information, and a great deal of supposition, the accuracy of what we're about to see is open to question."

Pem-Da frowned, willed Dal-Ba to shut-the-hell-up, and traded glances with Moder-Ta.

"Still," Dal-Ba continued stolidly, "the battle sim will serve to set the stage, acquaint everyone with the basic outline of what took place, and lay groundwork for the testimony ahead."

Better, Pem-Da thought critically, better but not perfect. The lights started to fade.

Hoskins was seated next to Norwood. He looked her way and she shrugged in reply.

Darkness descended on the room. Seconds passed. A pinpoint of light appeared, grew larger, and became a miniature sun. The orb started to move, slowly but perceptibly, tracing an orbit across what Norwood estimated was the area just below the ceiling. There was no way to be sure, however, since the light radiated by the sun did nothing to illuminate the room, a fact that mystified Norwood and made the presentation even more effective.

Stars appeared, popping into existence as if made by pinpricks through black paper, until they were everywhere, filling the space where the council sat, twinkling around Norwood's head, and covering the ceiling and deck.

Then, appearing from behind the sun and growing steadily larger, came a strangely shaped... asteroid? Planet? Norwood wasn't sure which. Whatever it was had man-made structures on its surface, structures that looked real, thanks to video taken by the Hudathan robo-spies, included in Niber-Ba's reports.

The object seemed to slow, grow larger, and hang suspended

in the middle of what she knew to be the room. Norwood felt her perspective change to that of someone orbiting along with the planetoid, so she seemed to be stationary while everything else continued to move.

Thanks to the god-like position she occupied, Norwood could see storage tanks, antenna farms, crawlers, robots, miners, techs, and cyborgs, all going about their business, oblivious to the tiny mechanisms that dogged their tracks.

Then came the Hudathan ships, closing in to attack the planetoid's surface, destroying everything in sight. Some of the pictures were computer simulations, but some were real, taken by the attack craft themselves and fed to their mother ships. So Norwood knew, as did every other human in the room, that this was real.

But there was opposition as well, for many of the fighters were destroyed, and many of the Hudathan troops were killed. And killed, and killed. Norwood was amazed that her fellow humans could inflict so much damage and that the Hudathans could take it.

So it went, attack after attack, until remote-controlled ships were launched, and the Hudathan fleet was destroyed.

There was distortion, of course, both in the amount of destruction inflicted on the humans and in the strength of their forces, but the outcome was the same. Once seen, the presentation left little doubt as to the severity of Spear Three's defeat or the relative insignificance of the planetoid in question.

The impression was so strong, in fact, that Poseen-Ka felt a mantle of hopelessness settle over his shoulders as the lights came up, and wondered if he should simply plead incompetent and be done with it. Never had he seen a more disturbing sight than the destruction of so many good ships and the loss of so many Hudathan lives.

But did mistakes made by one commander, and the ensuing destruction of a single spear, signal the failure of his entire strategy? Or was the battle what it appeared to be? A single defeat within a greater framework of success. Poseen-Ka felt his resolve harden and kept his eyes straight ahead.

Baldwin, seated opposite his fellow humans and next to

Moder-Ta, felt triumphant. The battle sim was more damning than anything he could have imagined. With what weak and ineffective weapons would Poseen-Ka defend himself? No, the rest of the inquiry would be little more than a joke, leading to an almost certain victory.

He leaned back in his chair, allowed a smirk to steal across his face, and watched Norwood whisper something to the fool Hoskins. He resented the easy familiarity that existed between them, and more than that, the companionship they had and he didn't. Later, after Moder-Ta took charge, they would be his. To do with as he pleased. The thought felt good. He hugged it close.

"So," Dal-Ba said gloomily, "the facts, to the extent that they will ever be known, have been placed before us. A battle was fought and subsequently lost. The question remains: Was the loss of Spear Three simply an unfortunate incident within the framework of an otherwise successful strategy? And solely the fault of that unit's commanding officer? Or was the loss of Spear Three indicative of a larger failure? A strategy so flawed that it will lead our forces to even more defeats in the future? If so, the officer who devised that strategy and continues to use it is guilty of gross incompetence and must be disciplined. That is the business of this court: to establish that officer's guilt, or to proclaim his innocence, and having done so, to take the appropriate action. Lance Commander Moder-Ta will give his arguments first, followed by War Commander Poseen-Ka. Are there questions? No? That being the case, Lance Commander Moder-Ta may proceed."

Confident that his case was practically airtight, Moder-Ta stood and read his opening statement. Most of it was boring, consisting of a blow-by-blow account of the battle they had just seen, some carefully chosen statistics, and other not especially interesting quotes, opinions, and judgments.

The presentation was so boring, in fact, that Poseen-Ka saw Sector Marshal Isam-Ka's left eyelid start to droop. It was impossible to tell what the officer's right eyelid was doing, since it was hidden by a Mack eye patch, but chances were that it was drooping too. Isam-Ka was falling asleep, a fact that wouldn't have mattered much, except that he was the one member of the court that Poseen-Ka could rely upon. Not because they were members of the same clan, which they were, but because the glue of military politics held them together.

Like Poseen-Ka, the sector marshal favored deliberate advance over slapdash leaps, had done so throughout his career, and was unlikely to change his mind at this late date. So, with Pem-Da opposed to his interests, and Dal-Ba leaning in that direction, Isam-Ka became critical. What if he missed an important piece of testimony? Or was dead to the world at the moment when Poseen-Ka needed him most? Poseen-Ka hurled thoughts at the other officer and willed him to stay awake. It didn't work.

Finally, with his statement read and safely behind him, Moder-Ta turned to his witnesses. Baldwin was first.

The Hudathans made no attempt to swear him in as a human court would have done. After all, why bother? Any witness worth his or her salt would give responses favorable to them and it was the court's job to sort that out.

Nor was Baldwin asked to move to another part of the compartment, stand, or otherwise change the position of his body. He did sit up, however, and felt the translator thump against his chest. He looked into Moder-Ta's eyes. They were as hard as stone.

"So, Colonel Baldwin, you are an officer of some experience and have seen the evidence. What do you conclude?"

Moder-Ta had used his military title! For effect, yes, but it was a first and Baldwin felt his spirits soar. He forced himself to concentrate.

"The objective, a third-rate industrial asteroid, should've been bypassed and dealt with later. Failing that, Spear Three's commanding officer should've launched an all-out attack, what you would call the 'Intaka.' Had he done so right away, the humans would have been unable to launch a counterattack on your battleships."

Moder-Ta eyed the members of the court to make sure they were listening and was pleased to see that Isam-Ka had opened his eyes. He summoned what he hoped was an objective expression.

"You are too modest, Colonel. Members of your race won a great victory. They fought against overwhelming odds and won.

Based on their performance, War Commander Poseen-Ka might argue that every outpost poses a threat. A threat that must be successfully dealt with before the overall war effort can proceed."

"And he'd be wrong," Baldwin argued calmly. "Your forces have taken dozens of worlds, hundreds of outposts similar to the one under discussion, and literally thousands of lesser settlements. None of them put up a creditable defense."

"Ah," Moder-Ta said, "but the war commander has an answer for that argument as well. He points out that most of your naval forces ran rather than fought, and suggests that they are waiting to ambush our fleet and administer the blow of death. How would you respond to that?"

"I'd say it was absurd," Baldwin replied contemptuously. "The Emperor is insane, his government is riddled with corruption, and it takes them forever to make a simple decision. That's why you must attack now. *Before* they can organize the kind of ambush the war commander envisions. To wait is utter madness. Some sort of competent leadership is sure to emerge eventually, and when it does, the military will come around. And, due to the fact that their fleet is virtually intact, you'll have a fight on your hands. Imagine what happened to Spear Three, only multiplied a hundred times."

Norwood felt a sinking sensation in the pit of her stomach. She wasn't so sure about the Emperor, but the rest was true, or could be true. What if the Hudathans believed him? What if Poseen-Ka was replaced? The Hudathans would bypass planets like Frio II, devour the empire in huge bloody gulps, and annihilate her race.

Of course Poseen-Ka might win the war as well, but his strategy provided for at least the possibility of a defense, and something was better than nothing.

Spear Commanders Two and Five testified after that, risking their careers on the strength of promises made by Moder-Ta, and echoing each other's comments. Neither seemed very enthusiastic.

But enthusiastic or not, they allowed Moder-Ta to put them through their paces, endorsed his point of view, and added their weight to the opposition. The fact that they dared to oppose Poseen-Ka, or were desperate enough to do so, would damage his credibility. Of course Spear Commanders One and Four offset their testimony to some extent, sitting as they did on Poseen-Ka's side of the room, staring balefully at their peers.

Poseen-Ka struggled to hide his anger and swore a silent oath to deal with Commanders Two and Five later. Assuming he was alive to do so.

Dal-Ba squinted in Moder-Ta's direction. "Do you have anything to add?"

Moder-Ta made eye contact with each member of the court in turn. "Yes, I would like to say that your decision will influence more than a single officer's career. If War Commander Poseen-Ka remains in command, and continues his present strategy, we could lose the war. Millions of Hudathan lives could be lost, but worse than that, the survivors would be little more than slaves. The outcome is up to you."

Hoskins had learned a lot about the Hudatha since Norwood had walked in out of the snow, and was filled with admiration for Moder-Ta's skillful use of racial psychology. If the other Hudatha were even half as paranoid as Norwood claimed they were, his arguments would have a telling effect.

Dal-Ba looked especially sober. "Thank you, Lance Commander Moder-Ta. You may return to your seat. The time has come for War Commander Poseen-Ka to present his arguments. You may proceed."

Poseen-Ka stood and moved away from both his chair and the vulnerability that it signified. He drifted towards Isam-Ka and made eye contact with Dal-Ba.

"Thank you. I would like to open my arguments by providing the court with a summary of the war effort."

The lights dimmed once again and darkness filled the room. A three-dimensional diagram appeared at the center of the room. In contrast to the mix of computer simulation and actual video used by Moder-Ta, this presentation was entirely symbolic.

Clusters of red spheres represented human-controlled planets, clusters of green spheres stood for Hudathan worlds, and a scattering of blue deltas symbolized Spears One, Two, Four, and Five.

Poseen-Ka started to talk as soon as the model was in place.

He told the court about the attack on Worber's World, and on subsequent worlds, and how the fleet had won each battle. And as he talked red spheres turned to green, each one giving silent testimony to the effectiveness of his strategy, and adding weight to his arguments.

"And so," Poseen-Ka concluded, "my actions can be justified with a single word, and the word is 'success.' Yes, mistakes were made, yes, I lost Spear Three, but consider the overall context. Think about an overall casualty rate below computer projections. Look at the worlds that were part of the human empire and now glow green. Consider the fact that our backs are protected by Hudathan-held planets, that our supply lines are unchallenged, and that our homeworld is safe. Furthermore, if it were not for the fact that my commanders are here testifying both for and against me, we would have even more victories to celebrate."

The officers looked, and couldn't help but be impressed, because the green spheres were like a wedge pointing at the heart of the Human Empire. Not even Pem-Da could deny what Poseen-Ka had accomplished, and momentarily wondered if the other officer was right. But no, an ambush always looks good until you're in it, and then it's too late. Besides, he had committed both his honor and his prestige to pulling Poseen-Ka down, and there was no backing out. He frowned.

"An excellent presentation," Isam-Ka said, signaling his support and filling Dal-Ba's veins with ice. If Pem-Da was opposed to Poseen-Ka, and Isam-Ka had decided to support him, then where did that leave him? With the deciding vote, that's where. A vote that could cost him everything he had worked so hard to achieve. Which officer had the most supporters within the high command? In the triad itself? The questions whirled through his mind and caused his hands to shake. The lights came up and he slid them under the table.

"Thank you, Sector Marshal Isam-Ka, but my strategy has been questioned. Lance Commander Moder-Ta sees no need to protect our backs, to defend our lines of supply, and urges us to leap blindly forward, striking at the enemy's heart while preempting the Intaka. But such a view presupposes that the humans have been inactive, and I intend to challenge that assumption."

Hoskins shifted his weight from one side of the oversized chair to the other and wondered if he'd done the right thing by providing the information the Hudathan was about to use. Favoring Poseen-Ka over his opponents was akin to choosing one dire beast over another. Both wanted to devour you; the only questions were where to start and when to do it.

Such distinctions might seem valid now, and had been sufficient to save the survivors of Frio II, but how would they look at his court-martial? Assuming he lived long enough to have one. Then it would be *he* rather than Poseen-Ka who faced a court of inquiry and awaited the outcome.

The lights dimmed only slightly this time as four documents appeared on the wall opposite the court. There were two originals, both of which were in standard, and two translations. The Hudathan script consisted of pictograms similar to those that Norwood had seen throughout the ship.

Poseen-Ka had hit his stride by now and seemed more like a commanding officer briefing his staff than a defendant pleading his case, a stratagem that made him seem part of the court rather than the subject of it. He pointed a small device at the wall and an arrow appeared.

"As you can see, the first document, the one from NAVCOM Earth, instructs the forces on Frio II to withdraw and head for the inner planets, an order that could suggest either cowardice or a gathering of forces, and would be consistent with what human forces have done up until now.

"Interestingly enough, however, the second document, the one from LEGCOM Algeron, instructs them to ignore the first set of orders and hold. This in spite of the fact that LEGCOM Algeron is a subordinate command structure that normally takes directions from Earth."

Poseen-Ka turned towards Hoskins.

"Lance Commander Moder-Ta saw fit to call on human testimony, so tell us, Major Hoskins, how do you interpret those conflicting orders?"

Hoskins swallowed the lump that had formed at the back of his throat. A hand went to the translator that hung from his neck.

"I have no way to know for sure, but I assume that LEGCOM Algeron favors a different strategy than that advocated by NAVCOM Earth, and has decided to go its own way."

Poseen-Ka could have asked a follow-up question, but didn't, preferring to let the news sink in instead.

All three of the judges looked at each other in alarm. This was a brand-new piece of information, carefully hoarded, and used to great effect. A split in the human command structure! Even the triad itself would take notice. But what did it mean?

Pem-Da was furious that Moder-Ta had allowed himself to be outmaneuvered and said so with a scathing look. The energy was wasted, however, since Moder-Ta had aimed a similar expression at Baldwin, who had turned white as a sheet.

Poseen-Ka was well aware of the discomfort that he'd caused but pretended to be above such things. The questions continued.

"Describe the planet Algeron."

Hoskins felt cold all over. He sat at attention. "I refuse to provide you with information about the planet or its defenses."

Poseen-Ka looked stern.

"Nor did I ask you for such information. Tell the court what LEGCOM Algeron means. I ask nothing more."

Hoskins shrugged. "It means Legion Command, Algeron."

"Yes," Poseen-Ka hissed softly. "Legion Command, Algeron. Headquarters for the Imperial Legion! A world already under surveillance by our long-range scouts. A well-fortified planet, with no civilian population to worry about, that intends to fight us. Why? And in cooperation with whom?"

Poseen-Ka turned and pointed an accusing finger at Moder-Ta. "Tell us, Lance Commander Moder-Ta, is this the kind of world you would have us bypass? Is this the kind of world that you would leave between our fleet and the homeworld? Is this the kind of world you want me to deal with later?"

Moder-Ta opened his mouth but nothing came out.

Completely in command now, Poseen-Ka whirled towards the hatch and rapped out an order.

"Bring him in."

The hatch hissed upwards and a medic entered the room. He was closely followed by a power-assisted stretcher and a second medic. A third of the stretcher had been raised so the heavily bandaged pilot could sit up. He tried to salute. The first medic helped him complete the motion.

"I give you Flight Officer Norbu Seena-Ra, the single surviving member of Spear Three, the only real battle with the humans. We would know nothing of the final battle were it not for Seena-Ra's heroic efforts to bring us the news. He's much too weak to give prolonged testimony, so I will limit myself to three questions."

Poseen-Ka walked over to the stretcher and placed a hand on the pilot's arm. The pilot's burned face had been covered with lab-grown skin. Bandages offered some protection and held the artificial tissue in place. The war commander looked down and made contact with two pain-filled eyes.

"Tell us, Flight Officer Seena-Ra, how did the humans fight?"

The pilot's voice was little more than a croak and, had it not been for the almost total silence in the compartment, would have been impossible to hear.

"The humans fought like devils."

"Did they have weapons or capabilities that you would consider to be unusual?"

"They had cyborgs, huge things that could destroy aircraft and troops alike, and stalked the surface like killer robots."

"One more question," Poseen-Ka said, "and you can return to sick bay. The soldiers and the cyborgs... what unit were they from?"

Seena-Ra rolled his eyes. The words seemed to fall from his mouth like stones. "They were members of the Imperial Legion."

"Thank you."

Poseen-Ka turned towards the court as the pilot was wheeled from the room.

"So there you have it. Lance Commander Moder-Ta, and those who agree with him, would have us bypass the very world on which many of the Human Empire's most effective troops are headquartered. And they would have us do so while completely ignorant of whatever traps are being laid. Yes, we must fear an ambush, yes, we must fear the blow of death, yes, we must move aggressively. But *not* by foolhardy leaps into the unknown, *not* by abandoning a strategy that has been successful, and *not* by ignoring the natural conservatism that has protected our race for so long. Thank you."

So saying, Poseen-Ka strode to the middle of the room, took his seat, and stared straight ahead. He'd left some witnesses uncalled, but their testimony would be assumed, so he felt comfortable with that decision. Yes, Poseen-Ka decided, he'd done the best he could and it was time to quit.

There was a long moment of silence as everyone present absorbed what he'd said.

Norwood felt something akin to victory.

Hoskins worried about the effect of what he'd done.

Baldwin felt rage bubble up from deep inside.

Moder-Ta wondered how many days he had left.

And Pem-Da made the decision to salvage what he could.

Dal-Ba cleared his throat. The choice would be easier than he'd thought.

"Thank you, War Commander Poseen-Ka. Having heard testimony both for and against the officer in question, and having considered all of the evidence, the court is ready to vote. Sector Marshal Isam-Ka?"

"Not guilty."

"Grand Marshal Pem-Da?"

"Not guilty."

Dal-Ba gave an involuntary blink of surprise but was otherwise impassive.

"Thank you. And since my vote is 'not guilty' as well, let the record show that War Commander Poseen-Ka has been exonerated of all charges against him and restored to his command. This court of inquiry is now adjourned."

It was then that Baldwin came to his feet, gave an incoherent bellow, and charged Poseen-Ka. The Hudathan was waiting when the human arrived, decked him with a single blow, and ordered his bodyguards to haul the unconscious body away.

Their usefulness at an end, Norwood and Hoskins were escorted out of the compartment and led away.

Moder-Ta, along with Spear Commanders Two and Five, followed. With a war on, and Poseen-Ka in command, their prospects were suddenly bleak.

That left Pem-Da, Isam-Ka, Dal-Ba, and Poseen-Ka himself.

"So," Pem-Da said, forcing a jocularity that he didn't feel, "what next?"

Poseen-Ka looked through him as if able to see something beyond. There was no humor in his voice or mercy in his eyes.

"Next comes Algeron, and after that, Earth itself."

20

Planet Algeron, the Human Empire

The VIP suite boasted dark red walls, gold trim, and ornate handcrafted furniture. Regimental emblems had been framed and hung on the walls along with a selection of ancient hand weapons and some bloodstained flags. It made for a rather somber setting and Chien-Chu would be glad to escape it. He put his hands on his daughter-in-law's shoulders and looked into her eyes. They were level with his.

"Are you sure? Twelve ships have dropped hyper during the last hour. Scolari will deliver an ultimatum of some sort, St. James will refuse, and the marines will land." He shrugged. "After that who knows. The Legion stands a good chance... but nothing is certain."

Natasha forced a smile. "Yes, I'm sure. I can be useful here. The Cabal needs a representative on Algeron. You said so yourself. Besides, based on what I've heard during the last few

A pair of marine guards crashed to attention as she approached the operations center. The heels of their right boots hit the deck at precisely the same moment that their Class IV assault rifles went vertical. Scolari nodded her approval, taking pleasure in the recognition of her rank and the precision with which it was rendered.

The hatch slid aside and Scolari entered the ops center. All three watches were present, bringing the total number of people in the compartment up to thirty or so, making things a bit crowded.

Like Scolari, the ops center staff wore lightweight pressure suits that would automatically inflate if the compartment was holed. Their helmets, which were transparent, hung down around their faces like folds of translucent skin. They looked more alien than human as they hunched over their screens and muttered into their microphones.

An officer materialized at Scolari's elbow. His name was Wheeler and his normally attractive features looked grotesque through the heavy-duty plastic. The helmet muffled his voice.

"Welcome to the ops center, Admiral. Captain Kedasha is making her rounds. We're right on schedule."

Scolari nodded her approval. "Any sign of the transports?"

Wheeler knew what she meant. The transports sent to evacuate the Legion had never been heard from again.

"No, ma'am. The intelligence reports were accurate. The ships are gone."

Scolari nodded again. Lieutenant Colonel Vial had been correct. St. James *had* loaded the transports with reinforcements and sent them to the rim worlds. Good. The Hudatha would cut them down to size and make her job that much easier.

A com tech wormed his way through the crowd and whispered something in Wheeler's ear. He turned to Scolari. "One of our scouts reports that a ship has lifted and is headed out-system."

"Profile?"

The tech whispered something more in Wheeler's ear.

"A relatively small Class IX courier or yacht."

"Let it go. We have bigger fish to fry."

The tech nodded and disappeared into the crowd.

"We're in com range?"

Wheeler nodded. "Yes, Admiral. Easily."

"Excellent. Get General St. James on-screen. I want to talk to him."

It took five minutes for the signal to reach Algeron, another five to find St. James, and five more to get him on-screen. He wore a crisp set of camos and his face looked bleak. Scolari saw combat-equipped legionnaires moving around in the background and knew that his forces were as ready as hers. More so since the planet was fortified.

"Hello, Admiral. Nice of you to drop in."

Scolari squinted through plastic. She could feel everyone in the operations center staring at her. She was conscious of how her statement would sound to the Emperor, to the public, and to the historians who would study the campaign.

"I'm only going to say this once... so listen carefully. You have been charged with dereliction of duty, refusal to obey lawful orders, incitement to mutiny, and high treason. On behalf of the Emperor, and in accordance with the relevant military codes, I hereby relieve you of command, and order that you step down. You will surrender yourself to the military police and be confined to quarters until I arrive. Lieutenant Colonel Andre Vial has been appointed to take your place."

Only those who knew St. James extremely well would have noticed the slight tic in his right eyelid and understood what it meant. His expression was otherwise unchanged.

"Lieutenant Colonel Vial is somewhat incapacitated at the moment. It seems that my intelligence people caught him trying to load and launch an unauthorized message torp. As for stepping down and surrendering myself to traitors, the answer is no. The Legion will stand against tyranny even if it comes from within."

Scolari's jaw worked and her fists were clenched into balls of bony flesh. "Then say your prayers." The Admiral made a cutting motion with her right hand and the video snapped to black.

Bio bods, cyborgs, and vehicles of all sorts had poured out of Fort Camerone for hours now. Radios crackled, orders snapped, engines revved, servos whined, boots stamped, and gears ground as they headed out into the wastelands. The lights that normally lit the parade ground had been extinguished, but the sun was in the process of rising, so it was possible to see.

Long dark shadows slanted down from the walls, rippled across the jam-packed grinder, and gave Booly a place to hide. Escaping from the base hospital had been as easy as walking away. Now came the hard part: breaking his word of honor, betraying those that trusted him, and discarding his way of life. But if desertion was horrible, then the other possibility was even worse.

Windsweet had filled a space that he hadn't even known existed, and having done so, had left an emptiness that only she could fill.

Booly had been thinking of her as General St. James pinned a medal to the front of his hospital robe, had dreamed about her that night and every night that followed, until it seemed as though he thought of nothing else and would explode if he didn't see her, hear her voice, smell her perfume, or touch the fur that covered her body.

Booly's breath came in short shallow gasps and his heart beat like a trip-hammer. His shoulder ached, nausea filled his stomach, and fear weakened his knees. To desert now, on the very eve of battle, was to sever all ties with the Legion and become an outcast. He would be hunted by aliens and humans alike, forced to scavenge a living from the surface of a harsh planet, all because of someone he should never have even known, much less loved.

But no matter what he told himself, no matter how much he tried to suppress the feelings, they wouldn't go away. So he would trade what he had for what he couldn't live without, and willingly pay the price.

A platform surfaced and a company of Trooper IIs clanked off. Some bio bods were right behind them. Elements of the 1st RE under the command of Colonel "Crazy Alice" Goodwin. She marched at the head of the troops, her badly scarred face a symbol of the sacrifice that she was willing to make, and expected others to make as well.

Booly waited for the legionnaires to climb into the waiting APCs, drifted out of the shadows, and marched briskly towards a heavily loaded hover truck. He carried a field pack stuffed with E-rations, twice the normal amount of ammo, and a brand-new assault rifle. He opened the passenger-side door, threw his gear inside, and climbed into the cab. It smelled like stale cigarette smoke. The driver was surprised but cordial.

"Hi, Sergeant Major… need a ride?"

"Yeah, the brass had me on an administrative shit detail. Just busted loose. Have you seen Legaux? Or any of his staff?"

The driver wore a kepi tilted towards the back of his head. A cigarette rode the top of his left ear, and thick red eyebrows wiggled as he talked.

"I didn't see him, but the 1st REC pulled out about three hours ago, or so I heard. A good thing too. Wouldn't want the swabbies to catch the borgs in a trap. Don't know where they headed, though… so I might take you in the wrong direction."

Booly nodded. "Well, the way I figure it, somewhere's better than nowhere, so let's go."

Radios crackled and the column started to move. The truck in front of them rose on its fans. Grit sprayed sideways and rattled on the windshield. Turbines whined, the truck wobbled, and the cab tilted forward. The main gate came and went. The fortress and everything it stood for disappeared behind them.

The mobile command post (MCP) consisted of three linked units, each with its own set of tracks and individual power plant. The vehicle, custom-designed for use on Algeron, looked like a segmented beetle as it crawled up and over gently rounded hills or waddled through low-lying gullies. A squad of six Trooper IIs accompanied the huge vehicle, scouting ahead and protecting its flanks.

Boulders popped under the MCP's considerable weight and peppered the undercarriage with rock shrapnel. One of these, larger than the rest, caused module 2 to lurch sideways. Natasha lost her balance, slid toward the edge of the jump seat and grabbed for a handhold. It made her conscious of where she was. The sights, sounds, and even the smells were foreign to her.

Module 2 functioned as a defensive nerve center and used

encrypted radio transmissions to stay in touch with sensor stations all over the planet. A single aisle ran down the vehicle's axis. Rows of computer-controlled equipment and camo-clad technicians sat to either side. It was their job to take raw intelligence, put it through sophisticated computer programs, and feed the resulting summaries to module 1, where St. James and his staff used the information to plot strategy.

Tactical problems, like those handled in module 3, relied on the sensor stations for data, but were dealt with by an artificial intelligence known as "Bob." It was Bob's job to counter incoming missiles, attack ships, and energy weapons that could reach down from space itself. Since the Legion had no air or space force of its own, Bob's role was especially important, with most of his processing ability being dedicated to antiaircraft activity.

Natasha knew that a second MCP, identical to the first, and under the command of St. James's XO, Colonel Edwina "Ed" Jefferson, was also on the loose, maintaining complete radio silence, but ready to take over should the first unit be destroyed.

They were new facts, new realities, completely unlike anything Natasha had dealt with before, as strange as the heavily starched camos she wore.

"Would you care for some coffee?"

The question came from a master sergeant. She had large expressive eyes, creamy brown skin, and flashing white teeth. The module rocked slightly but her hand stayed steady as a rock. The cup had a lid to prevent spills. A tendril of steam twisted its way up from a small slit.

Natasha accepted the cup. "Yes, thank you."

The legionnaire nodded and leaned against an equipment locker. She had a mug of her own.

Natasha sipped the piping hot liquid and held the cup between her palms. Warmth seeped into her hands. The module lurched sideways and a few drops of coffee escaped the lid.

The master sergeant smiled sympathetically. "Not to worry, ma'am. The terrain will become smoother soon and stay that way till we reach the foothills."

Natasha took another sip of her coffee. "What then?"

The legionnaire smiled. "Then we slip into one of many

prebored tunnels, connect the MCP to a batch of prelaid cables, and slam the back door."

"Slam the back door? What does that mean?"

"Simple," the other woman replied cheerfully. "We blow the hillside and use a few hundred tons of rock to seal ourselves in."

Although Natasha had no military training to speak of, she had no trouble understanding the logic involved. The enemy might or might not know about the mobile command posts and the prebored tunnels, but even if they did, they wouldn't know which hidey-hole the Legion had used, and, with tons of rock sealing them in, the command staff would be safe from anything short of a direct hit by a baby nuke. Not only that, but specially protected radio and cable facilities would ensure their ability to communicate. She thought of one potential problem, however.

"But how do we get out?"

The legionnaire shrugged. "The Pioneers will dig us out, or failing that, we'll abandon the command post and use escape tunnels already in place."

Someone called her name, so the master sergeant nodded in Natasha's direction and headed towards a well-padded chair. A mike swiveled in front of her mouth as if folded around her. The tech sitting to the woman's right said something and she laughed in response.

Natasha envied their companionship and found herself thinking of Leonid. Guilt rolled over her like a wave. Her husband had been dead how long? Weeks? Months? She tried to calculate all the variables involved and quickly gave up. A month seemed about right. Not much time really, and she had already betrayed him, if not physically then emotionally, for she had every intention of pursuing the relationship with St. James wherever it might go.

Sergi knew how she felt and approved. Natasha was sure of that. If her ex-father-in-law approved, there was nothing to worry about, was there? And what did it matter with death all around?

The module lurched, the deck slanted down, and Natasha hung on. What would be, would be.

* * *

Booly waited until a rock slide brought the convoy to a jerking halt, thanked the driver for the lift, and jumped to the ground. He didn't know what the younger legionnaire thought about his sudden departure, nor did he care. No, it was not for corporals to ask such questions or for sergeant majors to answer them. Too bad his rank wouldn't mean much out in the wastelands.

Three day-cycles and two night-cycles had passed since their departure from Fort Camerone. The sun had started to set, the air tasted clean after the stuffiness of the cab, and gravel crunched beneath his boots.

Vehicles were lined up bumper-to-bumper for more than a mile, sitting ducks for low-flying aircraft. Officers and noncoms swore, burning the airwaves with their invective, trying to clear the jam by force of will. It was too late. The rearmost vehicles were backing up, but by the time they got far enough back to do some good, the obstacle would have been removed.

Cyborgs were dispatched to cover both flanks, prayers were said, and electronic eyes swept the heavens. The swabbies hadn't dropped into orbit yet, or so intelligence claimed, but nobody trusted them.

Engines growled as heavy equipment moved up to clear the slide and hundreds of troops left their vehicles. Some stretched, and told each other lies about their sexual prowess, while the rest moved out into the surrounding ravines in search of some privacy. Booly joined them.

Weapons were SOP for such excursions, but packs were the exception. Booly received more than a few quizzical looks. Still, if the sergeant major wanted to lug fifty or sixty pounds of extra weight around, who were they to object?

Booly found that it was relatively easy to slip into a side ravine, check his back trail, and disappear into the quickly gathering darkness. After that it was a simple matter to find a crevice, sit down, and wait for the Legion to go away. It took the better part of an hour, but the shouts, bursts of radio traffic, and engine rumble finally died away.

A Trooper II, on the lookout for bandits and stragglers, crunched its way down a dry riverbed but neglected to scan

Booly's crevice. The pod steps died away and allowed complete and utter silence to fall over the land. Booly discovered that he had never felt so all alone.

The ridge made a perfect vantage point. The Naa chieftain wriggled forward, brought the binoculars to his eyes, and zoomed in. It was nearly dark, but the Legion-issue glasses did an excellent job of gathering what light there was and amplifying it.

Wayfar Hardman watched the earthmovers scrape out shallow trenches and saw the quads settle into them like ground-nesting brellas. The "Rulu," or attack from beneath the ground, was one of the Naa's favorite tactics, and the chieftain gave a grunt of approval. Dug in, and covered over with loose soil, the cyborgs formed a nearly impregnable cluster of mutually supporting fire bases.

No, Hardman corrected himself, not impregnable, since the Legion had never used such tactics against the Naa. Nor had they needed to, since no tribe or combination of tribes could stand against such massed strength.

Of equal interest was the fact that similar things were taking place at a variety of locations, none of which had any special bearing on his people, but had been frequented by humans in the past. Places where holes had been dug, mysterious boxes had been buried, and humans visited once or twice a year.

Hardman had issued orders to excavate one such box in hopes of finding a weapons cache but had lost three of his best warriors in the ensuing explosion.

So what was happening? And whom did the humans fear? Whoever it was had to be as strong or stronger than they were to justify such extreme precautions. Anyone who was that strong would represent a threat to his people as well, since they could be killed in the cross fire.

The aliens who called themselves "Hudathans" seemed like the likeliest possibility, but who knew for sure? A race such as the humans were likely to have multiple enemies, *must* have multiple enemies, or why have so many warriors?

For the first time, and much to his own surprise, Hardman

wished that Booly had stayed. Though somewhat strange, and a bad influence on Windsweet, the human was a competent warrior. The fight with Surekill proved that. Booly would know what these activities meant and be able to provide advice. But the legionnaire was gone and that was that.

Hardman pushed himself backwards, felt gravel slide under his chest, and got to his feet. Rocks littered the plateau. It was necessary to jump from one to the next. All were warmed by the sun every other hour. Heat-sensitive ganglia located in the soles of his feet helped identify the largest and, in most cases, the most stable rocks.

Hardman's dooth caught his scent and snorted a greeting. The chieftain snorted in reply, vaulted into the saddle, and urged the beast forward. Three of his most trusted warriors moved with him.

A storm was gathering, and even a fool knows that the best place to seek shelter during a storm is deep, deep underground.

The atmosphere reminded St. James of a primitive church, with screens where the altars would be, each tended by its own priest or priestess, all of whom were in communication with the gods.

Except that these gods were flesh-and-blood human beings, located hundreds or even thousands of miles away, and none were immortal or armed with supernatural weapons.

St. James sat at the front end of module 1 with his back to the airplane-style control compartment. The command chair hugged the officer in its black embrace, whining softly, as it cushioned him from the effects of the explosion.

An empty coffee cup clattered to the deck and someone swore. A voice whispered in his ear.

"The back door is closed, sir. All stations are in the green."

"Roger. Crank her up. Give me a sitrep, please."

Information flooded the legionnaire's mind. Scolari's forces were in orbit. Energy beams had started to probe the surface, assault craft had been launched, and drop ships were falling through the atmosphere. Facts, figures, reports, and commentary were processed and fed through St. James's headset. The Second Battle of Camerone had begun.

* * *

Scolari basted in her own sweat. The pressure suit kept everything in, including the smell of her own body. The officer blinked her eyes. It felt as if they were lined with sandpaper. How long had she been in the ops center anyway? A long time. Sleep beckoned but she pushed it away. Her subordinates were fools and would ruin everything if left on their own. The plans were the key. She reviewed them one last time.

All Imperial forces were required to file primary, secondary, and tertiary battle plans on any installation classified as "Triple A" or better, and the Legion was no exception.

Ironically enough, all three plans had been drawn up by the traitor Mosby prior to her assignment on Earth. All had one thing in common. Consistent with their absurd traditions and notions of honor, the Legion planned to defend Fort Camerone to the death.

According to the schematics, drawings, and other materials on file at NAVCOM Earth, the fort would be a hard nut to crack. It was a hardened, mostly subterranean complex, equipped with thickets of missile batteries and energy cannons that could reach the upper atmosphere. Having no air arms to speak of, and rightfully fearing those who did, the Legion had invested a great deal of money in antiaircraft technology.

So it was this commonality, this insistence on defending Camerone, that Scolari planned to exploit. By concentrating her attack on the fortress, and reducing it to rubble, she would kill the monster's brain and destroy the majority of its strength at the same time. Casualties would be high, but the price would be worth it.

The very thought of it refreshed Scolari's mind and sent adrenaline pumping through her veins.

Death reached down from the sky, found Fort Camerone, and caressed it with fire. Computer-guided missiles came first, blowing holes in the steel-reinforced concrete, preparing the way for the smart bombs that followed.

Any one of the bombs would have leveled the complex had

Scolari's forces been authorized to use nuclear weapons, but the Emperor had expressly forbidden them, pointing out that Algeron belonged to *him* and might come in handy someday.

So the fortress died the death of a thousand cuts, crumbling a bit at a time, until both it and what had formerly been Naa town ceased to exist. But the destruction was far from one-way, as salvos of self-directed missiles rammed their way up through the atmosphere to hit the troop-packed drop ships as they plummeted downwards.

It was only later, when it was too late to make much use of the information, that a computer would notice that the fortress had made little or no attempt to intercept the missiles directed towards itself, and had used every weapon it had to destroy the incoming troopships. The fort's ability to attack such vessels was eventually neutralized, but not before 26 percent of the marines in the first wave were killed. Scolari was furious.

The words were flat and unemotional. St. James wasn't sure who had uttered them and decided that it didn't matter.

"All of Fort Camerone's offensive and defensive weapons systems have been destroyed. At least a brigade of marines has landed and is digging in."

St. James mustered some saliva and rolled it around his mouth. The muscles along the top of his shoulders hurt and his right foot had fallen asleep. He worked it back and forth.

"Casualties?"

He recognized the voice this time. It belonged to an intelligence officer named Tarker.

"We have two casualties, sir, both deaders, killed when their scout car went off a cliff."

St. James swore silently. A goddamned accident. Such things were inevitable with so many men, women, and cyborgs milling around, but it was unfortunate just the same. He'd hoped for a zero casualty rate going into phase two, and would've had one too, except for the errant scout car.

Knowing that Scolari could access the battle plans filed on Earth, and knowing that they focused on defending Camerone,

St. James had decided to sacrifice the entire installation, while preventing as many marines from reaching the surface as he could. With that strategy in mind the legionnaire had evacuated every single human being and Naa from Fort Camerone *prior* to Scolari's attack. Now with the marines on the ground, and his forces almost completely intact, it was time to turn the tables.

Way out in the wastelands, more than a thousand miles from the spot where Mobile Command Post One had burrowed its way into a hillside, something moved. The vibrations it made were transmitted through the soil around it to a nearby burrow. Roused from its sleep a buka nuzzled her thumb-sized pups, found everything was okay, and yawned. And, having felt the vibration many times before, went back to sleep.

Above the ground, where the eternal winds whipped across the rock-strewn plains, a metal rod poked its way up through the gravel, gave birth to a microsecond-long burst of coded radio traffic, and retreated underground.

This particular transmission meant nothing at all, and was intended to confuse the enemy, but other similar bursts of code *did* have meaning, and the Legion started to stir.

First came their mechanical minions, tiny robots that crawled, hopped, and flew around the marines, collecting information and passing it along to low-powered relay stations that took the intelligence and sent it to MCP One and Two via hardened cable. Many of the robots were identified and destroyed, but those that survived kept on reporting.

Which is how Colonel Pierre Legaux knew that six companies of Imperial marines were in the process of setting up a defensive perimeter around an area just east of what had been Fort Camerone.

Since the size and shape of the perimeter suggested a rough-and-ready airstrip, he knew it was likely that the jarheads planned to land reinforcements, followed by a wing of atmospheric fighter-bombers, followed by god knows what else. Armor probably.

Now, if there's anything that an armored officer hates more than attack aircraft, it's enemy armor, and Legaux was no exception. The grunts would have to die, and that being the case, there was no point in waiting around while they got stronger. Legaux made a plan, ran it by his company commanders, and fed it to MCP One. Authorization arrived ten seconds later.

Villain, along with an entire company of Trooper IIs, had been buried four feet underground. And why not? Her brain, the only remaining portion of her original anatomy that required oxygen, got more than enough from a pair of tanks located where a bio bod's kidneys would be.

The idea of being buried alive bothers most people, including Villain. But the fact that she was strong enough to break through the surface on her own helped to lessen the cyborg's fears, as did the knowledge that an ultralow-frequency radio link tied her to the rest of the company, four of whom were buried no more than five or six yards away.

And so it was that she was able to relax while sleep tugged her downwards. Villain had been through the dream so many times by now that she no longer feared it. Even as she lifted the cool-case and carried it towards the front of the store, she knew what would happen next.

She saw the customers, rejected the woman as unimportant and focused on the man. It was strange to see Perez-Salazar the way he'd been then, good-looking in an underfed sort of way, silly in the ball cap and wraparound sunglasses. She felt her heart beat a tiny bit faster and forced a smile.

"May I help you?"

"Yeah," Perez-Salazar said, "keep your hands where I can see 'em and give me everything in the till."

Conners-Villain shook her head. "Go ahead and shoot... you will anyway."

She watched the gun come up, watched him aim it at her chest and heard the hammer fall. *Click*. Nothing happened. Perez-Salazar looked confused. Villain laughed, and was still laughing when the orders came over her radio.

"Roller One to Roller Team. Rise 'n' shine, jerk weeds, we've got grunts to grease, and the colonel's in a hurry."

The voice belonged to Roller, who, along with five bio bods, was holed up in Gunner's cargo compartment. The atmosphere was more than a little ripe by now and the noncom would be glad when they could pop a hatch. His next order was directed at Gunner.

"Roller One to Roller Two... time to rock 'n' roll."

Gunner sent a pole-mounted sensor up through the surface of the ground, took a quick look around, and followed with the gatling gun. It would provide covering fire in case of an attack. Then, gathering his strength and directing it to his legs, the quad stood. Dirt erupted upwards, sprayed in all directions, and streamed downwind.

The other quads did likewise, like crabs emerging from the sand, their sensors sweeping the sky for signs of threat. Then, like zombies rising from their graves, the Trooper IIs sat up and scrambled to their feet. Systems checks were run, air jets were used to blow dirt from moving parts, and intelligence was downloaded to on-board computers.

All of the information gathered by the Legion's robots had been combined to create a composite map. The marines, their positions, the perimeter, and the implications thereof were crystal-clear. So was the fact that "B" Company, 1st REC, was ideally positioned to attack the jarheads, being only ten miles to the north and screened by some low-lying hills. Speed would be of the essence, however, since the Navy's orbital spy-eyes would detect them within the next ten minutes or so and dispatch attack craft to their position.

Knowing that his troops understood the situation just as well as he did, Colonel Legaux wasted no time on unnecessary instructions, and gave a single order.

"Charge!"

Mounted behind a Trooper II named Hanagan and possessed of a body only slightly more natural than the one he rode, Legaux looked like some sort of mythical war god charging into battle. He wasted no time looking backwards, nor did he need to, since every borg in his command was traveling at flank speed. The attack involved three companies of cyborgs, totaling 296 Trooper IIs, 26 quadrupeds, and 168 bio bods, some of whom rode inside the quads, while the rest hung onto Trooper IIs. They made an impressive sight loping towards the enemy, pennants whipping in the wind, dust rolling up to fill the air.

All the borgs, with the exception of a quad and a pair of Trooper IIs with mechanical difficulties, traveled at approximately forty-five miles an hour, which meant that they covered the intervening distance in a little over ten minutes. And, given the fact that the 1st REC rolled over the jarheads' outlying sentry posts about the same time as word of the attack arrived from orbit, the air threat was temporarily neutralized. The brass knew that once the two forces were intermingled, an air attack would do as much damage to the marines as it would to the legionnaires.

So, unless the ranking grunt, a major named Hu, wanted to call in an air strike on her own position, she didn't have much choice but to fight the legionnaires on their own terms, and the 1st REC took full advantage.

The countryside seemed to sway and jump as Villain ran. The hills grew larger, the ground sloped upwards, and tracer stabbed down from the ridge. A cyborg stumbled, slammed facedown in the dirt, and skidded to a halt. It had been a lucky shot but telling nonetheless. Villain traced the bullets to their source, ran a lightning-fast solution, and fired a shoulder-launched missile. There was a flash of white light followed by the sound of an explosion. The tracer stopped.

"Nice shootin'."

Salazar had moved up on Villain's left and positioned himself to protect her flank. She started to snap at him, remembered the dream, and thought better of it.

"Thanks, Sal. Watch your ass."

"I like yours better."

"Shut the fuck up and pay attention to what you're doing."

She could almost hear his grin.

"That's my baby."

Gunner chose the point where two hills came together, knowing it would be easier to negotiate, and more likely to get him killed. Surely it was his turn to burn, to die like his family before him, to join them in the great hereafter. After all, he'd earned it hadn't he? Damned right he had.

Gunner dropped his bio bods, stepped out onto the plain, and opened up with everything he had. Missiles raced out of his launchers, found targets, and destroyed them one at a time. His quad-mounted energy cannon probed the rocks, found ceramic armor, and cooked the flesh inside, as the gatling gun swiveled right, locked onto an APC, and turned it to scrap.

Then, feeling sure that he'd drawn enough attention to himself, Gunner illuminated the bull's-eyes on either side of his hull. The lights were a new wrinkle, added only recently, and almost sure to have the desired effect.

Fully aware that they'd be forced to face the Legion's cyborgs, and more than a little concerned about that possibility, the marines had been issued double the normal complement of fire-and-forget shoulder-launched missiles. These were put to use with devastating effect.

Gunner took five SLMs within seconds of illuminating the targets on his sides and felt his entire body shake as secondary explosions followed the initial impacts. System after system went down, until he could no longer move. The incoming fire slackened as he went down.

No! he screamed. I'm still alive! Fire, damn you, fire! But the marines had more than enough targets, and turned their attention to those that moved, leaving the blackened hulk to sit where it was, smoke pouring from its belly, weapons useless.

Gunner disengaged his spider-form from the larger quad body, scampered free, and waited for some enterprising marine to shoot him. None did. Depressed, and still very much alive, he made his way back towards one of the predesignated assembly areas.

Villain and her fellow cyborgs felt all-powerful as they strode through the marine defenses, dealing death with both arms, stepping over piles of dead bodies.

Later, when the battle was over, she would remember what it felt like to die and wonder about what she'd done. But not now while bullets flattened themselves against her armor, and friends vanished inside yellow-red explosions, and hate pumped chemicals into her brain, and voices screamed in her nonexistent ears.

"Watch him. Roller Six! He's toting an SLM!"

"Damn! Look at that sucker burn!"

"Roller Eight's down... I'm pulling his box..."

"I have an APC on bearing two..."

"Wait a minute... cease fire... cease fire, damn you! They're waving a white flag."

It took a conscious effort to stop firing, to stop killing, and see the scraps of white cloth that fluttered in the breeze. Villain saw a pair of men's shorts and laughed.

The message torp had started its journey in normal space, jumped hyper out near Jupiter, and dropped well clear of Algeron. One of Scolari's scouts had homed on its radio beacon, had pulled the device aboard, and hightailed it for the flagship.

Once aboard, codes were entered via an external jack, and a hatch popped open. The data cube was extremely small but capable of carrying an enormous amount of information. The color, plus the code stamped on the plastic casing, screamed *"High Priority—command eyes only."*

A crypto tech, accompanied by two heavily armed marines, carried the cube to the ops center, where it was handed over to Scolari herself.

Curious, and grateful for an excuse to retreat to her cabin, Scolari accepted the cube and left. It was only when the hatch was safely closed and she was all alone that the naval officer removed the pressure suit. She wrinkled her nose. What a horrible stink! What should she do? Shower? Or play the cube?

Curiosity won out. Scolari walked over to her desk, dropped the cube in the player, and pressed her thumb against the recognition plate. A fog appeared over her desk, swirled, and took on form. The Emperor looked years older than when she'd last seen him and extremely tired. He looked straight into her eyes.

"Hello, Admiral. Things are going well, I trust. The same can't be said for things here on Earth unfortunately. A group calling itself 'The Cabal' broke Mosby and her legionnaires out of prison yesterday. They are well armed and headed this way. Those elements of the Navy and Marine Corps not with you continue to stand by me. They may require some assistance, however, so I'm ordering you to withdraw and return to Earth."

The Emperor started to turn away and looked back again. He smiled crookedly.

"Oh, and one more thing. I'd hurry if I were you."

Contrails made white streaks across the sky and missiles rose to meet them as Hardman arrived in his village. The ride had been long and hard, frequently interrupted by the need to hide from both the Legion and the sky soldiers. Both had a tendency to fire at shadows.

But finally, after many wasted hours, Hardman made his way home. Shootstraight and the other warriors had already shooed most of the females and cubs underground and done what they could to camouflage the village. They knew that just as they could *feel* warmth through the soles of their feet, the humans could *see* it through the eyes of their machines, and send death to find it.

So all fires had been extinguished, the dooth herds had been released into the mountains to forage for themselves, and no one ventured outside except at night.

The chieftain slipped into the village at twilight, released his dooth, and sought his home. Tired though he was, some clean clothes, a good hearty meal, and a mug of ale would set him right.

The entry had been covered with a large basket filled with dirt. Hardman lifted a corner, slid inside, and made his way down into the living area. He used a flashlight to find his way.

Hardman knew that most of the villagers would be in the underground cavern, so didn't expect to find anyone at home, but called anyway. Windsweet would be frightened if he appeared without warning.

"Windsweet? Shootstraight? Anybody here?"

There was no reply. His normally cheerful home was silent and empty.

Hardman passed the now cold fireplace and made his way into the corridor that circled the living area. He stepped into Windsweet's room. She was gone, but the smell of her lingered behind. The flashlight caught and held the carefully polished writing slate. Hardman walked over and picked it up. The note was addressed to him:

Dear Father,
Booly came back. He wants me and I want him. We know that our relationship will be difficult, that it may end in tragedy, but are helpless to stop ourselves. I am sorry about the pain I caused you and wish the gods had blessed you with the daughter that you deserve.
Love,
Windsweet

The Naa chieftain read the note over and over, let the slate fall to the floor, and held his head in his hands. He hadn't cried since his wife's death. The tears flowed for a long time.

The company of Pioneers, with help from some sturdy-looking robots, were hard at work enlarging the tunnel that housed MPC One. A side cave had been dug and turned into a makeshift meeting room.

Natasha, feeling less out of place than she had a few days before, sat on a cable reel with her arms wrapped around her knees.

Crazy Alice, her right arm resting in a bloodstained sling, sat on a folding chair. Her pencil pushers had been forced to go one-on-one with a marine recon unit. They hadn't won, but they hadn't lost, and she was damned proud.

Colonel Legaux, his metal parts gleaming with reflected light, preferred to stand. The battle for the marine airfield spoke for itself.

Iron Jenny had led the 13th DBLE against a mobile landing force and fought them to a standstill. She sat on a .50-caliber ammo box and looked fresh as a daisy.

Colonel Ed Jefferson leaned against the dirt wall, arms folded in front of her, a frown on her face.

"Where's Tran?"

"Dead," St. James answered as he came into the room. "Killed in action when the 2nd REP took on a battalion of marines in the southern hemisphere."

Jefferson's frown deepened. "Shit."

"Yeah," St. James agreed. "That about sums it up. We lost a lot of good men and women over the last few days."

"And kicked some serious butt," Jenny put in happily. "The grunts ran like hell."

Everyone knew that the diminutive officer was referring to the fact that the marines had departed as suddenly as they had come, breaking off all contact, lifting as quickly as they could. Not only that but the warships had left as well, leaving two scouts to keep an eye on them.

St. James looked Jenny in the eye. "That's one way to look at what happened... but I'm not so sure. We put up a good fight, yes, and might have won. But when? A week, two, if things went well, but victory was never certain. No, I think they pulled out for some other reason."

"Like what?" Legaux asked.

"Like a direct order from the Emperor himself," St. James replied.

"But why?"

St. James shrugged and looked towards Natasha. "It's only a guess, mind you, but the Cabal had plans to release Marianne from prison, and that could have triggered a recall."

"It sure as hell could," Alice growled. "The Emp would freak."

"Yeah," Ed said happily. "He sure would."

"So what now?" Jenny asked.

"Get ready for the next battle," St. James said grimly. "The marines could return, or even worse, the Hudathans could arrive. One of Pierre's people, a Sergeant Major Booly, watched the Naa torture a Hudathan agent to death."

"*Ex*-Sergeant Major Booly," Legaux said bleakly. "He deserted."

St. James raised an eyebrow. His voice was as cold as an Arctic gale. "Really? Well, he'll turn up sooner or later, and when he does, shoot him."

Natasha, unused to the ways of the Legion, was shocked. To hear the man she loved, or thought she loved, casually sentence someone to death troubled her. Had she been wrong about him?

"So," Ed asked, "how would you rate our chances if either one of them attacks?"

St. James spread his hands. "We're okay for food and ammo, ditto the fuel and parts, but short on people. Between the reinforcements sent to the rim and the casualties suffered during the last few days, we're very thin on the ground. So thin that either force could beat us within three or four days."

The ensuing silence lasted a long, long time.

21

Planet Earth, the Human Empire

Smoke boiled up from the city of Lancaster and stained the sky black. A breeze, just in from the Pacific Ocean, pushed the haze towards the east. The cloud made a fitting backdrop for the drama being played out on the street in front of Palmdale's municipal building.

Bullet holes marked the structure's marble facade, windows gaped empty, and uniformed bodies lay where they had fallen. The Legion's dead had been buried, so these were clad in marine green or police blue. Good men and women for the most part, following orders from on high, and dying for no good reason.

Marianne Mosby, commanding officer of the Legion's free forces on Earth, stood at the top of a long flight of stairs. She felt the wind tug at her uniform and looked down into the square. A statue of the Emperor stood on a pedestal, its head missing, an arm pointed towards the stars. In joy? As a warning? It was impossible to tell.

Most of Mosby's forces were elsewhere, fighting their way towards the Imperial Palace, but 250 men and women stood before her, witnesses to what would happen.

They might be dressed in the remnants of prison uniforms and armed with a wild assortment of weapons, but her legionnaires looked like what they were. Soldiers. But like all soldiers, especially those recruited from the bottom of society's barrel, some were better than others. In the wild semi-crazed days since their escape from prison, there had been incidents of theft, rape, and yes, murder. Actions for which no leniency could or should be shown. Colonel Jennings, her XO, stood toward the bottom of the stairs and read the findings.

"... And so," Colonel Jennings concluded, "having been tried and found guilty, you are hereby sentenced to death. May god have mercy on your souls." The words had been amplified and echoed back and forth off the surrounding buildings.

The five men and women stood on the roof of a large hover truck. A decal in the shape of an enormous loaf of bread graced its side. Their hands had been tied behind their backs and nooses placed round their necks. Yellow rope, like the kind sold in hardware stores, led up and over a gracefully curved light standard. None wore hoods.

Mosby forced herself to examine their faces. One, a private named Torbo, looked familiar. The rest were strangers. A woman with multicolored tattoos on both arms tried to spit on Jennings. She was thirty yards short. The officer turned and looked in Mosby's direction. She felt herself nod.

Jennings gave an order and a pair of legionnaires, both equipped with drums that said "Palmdale Tech" along their sides, started a steady rhythm. Turbines screamed, pieces of paper skittered sideways, and the truck came off the ground. It wobbled slightly and a man started to fall. A companion moved in to prop him up. The truck moved forward. The legionnaires stumbled off the roof one at a time. Their necks snapped as they hit the end of the rope. They swung from side to side, their boots arcing through the air.

Mosby felt sick to her stomach but kept her face impassive. It was horrible, but as Chien-Chu had pointed out the day before, so were the crimes they had committed. There was a political component too, because if the Cabal was to have any hope of toppling the Emperor, they needed popular support, support that would be hard to come by if her troops raped and murdered the very people they had to protect. No, it had to be done, but the executions were a stain on an otherwise successful effort.

The revolt had begun when a specially trained cadre of corporate security people had dropped out of the sky and into the middle of the prison's parade ground. The attack occurred when Commandant Tough Shit Gavin had least expected it, right during the heat of the day, when the legionnaires were busy "walking the wall" from one end of the grinder to the other.

The first indication that something was wrong came when ten lighter-than-air freight platforms appeared on radar and ignored all attempts at communication. Gavin could have launched antiaircraft missiles or called for air support, but didn't. Yes, the platforms had entered restricted airspace, and yes, they had revised to acknowledge his calls, but they were clearly civilian. Hell, they had "Chien-Chu Enterprises" painted across their flanks in twenty-foot-high letters, for god's sake. No, it was a mistake of some sort, and one he would soon straighten out.

Mosby remembered feeling a sense of satisfaction as the big black shadows drifted across the parade ground, knowing the time had come, knowing her people were ready. She remembered how the exoskeleton-mounted guards had tried to herd them inside, how they had screamed when the legionnaires pulled them down, how it felt to hit them with her fists.

No mercy was shown to the yard's guards, or to those that spilled out of the armory, weapons chattering as they machine-gunned the crowd. Hundreds died that day, swept away in the storm of lead, but thousands had survived, and, armed with weapons dropped from above, began to fight. Black-clad security troops had joined them, repelling down from the hovering platforms, firing as they came. The battle was over a scant one hour and fifteen minutes after it began.

Mosby had searched for Gavin, planning to kill him with her own bare hands, but arrived too late.

A group of specially trained security people had located the prison's computer-controlled life support system, liberated the brain boxes stored there, and plugged them into their cybernetic bodies. Within minutes Mosby's forces were 362 cyborgs stronger. All of the quads and most of the Trooper IIs left the prison to defend against the possibility of a counterattack, but five went in search of Gavin. They found him cowering in a corner of his office.

There were various rumors about what they'd done to him, but Mosby had seen the body and had a theory of her own. She thought the borgs had played catch with him. She imagined Gavin being thrown back and forth until the trauma killed him.

The blood-smeared office seemed to support her hypothesis, as did the commandant's broken-doll body, but she'd never know for sure.

Jennings appeared at her elbow. Glass crunched under his boots. He gestured towards the bodies. "Shall we cut them down?"

Mosby looked and shook her head. "No, not today. I want people to see and remember."

Jennings nodded. He needed a shave but looked good anyway. Mosby hadn't thought about her appearance in days.

A sergeant major dismissed the troops. They broke into groups and headed for the mismatched convoy that waited nearby. A trio of Trooper IIs faced outwards watching for trouble. Jennings gave her a quizzical look.

"So, what's next?"

Mosby looked towards the south, where the ancient city of Los Angeles had stood hundreds of years before, and the Emperor's mother had made her home. She couldn't see the high-rise towers but knew they were there. She smiled.

"It's time to visit an old friend of mine. The same one that threw us into prison and sent the Navy against Algeron."

Jennings nodded. "Sounds like a plan. Let's go."

Exactly why the complex had been constructed, and left off the building's architectural drawings, was known only to Madam Dasser and her immediate family. But whatever the reason, it made a rather handy headquarters, and being located only miles from the Imperial Palace made it even more secure, since the Emperor's secret police had searched the structure above countless times and declared it clean. That, plus the fact that the building was owned by a front company not known to be part of Dasser Industries, meant the Cabal had a place to gather.

Chien-Chu found himself an unknown number of stories underground, sitting in a darkened room, viewing video of what had once been his estate. Nola sat beside him and did her best not to cry. The Cabal had grown since the early days, adding hundreds of new members, but the executive committee had been limited to only five people. All were present and wore the usual loose-fitting robes.

The holo had been shot twenty-four hours after the secret police had attacked and there wasn't much left to see. The house and all that it contained had been blown up. Then, to make sure that Chien-Chu got the point, the wreckage had been burned. Two of the chimneys still stood, as did a ragged section of brick wall, but the rest of the place had been reduced to little more than blackened rubble. Smoke drifted up from a fire that still burned somewhere beneath the debris.

"I'm sorry," Madam Dasser said, "but my estates were targeted as well."

"And mine," Ari Goss added.

"Mine too," Zorana Zikos said.

"And ours," Susan Rothenberg put in.

Chien-Chu sighed. "It was to be expected, I guess. We had to come out in the open, and the moment we did, they attacked."

Nola noticed something that struck her as both sad and funny. She made a choking sound. "They missed something, though…"

Madam Dasser turned in her direction. "They did? What?"

Nola pointed to the holo. "Look… Sergi's sculptures are completely untouched!"

They saw that the rusty metal plates the merchant had welded together stood exactly as they had before, and laughed.

"Perhaps the secret police assumed that someone had already destroyed them," Zikos said dryly.

Chien-Chu smiled and took his wife's hand. "Laugh if you

will, but at least I have a second career, and how many of you can say the same? We can't be revolutionaries forever, you know."

"Sergi has a point," Rothenberg said. "We must plan for success. What happens when the Emperor is deposed?"

"We're a long way from having to worry about that," Goss said soberly.

"Maybe," Madam Dasser replied, "and maybe not. Let's take a look at the report that our combined intelligence and marketing research staffs put together."

She touched a button and the holo dissolved into a thousand shards of light. They swirled, chased each other in circles, and came back together. A set of eight summaries, graphs, and charts appeared in front of them, and being business people, they sat up and paid attention. Dasser narrated.

"Here's the way things look. The good news is that cross-cultural, multi-location opinion research indicates that the public agrees with our plan to fight the Hudathans out on the rim, and want new leadership. Once we got around the Emperor's propaganda machine and gave the population some real news, billions of people came over to our side. The stuff from Spindle was especially effective. Citizens want military action and they want it now."

"So what's the bad news?" Zikos asked cautiously.

"The bad news," Dasser answered, "is that the people don't trust us. Crazy or not, the Emperor represents stability, and people like that, especially when compared to people like us. Here, take a look at this." She used a light wand to highlight some statistics. "Because we're business people and fit the common definition of 'rich,' they're afraid of what we might do *after* the Emperor is deposed."

"Which makes perfect sense," Chien-Chu said softly.

"But it's not fair!" Rothenberg exclaimed. "We risked everything! The Emperor closed our companies, destroyed our homes, and sentenced us to death!"

"So I'll bite," Zikos said grimly. "What's the answer?"

Madam Dasser grinned. "Our communications people recommend a phased approach. They point out that a cabal made up of faceless men and women, all of whom have questionable motives, is inherently more threatening than a single person. Especially within a society where all authority has been invested in a single individual for such a long time."

"So we should choose a front man," Goss said thoughtfully.

"Or *woman*," Rothenberg said stiffly.

"Exactly," Dasser agreed. "The communications people further recommend that this person be the member of the Cabal who has the warmest personality index, the least threatening physique, and the greatest similarity to cross-cultural icons such as the Buddha, Mahatma Gandhi, the late Empress, and Santa Claus."

Everyone in the room looked at Chien-Chu. He held a hand up in protest. "No!"

But a vote was taken and a spokesperson was chosen.

Sun streamed in through the pyramid's transparent sides, warmed the Emperor's back, and threw his shadow across his mother's tomb. Fascinated, he raised his arms, watched his duplicate take on the shape of a cross, and made it move. He had come to talk with her, to ask her what to do, but the voices made it hard to think. They were fighting again, arguing over what he should do, but never coming to any sort of conclusion.

"He's insane, you know."

"And who wouldn't be with a fruitcake like you running around inside his head?"

"Stop it! We must cooperate, work as a team, or the entire empire will be lost."

"So?"

"So the Emperor could be killed. If he dies, we go with him."

"Sounds good to me," another voice said grimly. "Anything would be better than this."

"Your Highness?"

It took the Emperor a moment to realize that this particular voice had originated from outside the confines of his own mind. He allowed his arms to fall. The voices died to a whisper.

"Yes?"

"The Legion has forced their way into the city. They will be here in an hour or two."

The face looked familiar. The Emperor forced himself to concentrate. "Admiral Scolari! What are you doing here? I sent you to Algeron."

Scolari forced herself to remain calm. It was as bad as she had heard... maybe worse. "You ordered my return, Your Highness, and judging from what I've seen, it was an excellent idea."

"Oh," the Emperor said vacantly. "Of course. Sorry about that, it slipped my mind."

"Yes, Highness," Scolari replied dryly. "Now, with your permission, I suggest that we depart for the spaceport. Your Highness will be a great deal safer up in orbit."

The Emperor brightened. "Up in orbit! Yes. That would be fun. Let's go."

Scolari felt depressed as she followed the Emperor up a flight of steps, through a blastproof door, and out into the afternoon sun. The return trip had been long and stressful. What would the Legion do while she was away? Where would the Hudathans strike next? And what awaited her on Earth? The reality was worse than anything she'd imagined.

The Emperor had slipped further into madness, the Cabal had come out into the open, Mosby was on the verge of occupying the Imperial City, and the rest of the military were sitting on their hands. Well, most were anyway. Some commanders had done what they could.

A fighter screamed by a few hundred feet overhead, launched missiles towards Mosby's forces, and stood on its tail. Sun glinted off the plane's canopy as it fought for altitude.

Scolari squinted upwards, searched for the plane's insignia, and winced when a quad-launched SAM hit the aircraft and blew it up. Flaming debris tumbled through the air and fell on some government buildings. One caught fire and more sirens joined those already bleating in distress.

Damn those cyborgs anyway! The moment this was over, Scolari would track them down, kill them one by one, and start her own cyborg corps.

Two squads of heavily armed marines closed in around them as they walked towards the waiting vehicles. Scolari had considered a chopper but decided against it for security reasons.

Like the fighter, a helicopter would have been vulnerable to all sorts of ground fire. The Emperor seemed oblivious to the danger that surrounded him.

Doors slammed and engines revved as the convoy headed out. The streets were empty. The bureaucrats had gone to ground and were hiding deep within their comfortable caves waiting for a winner to emerge. Then they would appear one by one, swear allegiance to whatever was handy, and go back to work. It made Scolari sick.

The command car bounced over something hard and the Emperor stared out the window.

Mosby entered the palace mounted on a Trooper II named Logan. She shifted her weight from side to side as the cyborg made his way up the steps, scanned for signs of opposition, and finding none, proceeded inside. His pods made a thumping noise as they hit the hardwood floors, and unprotected by the pads normally worn inside buildings, left dents in the wood. Bio bods, their weapons at ready, were right behind.

Mosby had expected stiff resistance, but the marine guards had deserted their posts or been ordered to withdraw. Both possibilities were fine with her. There had been more than enough killing. What she wanted was the Emperor. Not to kill him, since that might create a martyr, but to tell him it was over. Not that she was likely to get the chance. The palace seemed deserted.

The ballroom, empty of all life, passed on her left. Yellow sunlight slanted down from the high arched windows on her right.

Logan ignored the elevator and took the access stairs. Mosby ducked as the Trooper II passed through doorways. The motion involved in climbing stairs threw the officer back and forth, but the harness held her in place. A squad of bio bods followed along behind.

Logan paused in front of a fire door, checked for trip wires, and pulled it open. The second floor was just as deserted as the first. A long hallway led right and left. Impressionistic paintings, each worth a fortune, marched in both directions.

"Hold one."

Logan held while Mosby pulled the com lead and triggered the harness release. Her combat boots thumped as they hit the floor. A sergeant approached. He wore armor taken from a dead marine and his features were invisible behind reflective plastic.

"Orders, General?"

Mosby jerked her thumb to the left. "Take your squad and search everything from here down. Logan and I will take the other half."

Jennings had instructed the sergeant to "stay with the general at all times," but an order is an order, and there wasn't much he could do. The sergeant swallowed hard.

"Yes, ma'am."

The bio bods did it by the book. One trooper to the left of the door and one to the right. None of the rooms were locked.

Mosby and Logan approached things in a different manner. She watched while he opened the doors. Room after room was empty. The Emperor's quarters were directly ahead. Mosby felt her heart beat a little faster. The cyborg opened the double doors and stepped inside. She followed.

The room where the Emperor had met with Chien-Chu, Scolari, Worthington, and herself was exactly as it had been that night except that the gas-fed fire had been extinguished, light streamed in through the rectangular windows, and it was otherwise empty. She felt disappointed and knew it was silly. Something whirred. Logan turned towards the sound and raised his weapons. Mosby pulled her sidearm. A section of bookcase slid aside and the Emperor stepped through. He wore a loose-fitting pajama-like outfit and looked as handsome as ever. He smiled as if encountering a general and a Trooper II in his study was the most natural thing in the world.

"General Mosby... how nice of you to drop in. I see you've been working out. Would you like to see our gym?"

Emotions chased each other through Mosby's mind: the shock of his unexpected appearance, the same attraction she'd felt before, and disappointment as she realized that it wasn't really him. Because while the clone might *look* like the Emperor, he'd led a much more sheltered life and exuded the simplicity of a child. She remembered some of the things the three of them had done together and blushed.

"Where's the Emperor? The *real* one?"

The clone raised a carefully tended eyebrow and shrugged. "He rarely tells me anything."

Mosby thought for a moment then motioned with her gun. "You're under arrest. Step into the hall."

The clone frowned. "Why?"

"Because I'll shoot you if you don't."

The clone moved towards the hall. He eyed the legionnaires. "Are you going to kill me? He threatens to kill me all the time."

Mosby shook her head.

"No. I plan to use you. The same way he did."

"And then?"

"And then you can do whatever you want... except for a career in politics that is."

"Oh," the clone replied happily. "That sounds like fun."

The Emperor's yacht was the same size as a battleship and as heavily armed. They had just come aboard and were striding towards the operations center when the first piece of bad news arrived. It came in the form of a printout carried by a pimple-faced ensign. He was intercepted, cleared by a pair of marines, and allowed to catch up.

"A message from the captain, Admiral. It just came in."

Scolari snatched the message from the youngster's hand, glanced at the Emperor, and saw no signs of interest. She sighed. Usurping the throne and having it dumped in her lap were two different things.

Scolari read the message, then read it again. The news was anything but good. Ships had dropped hyper off Algeron. Her scouts had gone in for a closer look and ran head-on into the lead elements of a Hudathan task force. One of her scouts had been destroyed. The other had launched a message torp and run for its life. There was no way to know if it had escaped or not.

Damn! The Hudathans would polish off what was left of the Legion, jump inwards, and strike for the empire's heart. Then, rather than the massive fleet that she'd imagined, they'd find easy pickings instead.

Guards snapped to attention as they entered the ops center and the ship's captain rose to greet them. He was a middle-aged man, tall and thin, and had the unctuous manner of an undertaker. He hurried forward.

"Your Highness! Admiral Scolari! Welcome aboard. The crew is honored by your presence. I will do everything in my power to—"

"Shut the hell up," Scolari growled. "I haven't got time for your ass-kissing bullshit."

An intelligence officer inched her way forward. "Captain?"

Still smarting from Scolari's rebuke, Captain Kresner lashed out at her. "Yes, Lieutenant? What the hell do you want?"

Her voice was hesitant. "Over there, sir, on screen two."

Scolari looked and felt her heart jump into her throat. The shot showed the Emperor, or an exact likeness, sitting on his throne. An electronic key had been inserted towards the bottom of the frame. It said, "Live."

Scolari's voice cracked like a whip. "Silence! Bring the audio up!"

"And so," the clone concluded, "I have decided to step down from my position as Emperor in favor of a transitional government led by those known as 'The Cabal.' The Hudathan menace must be dealt with first but when that's been accomplished, they have agreed to empire-wide elections. So I urge you to follow the Cabal's lead, to support our troops and ignore those who would lead you astray. Thank you."

"That isn't me," the Emperor said dully. "That's my clone."

"Not anymore," Scolari answered wearily. "Perception is reality, and since your clone was a closely guarded secret, people will treat *him* as the Emperor and you as an imposter."

The Emperor was silent for a moment. Something changed behind his eyes, as if his more rational self had momentarily gained control and was taking charge.

"Unless…"

Scolari felt suddenly hopeful. "Yes, Highness? Unless what?"

"Unless we find the Hudathans, make peace, and save the empire from war."

Scolari took a deep breath. The Emperor's plan was so outrageous that it just might work. They would approach the aliens, negotiate the best terms they could, and stay in control. Not a win, but not a loss, and a lot better than nothing. She smiled.

"An excellent plan, Your Highness. Captain... prepare to break orbit."

22

Medals are often won by people who screw things up... then fight like hell to get out of it.

LIEUTENANT COLONEL "SMOKER SIX" MERRITT
United States Army
Somewhere in Saudi Arabia, Planet Earth
Standard year 1991

Planet Algeron, the Human Empire

Loose gravel slid out from under the dooth's hooves, the animal backed away from the precipice, and Wayfar Hardman swore. The snow had turned to sleet and attacked the scarf that covered the lower part of his face.

The dooth found firmer footing and refused to move. The chieftain jerked the creature's head around and kicked its barrel-shaped sides. Slowly, and with a good deal of grunting, the dooth picked its way upwards. Rocks scraped by on Hardman's right, some marked by ancient tools, the legacy of ancestors long dead.

Damn Windsweet anyway, for leading the human up here and forcing him to follow. He was too old for such trails and saw no purpose in them anyway, ending as they inevitably did on some high and rocky plateau.

Still, there was some sense in it, he supposed, since the two of them were outcasts, unlikely to gain admission to an established village, a fact that still made him feel guilty. So, with bandits to avoid, and the Legion to watch for, the high country offered a rough and ready sanctuary.

A piece of rock projected outwards. Hardman let the reins fall slack, allowed his mount to edge her way around it, and reassumed control. The trail opened up a bit after that, and the Naa was about to kick the animal in her sides when a rifle shot rang out. A rock bounced into the air, tumbled end over end, and fell from sight.

"Hold it right there."

Hardman pulled back on the reins. The dooth came to a halt. The chieftain held his hands chest-high and palms-out. The wind ripped his words away.

"This is not the sort of greeting I expect from my future son-in-law!"

There was a pause followed by another order. "Unwrap your scarf."

Hardman did as he was told and felt hundreds of tiny ice-cold cannonballs pepper his face. The voice was closer now but the Naa kept his eyes straight ahead.

"Are you alone?"

"Yes."

"Good. Follow the trail. I'll be along in a while."

Hardman rewrapped his scarf, kicked the dooth into motion, and grinned. Booly trusted no one and that was good. His daughter's life would depend on it.

The trail wound through the site of an ancient rock slide. Hardman could see where Booly and Windsweet had pushed some of the more recent boulders off the path, and he marveled at their energy.

Once past the rock slide, the trail shelved sharply upwards, turned through a rocky defile, and ended on a windswept plateau. A thin coating of sleet had turned everything white. Tumbledown stone walls showed where ancient windbreaks had stood. The people who had lived there had been very tough, or so desperate they had preferred the rigors of the heights to the dangers below.

A rock bounced off his shoulder. Hardman smiled. The human, accustomed to endless supplies of ammunition, had fired a warning shot. His daughter, knowing that every bullet was precious, had thrown a stone instead. Her voice was thin but determined. He could see the handgun from the corner of his eye and it was rock steady.

"Show your face."

Hardman unwrapped the scarf.

Her voice was hesitant. "Father?"

Hardman felt a lump form in his throat. He spoke around it.

"Who else would ride all the way up here for a cup of your tea?"

Hardman swung his left leg over the dooth's woolly neck and hit the ground just as his daughter threw herself into his arms. She pressed her face against his chest. The smell of her filled his nostrils and he was glad that she couldn't see his tears. He used the top of her hood to wipe them away.

"So you chose to live the life of brellas rather than buka."

Windsweet laughed and reminded him of the cub that had played around his feet. "Come! I'll serve the tea you came for!"

"In a moment," Hardman admonished. "First the supplies I brought you… then the dooth."

They had barely unloaded two enormous saddlebags full of food when Booly appeared. His winter whites rendered him almost invisible against the sleet-covered rocks. The males eyed each warily, neither sure of what to say, both wishing for some sort of divine intervention. It was Hardman who held his hands palms-out. The words came more easily than he'd thought they would.

"My daughter loves you, human, and that's good enough for me."

Booty grinned and placed his hands against the chieftain's. Their fingers intertwined. "Thanks, Wayfar… and I have a name. It's Bill Booly."

Hardman scowled. "That's not a name… it's a collection of sounds. Longrun Banditkill. Now, that's a name."

Booly shook his head in mock surrender, led the chieftain's dooth into the cave where their own animals were quartered, and left it to chew on a bundle of dried grass.

They had taken the best of the underground dwellings. A

doothskin blocked most of the wind and a spiral stairway led down to the common room. The interior was spacious, but not overly so, and a dooth-dung fire glowed in the ancient fireplace. There was very little smoke, but what there was trickled up through a funnel-shaped chimney and was vented to the outside. Colorful blankets were hung here and there. Booly and Windsweet had worked hard to make the space pleasant and Hardman was impressed. The human dumped one of the saddlebags into an alcove and he did likewise.

"This is nice, very nice, just right for an aging father. I'll bring my things and move in."

Windsweet laughed and beamed her pleasure. This was a dream come true. To have both of them there, and reasonably happy with each other, was all she could possibly hope for. Except for the little one, of course… and only she knew about him.

"Come," Booly said, beckoning Hardman to a place by the fire. "Warm yourself and tell us about the journey. How did you find us?"

Hardman took his coat off and held his hands to the fire. He grinned. "It was like following one of the roads that the Legion builds. A blindfolded cub could have done it."

Booly gave a snort of derision. "Maybe, if I'd been alone, but Windsweet led the way."

Hardman chuckled. "That explains it, then. The truth is that it took me quite a while to find you. My daughter can make life extremely difficult when she wants to. Something you'll discover for yourself in the very near future."

Windsweet made a face from across the room, Booly laughed, and wonderful smells filled the cavern as dinner started to simmer. It was only after they had eaten and were sitting or lying around the fire that the conversation turned serious. Booly made the question sound like a statement.

"There was fighting. We saw contrails when it was light and the flash of explosions when it was dark."

Hardman signaled his agreement. "True. Other humans came. They destroyed the fort and fought many battles."

Booly felt a tightness in his throat. "They destroyed Camerone? Never!"

"'Never' is the time of fools," Hardman said levelly as he used a bone to pick his teeth. "Trust me when I tell you the fort was leveled. But it sounds worse than it actually was, since every single human left the fort *prior* to its destruction and took the riffraff from Naa town with them."

Booly remembered how it had been with thousands of troops and hundreds of vehicles pouring out of the fort. He had assumed that the Old Man would defend Camerone to the death, which showed how much he knew. Chances were that the Navy and Marine Corps had believed the same thing. If so, they had wasted a lot of time, energy, and lives attacking something of little strategic value. He grinned.

"So who won?"

Hardman looked Booly in the eye. "You tell me, human. The others left and the Legion remains. That looks like a victory to me. But in a war where worlds are valued as villages, and entire solar systems stand for continents, who can say? And the smelly ones will present difficulties as well."

"Smelly ones?"

"He means the Hudatha," Windsweet said, wrinkling her nose. "The ones Surekill captured smelled horrible."

Booly sat up in alarm. "You've seen more of them?"

"Yes, many more," Hardman affirmed. "They land all the time. And spy machines too. It's the same in the south. The most recent arrivals said interesting things before the flames consumed their words."

Booly remembered how the Hudathan had screamed as he fell into the pit. He felt sick and Windsweet had turned away. "What did they say?" he asked.

Hardman was silent for a moment as if choosing his words with great care. "They said their ships are as numerous as the stars... that they will strike soon... and the Legion will die."

Guilt rose to pull Booly's spirits down. He should be there when the Hudathans struck, fighting shoulder-to-shoulder with his comrades, not here cowering in a cave.

Hardman watched, gauging the human's reactions, guessing at his emotions. His voice was calm. "You could help them."

Booly showed a flicker of interest. "Really? How?"

"My scouts tell me that while the Legion fought bravely and sent many warriors to the next world, they suffered heavy casualties. That, plus the fact that many legionnaires were shipped off-planet during the last month or so means they will be severely outnumbered."

Windsweet had told Booly about her father's spies, but he still marveled at the extent of the chieftain's intelligence network. "So?" he said.

"So the Legion could use some help, allies who know every nook and cranny of the planet's surface, and are proven warriors." The last was said with obvious pride.

It took Booly a moment to realize what Hardman was suggesting. It didn't make any sense. "You mean it? The Naa would fight with humans? But why? You fought the Legion for years. Here's your chance to be rid of them once and for all."

"But at what price?" the chieftain countered. "It's true that humans occupy our planet, but only a small part of it, and they smell good. Most of the time anyway."

Windsweet laughed and so did Booly. The truth was that the Naa's culture and the Legion's culture were complementary. That, plus the fact that the Legion had never allowed colonists on Algeron, meant the natives had been spared the horrors of full-scale colonialism. But that was something Booly saw no reason to go into.

The legionnaire frowned. "What about the southern tribes? How do they feel?"

"The same way," Hardman replied. "They too will fight. But only until the Hudathans are vanquished. Things must return to normal after that."

Booly was surprised. He'd never heard of such cooperation outside the area of commerce. And how were the two groups communicating with each other?

"The passes remain closed," Booly pointed out. "How do you know the southern tribes will cooperate?"

Hardman grinned. "The Legion has supplied them with some excellent radios over the years. The southern tribes are adept at copying such things and making more."

It made perfect sense and Booly wondered why he hadn't

thought of it before. He'd seen no hint of such technology in Hardman's village but hadn't looked for it either. It seemed that Naa had anticipated the possibility of an escape and concealed some of their capabilities. Obviously, there were things Windsweet had neglected to mention as well. He looked at her and received an innocent smile in return.

"So," Hardman said pragmatically, "contact the Legion and let's get to work."

Booly looked away. "I wish I could... but they'd shoot me."

Hardman smiled. "Not necessarily. I hereby designate you, Longrun Banditkill, as emissary for the Naa tribes."

Booly started to object, had second thoughts, and let them flow. The idea made sense. By working together the Legion and the Naa *might* defeat the Hudathans. That would go a long way towards reducing the guilt he felt. It wouldn't hurt later on either, when the war was over and he lived among the Naa. Which led the human to another thought: Why settle for a temporary alliance? The Naa might have sufficient leverage to gain additional incentives, like better medical care, technical assistance, or who knows? Total independence wasn't out of the question. Not only that, but he had an idea that would allow him to contact St. James quickly, efficiently, and with very little risk to himself. He nodded slowly.

"You know what? I think it could work."

War Commander Niman Poseen-Ka held the bubble-shaped terrarium up to the light. The recurved road crossed the bridge just so, entered the village at exactly the right point, and turned into the main street. Each building was positioned just as he remembered it, a little better than reality, but so what? The terrarium modeled his world the way it could've been had it been more predictable. Or was it simply his mood? He felt good, very good, and why not? The court of inquiry had gone his way, his strategy had been vindicated, and the upcoming battle would provide the perfect opportunity to rid himself of the traitorous Moder-Ta, Spear Commanders Two and Five, and the human called Baldwin. Yes, life was good.

Poseen-Ka placed the terrarium on his desk, stood, and walked over to the view port that graced one wall of his cabin. The planet Algeron filled most of it. It was an unusual planet with a single world-spanning continent and towering mountains. And while different from Hudatha, it was similar as well. So much so that it might be worth colonizing, a possibility that caused Poseen-Ka to forbid the use of nuclear weapons and plan a conventional attack.

That a human fleet had already destroyed the planet's major military base took some of the fun out of it, but the recon units assured him that many of the troops had escaped and would put up a creditable tussle.

And, he knew, this contingent of humans included the same sort of cyborgs who had played such an important role in the destruction of Spear Three and the defense of outposts like the one on Frio II.

Yes, he looked forward to battle ahead, but must be careful. The humans had proved themselves to be extremely resourceful in the past and would be fighting on their home turf. He had accused others of overconfidence and must be sure that he avoided the same error himself. That was why he'd wait until his entire fleet had emerged from hyperspace before undertaking the sort of all-out attack that the ill-fated Niber-Ba should have launched but hadn't.

Still, the Hudathan couldn't help but feel optimistic, and allowed himself some additional time with the terrarium.

The air-conditioning whispered incessantly, the lights never blinked, and the minutes rolled off the wall clock with relentless precision. The aliens had been in orbit for some time now, gathering their forces, preparing to wipe the Legion off the face of Algeron. There had been no attempt to communicate, no offer of terms, just the steady, almost insulting infiltration of Hudathan scouts, robots, and spy-eyes.

That, plus the fact that St. James had been living in the mobile command post for weeks now, made him tired and irritable. Natasha's presence only added to his frustration, since he would have preferred to spend his time with her rather than his work. So, while the answer was surly, the com tech got off lightly.

"What now?"

The com tech, a vet with ten years in, didn't even flinch. "We have an anomaly, sir. A man who identified himself as ex-Sergeant Major William Booly crashed net three. We jerked his file, found he was AWOL, and asked enough questions to confirm his identity. He wants to speak with you."

St. James frowned. "But how?"

"He dug his way down to relay station 856-K, disarmed the booby traps, and used the handset. It seems he led the patrol that buried this particular unit."

"Tell him to shoot himself. It'll save us the trouble."

The com tech stood her ground. "He claims to speak for the unified tribes, sir."

"Tribes? Unified? Since when?"

The com tech shrugged. "Beats me, sir. The sergeant major claims they came together and are willing to fight the Hudathans."

Could it be true? It would make a tremendous difference if so. St. James felt his fatigue drop away.

"I'll talk to him. Which channel?"

"Six, sir."

St. James touched a button and spoke into his mike. "Booly?"

The voice at the other end sounded as crisp and clear as if Booly were sitting by his side.

"Hello, General. Thanks for taking my call."

"What's this crap about unified tribes and fighting the Hudatha?"

The pit was about eight feet deep. The relay station consisted of a green box no larger than a foot locker. Hardened cables entered the unit on one side and exited on the other. Robo trenchers had laid mile after endless mile of the stuff, which meant that the Legion would have excellent communications even if every frequency on the spectrum was jammed.

Booly leaned back against the side of the pit and felt cold seep through the back of his jacket. It had taken more than eight hours to dig their way down to the relay station and another two to disarm all the booby traps. His muscles ached, his hands were blistered, and the Naa had started to stay upwind of his sweat-soaked clothes.

"It isn't crap, sir. The Naa have an intense dislike for the Hudathans and are willing to fight."

Excited by the prospect of reinforcements, St. James allowed himself to momentarily forget Booly's status as a deserter.

"I'm glad to hear it. We could use some help. Tell me, Sergeant Major, how many warriors could the Naa supply?"

"Approximately 250,000, sir."

"What about arms?"

"The usual mishmash of their own stuff combined with ours, sir."

St. James thought out loud. "Well, we can't arm them all, but we can sure as hell supplement what they already have. What about command? Will they take orders?"

Booly tried to ignore the fact that Hardman and Windsweet were staring down at him from the surface, that the cold had penetrated his clothing, and that his hand was shaking. The next part would be tricky, very tricky, and he would have to be careful.

"Well, sir, that depends."

"Depends? Depends on what?"

Booly had been taking orders all his adult life and to defy an officer was extremely difficult. He swallowed hard. "It depends on who gives the orders." It took a conscious act of will to leave "sir" off the end.

St. James felt his fingers dig into padded leather. The words were clear. The Naa would take orders, but only from Booly, and only if certain demands were met. Anger rose and threatened to spill over into his voice. He forced it down. There was too much at stake to call Booly the names he deserved. But any sympathy for Booly's plight, any tendency to forgive what he'd done, was irrevocably erased. His voice was as cold as mountain snow.

"I see. And who would they listen to?"

Booly rewrapped his fingers around the handset "They'll listen to me."

St. James tried to resist sarcasm and failed. "I'm not surprised."

Booly heard the sarcasm and felt the pain. "Believe what you will, General, but the Legion will survive, and that's what counts."

"Is it?" St. James demanded. "You don't want anything in return? A pardon? Money?"

"No. But I do want things for the Naa. Ongoing support for families who lose breadwinners. Medical attention for their wounded. And compensation for the Legion's use of Algeron."

St. James was surprised. The requests were moderate and obviously fair. And the guarantees he had expected were missing. Why? Then he understood. Once armed, the Naa would have the ability to demand what they wanted, and Booly knew that. St. James sighed. It was a damned good thing that most deserters were less capable than Booly.

"Agreed. Stay where you are and I'll have a fly-form pick you up. We can't have a deserter leading allied troops, so I'll second you to the Naa, with the temporary rank of major. And Booly…"

"Sir?"

"When this is over… you'd better make damned sure that we never run into each other."

"Yes, sir."

23

War is the remedy that our enemy has chosen; therefore, let them have as much of it as they want.
GENERAL WILLIAM TECUMSEH SHERMAN
NORTHERN ARMY
Standard year 1861

Planet Algeron, the Human Empire

The Emperor's yacht had no more than left hyperspace before it was running for its life. The whole system was swarming with Hudathan vessels, and powerful though it was, the human ship was no match for their combined strength. It wasted little time making contact.

Curious, and somewhat amused by the enemy's electronic bleatings, War Commander Niman Poseen-Ka ordered his ships to hold their fire. They did so, but continued to move in, until the human vessel was completely englobed. It was then, as the humans nattered on about peace talks, treaties, and the possibility of bilateral trade agreements, that the Hudathan sent for Colonel Natalie Norwood. Of the humans he'd met thus far she made the most sense.

Norwood was surprised by the summons, and curious as to what was happening, since no effort had been made to keep her or the other prisoners informed. The Hudathans were getting ready for battle—that much was obvious—but she knew nothing more than that. An escort comprised of four guards marched her through the now familiar corridors and up to the command center's airtight hatch. It disappeared into the ceiling. The Sun Guards were still mindful of what she'd done to Keem-So but made no effort to intervene.

The command center's interior was just as she remembered it. The compartment was oval in shape, with fifteen wall niches, and a huge holo tank at its center. The device depicted a five-planet solar system and a host of tiny ships, many of which were gathered around a flashing green globe. Poseen-Ka came forward to greet her.

"Greetings, Colonel. You are looking well… or I assume so anyway."

It was a joke, the first one Norwood had heard Poseen-Ka tell, and she laughed politely. "Yes, thank you."

Poseen-Ka gestured towards the long, gently curved wall screen. Admiral Paula Scolari took up a third of its surface. She continued to talk about peace in spite of the fact that the Hudathans had shown no interest in what she was saying. The Emperor stood beside her, eyes focused on something only he could see, features hanging slack.

"These individuals claim to be high-ranking members of your government. The man claims to be the Emperor, and in spite of actions to the contrary, the woman represents herself as War Commander Scolari. I assumed they came for honorable deaths, and was about to grant their wish, when they started to run. No sooner had we closed with them than they started to babble about a cessation of hostilities, something called a 'truce,' and trade agreements." The Hudathan seemed truly amazed. "Tell me, Colonel. Are they really your leaders?"

Norwood looked up at the screen, remembering how millions had died, hating the people she saw with every fiber of her being.

"Yes, those are our leaders. Pathetic, aren't they?"

"Truly," Poseen-Ka replied, ignoring Scolari's latest demand for a response. "What are they trying to accomplish?"

Norwood shrugged stoically. "They know nothing of you, or

your people, and hope you will make peace."

"But why should we do that?" the Hudathan inquired. "We're winning."

"True," Norwood agreed sadly.

"So I should kill them?"

Norwood fought to keep her voice steady. "No. They are helpless and can do you no harm."

"Not now," Poseen-Ka agreed, "but what about the future? We have a saying: 'He who spares an enemy adds to the army that will bring him down.' "

"And we have a saying," Norwood countered. "'Do unto others as you would have them do unto you.'"

"Exactly," Poseen-Ka agreed, and said something in Hudathan. A thousand beams of light converged on the Emperor's yacht.

Norwood saw Scolari react, turn towards the Emperor, and vanish as the Hudathan beams overwhelmed the yacht's force fields and ruptured the hull. A fireball blossomed, ran out of oxygen, and disappeared.

Poseen-Ka was impassive. "You may go."

Norwood searched his face for some trace of humanity, realized how stupid that was, and turned away. If the guards thought the tears were strange, they didn't say anything.

A detachment from the 1st REC had been assigned to support a contingent of Colonel Ed Jefferson's 2nd REI. They were spread out along both sides of a broad U-shaped valley and heavily camouflaged. Villain could make out the vehicles, launchers, and quads, but just barely. Salazar was up ahead and yelled for her to follow. She waved an acknowledgment. Both observed the strict radio silence that Colonel Ed and her staff had imposed.

The Trooper IIs followed a narrow path up along the side of a gently rounded hill, past some jumbled boulders, and into a small clearing. Salazar had noticed it while on patrol the previous day and decided it was ideal.

Villain searched her surroundings for signs of life. She did it partially from habit and partially for fear of being discovered. Both had logged off for maintenance.

Salazar smiled inside his mind. "Nervous?"

"Hell, yes. What if someone sees us?"

Salazar shrugged. "Then they'll see a couple of Trooper IIs taking a break."

"You think it'll work?"

"Other borgs do it all the time."

"But this is *me*, damn it, and I *don't* do it all the time."

Salazar sat down and leaned against a rock. He patted the ground beside him. She paused for a moment before accepting his invitation. Her movements were large and ponderous. Different from the girl he'd seen behind the counter. He remembered how the gun had jumped in his hand, how blood had spurted from her chest, from *his* chest, before blackness pulled him down. For the millionth time he wished he'd done something else that day, blown his brains out, anything but enter the convenience store.

Villain looked at him and ignored the threat factors that popped up in the lower right-hand corner of her vision.

"I love you."

He'd heard the words before, but they surprised him nonetheless, as did the realization that he felt the same way. He reached out to touch her, his arm heavy with weaponry, his hand large and clumsy. Metal clanged.

"And I love you."

"Let's see it."

Salazar fumbled the dream box out of a storage compartment. The device was illegal and had cost him the equivalent of three months' pay. It wasn't much to look at. Villain saw a black cube, some rudimentary controls, and four leads. Each lead ended in a small cup-shaped device.

"How does it work?"

Salazar demonstrated by placing one of the cup-shaped devices against the side of his brain box.

"We each place a lead here, like so, and flip the switch. It works like the training scenarios they used on us in boot camp."

"Except we're in control."

"Exactly."

"What are the other two leads for?"

"In case you want to hook four borgs together all at once."

Villain shivered inside her mind. "Ugh."

Salazar looked into her scanners. It was impossible, of course, but he would have sworn that he saw something more than his own reflection there.

"Ready?"

"Ready as I'll ever be."

"Okay. Here goes."

Salazar placed one lead against his brain box and a second against hers. Magnets held them in place. He held the controls with one hand and placed the other over the switch. Servos whined as Villain placed her hand over his. He moved a huge sausage-like finger and the contacts closed.

The readouts that had become a part of Villain's normal vision disappeared. Fog swirled but nothing else happened. Salazar was nowhere to be seen.

"Sal?"

The voice came from nearby.

"Right here. Remember, reality is what you make it, so think yourself into the picture."

Villain tried. The fog eddied. She looked down at her Trooper II body and wondered why it was the same.

"Cissy?"

The cyborg's head came up at the use of her old name. He looked just as he had on the day he killed her, minus the sunglasses, of course, and the gun. Fear rose to constrict her throat.

"You're beautiful."

Beautiful? She looked down to find that the hard angular planes of her Trooper II body had been replaced by smoothly rounded flesh. Naked flesh. It felt strange to have breasts again. She blushed, and clothes appeared as quickly as she thought of them. The fear started to dissipate as pleasure seeped in to take its place. Villain, for that was how she continued to think of herself, twirled.

Memories came flooding back. Memories of what it felt like to be human, to move her limbs, to suck air into lungs, to taste, hear, feel, and see without electronic assistance. She laughed, and Salazar joined her, taking a flesh-and-blood hand in his and whirling her through an impromptu dance.

Villain felt wonderfully light, but tired with surprising suddenness, and remembered how weak a bio bod really is. Nothing like a cyber-form that could dance for days and never tire. She came to a stop. Salazar kept the grip on her hand. It felt good.

"What's beyond the fog?"

"Whatever you like. The more completely we visualize our surroundings, the more real they become."

Villain considered that. A place both of them were familiar with would be best. She thought about Earth and the Pacific Ocean.

"The beach, with surf and no people."

Salazar nodded. The fog swirled, grew transparent, and vanished. Miles of pristine beach appeared, backed by whitewashed condos, hotels, and mansions, empty of people. Sun beat down on her back, surf broke twenty yards out, and foam surged towards her feet. The leather pumps were silly and she wished them away. The sand felt warm and damp beneath her feet.

"Hello, baby."

Salazar had changed. He wore a loose-fitting blue shirt, white shorts, and slip-on tennis shoes. He looked handsome and she loved him. A flood of emotion rolled over her and was transformed into tears. Salazar took her in his arms. For the first time since her death Villain felt warm and secure.

She said, "I'm sorry."

"Don't be."

"We can have sex if you want."

"Next time, or the time after that. There's no hurry."

For the first time since her induction into the Legion Villain she felt truly happy. They were still together, still walking on the beach, when death fell from the sky.

Colonel Alex Baldwin sat sideways, wedged between two Hudathan soldiers, pondering his fate. The landing craft shuddered as it hit the outer layer of Algeron's atmosphere, slowed as friction warmed the surface of its hull, and jerked as a pair of short stubby wings were extended from the fuselage.

He remembered the military history classes that he'd been forced to take, and the soldiers who had volunteered for the Forlorn Hope at the siege of Badajoz, hacking their way through flesh and bone for a laurel-wreath badge or the chance of promotion. He imagined that he felt as they had. Dread, mixed with a terrible sense of elation, knowing that his decisions were behind him and nothing but the present remained.

Poseen-Ka wanted him dead, but had given him one last chance. Yes, he was a member of the almost suicidal first wave, yes, he would lead troops against a heavily defended target, but some chance is better than none. And a victory, snatched from the jaws of almost certain defeat, would entitle him to the same forgiveness granted Hudathans under similar circumstances. It wasn't much but would have to suffice.

Baldwin smiled grimly. There was something else as well. Everyone agreed that the Emperor was dead, and assuming that was true, he had already accomplished the first part of what he'd set out to do. He had proved his competency, made them sorry, and evened the score. The only thing missing was absolute power over those who had betrayed him, but the possibility remained, and he might have it yet.

The landing craft lurched as a SAM exploded nearby, but the human didn't even notice. His mind was far, far away.

Natasha had made herself a seat behind St. James. Everyone agreed that the Hudathans had the odds on their side, and that being the case, she preferred to die with someone she cared about. Besides, where better to track the battle than by looking over the general's shoulder?

St. James knew she was there, but his attention lay elsewhere. Information poured in through his headset and the visual displays that surrounded him. The voices were male, female, and computer-generated.

"Wave one has entered the atmosphere, sir. Existing glide paths suggest at least three hundred landing zones, most in the northern hemisphere. Waves two, three, and four are only minutes behind."

St. James felt his jaw tighten. It was a massive attack calculated to overwhelm his weakened defenses. And, as if that wasn't bad enough, the Hudathans had found a way to multiply the variables he'd have to track, thus spreading his forces over more territory. Divide and conquer. The axiom was as old as war itself. They key was to ignore the small stuff and keep his eye on the ball. He fought to keep his voice calm.

"Continue to track. Provide me with grid coordinates on anything battalion strength or better."

"Yes, sir."

Another voice whispered in his ear.

"'A' Company, 2nd REP, has located and engaged a force of Hudathan scouts. They were southbound on feeder road RJ2."

"Likely target?"

"Three possibles, sir. A Naa village in sector four, the underground ammo dump on the edge of five, or the missile battery at B-18."

"Anything from Jenny?"

"Yes, sir. She says not to worry, sir."

"Good. I won't. Next?"

"The orbital bombardment has begun, sir. The enemy is using both energy cannons and missiles to probe the hills in sector four. It appears as if they know about MCP Two and are trying to smoke it out."

"Use a land line. Tell MCP Two to button up and stay off the air until further notice."

"Yes, sir."

The next voice sounded female but belonged to a computer.

"The first wave has landed. We have three battalion-strength-or-better landing sites, sir. One in the south and two in the north. All three can be viewed on screen three."

St. James looked. He didn't like the landing in the south, but the northern sites concerned him more, since both were close to strategic targets.

The larger and more vulnerable of those was the fusion plant that had supplied Fort Camerone with most of its power, and while buried deep, was still vulnerable to attack. Though fairly well camouflaged, the heat generated by the plant and electromechanical activity around it would be visible from orbit. He had anticipated a move against the power planet, however, and had positioned a goodly portion of the 1st RE, along with elements of the 1st REC, to defend it.

Of yet more concern was the vast underground facility known as "Logistical Supply 2" (LS-2), which housed the only remaining cybernetic repair facility. The first, and primary, maintenance center had been destroyed along with Fort Camerone. Making the situation even more difficult was that he had counted on LS-2 escaping initial detection. But the Hudathan spy-eyes had proven themselves to be damnably efficient and it looked as though they'd found it. There were troops nearby, including some borgs, but not nearly enough. No, it looked as if the Naa would have to plug the gap, and he hoped they were up to the task.

"Get Sergeant... I mean Major Booly on the com."

"Yes, sir."

Seconds passed before Booly spoke. He was on radio rather than land line. "Banditkiller One. Go."

The deserter's code name stuck in the general's craw but he chose to ignore it. St. James cleared his throat and knew that the sound would be encrypted, routed hundreds of miles away, and broadcast via a relay station.

"Heads up, BK-One. The geeks have part of one wave on the ground with at least three more in-bound. Preliminary computer projections suggest more than three hundred drop zones—repeat, three hundred—with most in the northern hemisphere. Over."

There was a pause as if Booly were absorbing the news.

"Roger that, L-One. One wave on the ground plus three on the way. I recommend independent-command small-unit tactics against everything company strength and below. Over."

Booly was sticking to the game plan and St. James approved. There had been insufficient time to integrate the Naa into the Legion's forces and train them to fight as the humans did. Besides, their tribal structure, knowledge of the terrain, and experience as guerrilla fighters made them perfect for the task at hand.

"Roger that, BK-One. Remind your company commanders to activate their beacons. I'd hate to see an entire tribe wiped out because a quad thought they were geeks. Over."

The beacons, identical to those carried by the Legion's bio bods, were Booly's idea. Given the fluidity of the coming battle, and the independence of his subordinates, the potential for mistaken identities was enormous.

"Beacons. Yes, sir. Over."

"And another thing, BK-One... We have a battalion-strength landing party just east of LS-2. A mixed force of bio bods and borgs are in the area... but won't be able to hold it. Move your troops into position, make contact with Force Apple, and hold until further orders. Questions? Over."

"No, sir. Over."

"Good. Kick some ass. Over."

St. James broke the connection, prayed that Booly would hold, and moved on to the next set of problems.

The landing craft hit the ground with a distinct thump. Baldwin had been waiting by the hatch and was the first one out. His determination to lead from the front and take the same kind of risks they did, amused the troops and impressed them as well. Courage, be it human or Hudathan, was something they revered.

The ramp bounced under Baldwin's combat boots. One of the planet's weird one-hour-plus nights was under way and it was pitch-black outside. His Imperial-issue night-vision goggles made everything look green. The air was cold and smelled fresh. Gravel crunched as his troops spread out and took up defensive positions. Their skin had turned black in the cold and made them hard to see. There was no sign of opposition. Not too surprising, really, considering how many landing zones the Legion would have to deal with. Baldwin adjusted his helmet mike. The command frequency would override all other transmissions and leave no doubt as to who had spoken.

"The landing zone is safe. Ships two, four, and five may land."

The third drop ship had been destroyed in the upper atmosphere and pieces of it were still landing over a large section of the northern hemisphere.

There were no acknowledgments or any need for them. An order was an order.

The other ships had been hovering a hundred feet overhead, waiting for the all-clear, ready to provide suppressive fire. Repellers roared as the landing craft dropped into position and formed a fighting square.

Hatches hissed open, vapor out-gassed, ramps lowered, and troops poured forth. Vehicles followed, tracks clanking, engines growling. One stalled, sputtered, and died. A noncom swore. Orders were snapped and bodies moved. An armored personnel carrier backed up to the ramp and towed the supply truck out of the way. Thus freed, the rest of the vehicles rolled off and took their assigned positions.

Baldwin took one last look around. The landing craft had a lot of firepower and he hated to part with it.

"Arrow Commander Tula-Ba?"

Tula-Ba was Baldwin's second-in-command, a job he'd done his best to avoid, but wound up with anyway. Baldwin didn't know it, but Tula-Ba had been issued a small remote and could activate his implant if that seemed appropriate. The Hudathan was thirty yards away checking the perimeter.

"The spy-eyes and scanners are clear, sir."

"Good. Ships one, two, four, and five may lift. Thanks for the ride, and good luck."

The landing-craft pilots didn't believe in luck and made no reply. Repellers roared, the ships lifted, and the main drives were engaged. One minute they were there and the next minute they were gone.

Baldwin grinned. So far so good. The Legion had been kind enough to construct a road that passed within four miles of a cybernetic maintenance facility known as LS-2 and he wanted to thank them. He strode towards an armored command car.

"All right, Tula-Ba... load 'em up."

The cavern's interior was warm and cozy. Windsweet sat cross-legged before the fire. Aromatic incense burned in a bowl. Smoke wafted up around her head. Both Booly and her father had objected to her being alone, but Windsweet had insisted, pointing out that the villages would come under attack as soon as the Hudatha realized that the Naa were a threat.

But that wasn't the *real* reason she had stayed; no, the *real* reason had to do with the life in her womb and a desire to spend some time by herself. Like all females of her race, Windsweet had known her baby's sex from the start. The cub would be male, courageous like his father, strong like his mother. But what of his physical appearance? Would she give birth to a monster? Something so ugly no one could bear to look at it? There had been rumors of half-breeds born to the prostitutes of Naa town, but she'd never seen one. That was why she'd stayed: to pray for her loved ones and cast the Wula sticks.

The Wula sticks had been in Windsweet's family for generations, wrapped in brightly decorated dooth hide, and handed down from mother to daughter. To one unschooled in the arts of divination they might have been taken for so many polished sticks, some longer than others, all of the same diameter.

Windsweet inhaled the rich aroma of incense and reached for the package at her feet. She opened it carefully, reverently, as her mother had taught her to do, and spread the hide on the floor. It bore a design and would provide the sticks with a safe landing place.

Then, holding the Wula sticks with both hands, she raised them above her head and started to chant. It was a soft sound, conceived by females and denied to males.

The chant continued for a while, rising and falling in pitch, folding back on itself only to start anew. When Windsweet's beingness seemed to float outside of herself, and the moment felt right, she opened her hands and allowed the Wula sticks to fall. The clatter of wood on wood served to bring her back from where she'd been.

The sticks lay in a jumble, layered like the years in someone's life, and crossed like the tracks of a wandering dooth. The reading of the sticks was part art, part science, and called for complete concentration. Windsweet frowned and allowed her eyes to follow the topmost sticks down into the maze.

Many hours passed during which she learned that while

her child would look different, he'd be beautiful as well, and destined for a life among the stars. But there would be trouble too, and terrible danger, with no surety that he'd survive. But if he did manage to survive, the sticks told Windsweet that her son would bring great honor to both his peoples and be celebrated for centuries to come.

The Wula sticks told her nothing of Booly's fate, or of her father's, for she was afraid to ask. "There are," her mother had said, "many things we shouldn't know."

Rising from her place by the fire, Windsweet took a blanket and wrapped it around her shoulders. Making her way up along the spiral staircase, she slipped out through the doorway and onto the plateau. A breeze blew in from the west, ruffled her fur, and probed the blanket for holes. The sun was rising and contrails made claw marks across the blue sky.

The sun had just cleared the horizon and threw long black shadows across the ground. The scout, a Naa by the name of Farsee Softfoot, squatted. Booly, Roller, Hardman, and Shootstraight did likewise. Softfoot looked tired, which wasn't too surprising, since he'd been up for more than twenty-six hours and run more than fifteen miles cross-country.

"So," Hardman said, "what are the smelly ones up to?"

"They're coming this way," the scout answered matter-of-factly. He picked up a stick and drew an S-shape in the sand. "They're coming down the road like so. Should be here in three, maybe four hours."

"Shit," Roller said.

"Yeah," Booly agreed. "Three hours doesn't give us much time to get ready."

"How many of them are there?" Shootstraight asked pragmatically.

Softfoot squinted into the quickly rising sun. "About three hundred, give or take. A lot of them ride inside their vehicles so it's hard to tell."

Booly felt his heart sink. Three hundred! Against 27 bio bods, 12 borgs, and 120 Naa irregulars. Only slightly better than two-to-one odds. Still, it couldn't be helped.

"All right," he said, trying to sound confident, "three hundred it is."

"Actually three hundred and one," Softfoot said phlegmatically.

"What the hell does that mean?" Hardman demanded impatiently.

"The smelly ones have a human," the scout replied, "and judging from the way they treat him, he's in charge."

Booly's eyebrows shot towards the top of his head. "A human? It can't be!"

"Why not?" Hardman asked. "You left the Legion. Others could do likewise."

The chieftain's logic was impeccable and Booly was forced to agree. He avoided Roller's eyes. Assuming Softfoot's report was true, and he had no reason to doubt the scout, it meant the Hudathans had another advantage. A renegade would understand human tactics and be ready to counter them. More bad news. Booly did his best to ignore it and gestured for Softfoot's stick. Taking it, he drew a picture in the sand.

"Here's the road. It crosses the mouth of the valley like so. Assuming the Hudatha are heading for LS-2, they'll leave the road here and head down-valley. There isn't any road, but the path is wide enough for a single column of vehicles."

"What?" Softfoot grumbled. "I don't know the way to my own privy?"

Booly grinned. A legionnaire would never have said such a thing. Not to his face anyway.

"Sorry. I was thinking out loud. The objective is to stop them, well short of LS-2 if at all possible, and with a minimum of casualties."

"How 'bout an ambush?" Roller asked, pointing to Booly's trail. "We could lie in wait, trigger some mines, and hose 'em down."

"Good," Hardman said tactfully, "but not good enough. The trail is narrow, but the valley is wide, and the smelly ones could spread out."

"*Will* spread out from the start if they have any sense," Shootstraight put in. "Would *you* follow one of our trails?"

"Not if I could help it," Booly replied soberly, his mind

flashing back to the canyon and the ambush Hardman had sprung on him.

"Exactly," Shootstraight replied, taking the stick. "So here's what I propose. A canyon opens into the valley like so. As the smelly ones approach I lead a group of warriors out into the valley. I spot them, fire a few shots, and retreat."

"And they follow you up the canyon and straight into an ambush," Booly said, admiring the Naa's devious mind.

"An excellent idea," Hardman said proudly, and slapped his son on the back.

Roller frowned. "Maybe, maybe not. I don't know much about the Hudathans, but a human commander would send a patrol up the canyon while the rest of the battalion kept moving."

Booly nodded. "Good point. So let's give our friend time to detach whatever force he considers appropriate, blow the canyon behind them, and attack the force that remains. We have twelve borgs, and properly positioned, they should be able to eat the convoy alive."

There was a moment of silence while the rest thought it over. Hardman was the first to speak.

"It is good, very good. We will split his force, isolate the patrol, *and* take him by surprise."

Booly's knees had started to hurt. He stood and looked each one of them in the eye. "All right. We have work to do. Let's do it."

The human vessels came out of hyperspace so fast and attacked with such all-out ferocity that three Hudathan warships were destroyed during the first five minutes of battle.

Woken from a deep sleep, War Commander Poseen-Ka was called to the command center, only to find his fleet fighting for its life. What he saw in the holo tank, and what his officers told him, were his worst fears come to life.

Suddenly, and with the insight that sometimes comes with unexpected danger, he realized that he had succumbed to the very same overconfidence that he had so often warned against. With the Emperor dead, and the successful landings on Algeron, he had lowered his guard. In doing so he had paved the way towards the possibility of defeat. These humans had the will to fight and were doing a superb job of it. And, with a fleet to engage, his ground forces would be left without air support.

Well, Poseen-Ka thought as he strapped himself into his command chair, such are the ways of war. The ground troops will have to fend for themselves while I deal with the human navy.

The Hudathan's chair whirred as it tilted backwards into a semi-reclined position. He took information from the holo tank, compared it to computer-generated recommendations, and fought back.

The operations center hummed with carefully organized activity. The initial jubilation that had followed three kills in quick succession had disappeared, and a mood of quiet determination had taken its place.

Though distorted by their plastic pressure suits, the faces around Chien-Chu looked calm, as if they had looked death in the eye and come to terms with it.

This was the first battle Chien-Chu had been part of and he watched with interest, not just those around him in the operations center but himself as well, wondering how he'd react. Yes, he was frightened, a rather logical emotion, all things considered, but not to the extent that he'd feared. Not to the point of soiling his pants, gibbering like a fool, or trying to escape in a lifeboat. So that, plus the detachment of a noncombatant, allowed him to watch the battle with almost serene indifference.

The fact that they had caught the Hudathans by surprise was obvious, and a good thing too, considering the strength of their fleet. What had started as a fleet action had deteriorated into a number of separate brawls, some involving five or six vessels, others as few as two, all of them hard-fought.

His own ship, the *Imperial*, was slugging it out with a pair of cruisers, which though of lesser size, had enough combined strength to beat the battleship into submission.

Chien-Chu felt the entire hull shiver as a flight of missiles flashed outwards and, finding a momentary hole in a Hudathan force field, detonated on contact with the hull.

A nova blossomed and screens blanked as computers shut them down. Scattered cheers were heard but quickly disappeared as the second ship counterattacked with everything it had. Missiles raced outwards, were intercepted by other missiles, and blew up well short of their goal. Energy cannons spit coherent light, screens flared through all the colors of the rainbow, and fighters darted in and out looking for a point of weakness. The screens came up.

Chien-Chu saw one of the two-seaters stagger under the impact of an unseen projectile, tumble end over end, and blow up. He winced and looked away. It did little good. Death filled every screen.

He looked up to where Algeron filled most of a view port. Natasha was down there somewhere, living through god knows what, waiting for help to come. Well, it had, by god, it had.

A Hudathan ship shuddered as an internal explosion tried to rip it apart, went inactive, and drifted away. Chien-Chu cheered and others followed his example. Finally awoken from its self-induced stupor, the human race had responded and was taking its vengeance.

It was almost dark and the countryside was flooded with soft lavender light. Bare, and somewhat bleak during the day, the valley had been transformed into something beautiful. A rocky spire took on the semblance of sculpture, while a cliff was etched with light, and the skeleton of a dead bush became a plaything for the wind.

The spy-eyes came first, a dozen in all, drifting above the surface of the land like metallic seedpods, probing for signs of danger. Then came two computer-controlled robo-crawlers, both heavily armored, and capable of withstanding a major blast. If the Legion had laid mines up ahead, or prepared some sort of ambush, they would take the brunt of the attack.

The rest of the Hudathan vehicles followed one after another, preferring whatever dangers the trail might offer to the uncleared clutter of the valley's floor. The trail, following the path of least resistance, was hugging the valley's south side.

Baldwin swayed from side to side as the APC lurched over a rock. He was tired of standing in the hatch, of watching the miles roll by, of waiting for something to happen, but had no choice. The mission had been difficult to begin with, but the loss of air support made it downright dangerous. He wondered how the space battle was going and pushed the thought away. His attention belonged to the here and now.

As if to prove the truth of his assessment, there was movement up ahead. Riders mounted on what looked like woolly mammoths blundered out onto the trail, spotted the convoy, and loosed off a few shots. Then, figuring that discretion was the better part of valor, they returned the way they had come.

The spy-eyes sent belated warnings through the makeshift electronics that the Hudathans had grafted onto his standard-issue com gear, the robo-crawlers turned left and opened up with their machine guns, and Baldwin was thrown forward as his driver brought the APC to a sudden halt. Arrow Commander Tula-Ba asked the obvious question.

"Shall I send a dagger in pursuit, sir?"

Baldwin gave it some thought. Other units had reported attacks by the local sentients, some of which had done quite a bit of damage, but how serious could such a threat be? Memories came flooding back: Agua IV, the unending rain, and the indigs that never stopped coming—not until his career had been destroyed and his life ruined. The orders came of their own volition.

"Send two dags... and no prisoners."

"Yes, sir."

Half the order was unnecessary from Tula-Ba's point of view, since prisoners had no purpose and were therefore the exception rather than the rule.

Baldwin gave an order, the APC jerked into motion, and the column surged forward. It stopped at the point where ice-cold water emptied out of the canyon and made its way to the river that meandered back and forth across the valley. The sun had dropped to the horizon, and the canyon was dark, like the mouth of a mythical beast. Spy-eyes entered the darkness and quickly disappeared. Two dags consisting of twelve troopers each separated from the main column and went after them.

Baldwin waited for five minutes, and was just about to move out, when twin explosions shook the ground. Pillars of dirt fountained into the air, a spy-eye wobbled into a cliff, and a tidal wave of rock sealed the canyon.

In the twinkling of an eye Baldwin's force had been reduced by roughly 8 percent, for there was no doubt in his mind that the explosions were part of a carefully conceived plan, and the patrol would be wiped out. The muffled *thump-thump-thump* of a heavy machine gun served to verify his assumption. There were seconds in which to organize some sort of defense and he used them as best as he could.

"They will attack from the north! Turn towards the right! Keep moving but unload your troops!"

His orders were only half executed when Booly ordered his forces to attack. The quads went first, water cascading off armored backs as they rose from the river's bottom, and unleashed a salvo of surface-to-surface missiles. The range was less than a mile, so nearly every weapon hit its mark, and the Hudathans lost nine vehicles in the first thirty seconds of battle. Flames shot up through open hatches, turrets spun through the air, and troopers danced in cocoons of fire.

Gunner was shouting as he lurched out of the river, fired his energy cannon, and charged the Hudathans.

"Here I am! Shoot me! Kill me! Blow me up! Come on, you chickenshit bastards, you can do it, you can... "

The Hudathan missile launcher had been built to kill tanks. Three heat-seeking fire-and-forget missiles hit Gunner head-on, blew holes through his armor, and detonated inside his cargo bay. He felt a moment of warmth, followed by pain, followed by complete liberation. There was darkness, followed by light, and the family he had waited so long to see.

Baldwin saw the quad explode, heard himself scream, "Fire! Fire! Fire!" and felt the APC rock as the auto cannons fired in alternating sequence. He looked left and right. His armor was rolling now—what was left of it anyway—dodging boulders in the dark, and firing at anything warm.

Orange-red tracer drifted overhead. Explosions threw troopers into the air. Bolts of coherent energy sizzled back and forth. A quad stumbled, fell, and continued to fire. Flares went off, turned night to day, and fell from the sky with casual slowness. A Hudathan weapons carrier ran off a hidden ledge and pinwheeled across a sandbar.

Then a new threat appeared as man-shaped cyborgs rose from their various hiding places, extended their arms like sleepwalkers, and opened fire. Something hit the APC with a loud bang. It lurched but kept on going. Hot metal touched Baldwin's cheek and blood trickled down his neck. All of the hatred, all of the resentment, bubbled up, and something akin to madness gripped him. The war cry was equal parts joy and pain.

Booly rode a cyborg named Rogers. Villain was off to his right, with Salazar to his left. They advanced together, like giants from a children's story, stepping over boulders as if they weren't even there. The cyborgs fired their missiles, machine guns, and energy cannons and rarely missed. Vehicles exploded, weapons were destroyed, and Hudathans died.

Booly saw that the quads had punched a number of holes through the Hudathan line, leaving clusters of troops and vehicles behind. More aliens had rushed forward and were plugging the gaps. Booly spoke into his mike.

"BK-One to BK-Force. Watch the gaps. They're trying to plug them."

Cyborgs and bio bods alike redirected their fire and the Hudathans took more casualties.

The APC ran up onto a ledge, left the ground, and flipped on its side. Baldwin was thrown clear. He scrambled to his feet and looked around. Flares bathed the battlefield with an eerie light, vehicles burned like so many bonfires, and tracer floated by as if reluctant to reach its destination. Panic rose and tried to overwhelm him. He forced it down.

The threat was obvious. Once the line was broken, his troops would rally around the nearest armor, and his command would be reduced to isolated clusters. Defeat would certainly follow.

He gave the necessary orders and hoped they'd be followed.

"Hold the line! Plug the gaps! Don't let them through!"

The Hudathan troopers were tough and they rushed to obey Baldwin's orders. They had a plentiful supply of SLMs and used them to good effect.

Booly felt Rogers stumble as an SLM took a leg off. He tried to jump but didn't quite make it. The Trooper II hit hard, sat up, and continued to fire. Shaken but not seriously hurt, Booly hit the harness release. A quick check via his night-vision goggles showed that the Hudathan troops had filled most of the gaps and were holding the line. It was now or never. The Naa weren't much for radio procedure, so he let it slide.

"Okay, Hardman... take them."

The warriors rose up from the shelter of the riverbank and ran forward. Most had taken full advantage of the Legion's arsenal and were festooned with a wild variety of weapons and ammunition. They were like shadows at first, flitting from boulder to boulder like spirits of the dead, firing when sure of their shots.

But it wasn't long before the Hudathans spotted them, opened fire, and took their toll.

Sensing that speed would lessen the number of casualties that he took, Hardman ordered his forces to charge, and fired his assault rifle. Shapes rose to oppose him, flame stabbing at where he'd been, falling as his bullets cut them down. Then he was among them, their stench filling his nostrils, harvesting their lives one after the other.

The bullets came as an unpleasant surprise, entering through his back, exiting from his chest. It took the chieftain three seconds to die. It was more than enough time to fall forward and drive his knife through a Hudathan throat.

The Naa fought like demons, using skills honed through combat with the Legion, pushing the Hudathans back. The aliens held, and held some more, but a renewed assault by the surviving cyborgs made the critical difference. Salvaging what crew-served weapons they could, the Hudathans rallied around what was left of their armor.

Baldwin knew that defeat was certain as he backed away from the oncoming Trooper IIs and fired from the hip. He had seventy, maybe eighty troopers left, and it wasn't enough. He could fight on for a while but there was very little point in doing so. He used the command frequency. His voice was heard by every Hudathan still alive.

"You have fought honorably and bravely, but there is no hope of victory, and more deaths would be pointless. The humans not only accept prisoners of war but have a long tradition of treating them well, and may even send you home. Cease firing and place your weapons on the ground. I repeat, cease firing and place your weapons on the ground."

The troopers looked to their noncoms, received noncommittal gestures in reply, and did as they were told. The incoming fire continued.

Baldwin followed his own orders by placing his assault weapon on the ground. Then, switching from frequency to frequency in hopes of finding one that the Legion monitored, Baldwin declared his willingness to surrender. His fifth attempt met with success. An officer who identified himself as Major Booly agreed to a cease-fire, told Baldwin to meet him next to a burned-out quad, and ordered his troops to stop firing.

It took a moment to locate the quad. A flare went off and turned night to day. Baldwin thought it strange that the cyborg had a half-scorched bull's-eye painted on its right flank. A man he assumed was the major had started towards the wreck in the company of two Trooper IIs. Baldwin did likewise. He was about halfway there when Tula-Ba removed the remote from his belt pouch, aimed it at the human's back, and pressed a button.

Baldwin recognized the pain the moment that it began. Someone, Tula-Ba most likely, had activated his implant. They wanted him to die without dignity, to flop around on the ground like a just-landed fish, to scream for mercy. Well, they could frax themselves.

Baldwin did an about-face so that the Hudathans could see

him, jerking slightly as his muscles spasmed, and pulled the sidearm from its holster. He was proud of the way the weapon came up to his mouth, proud of the way he pulled the trigger, and proud of the way he died.

Baldwin slumped to the ground. There was total and absolute silence. Booly stepped behind Gunner's burned-out hulk, unsure of what had happened, half expecting the Hudathans to open fire. They didn't. Hesitantly at first, and then with growing confidence, they stood with palms outwards. Booly gave a sigh of relief, reminded Villain and Salazar to use their scanners, and waited for one of their officers to arrive. He wondered if any of them spoke standard.

Norwood gestured towards the lock and Poseen-Ka obeyed. He had little choice. A squad of marines surrounded him. Against all odds and logic the humans had prevailed.

It seemed impossible given the fact that they had initially allowed him to take hundreds of their worlds and kill millions of their citizens, yet it was true. Though vastly incompetent and mostly disorganized, the humans were talented soldiers. The apparent contradiction served to explain how they had forged their empire and why it had fallen apart. All things he would share with his superiors if he lived to do so.

The Hudathan stepped into the lock, waited for it to cycle closed, and stared at the bulkhead. There was an odd sensation in his abdomen and a distinct weakness in his knees. Poseen-Ka was afraid and, knowing that, wished that he was dead.

The lock opened, a marine poked him in the back, and he stepped out. It was the first time he'd been aboard a human battleship. Humans stopped, gaped in open amazement and watched him pass. Poseen-Ka remembered how Norwood had performed under similar circumstances and made a conscious effort to imitate her poise. He kept his head up, his eyes straight ahead, and his steps even. In spite of the fact that she hated him, and would cheerfully put a bullet through his head, the Hudathan felt better knowing she was there. Only she could understand the pain of his loss, the disgrace of being alive, and the loneliness of captivity. He knew it was wrong to feel that way about an alien but understandable in one as obviously flawed as he was.

A pair of marines snapped to attention as they approached the wardroom. The hatch slid open. The lighting was unpleasantly bright and the furnishings looked small and undersized. A mixed contingent of Navy and Marine officers backed out of the way. Poseen-Ka tried to place his back against a wall and stopped when a marine shoved him from behind. He tried to spot their commanding officer, the man or woman wearing the fanciest uniform, but couldn't find anyone that fit the bill.

The Hudathan was surprised when a diminutive man, who was clearly overweight, stepped forward and held his hands palms-outwards. He wore simple nonmilitary clothes and radiated the same kind of strength that Norwood did.

"Greetings, War Commander Poseen-Ka. I apologize for the fact that I'm unable to speak your language and compliment you for knowing ours. My name is Sergi Chien-Chu. Colonel Norwood informs me that your traditions are different from ours. She says that you tried to exterminate the entire human race and, given the chance, will try again. Is that true?"

Poseen-Ka thought about it for a moment, decided that the strange little human would see through whatever lies he told, and opted for the truth.

"Yes, that is true."

Chien-Chu nodded soberly. "Good. The truth makes a sturdy bridge. Let's see if we can cross it together."

24

About six miles south of Fort Camerone there is a military cemetery. The graves are arranged in concentric rings. There are hundreds of rings, and thousands of graves. At the center of the rings stands a fifty-foot stainless-steel obelisk. An identical inscription can be found on all four sides of the monument. It reads:

AND HERE THEY LIE, THEIR BLOOD FOREVER MINGLED,   THE
LEGION OF THE DAMNED.

Planet Algeron, the Human Empire

St. James had climbed the rocky spire so many times that doing so required hardly any thought at all. His hands and feet seemed to find the proper outcroppings, handholds, and fissures of their own volition. The journey was part play and part work, since he enjoyed the process, and could inspect the construction when he reached the top.

The final part of the ascent required the legionnaire to reach up, place both hands on a piece of overhanging rock, and pull himself up. He could have left a rope to make the task easier, but took pride in the strength involved, and enjoyed the element of risk.

He made the necessary reach, allowed himself to hang free, and pulled himself up. When his chin was level with the top of the ledge, it was necessary to hold with one hand while reaching forward with the other. He did so, felt the usual lurch in the pit of his stomach, and hooked his fingers into a crevice. Once that was accomplished, it was a relatively simple matter to swing his right leg up and over, pull himself away from the precipice, and roll onto his back.

He rested for a moment, completely unaware that Natasha had watched every move from the camp below, ready to call for help if he fell. She had disappeared by the time he stood and looked around.

A great deal had changed during the last few months. A war had been won, the first campaign anyway, winter had given way to summer, and Fort Camerone had risen from its own ashes. Though not complete, the underground complex had been refurbished, and three of the outer walls had been restored.

Rows of inflatable shelters started near the bottom of the spire and marched almost to the fort itself, where they gave way to the countless cranes, dozers, robots, cyborgs, and bio bods who labored to restore the damage done by Poseen-Ka and his fleet.

St. James smiled. The concept of turning what was left of Worber's World into a vast prisoner-of-war camp had originated with Colonel Natalie Norwood. The irony of it appealed to him, and to Chien-Chu as well, for the chubby little man had wasted little time in approving the proposal and assigning Norwood to implement it. Who better to entrust with such a weighty responsibility than the officer who knew the Hudathans best? And understood what they were capable of?

Yes, Worber's World was a good place to stash them while Chien-Chu and Mosby worked to strengthen the fleet, and the empire itself.

Thanks to the clone's abdication, the Cabal had experienced little difficulty in taking control, and in spite of his dislike for politics, Chien-Chu had been the almost unanimous choice to head the new government.

Refusing the title "Emperor," the former merchant had opted for "Chief Executive" instead, and insisted that he would resign the moment that the Hudathan threat had been fully neutralized. That could take years, of course, since Poseen-Ka's defeat had most likely served to reinforce their mass xenophobia, causing them to build new fleets.

St. James drew fresh air deep into his lungs. The Legion would be needed in the years ahead, as would the recruits drilling on the flat off to the right. Not just any recruits, mind you, but *Naa* recruits, who had requested and been granted the right to form their own regiment. A regiment to be officered with members of their own race.

Ex-Major Bill Booly had negotiated the agreement, using his newfound power as a chief of chiefs to obtain full citizenship for his adopted people, and the son who was on the way.

St. James still disapproved of Booly's desertion, but admitted that the ex-legionnaire had more than made up for it by his loyalty to the Legion and his successful defense of LS-2. Besides, having met Windsweet at her father's funeral, St. James had little difficulty understanding the attraction.

That reminded him of Natasha, the ring he had purchased, and the dinner planned for that evening. A brella squirted by, squeaked at the intruder, and headed for its nest. St. James smiled and started his descent.

ACKNOWLEDGMENTS

My thanks go to Joe Elder and Judy Travis for encouraging me to try something new, to Ginjer Buchanan for believing in it, to Dr. Sheridan Simon for his design of the Hudathan homeworld, the Hudathans themselves, the planet Algeron, the Naa, and the asteroid known as "Spindle," to Tony Geraghty, author of *March or Die*, Christian Jennings, author of *Mouthful of Rocks*, John Robert Young, author of *The French Foreign Legion*, and last but certainly not least, the legionnaires themselves, past, present, and future, who know what it is to fight for lost causes.

ABOUT THE AUTHOR

William C. Dietz is an American writer best known for military science fiction. He spent time in the US Navy and the US Marine Corps, and has worked as a surgical technician, news writer, television producer, and director of public relations. He has written more than 40 novels, as well as tie-in novels for *Halo*, *Mass Effect*, *Resistance*, *Starcraft*, *Star Wars*, and *Hitman*.